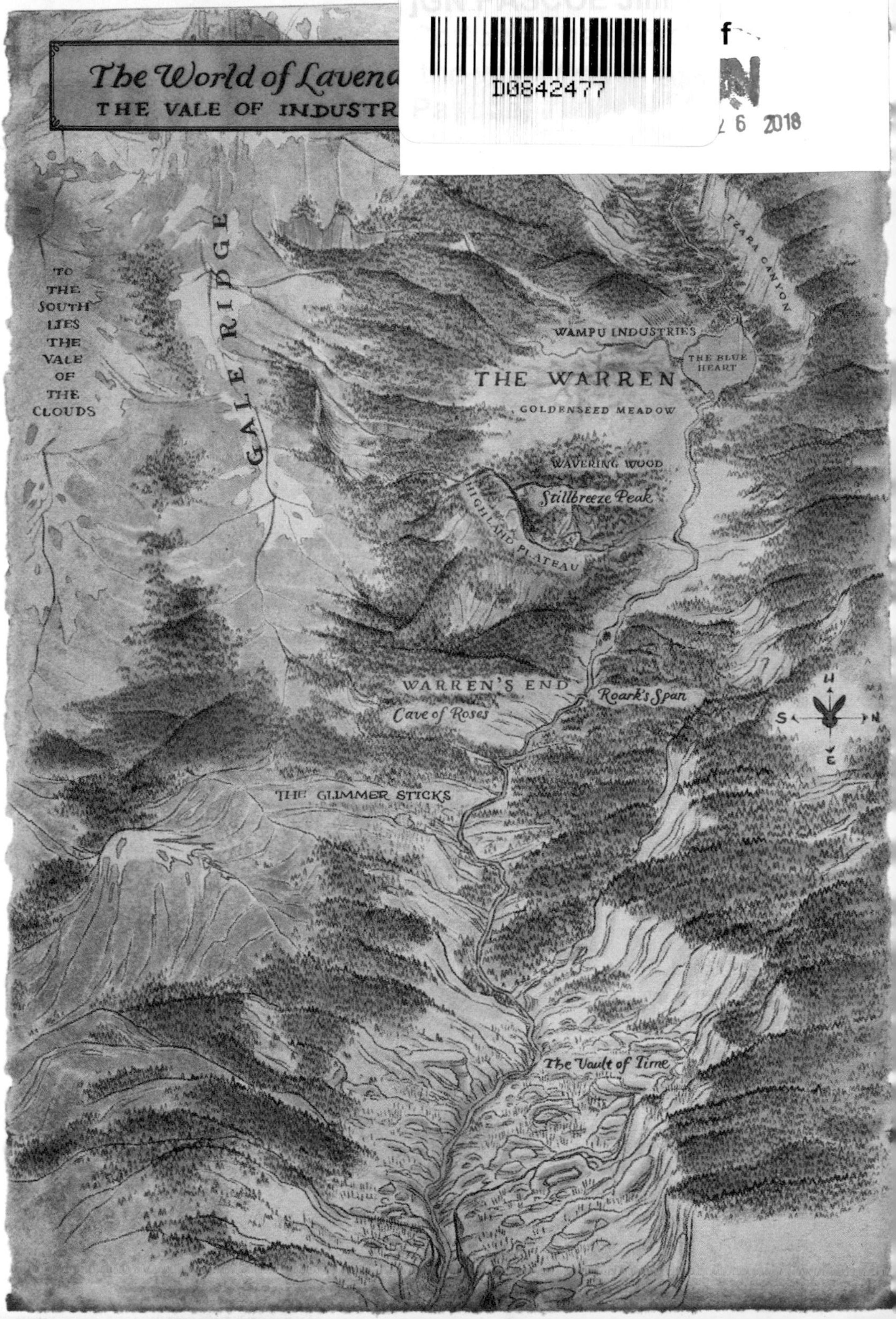
The World of Laven
THE VALE OF INDUSTR
TO THE SOUTH LIES THE VALE OF THE CLOUDS
GALE RIDGE
TZARA CANYON
WAMPU INDUSTRIES
THE BLUE HEART
THE WARREN
GOLDENSEED MEADOW
WAVERING WOOD
Stillbreeze Peak
HIGHLAND PLATEAU
WARREN'S END
Roark's Span
Cave of Roses
THE GLIMMER STICKS
The Vault of Time
S
N
E

COTTONS
THE SECRET OF THE WIND

THE COTTONS SERIES

BOOK ONE
THE SECRET OF THE WIND

BOOK TWO
THE WHITE CARROT

BOOK THREE
THE CURSE OF THE VALES

THE COTTONS
SECRET OF THE WIND

JIM PASCOE • HEIDI ARNHOLD

First Second

NEW YORK

TO THE YOUNG ARTISTS
OF THIS AND ALL OTHER WORLDS

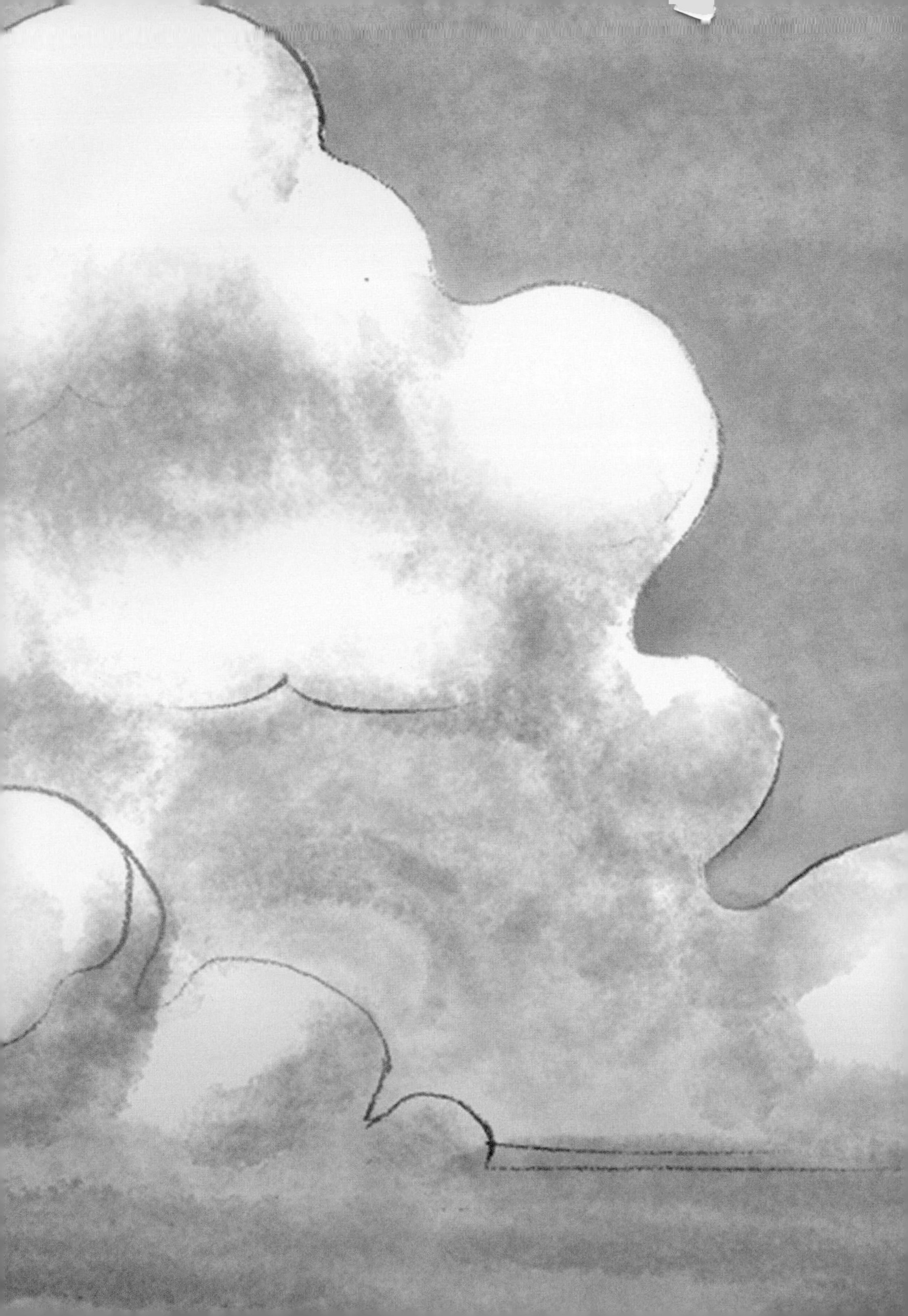

I

"*EVERYONE IS AFRAID OF SOMETHING*"

1.

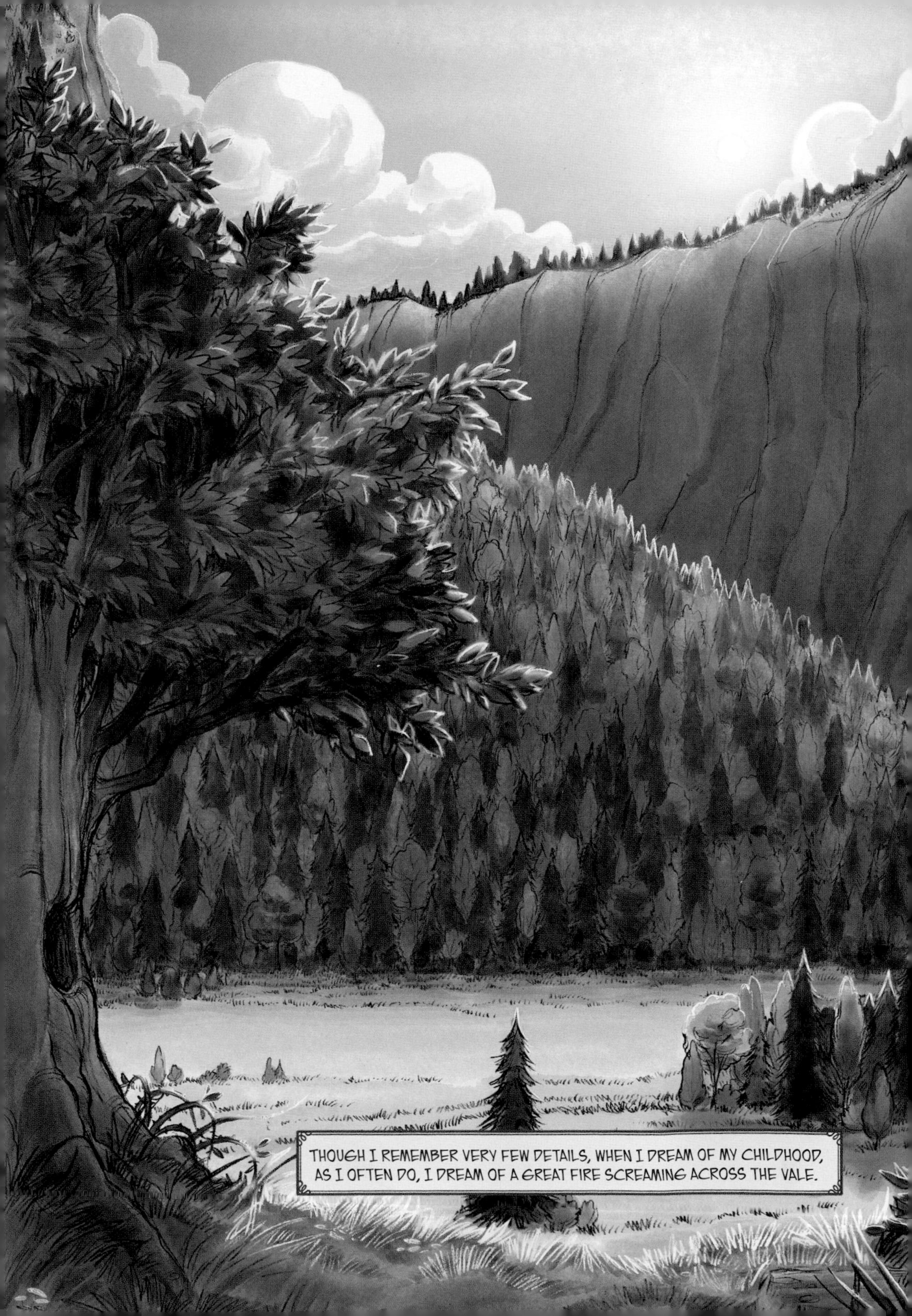
THOUGH I REMEMBER VERY FEW DETAILS, WHEN I DREAM OF MY CHILDHOOD, AS I OFTEN DO, I DREAM OF A GREAT FIRE SCREAMING ACROSS THE VALE.

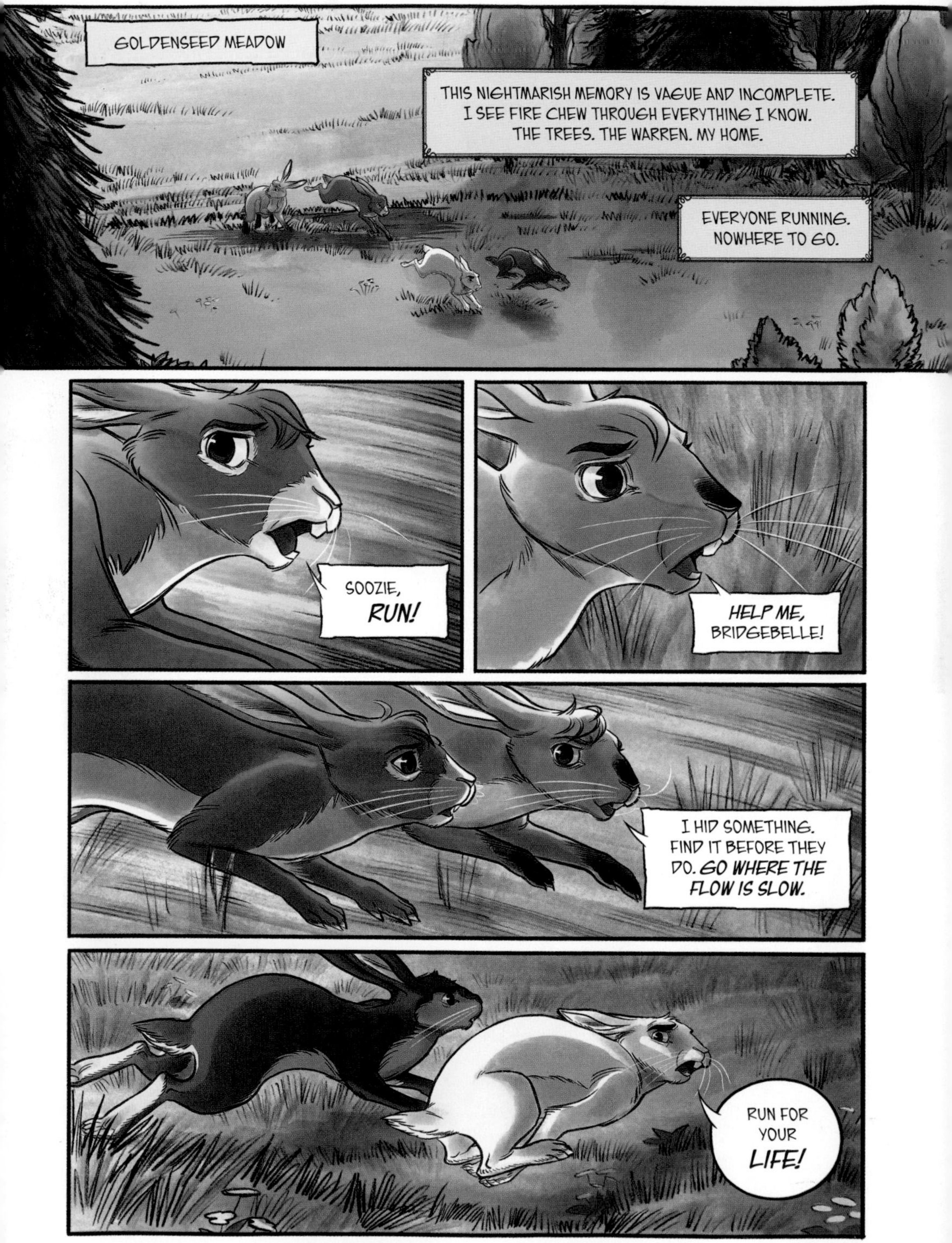
GOLDENSEED MEADOW
THIS NIGHTMARISH MEMORY IS VAGUE AND INCOMPLETE. I SEE FIRE CHEW THROUGH EVERYTHING I KNOW. THE TREES. THE WARREN. MY HOME.
EVERYONE RUNNING. NOWHERE TO GO.
SOOZIE, RUN!
HELP ME, BRIDGEBELLE!
I HID SOMETHING. FIND IT BEFORE THEY DO. GO WHERE THE FLOW IS SLOW.
RUN FOR YOUR LIFE!

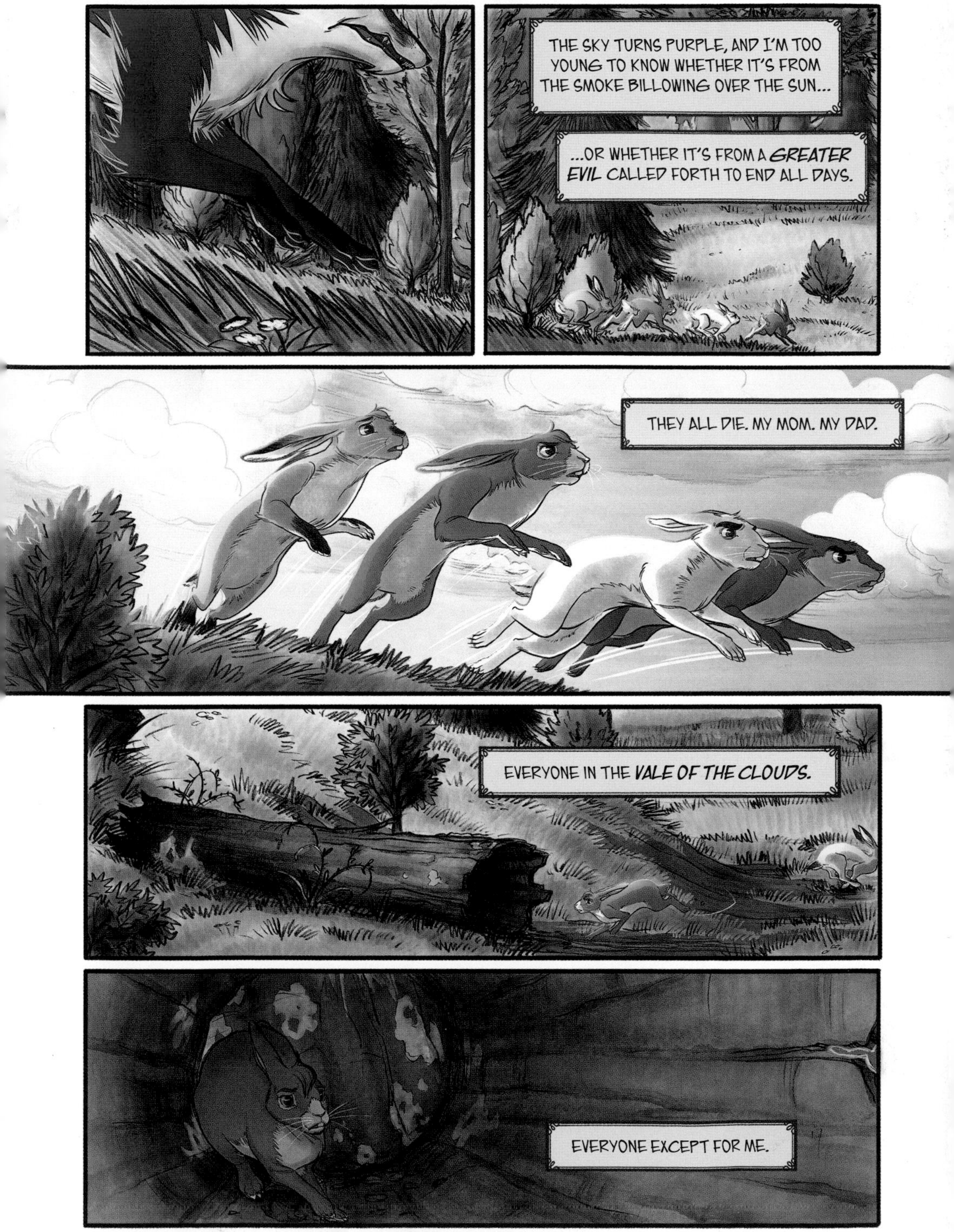
THE SKY TURNS PURPLE, AND I'M TOO YOUNG TO KNOW WHETHER IT'S FROM THE SMOKE BILLOWING OVER THE SUN...
...OR WHETHER IT'S FROM A GREATER EVIL CALLED FORTH TO END ALL DAYS.
THEY ALL DIE. MY MOM. MY DAD.
EVERYONE IN THE VALE OF THE CLOUDS.
EVERYONE EXCEPT FOR ME.

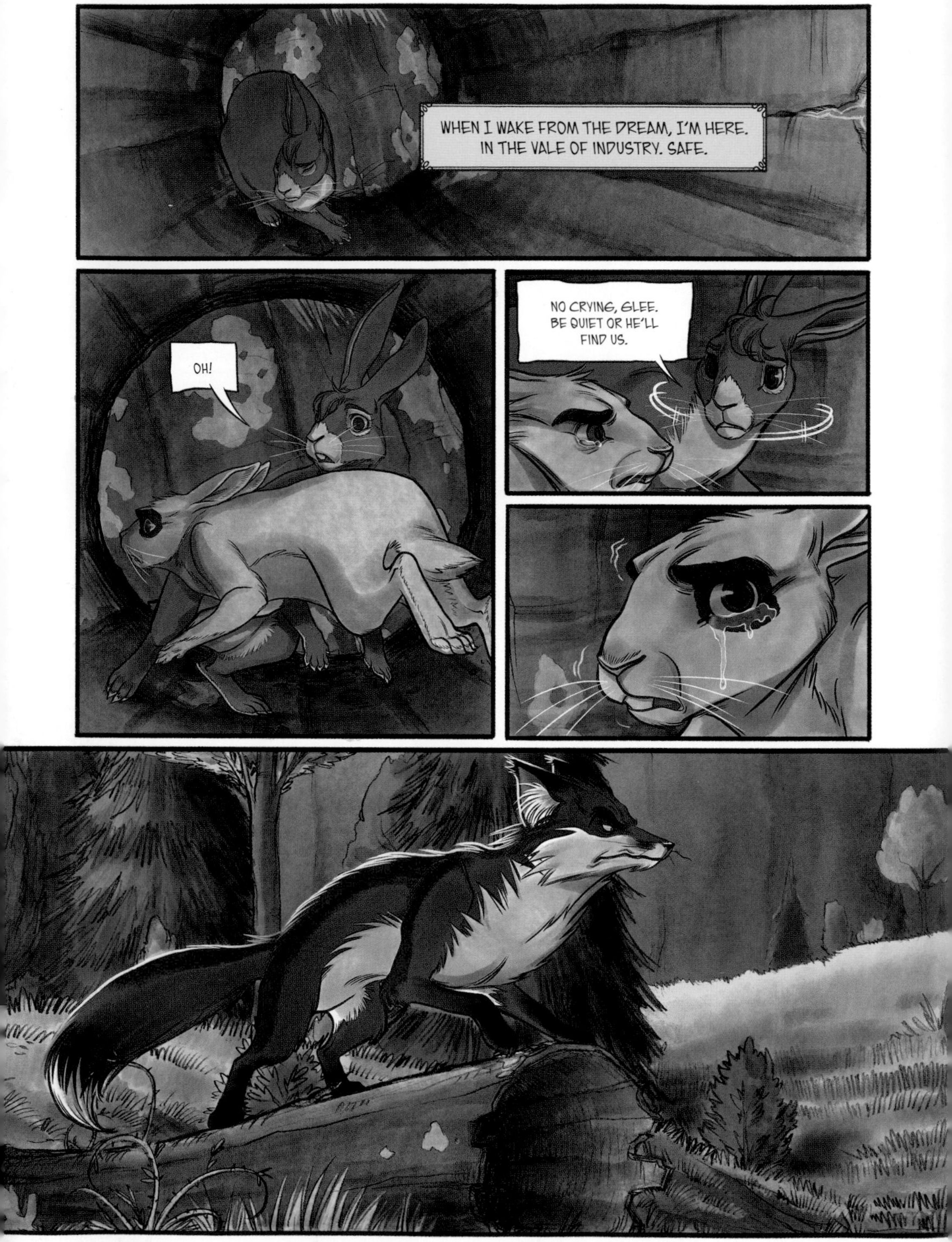
WHEN I WAKE FROM THE DREAM, I'M HERE. IN THE VALE OF INDUSTRY. SAFE.
OH!
NO CRYING, GLEE. BE QUIET OR HE'LL FIND US.

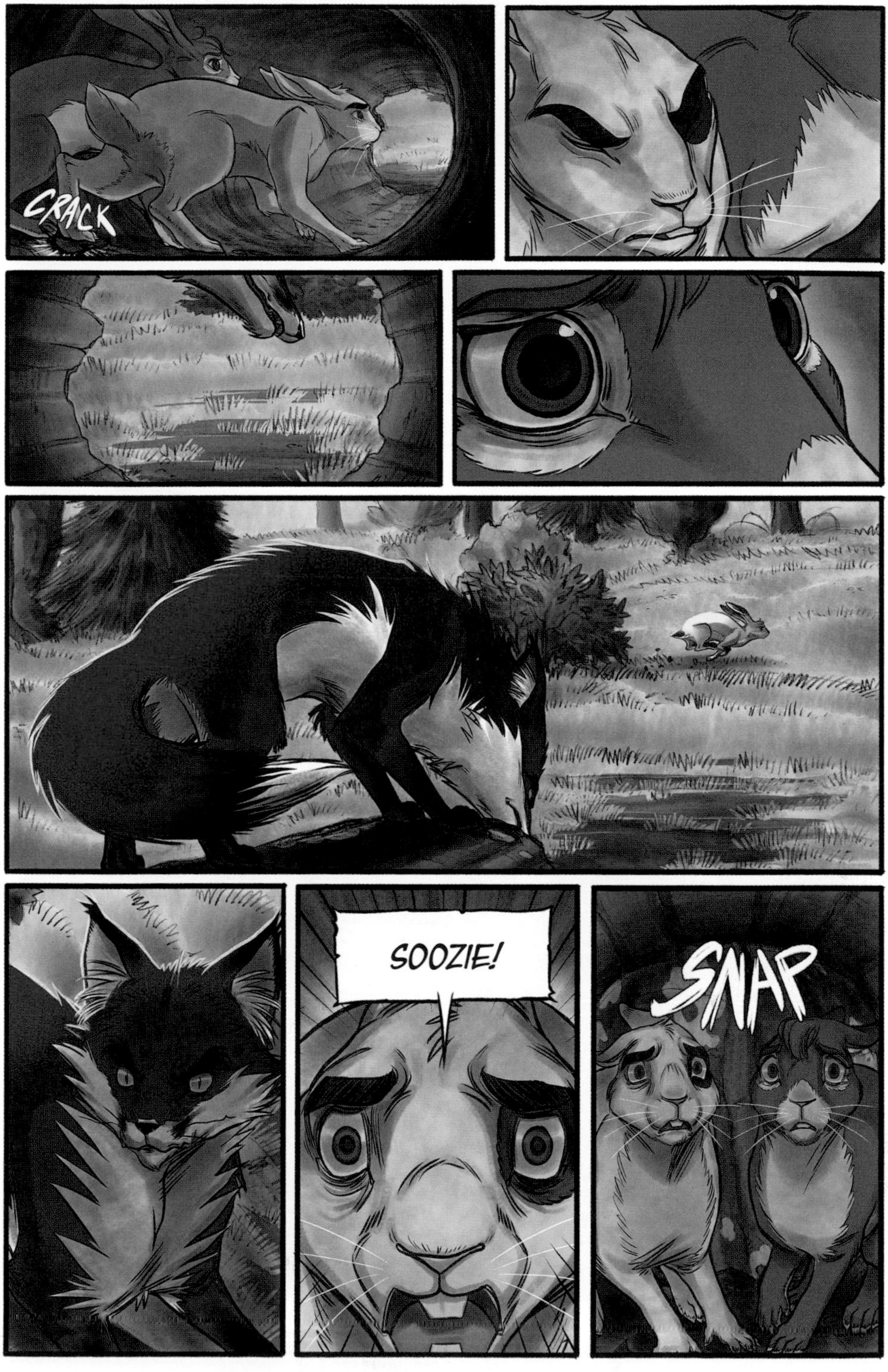
CRACK
SOOZIE!
SNAP

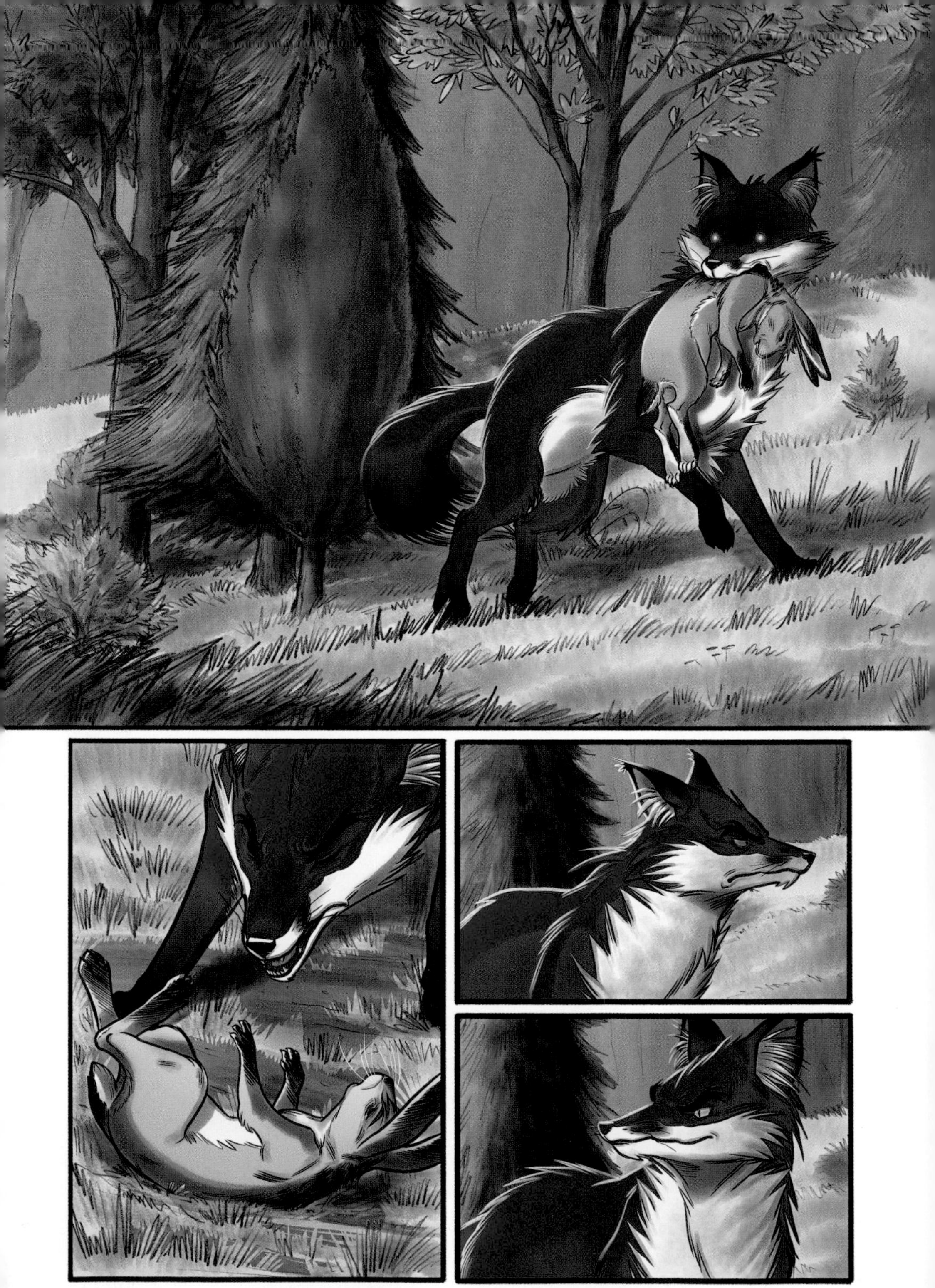

PERHAPS *NOW* YOU'LL LISTEN, MY LITTLE COTTONS.

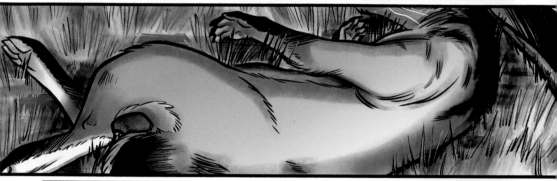

I HAVE PUT MY... *REQUEST*...TO YOUR CHIEF OF INDUSTRY.

BUT *WAMPU* REFUSED A REPLY.

WITH TODAY'S SHOW OF SERIOUSNESS, PERHAPS HE WILL BE...

...MORE ACCOMMODATING.

WIND IS LOVE. WIND IS LOVE. WIND IS LOVE.

LISTEN!

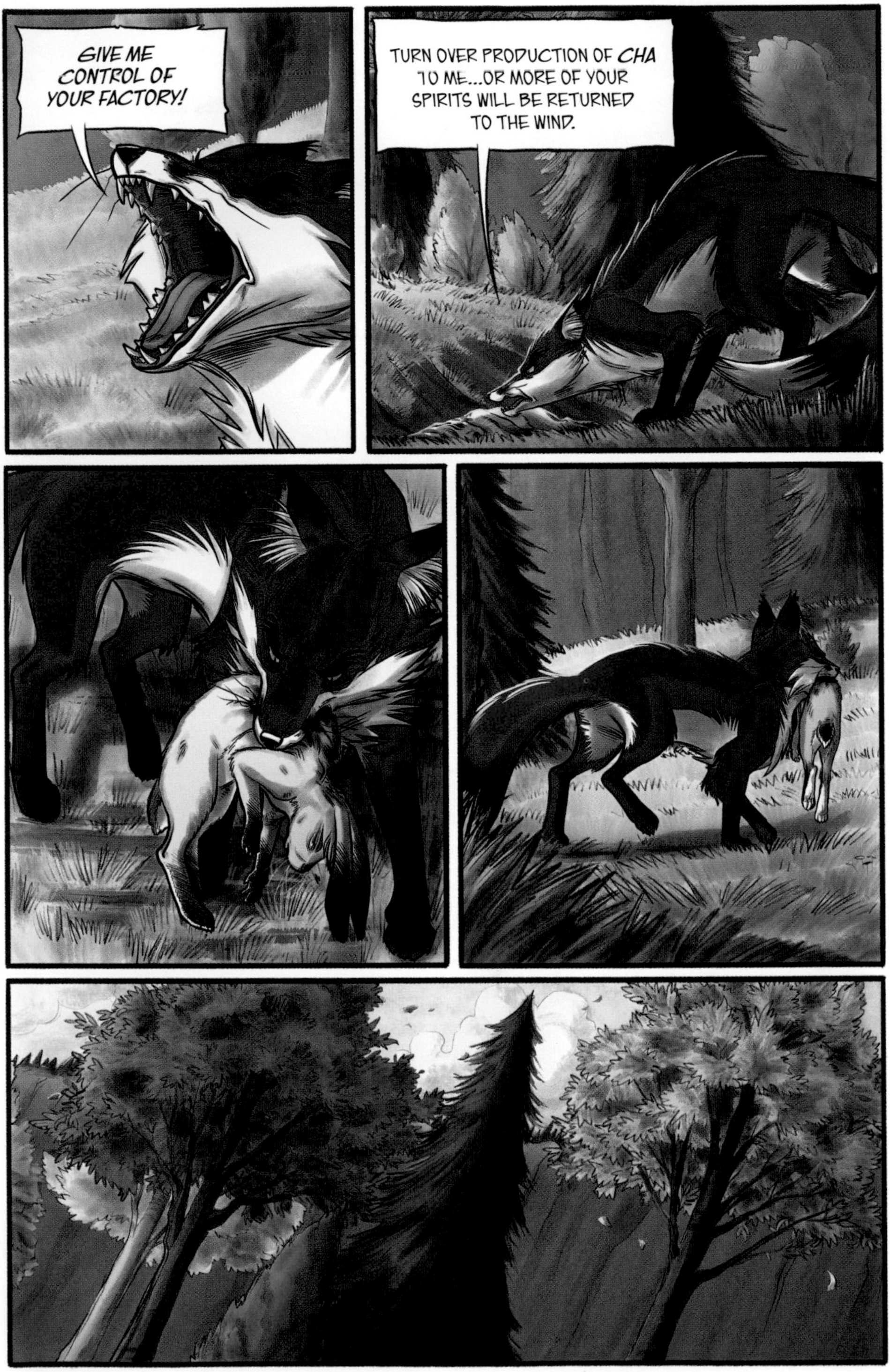
GIVE ME CONTROL OF YOUR FACTORY!
TURN OVER PRODUCTION OF CHA TO ME...OR MORE OF YOUR SPIRITS WILL BE RETURNED TO THE WIND.

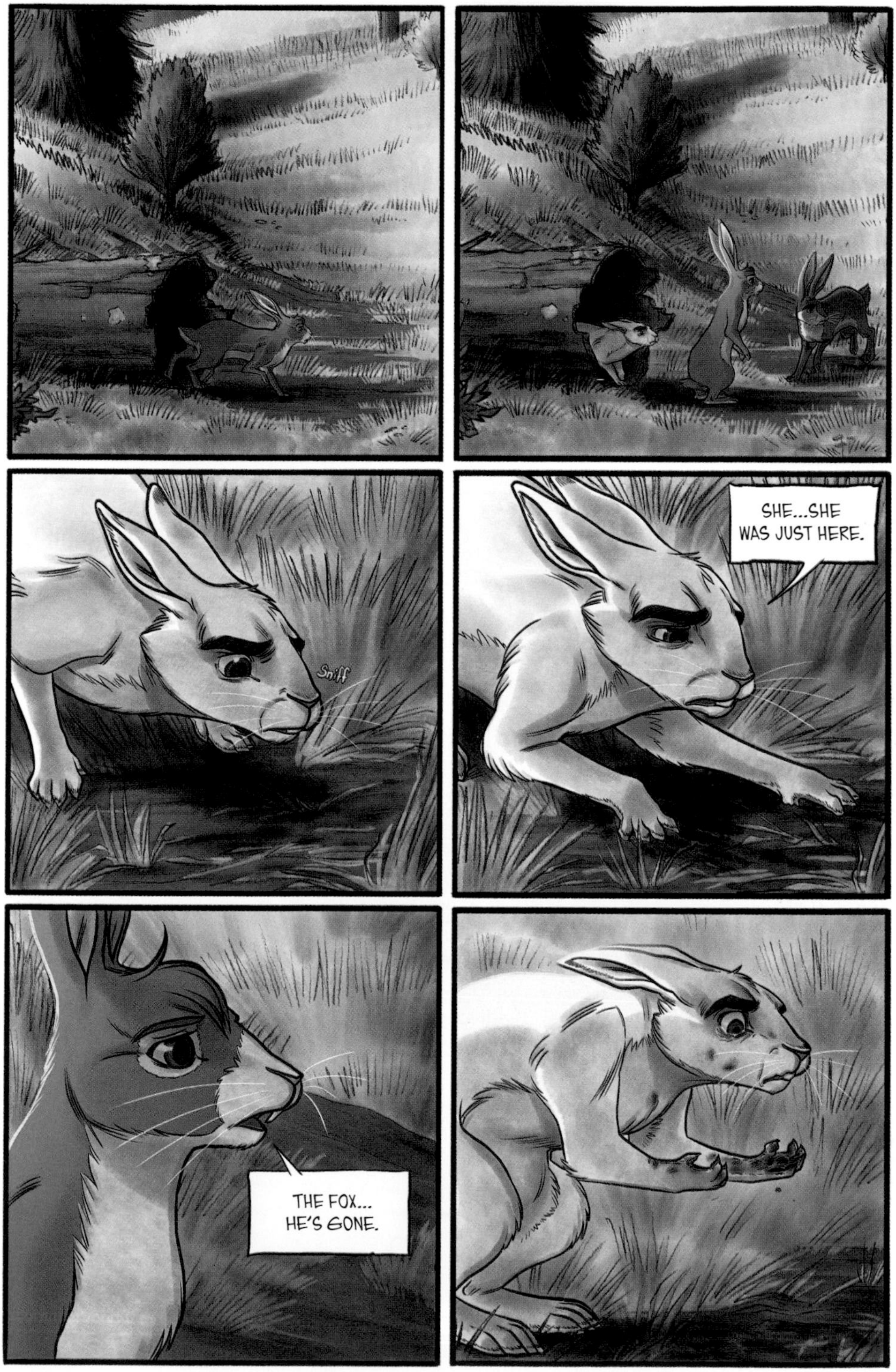
Sniff
SHE...SHE WAS JUST HERE.
THE FOX... HE'S GONE.

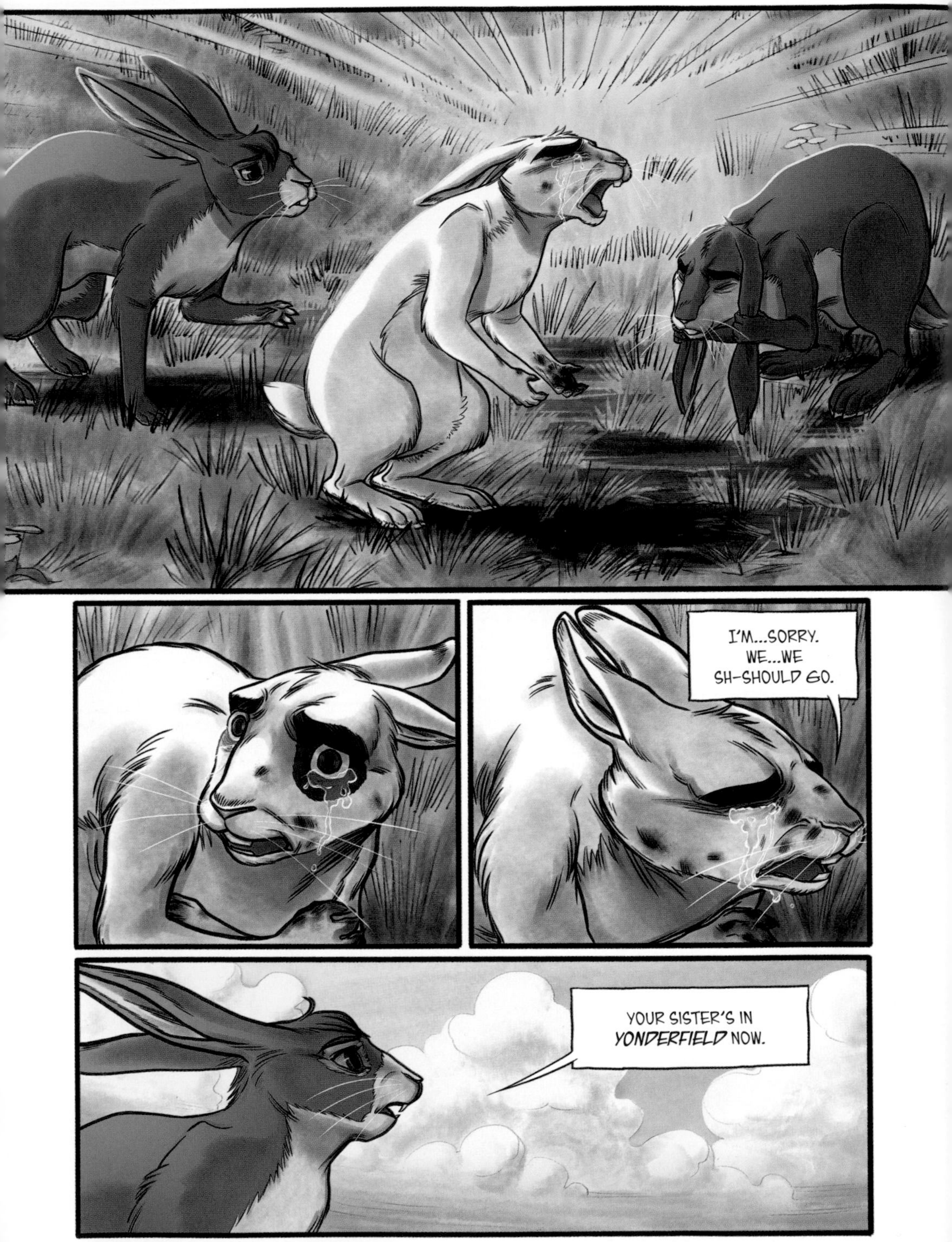
I'M...SORRY. WE...WE SH-SHOULD GO.
YOUR SISTER'S IN *YONDERFIELD* NOW.

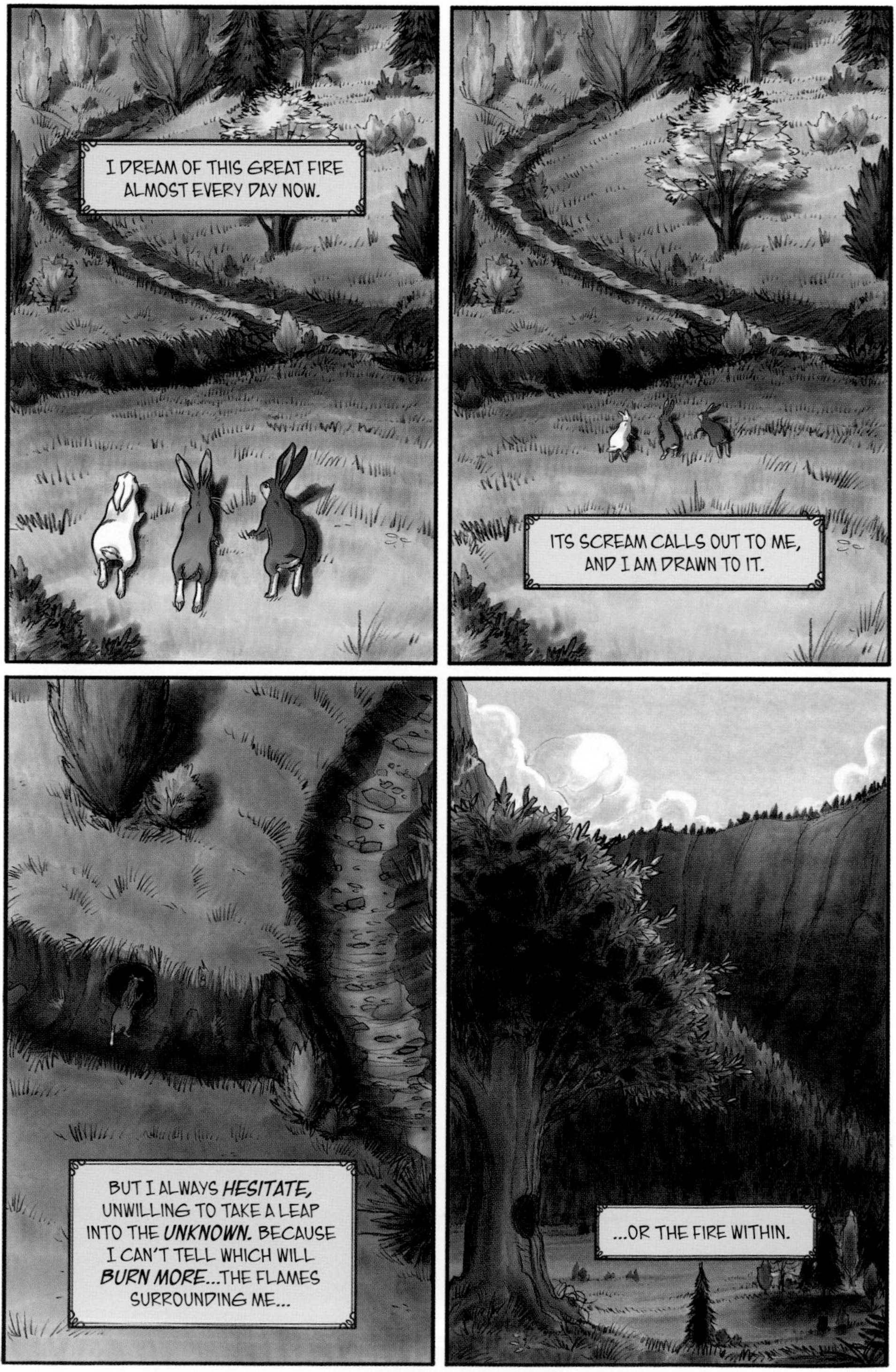
I DREAM OF THIS GREAT FIRE ALMOST EVERY DAY NOW.
ITS SCREAM CALLS OUT TO ME, AND I AM DRAWN TO IT.
BUT I ALWAYS HESITATE, UNWILLING TO TAKE A LEAP INTO THE UNKNOWN. BECAUSE I CAN'T TELL WHICH WILL BURN MORE...THE FLAMES SURROUNDING ME...
...OR THE FIRE WITHIN.

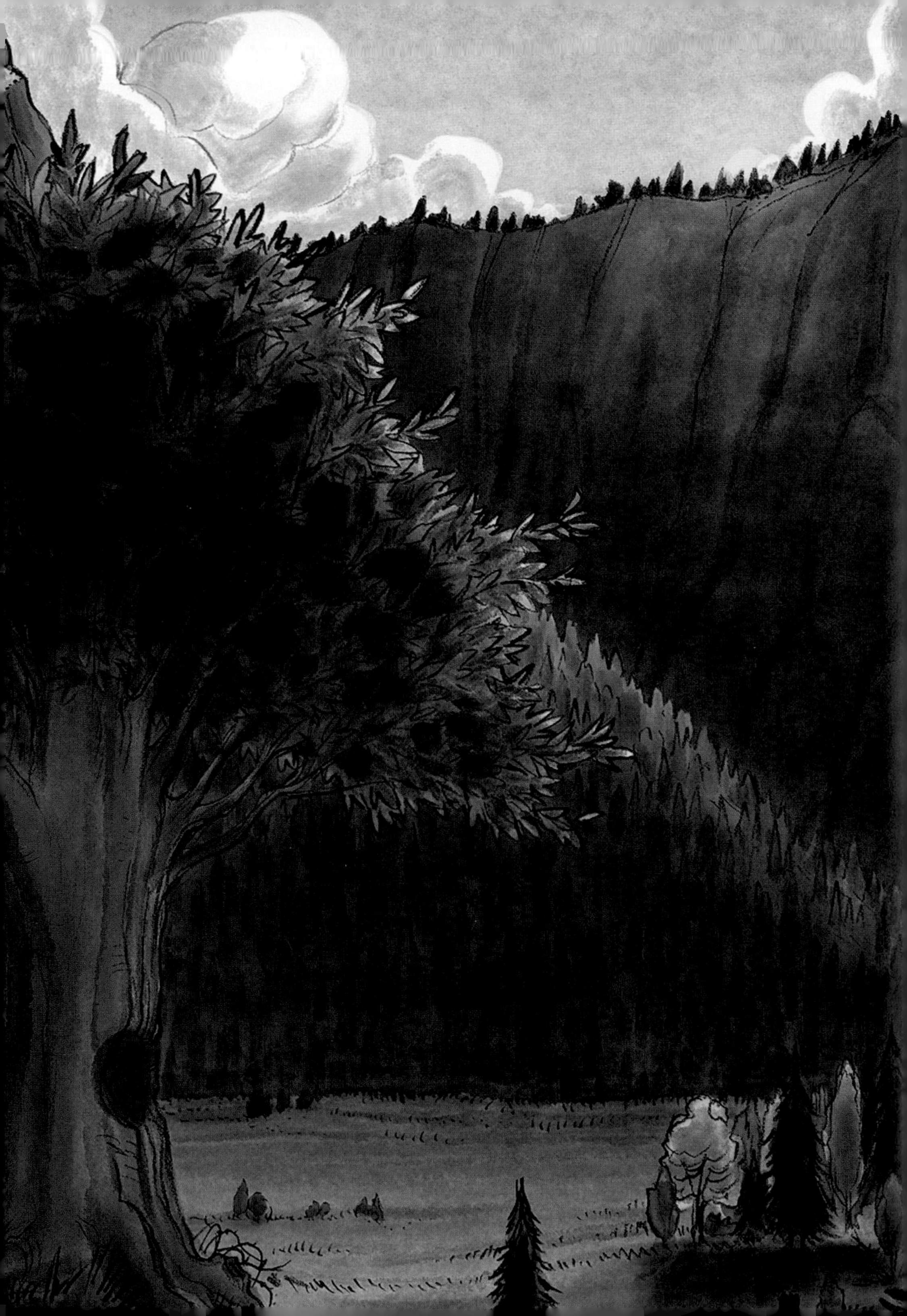

2.

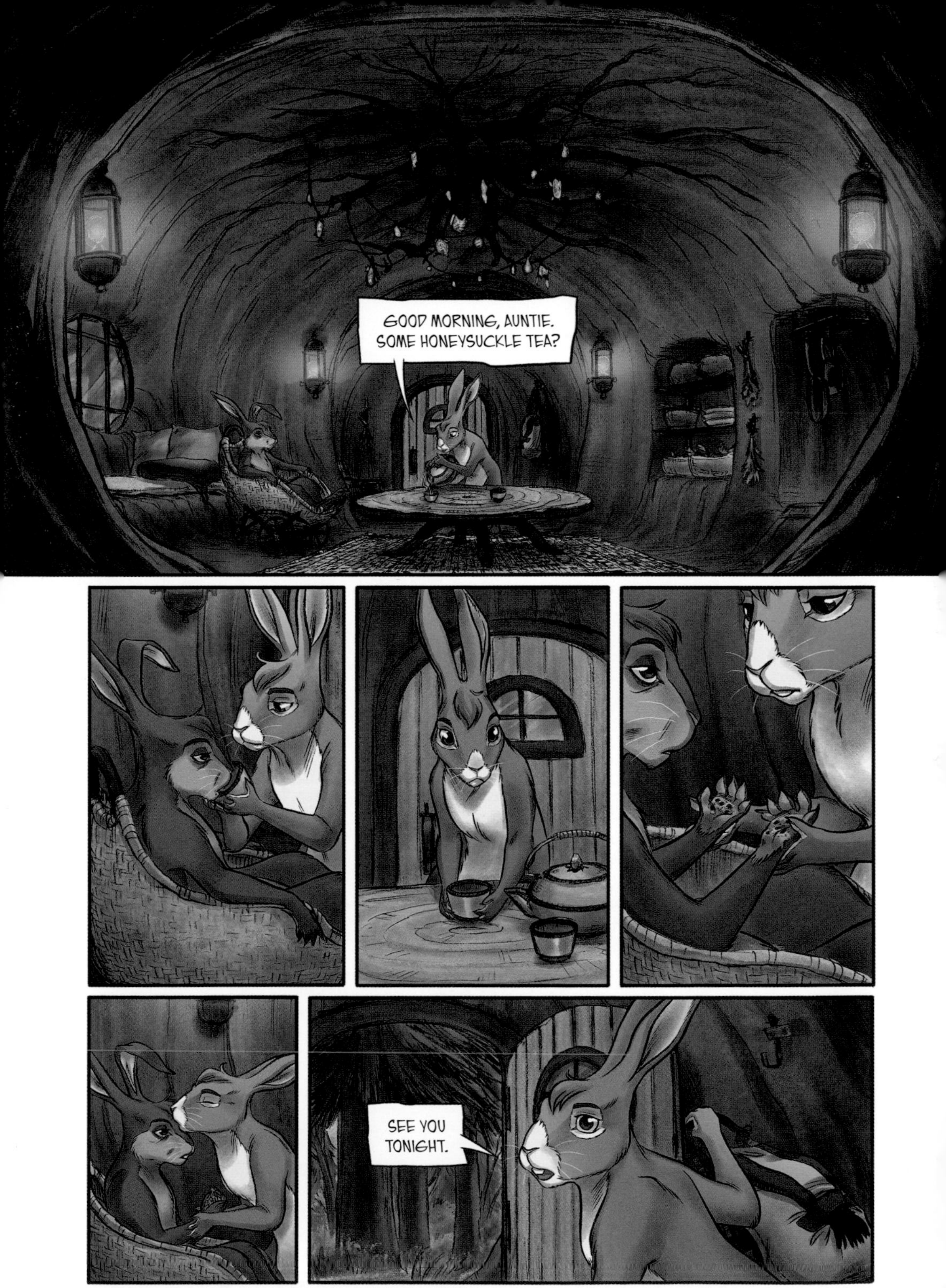
GOOD MORNING, AUNTIE.
SOME HONEYSUCKLE TEA?
SEE YOU
TONIGHT.

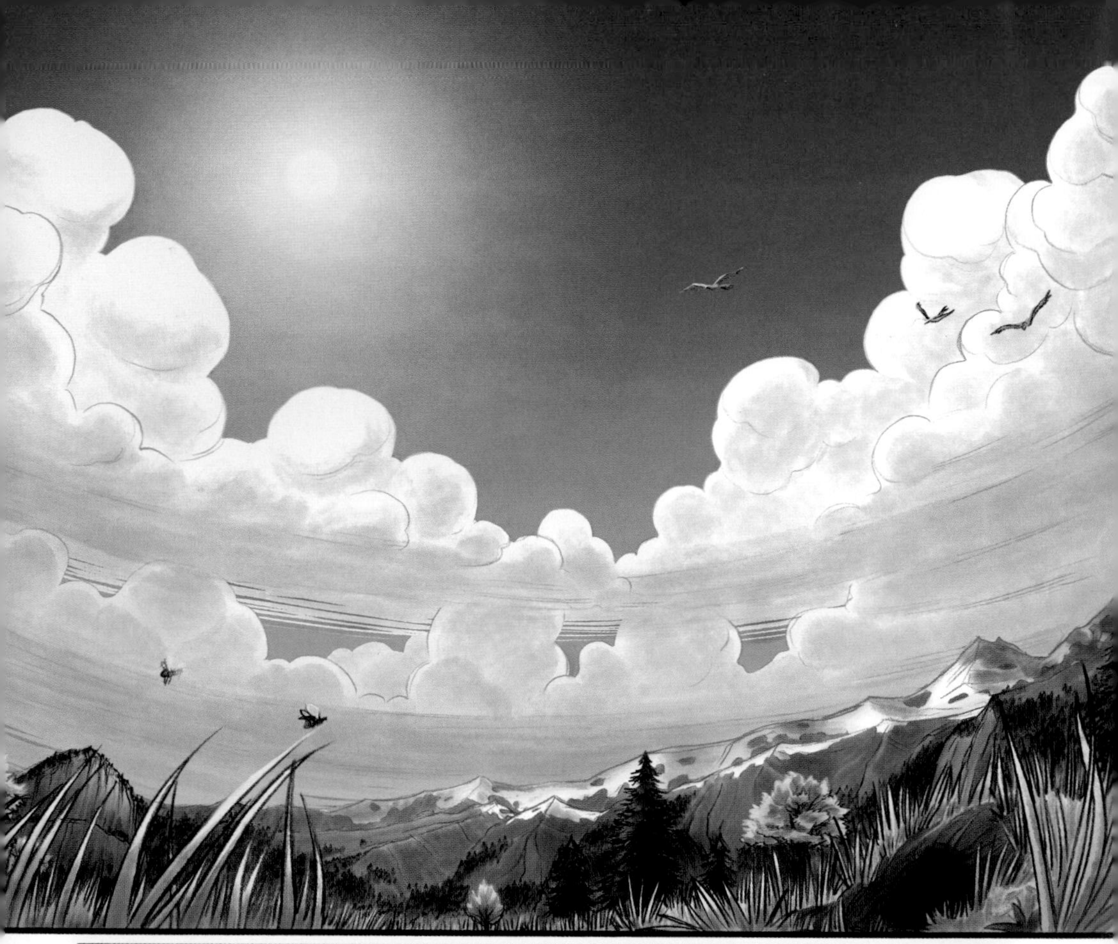

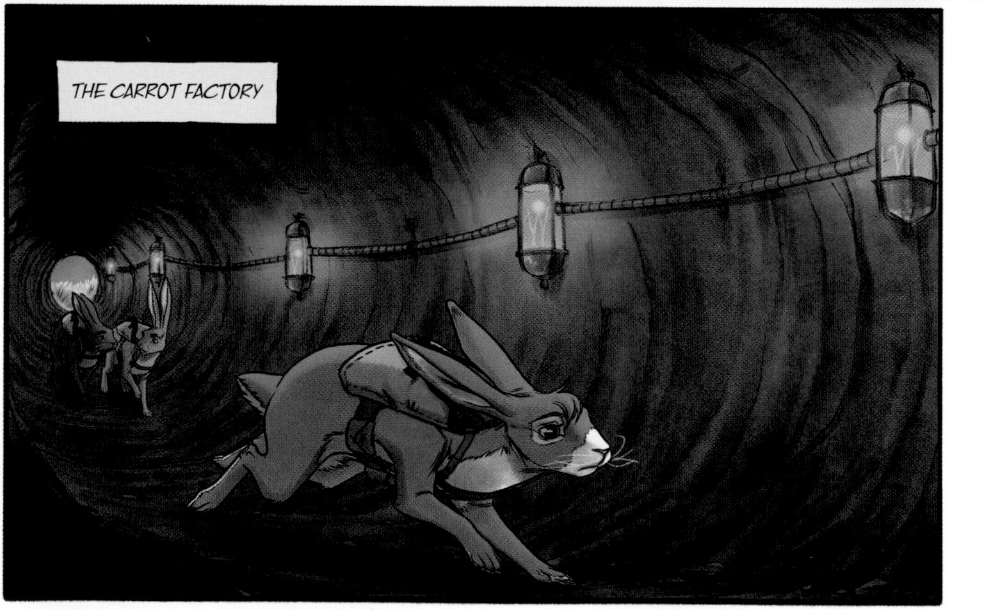
THE CARROT FACTORY

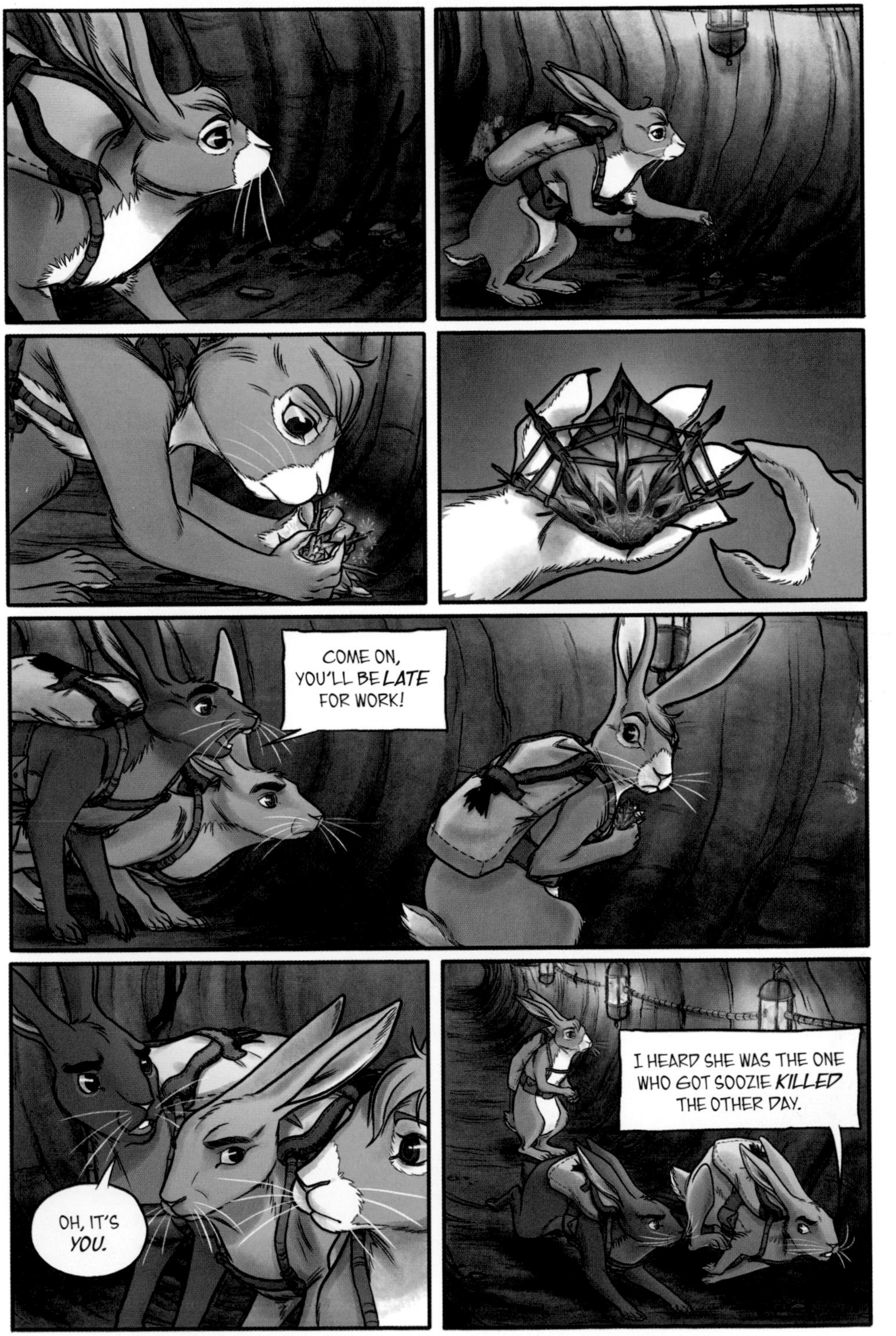
COME ON, YOU'LL BE *LATE* FOR WORK!
OH, IT'S *YOU.*
I HEARD SHE WAS THE ONE WHO GOT SOOZIE *KILLED* THE OTHER DAY.

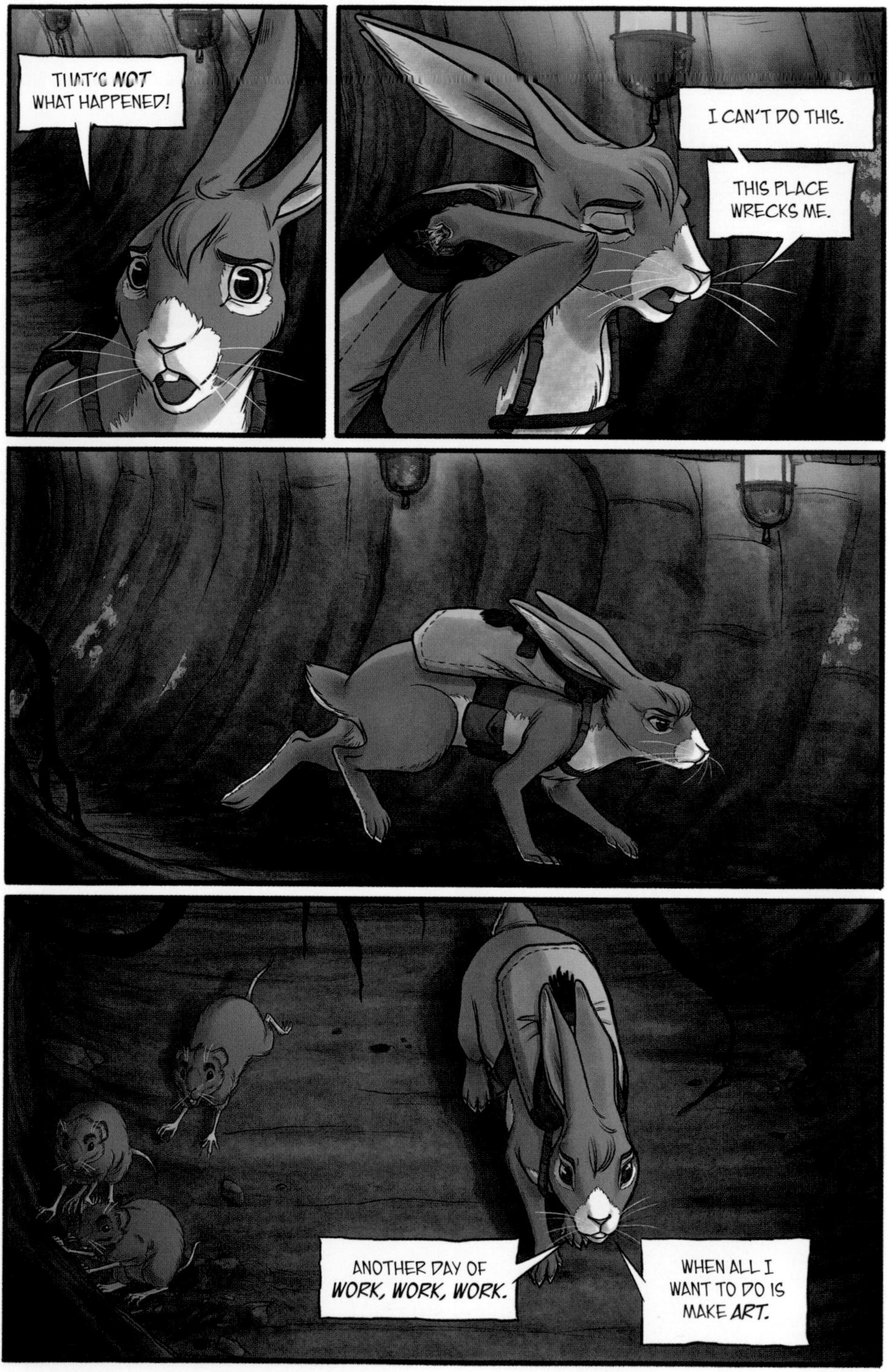
THAT'S **NOT** WHAT HAPPENED!
I CAN'T DO THIS.
THIS PLACE WRECKS ME.
ANOTHER DAY OF ***WORK, WORK, WORK.***
WHEN ALL I WANT TO DO IS MAKE ***ART.***

WHY, THANK YOU! I'M GLAD AT LEAST *YOU GUYS* RECOGNIZE MY TALENT.

...THOUGH I WISH *CROQUET* WOULD.

COME ON, DIGGERS, I CAN'T PLAY NOW. I HAVE TO WORK.

OKAY, OKAY. JUST *ONE* CRAFT. I THINK I HAVE ENOUGH CHA LEFT...

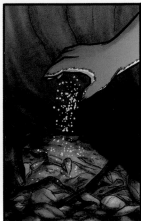

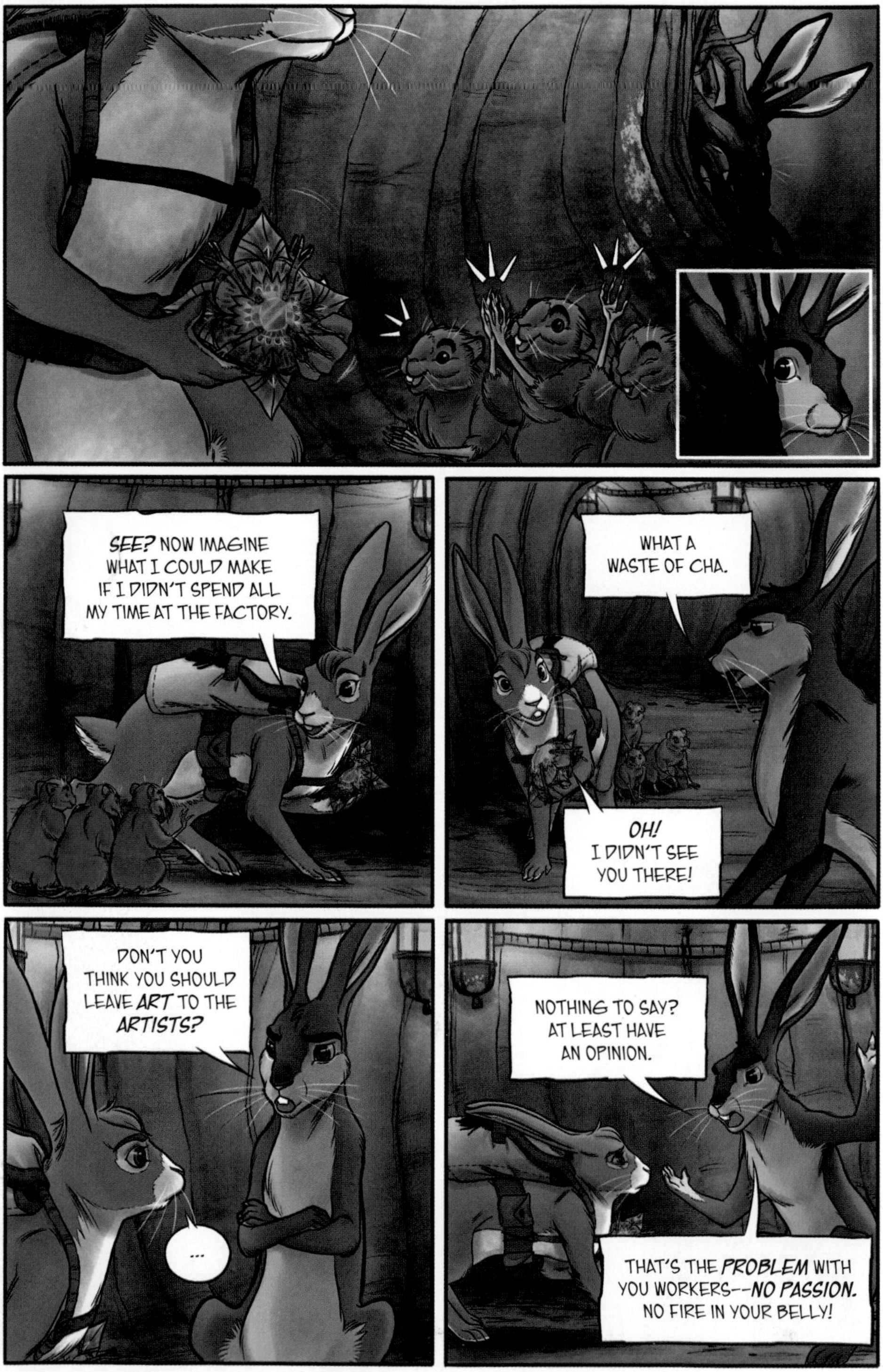
SEE? NOW IMAGINE WHAT I COULD MAKE IF I DIDN'T SPEND ALL MY TIME AT THE FACTORY.
WHAT A WASTE OF CHA.
OH! I DIDN'T SEE YOU THERE!
DON'T YOU THINK YOU SHOULD LEAVE ART TO THE ARTISTS?
...
NOTHING TO SAY? AT LEAST HAVE AN OPINION.
THAT'S THE PROBLEM WITH YOU WORKERS--NO PASSION. NO FIRE IN YOUR BELLY!

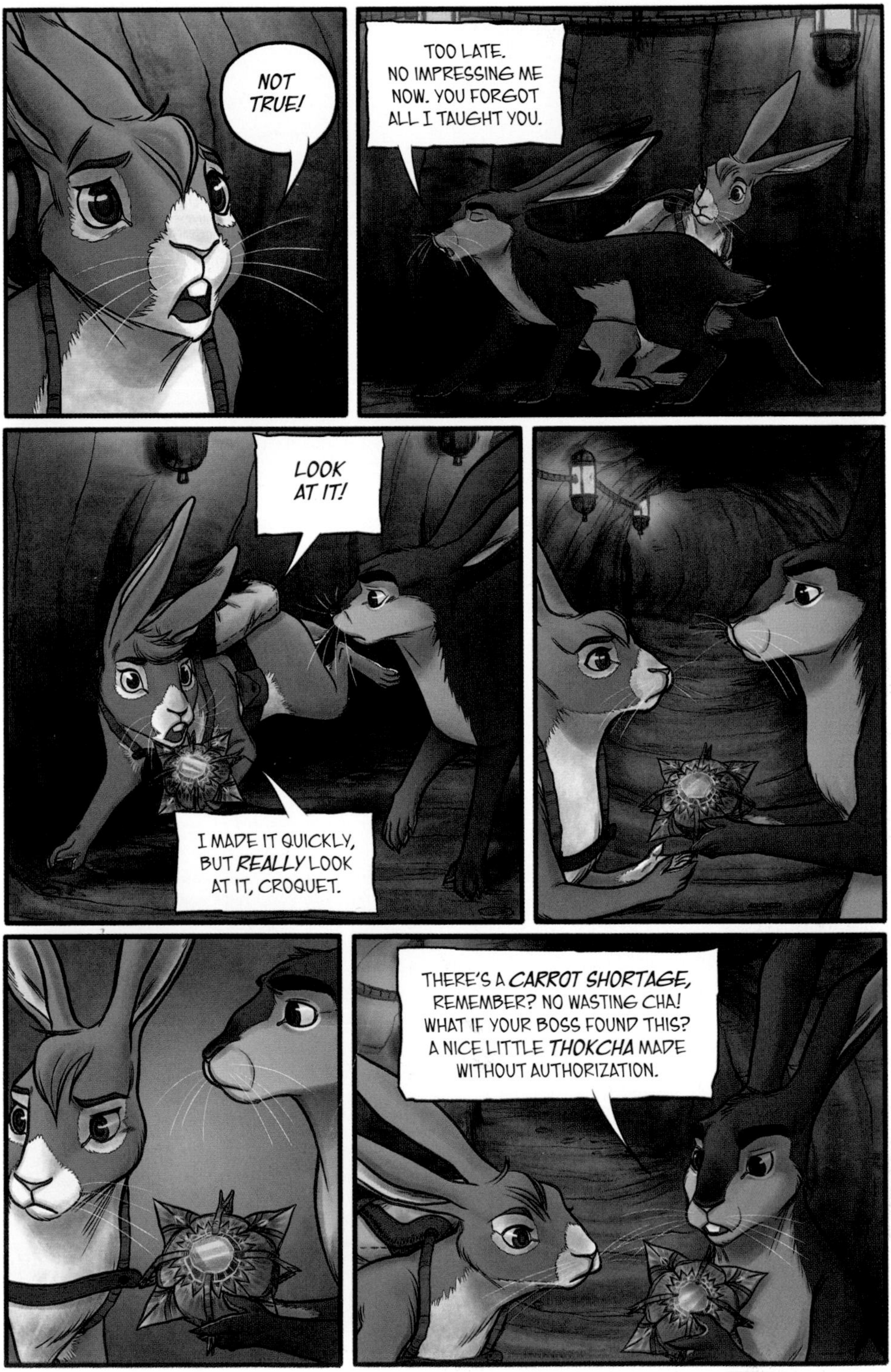
NOT TRUE!
TOO LATE. NO IMPRESSING ME NOW. YOU FORGOT ALL I TAUGHT YOU.
LOOK AT IT!
I MADE IT QUICKLY, BUT REALLY LOOK AT IT, CROQUET.
THERE'S A CARROT SHORTAGE, REMEMBER? NO WASTING CHA! WHAT IF YOUR BOSS FOUND THIS? A NICE LITTLE THOKCHA MADE WITHOUT AUTHORIZATION.

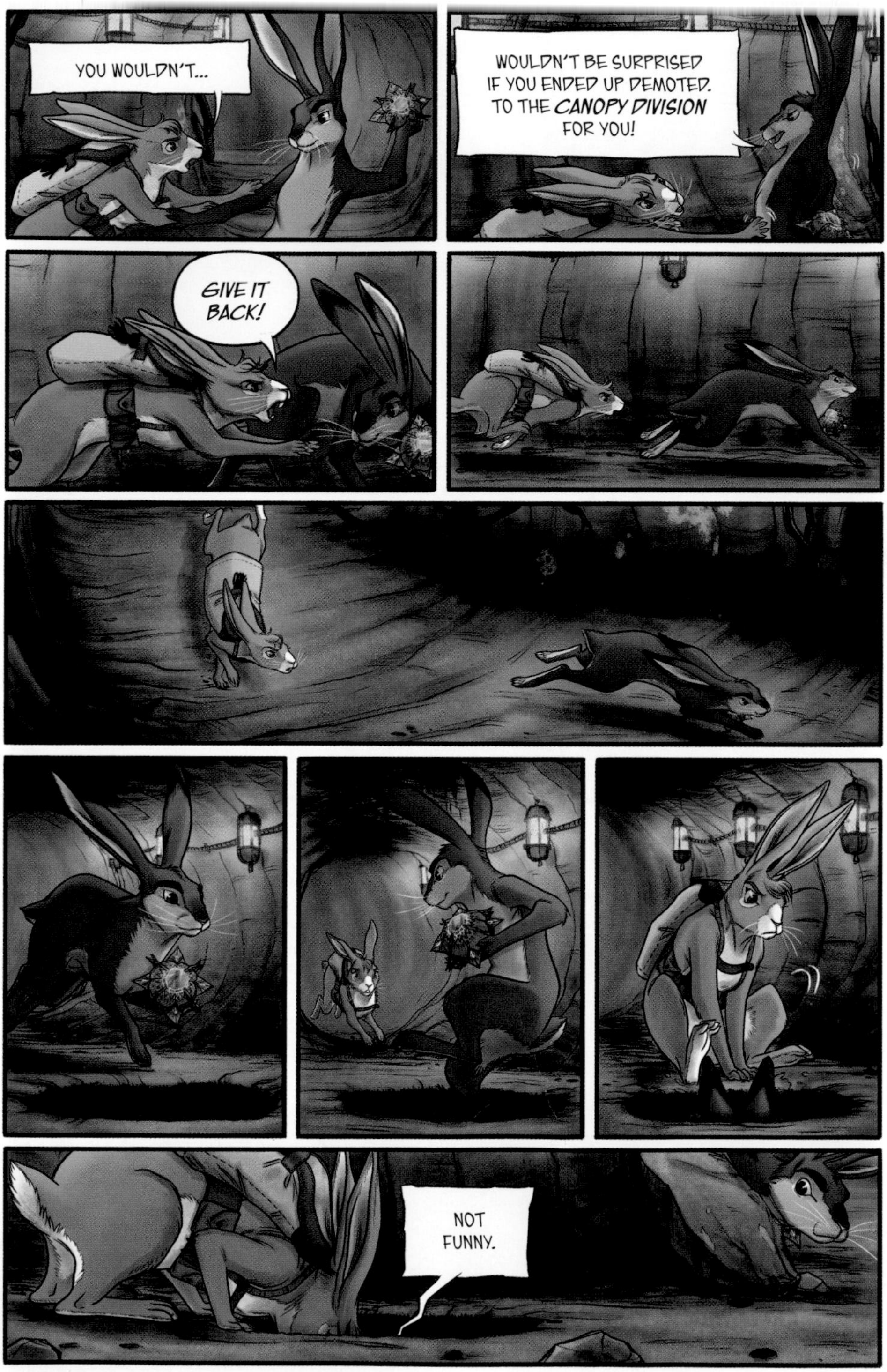
YOU WOULDN'T...
WOULDN'T BE SURPRISED IF YOU ENDED UP DEMOTED. TO THE CANOPY DIVISION FOR YOU!
GIVE IT BACK!
NOT FUNNY.

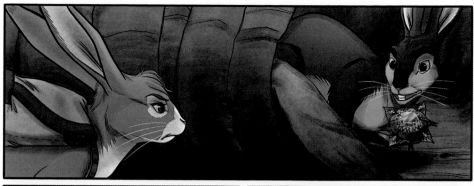

YOU WANT ME TO LOOK AT YOUR *THOKCHA?* LET'S SEE IT...

COME ON! IT'S WAY PAST MY START TIME!

TKK

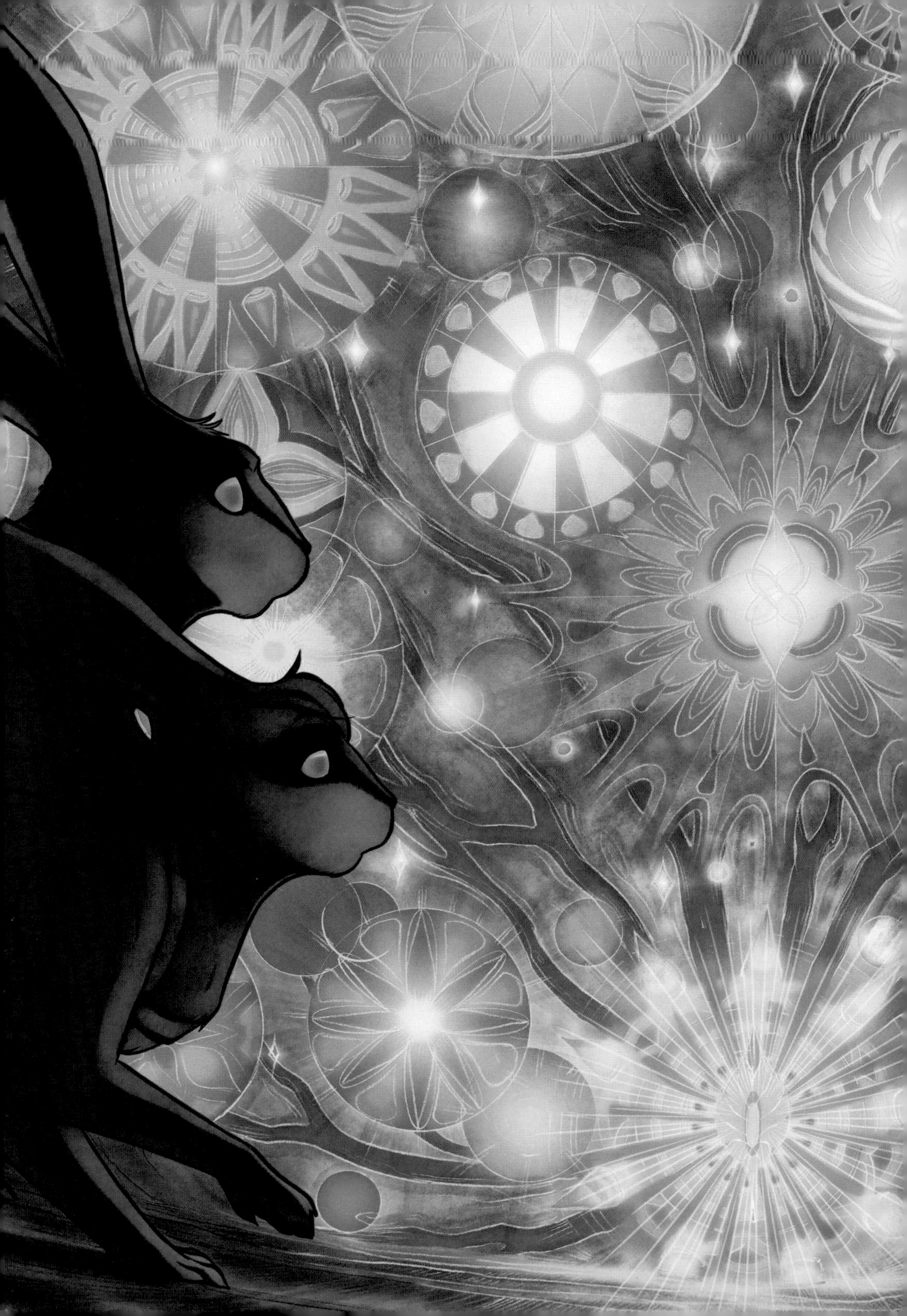

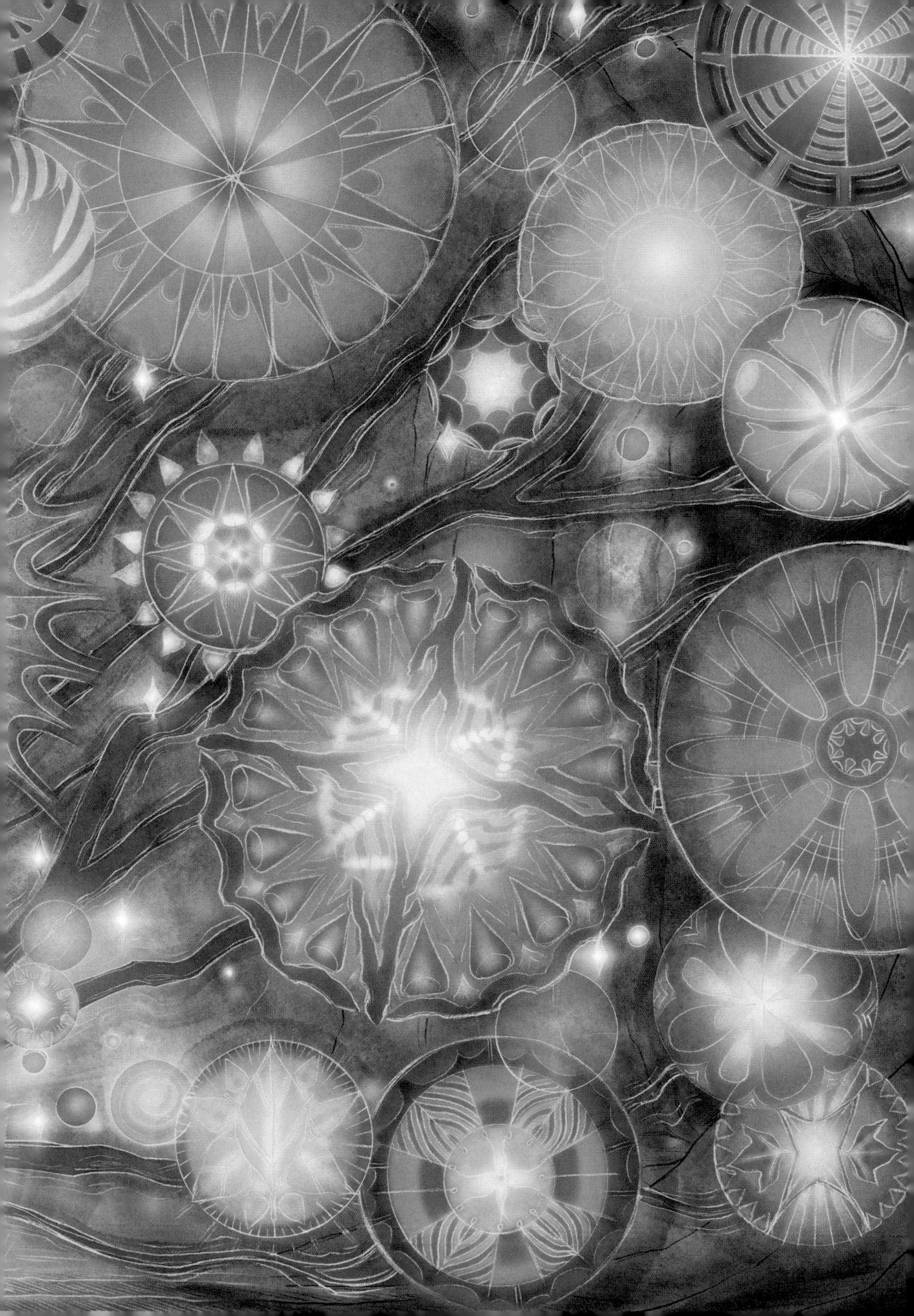

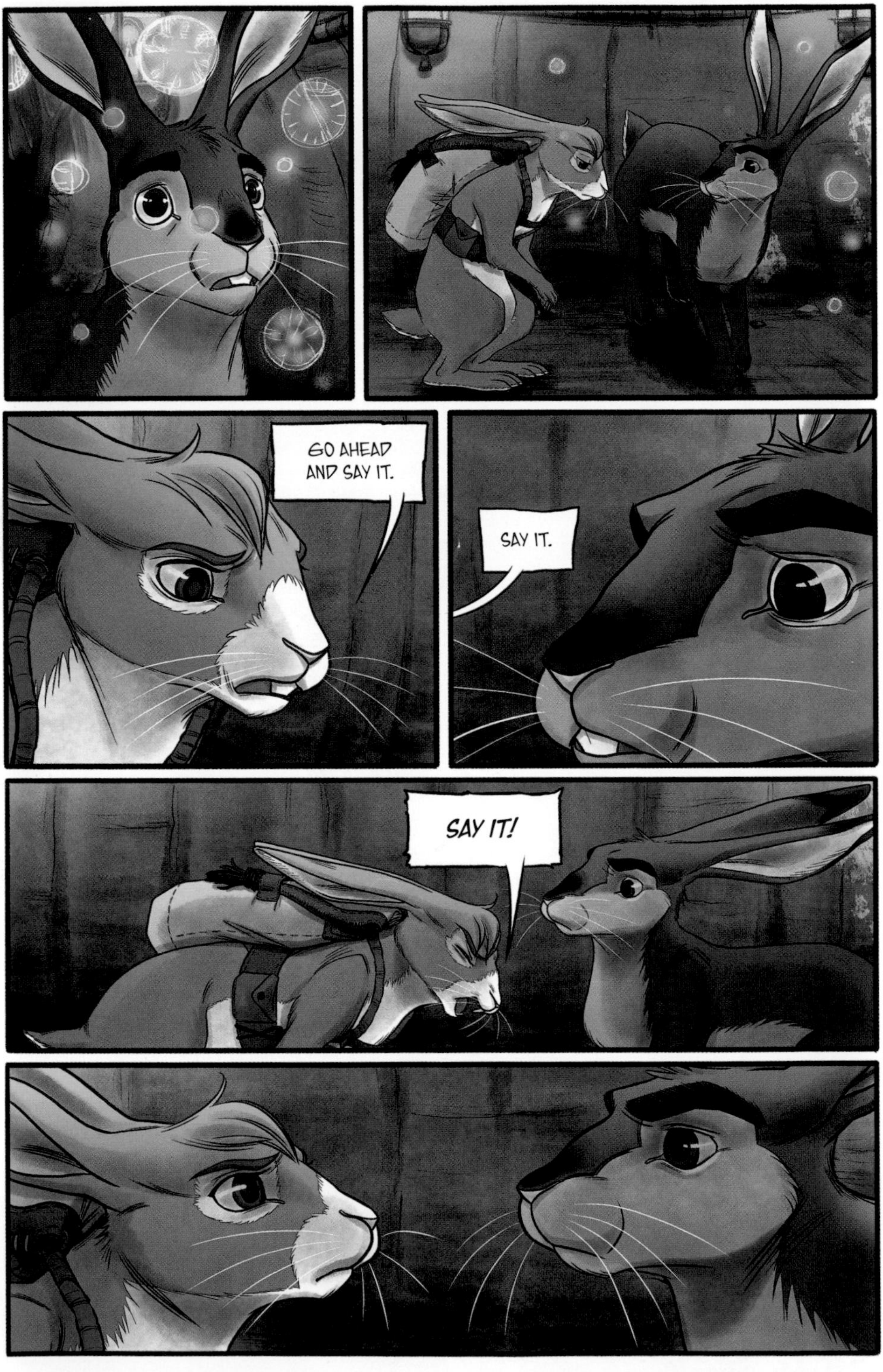
GO AHEAD AND SAY IT.
SAY IT.
SAY IT!

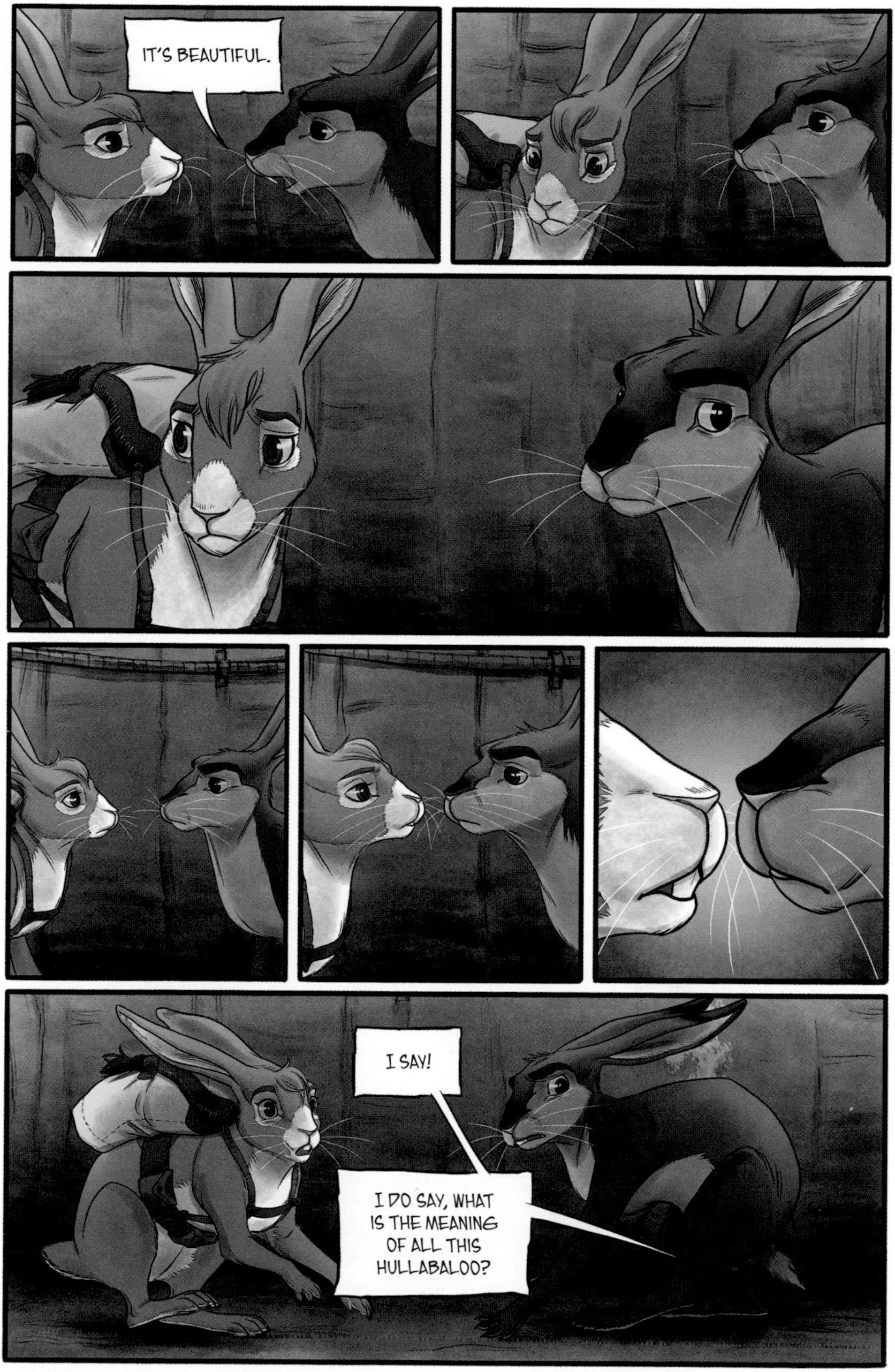
IT'S BEAUTIFUL.
I SAY!
I DO SAY, WHAT IS THE MEANING OF ALL THIS HULLABALOO?

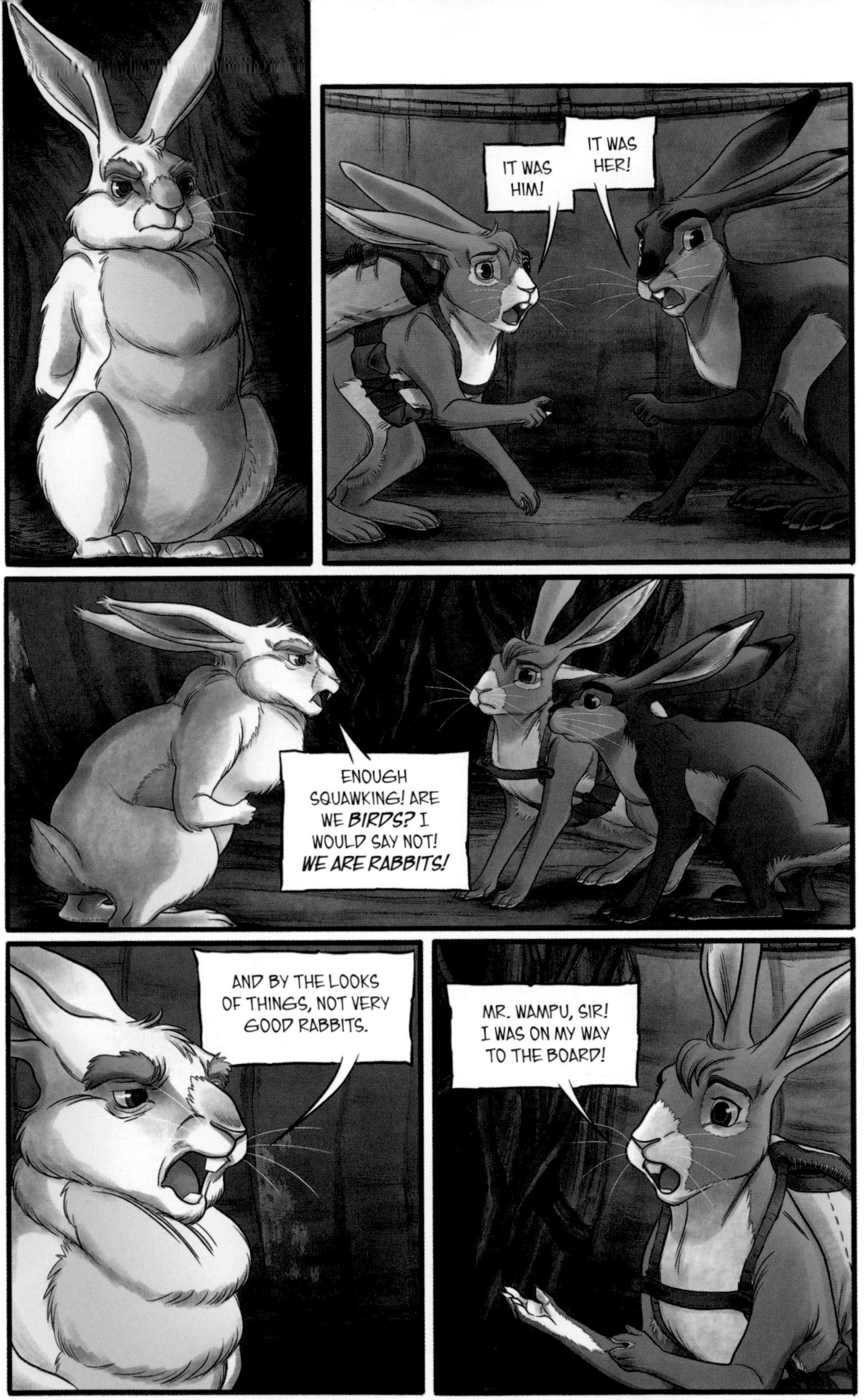
IT WAS HIM!
IT WAS HER!
ENOUGH SQUAWKING! ARE WE BIRDS? I WOULD SAY NOT! WE ARE RABBITS!
AND BY THE LOOKS OF THINGS, NOT VERY GOOD RABBITS.
MR. WAMPU, SIR! I WAS ON MY WAY TO THE BOARD!

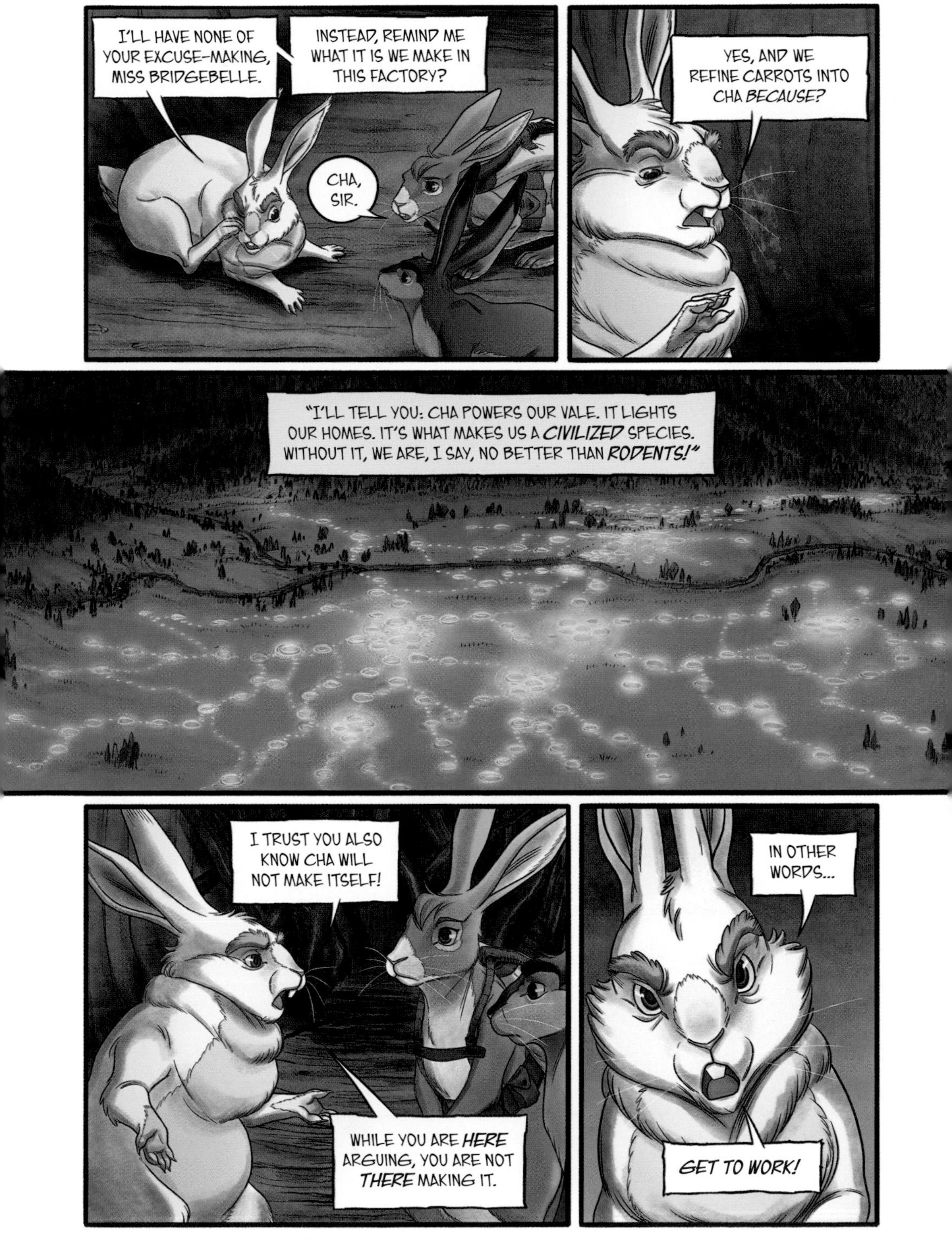

I'LL HAVE NONE OF YOUR EXCUSE-MAKING, MISS BRIDGEBELLE.
INSTEAD, REMIND ME WHAT IT IS WE MAKE IN THIS FACTORY?
CHA, SIR.
YES, AND WE REFINE CARROTS INTO CHA *BECAUSE?*
"I'LL TELL YOU: CHA POWERS OUR VALE. IT LIGHTS OUR HOMES. IT'S WHAT MAKES US A *CIVILIZED* SPECIES. WITHOUT IT, WE ARE, I SAY, NO BETTER THAN *RODENTS!*"
I TRUST YOU ALSO KNOW CHA WILL NOT MAKE ITSELF!
WHILE YOU ARE *HERE* ARGUING, YOU ARE NOT *THERE* MAKING IT.
IN OTHER WORDS...
GET TO WORK!

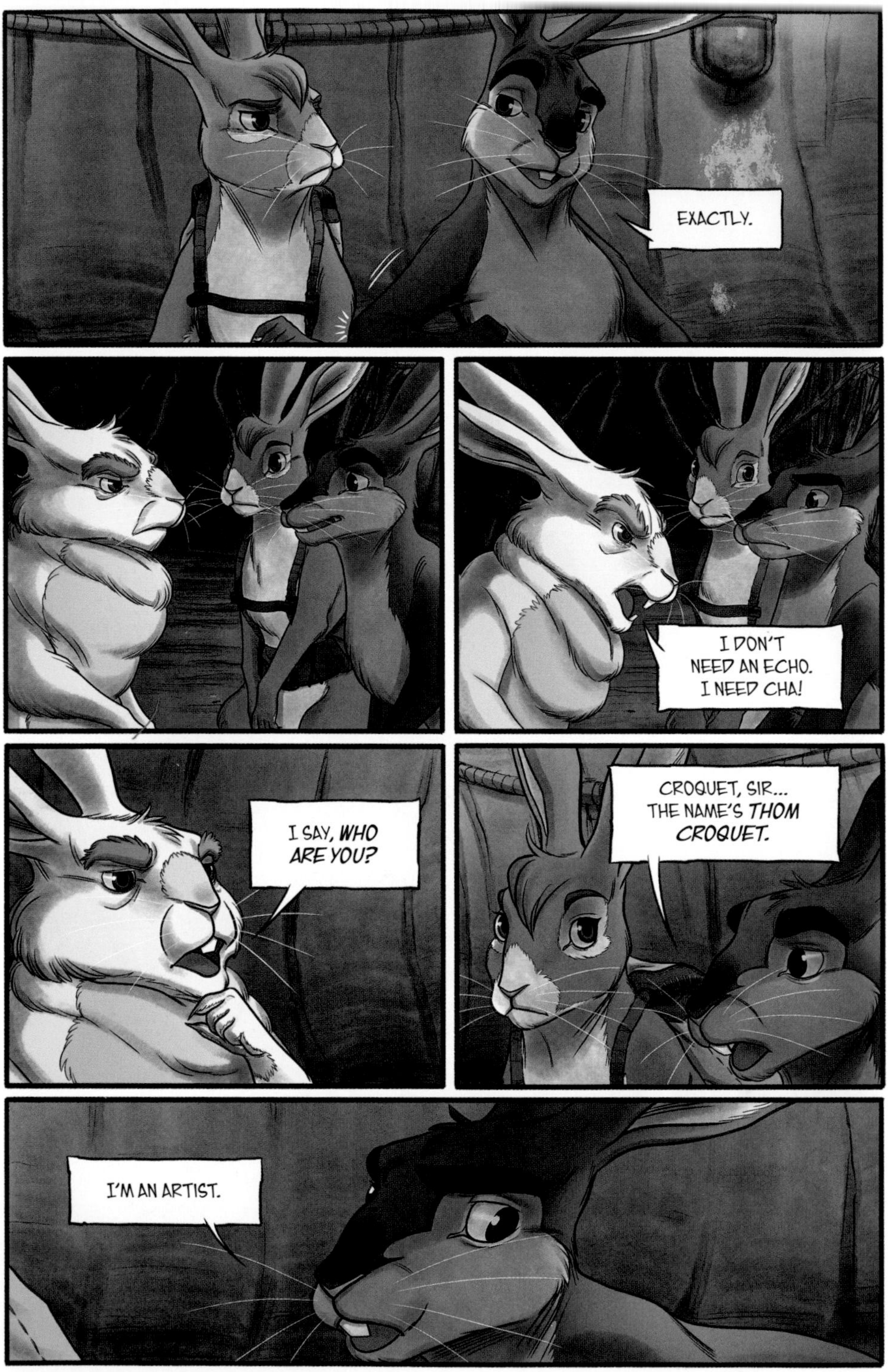
EXACTLY.
I DON'T NEED AN ECHO. I NEED CHA!
I SAY, WHO ARE YOU?
CROQUET, SIR... THE NAME'S THOM CROQUET.
I'M AN ARTIST.

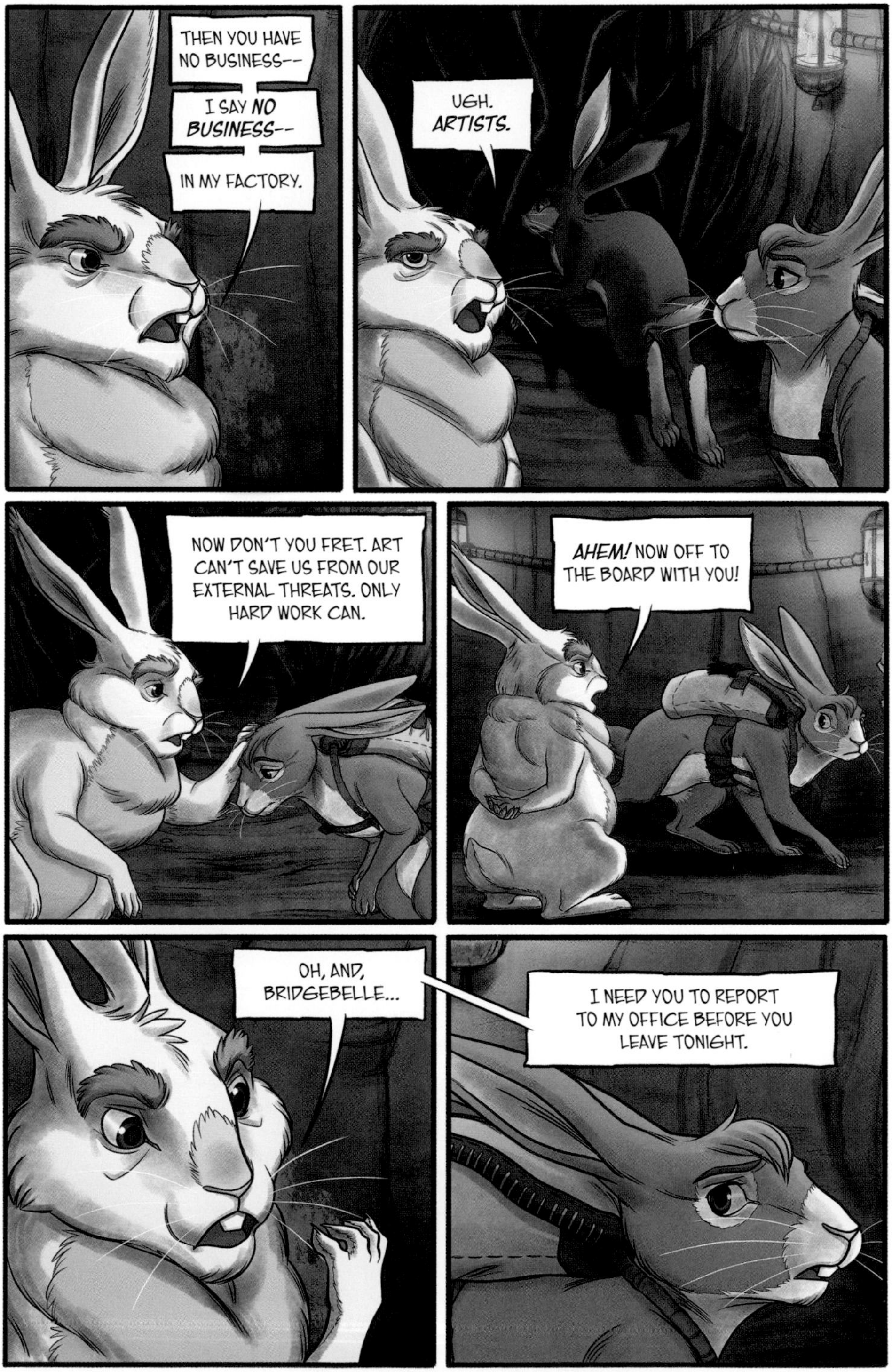

THEN YOU HAVE NO BUSINESS--
I SAY NO BUSINESS--
IN MY FACTORY.
UGH. ARTISTS.
NOW DON'T YOU FRET. ART CAN'T SAVE US FROM OUR EXTERNAL THREATS. ONLY HARD WORK CAN.
AHEM! NOW OFF TO THE BOARD WITH YOU!
OH, AND, BRIDGEBELLE...
I NEED YOU TO REPORT TO MY OFFICE BEFORE YOU LEAVE TONIGHT.

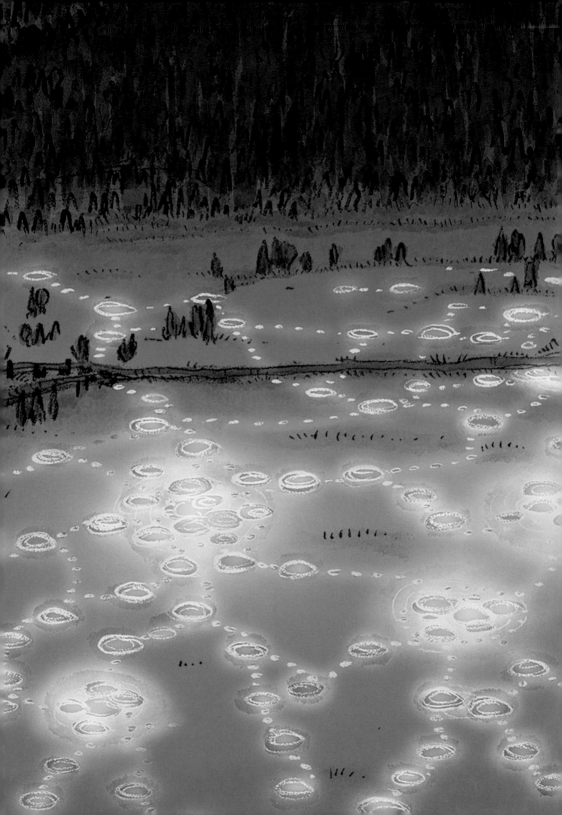

3. _____

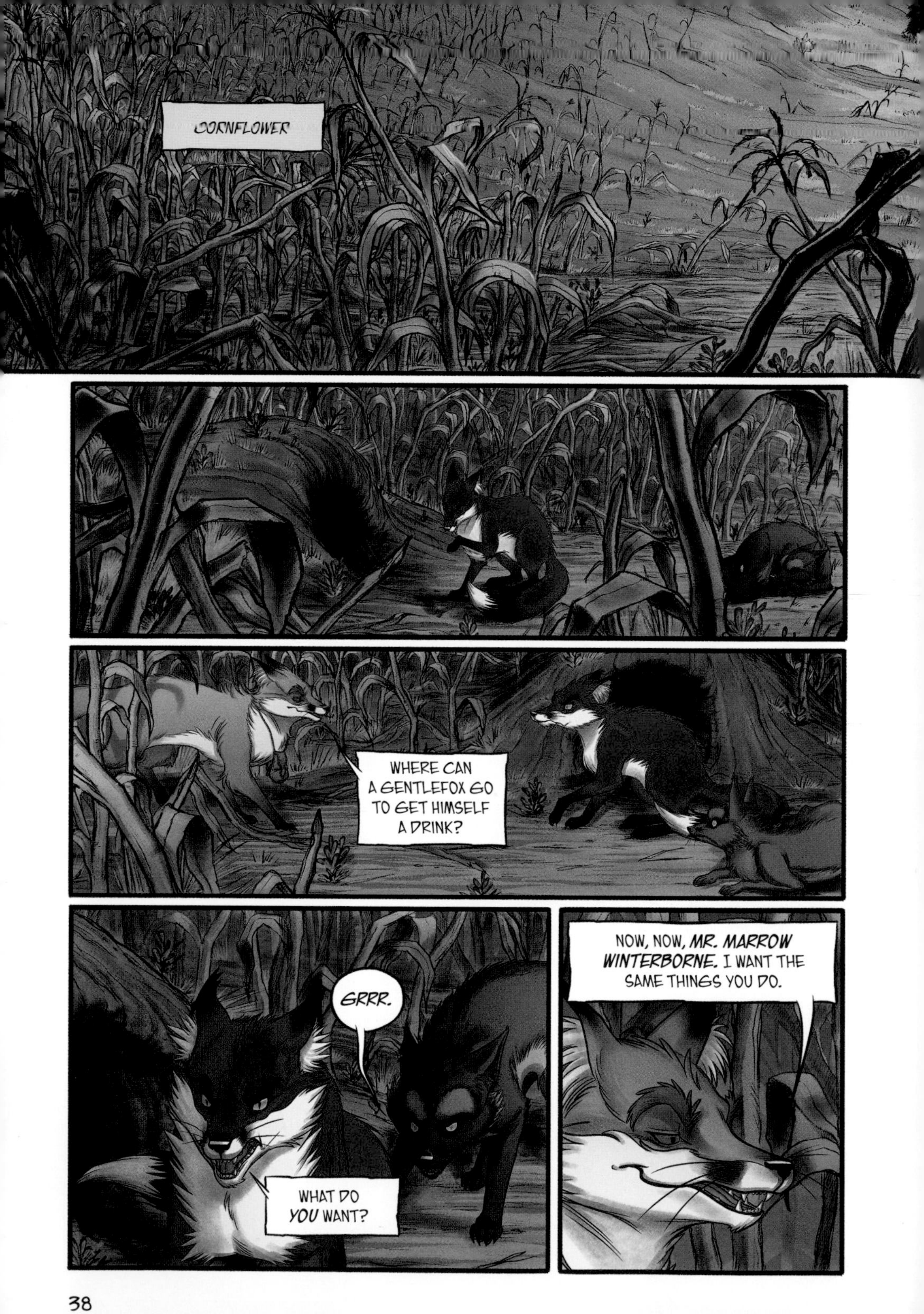
CORNFLOWER
WHERE CAN A GENTLEFOX GO TO GET HIMSELF A DRINK?
GRRR.
WHAT DO *YOU* WANT?
NOW, NOW, ***MR. MARROW WINTERBORNE.*** I WANT THE SAME THINGS YOU DO.

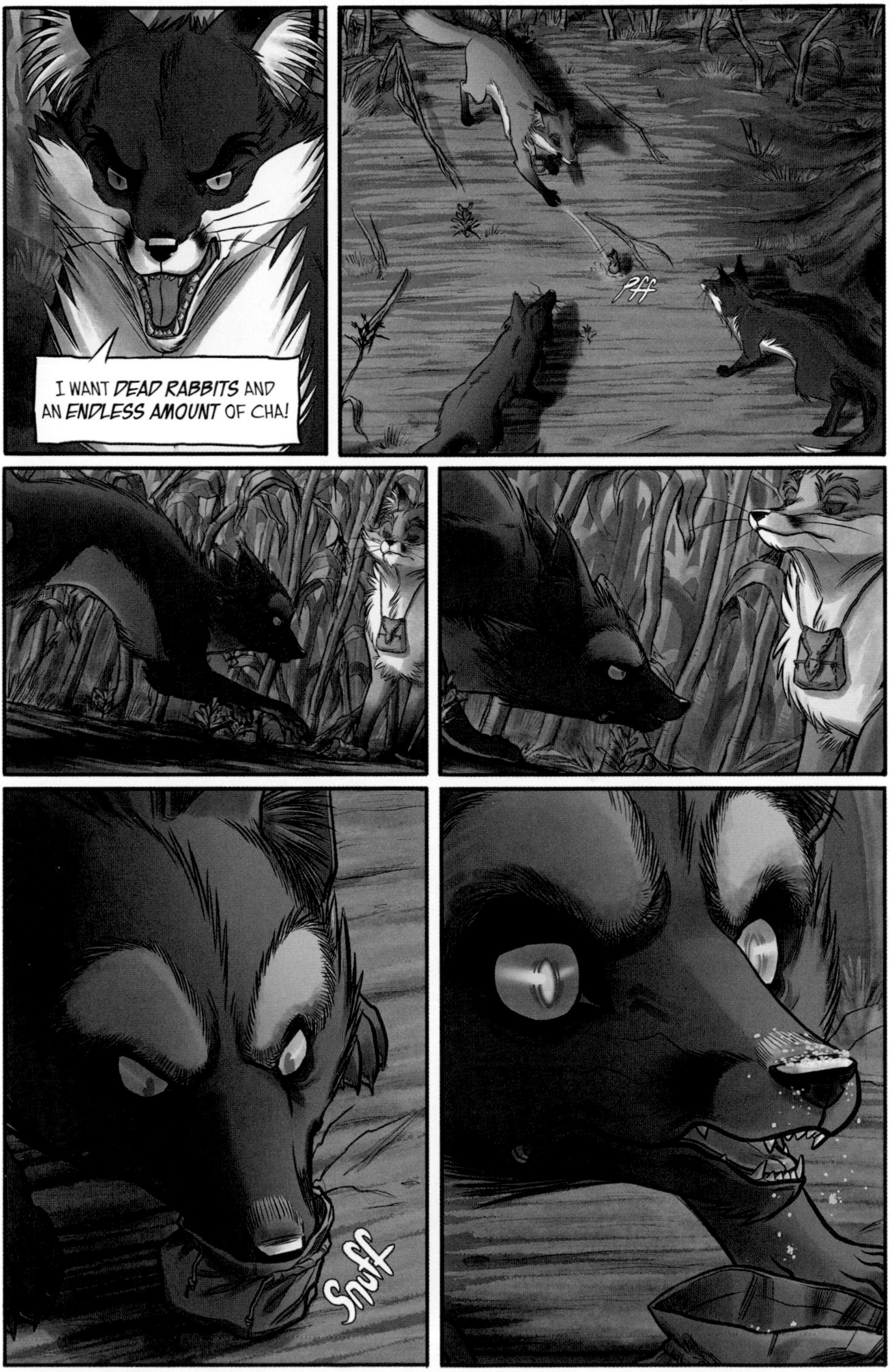

I WANT DEAD RABBITS AND AN ENDLESS AMOUNT OF CHA!
Pff
Snuff

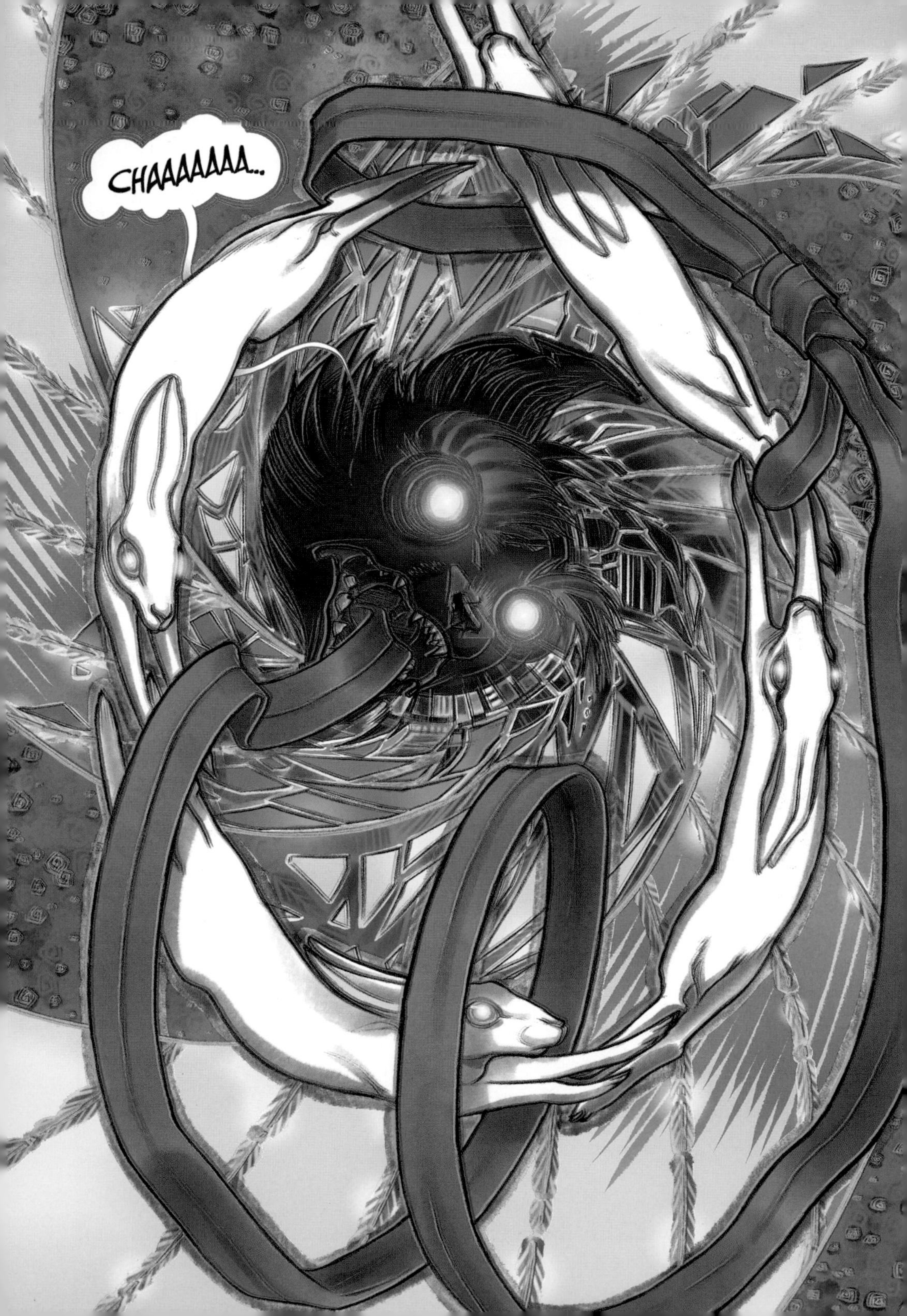
CHAAAAAAA...

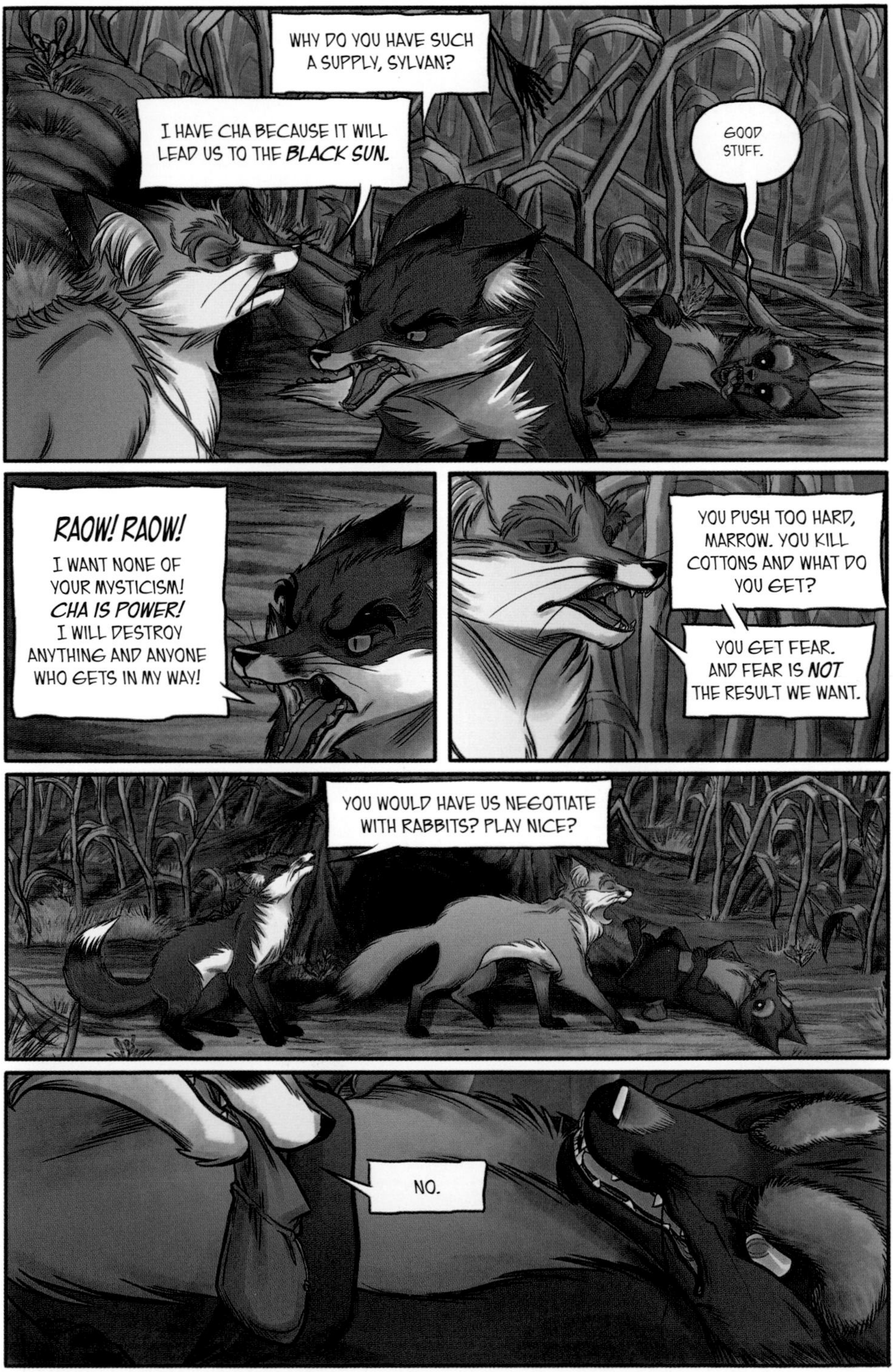

WHY DO YOU HAVE SUCH A SUPPLY, SYLVAN?
I HAVE CHA BECAUSE IT WILL LEAD US TO THE BLACK SUN.
GOOD STUFF.
RAOW! RAOW! I WANT NONE OF YOUR MYSTICISM! CHA IS POWER! I WILL DESTROY ANYTHING AND ANYONE WHO GETS IN MY WAY!
YOU PUSH TOO HARD, MARROW. YOU KILL COTTONS AND WHAT DO YOU GET?
YOU GET FEAR. AND FEAR IS NOT THE RESULT WE WANT.
YOU WOULD HAVE US NEGOTIATE WITH RABBITS? PLAY NICE?
NO.

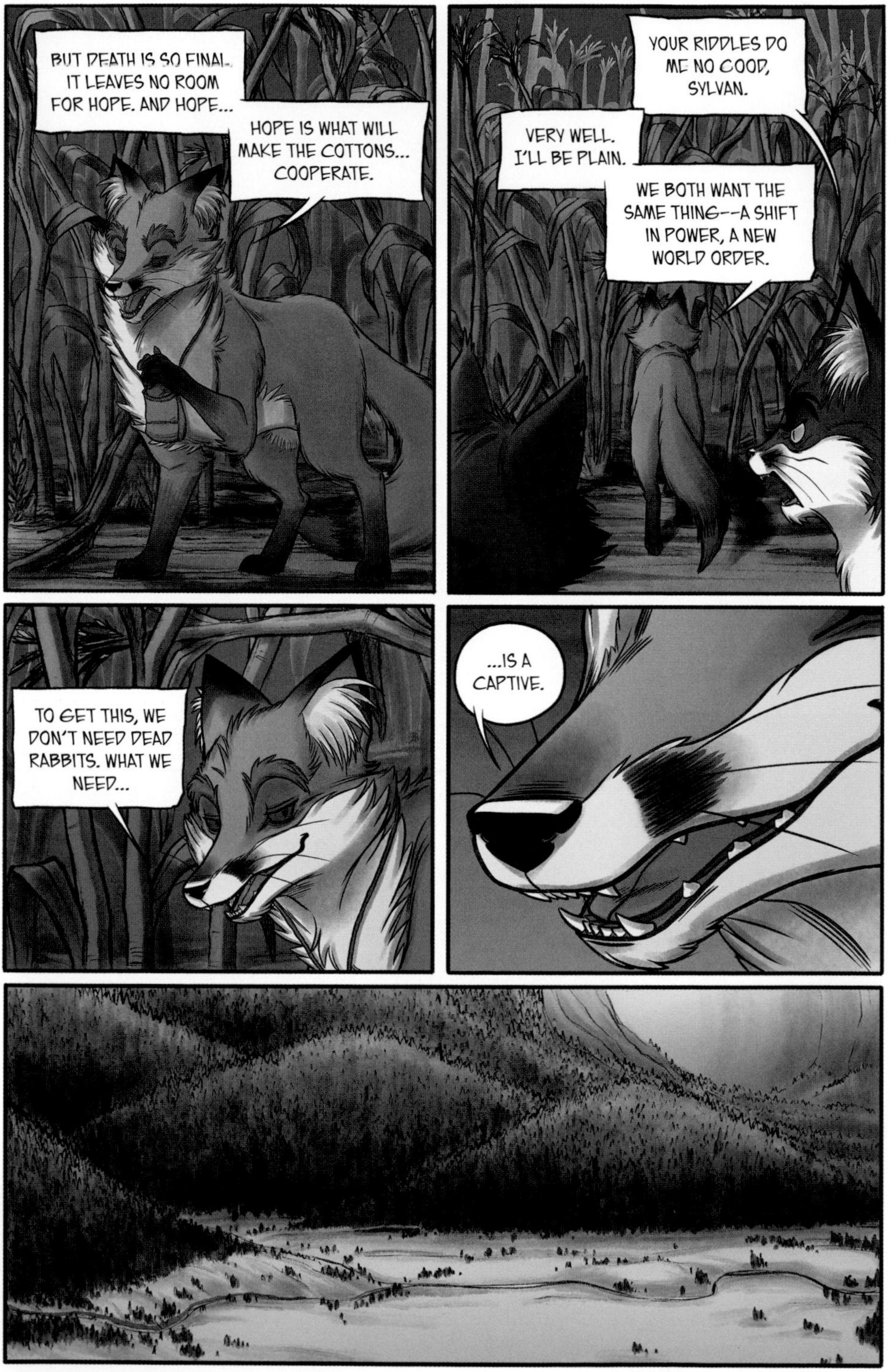
BUT DEATH IS SO FINAL. IT LEAVES NO ROOM FOR HOPE. AND HOPE...
HOPE IS WHAT WILL MAKE THE COTTONS... COOPERATE.
YOUR RIDDLES DO MC NO COOD, SYLVAN.
VERY WELL. I'LL BE PLAIN.
WE BOTH WANT THE SAME THING--A SHIFT IN POWER, A NEW WORLD ORDER.
TO GET THIS, WE DON'T NEED DEAD RABBITS. WHAT WE NEED...
...IS A CAPTIVE.

4.

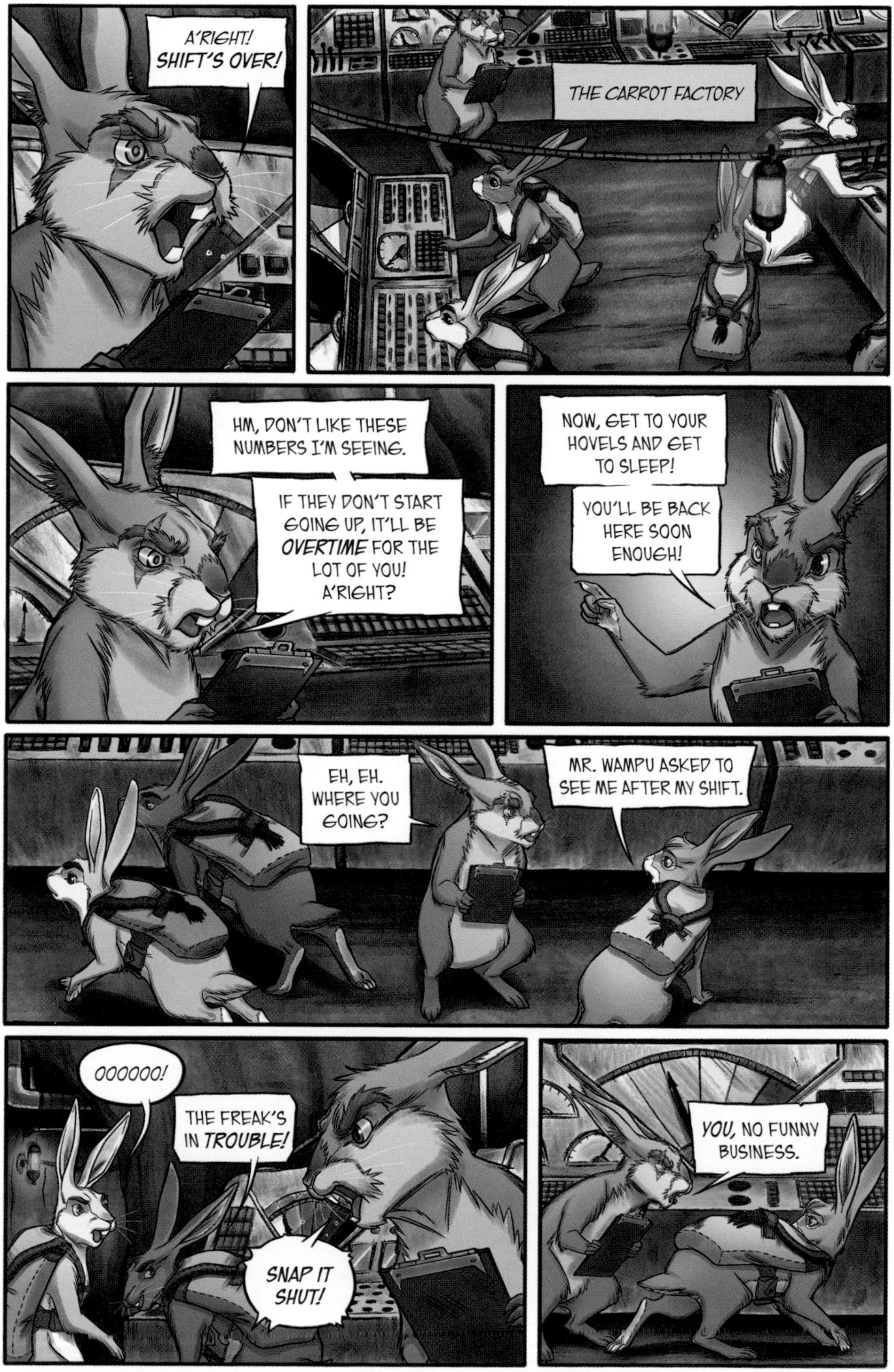
A'RIGHT! SHIFT'S OVER!
THE CARROT FACTORY
HM, DON'T LIKE THESE NUMBERS I'M SEEING.
IF THEY DON'T START GOING UP, IT'LL BE OVERTIME FOR THE LOT OF YOU! A'RIGHT?
NOW, GET TO YOUR HOVELS AND GET TO SLEEP!
YOU'LL BE BACK HERE SOON ENOUGH!
EH, EH. WHERE YOU GOING?
MR. WAMPU ASKED TO SEE ME AFTER MY SHIFT.
OOOOOO!
THE FREAK'S IN TROUBLE!
SNAP IT SHUT!
YOU, NO FUNNY BUSINESS.

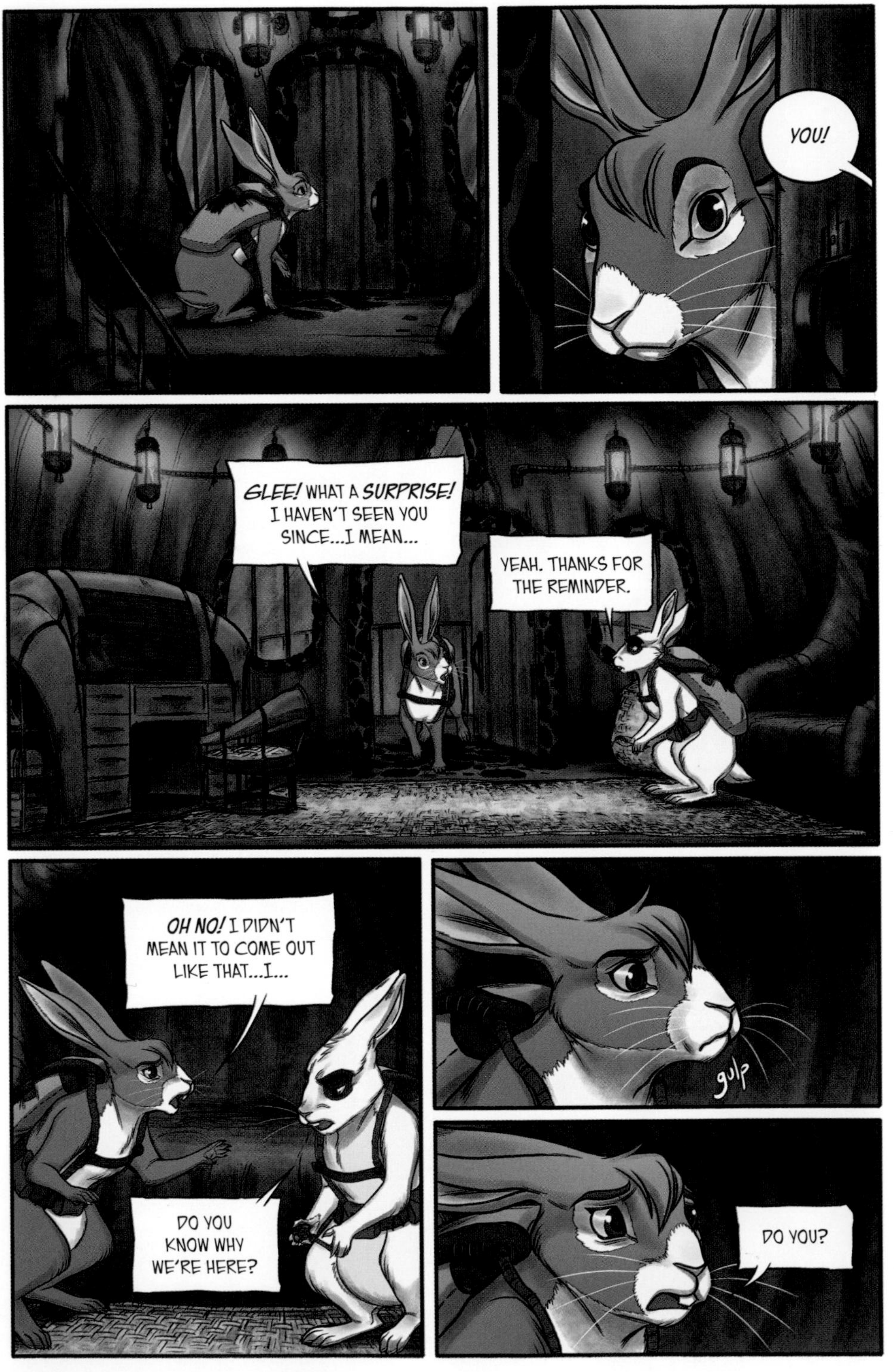
YOU!
GLEE! WHAT A SURPRISE! I HAVEN'T SEEN YOU SINCE...I MEAN...
YEAH. THANKS FOR THE REMINDER.
OH NO! I DIDN'T MEAN IT TO COME OUT LIKE THAT...I...
DO YOU KNOW WHY WE'RE HERE?
gulp
DO YOU?

WAIT! YOU'RE FROM THE *CANOPY DIVISION*, RIGHT?

...

THAT'S IT! I'M BEING *DEMOTED*.

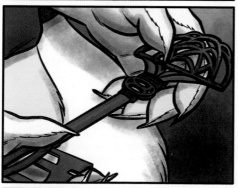

DID YOU HEAR WHAT HAPPENED THIS MORNING?

CROQUET MADE A *COMPLETE* MESS OF THINGS.

I CAN'T BELIEVE YOU. I CAN SEE WHY FOLKS THINK YOU'RE WEIRD.

THE FOX THREAT IS REAL. IF THEY TAKE OVER THE FACTORY, WE'LL ALL BE DOOMED.

SO GO AHEAD-- MAKE SMALL TALK ABOUT YOUR OLD TEACHER.

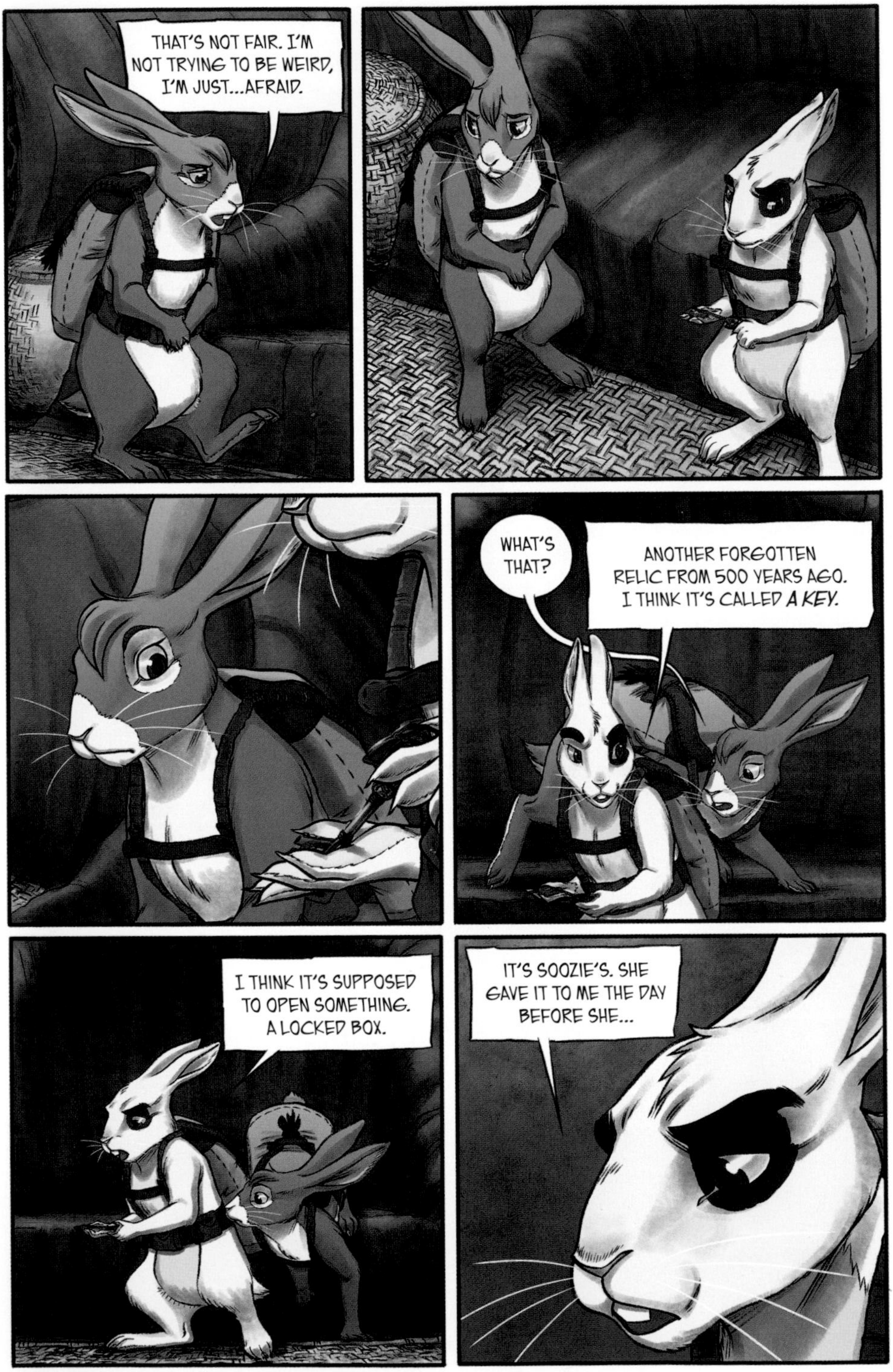
THAT'S NOT FAIR. I'M NOT TRYING TO BE WEIRD, I'M JUST...AFRAID.
WHAT'S THAT?
ANOTHER FORGOTTEN RELIC FROM 500 YEARS AGO. I THINK IT'S CALLED *A KEY.*
I THINK IT'S SUPPOSED TO OPEN SOMETHING. A LOCKED BOX.
IT'S SOOZIE'S. SHE GAVE IT TO ME THE DAY BEFORE SHE...

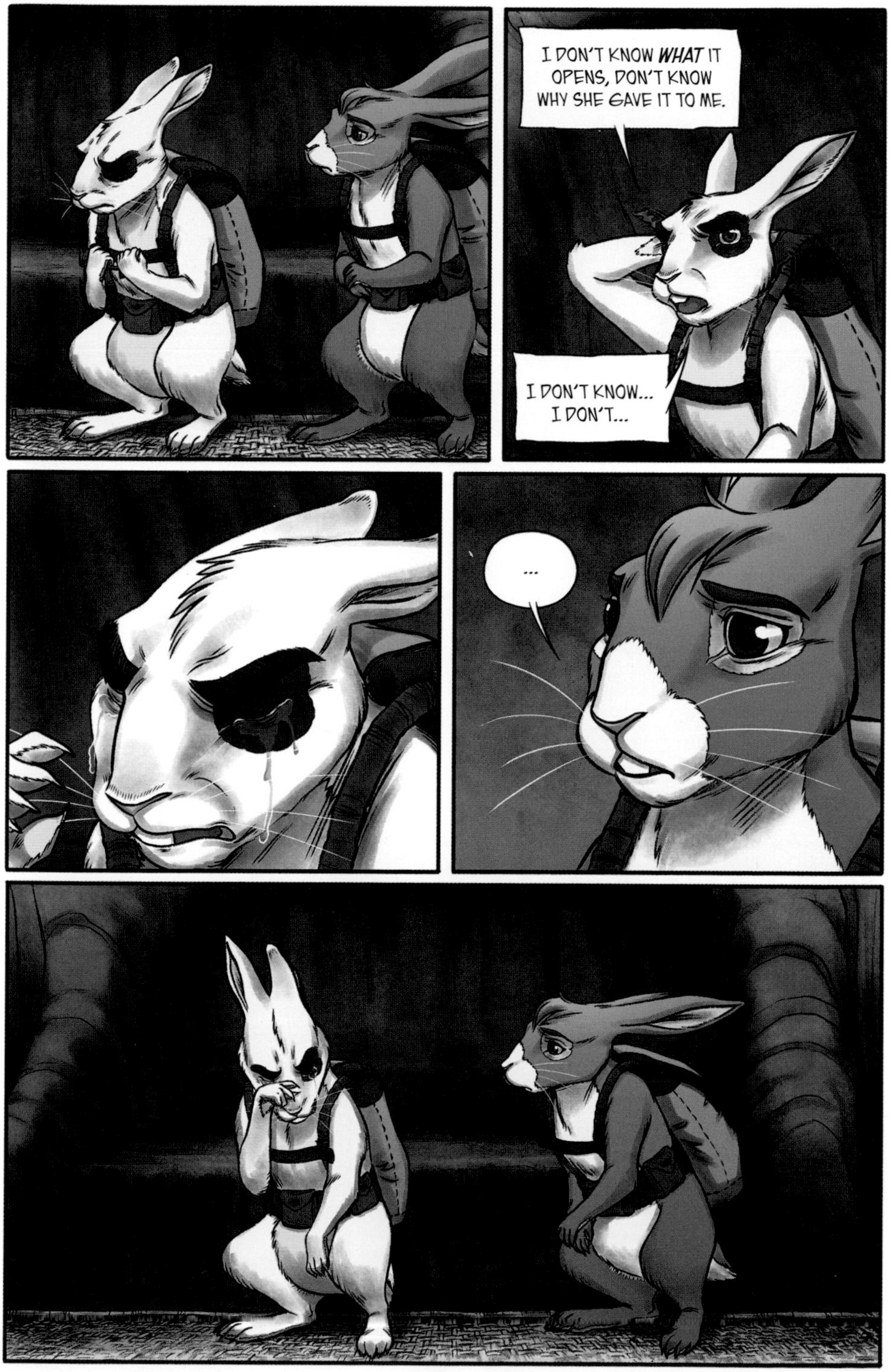

I DON'T KNOW ***WHAT*** IT OPENS, DON'T KNOW WHY SHE GAVE IT TO ME.
I DON'T KNOW... I DON'T...
...

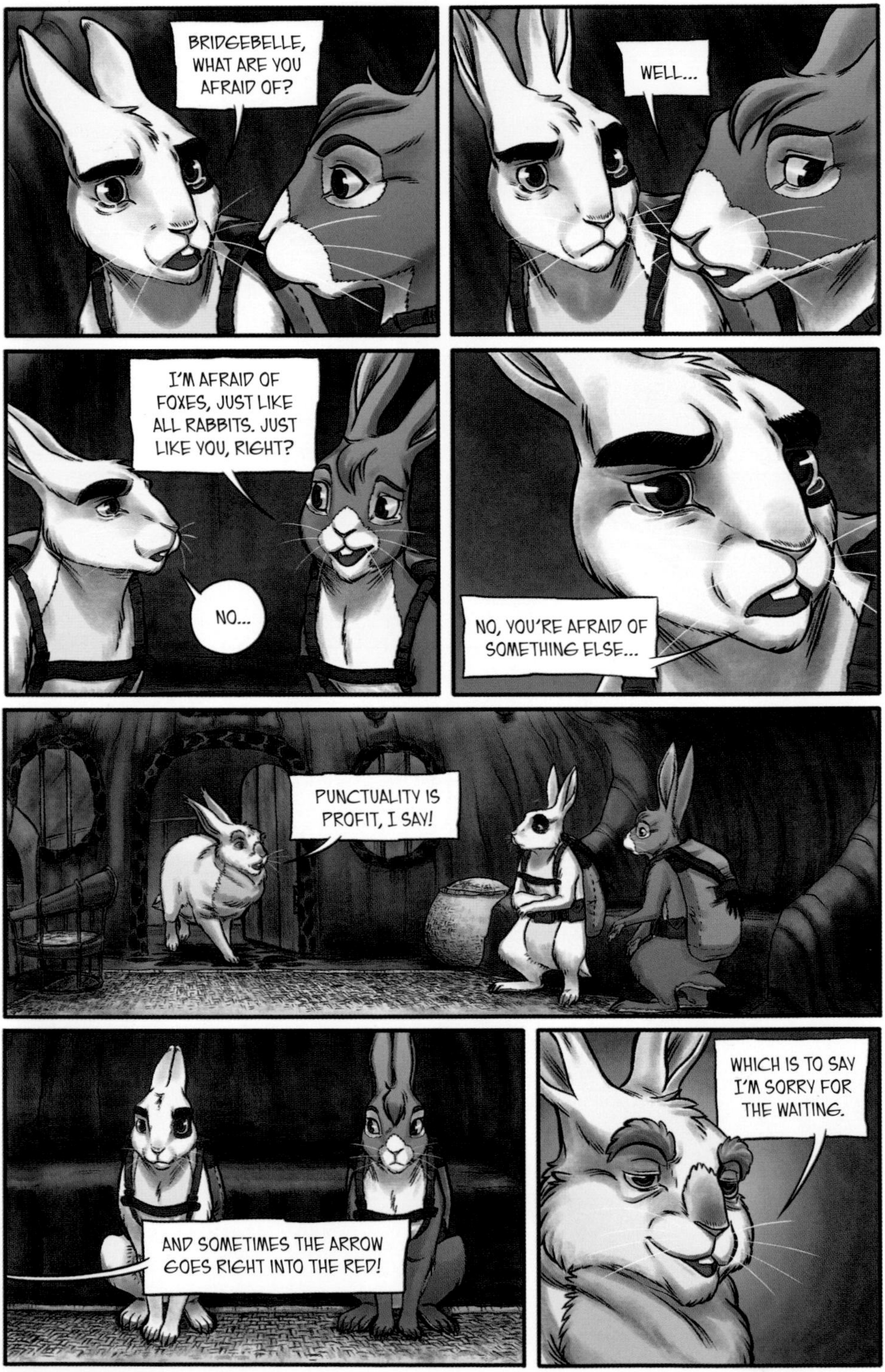
BRIDGEBELLE, WHAT ARE YOU AFRAID OF?
WELL...
I'M AFRAID OF FOXES, JUST LIKE ALL RABBITS. JUST LIKE YOU, RIGHT?
NO...
NO, YOU'RE AFRAID OF SOMETHING ELSE...
PUNCTUALITY IS PROFIT, I SAY!
AND SOMETIMES THE ARROW GOES RIGHT INTO THE RED!
WHICH IS TO SAY I'M SORRY FOR THE WAITING.

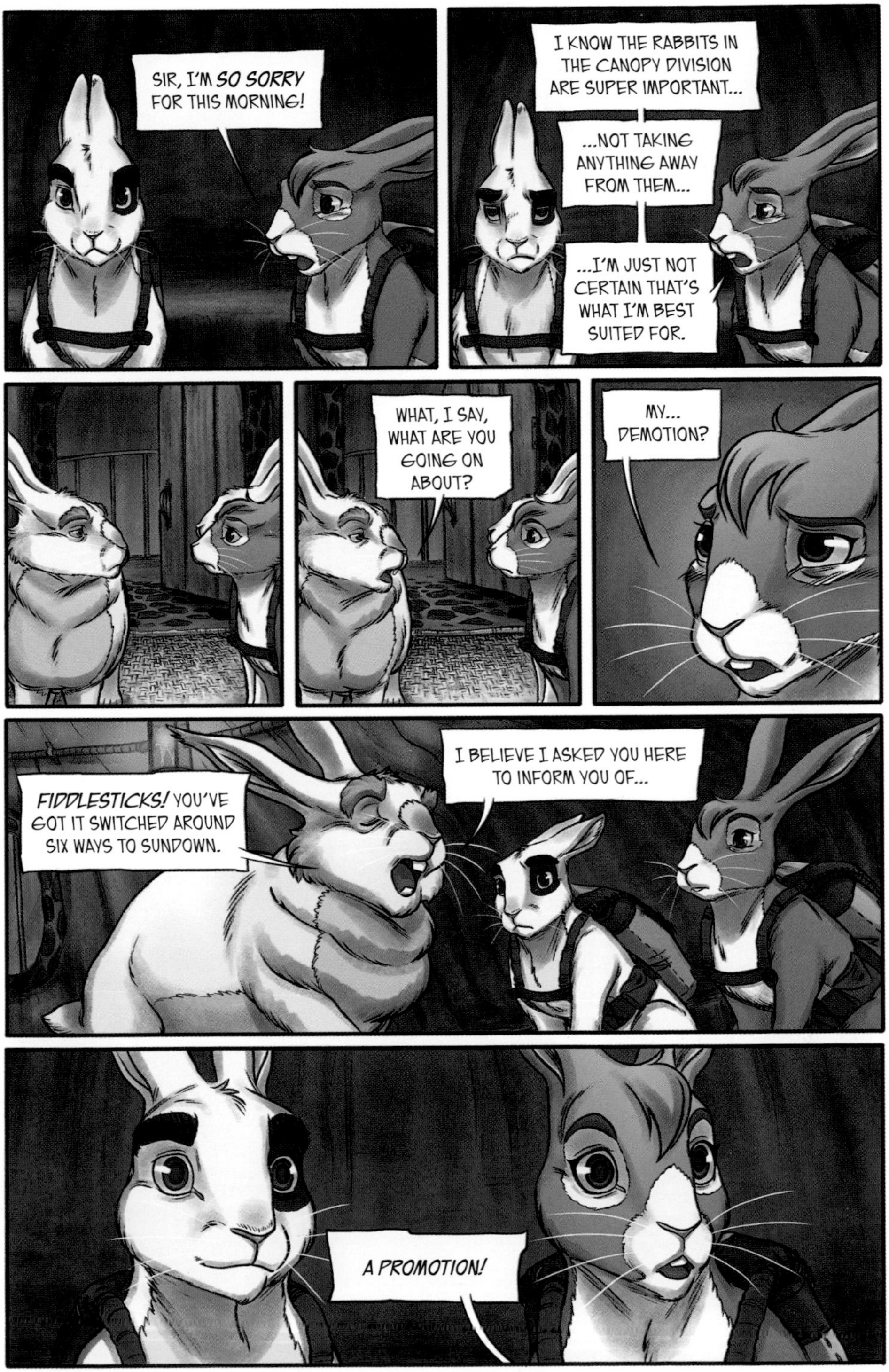

SIR, I'M *SO SORRY* FOR THIS MORNING!
I KNOW THE RABBITS IN THE CANOPY DIVISION ARE SUPER IMPORTANT...
...NOT TAKING ANYTHING AWAY FROM THEM...
...I'M JUST NOT CERTAIN THAT'S WHAT I'M BEST SUITED FOR.
WHAT, I SAY, WHAT ARE YOU GOING ON ABOUT?
MY... DEMOTION?
FIDDLESTICKS! YOU'VE GOT IT SWITCHED AROUND SIX WAYS TO SUNDOWN.
I BELIEVE I ASKED YOU HERE TO INFORM YOU OF...
A PROMOTION!

HEH.

SO WHAT'S HE DOING HERE?

I CAN *HEAR* YOU.

NOW THAT YOU ARE A MANAGER, YOU NEED SOMEONE TO MANAGE.

MR. GLEE HAS BEEN PROMOTED TO THE BOARD.

THANK YOU, SIR.

BRIDGEBELLE, I EXPECT GREAT THINGS FROM YOU.

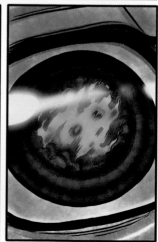

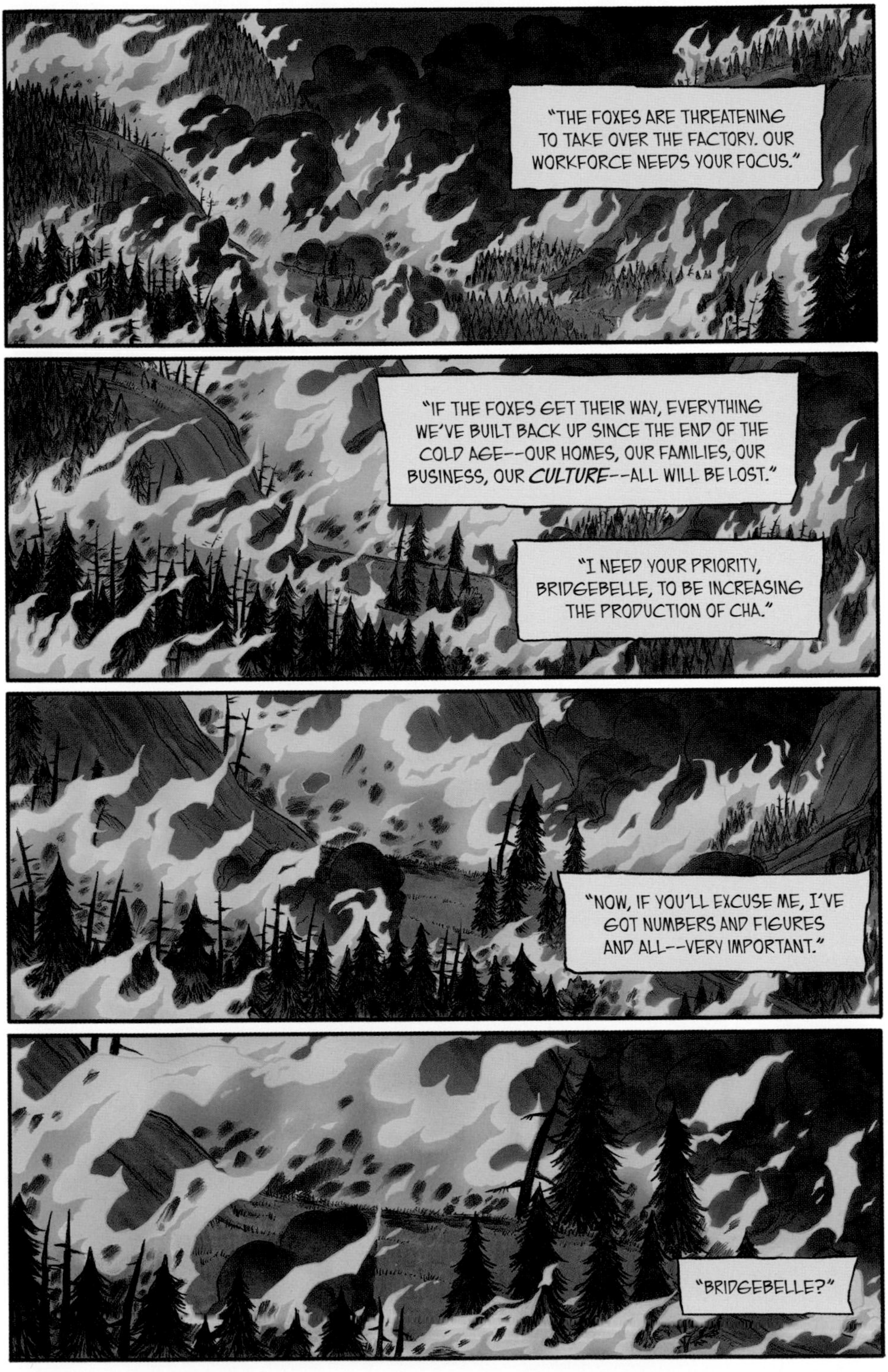
"THE FOXES ARE THREATENING TO TAKE OVER THE FACTORY. OUR WORKFORCE NEEDS YOUR FOCUS."
"IF THE FOXES GET THEIR WAY, EVERYTHING WE'VE BUILT BACK UP SINCE THE END OF THE COLD AGE--OUR HOMES, OUR FAMILIES, OUR BUSINESS, OUR *CULTURE*--ALL WILL BE LOST."
"I NEED YOUR PRIORITY, BRIDGEBELLE, TO BE INCREASING THE PRODUCTION OF CHA."
"NOW, IF YOU'LL EXCUSE ME, I'VE GOT NUMBERS AND FIGURES AND ALL--VERY IMPORTANT."
"BRIDGEBELLE?"

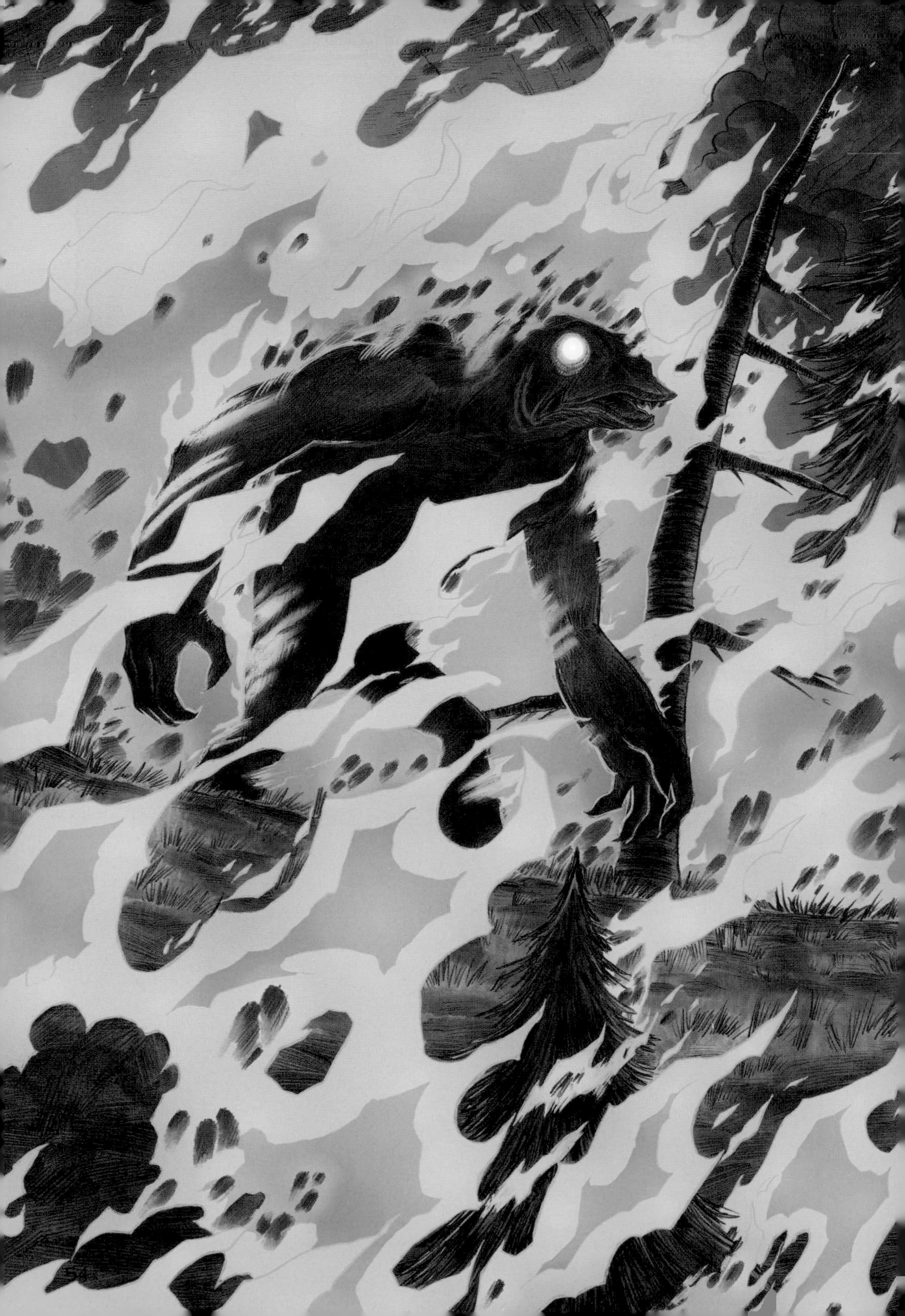

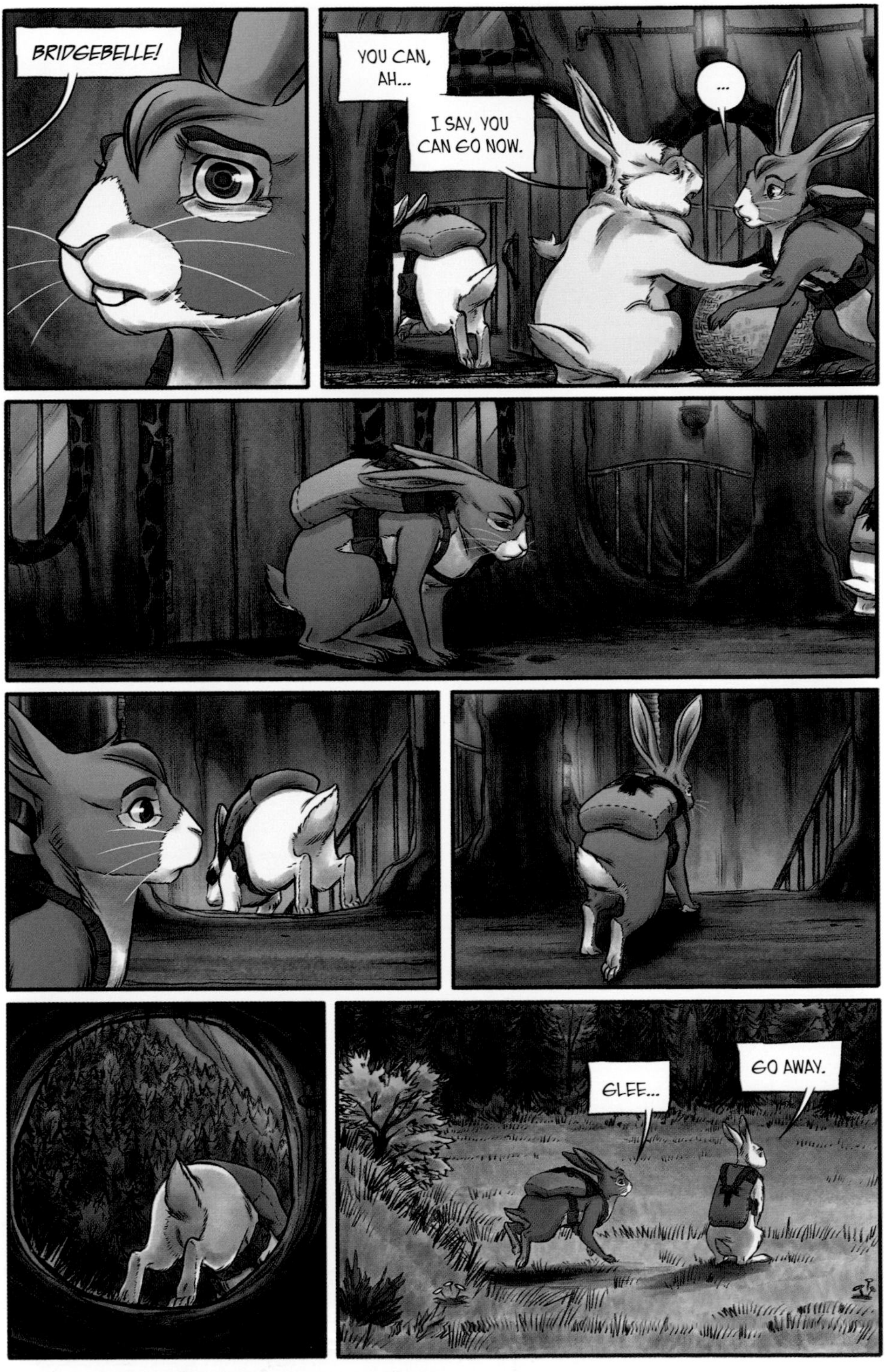
BRIDGEBELLE!
YOU CAN, AH...
I SAY, YOU CAN GO NOW.
...
GLEE...
GO AWAY.

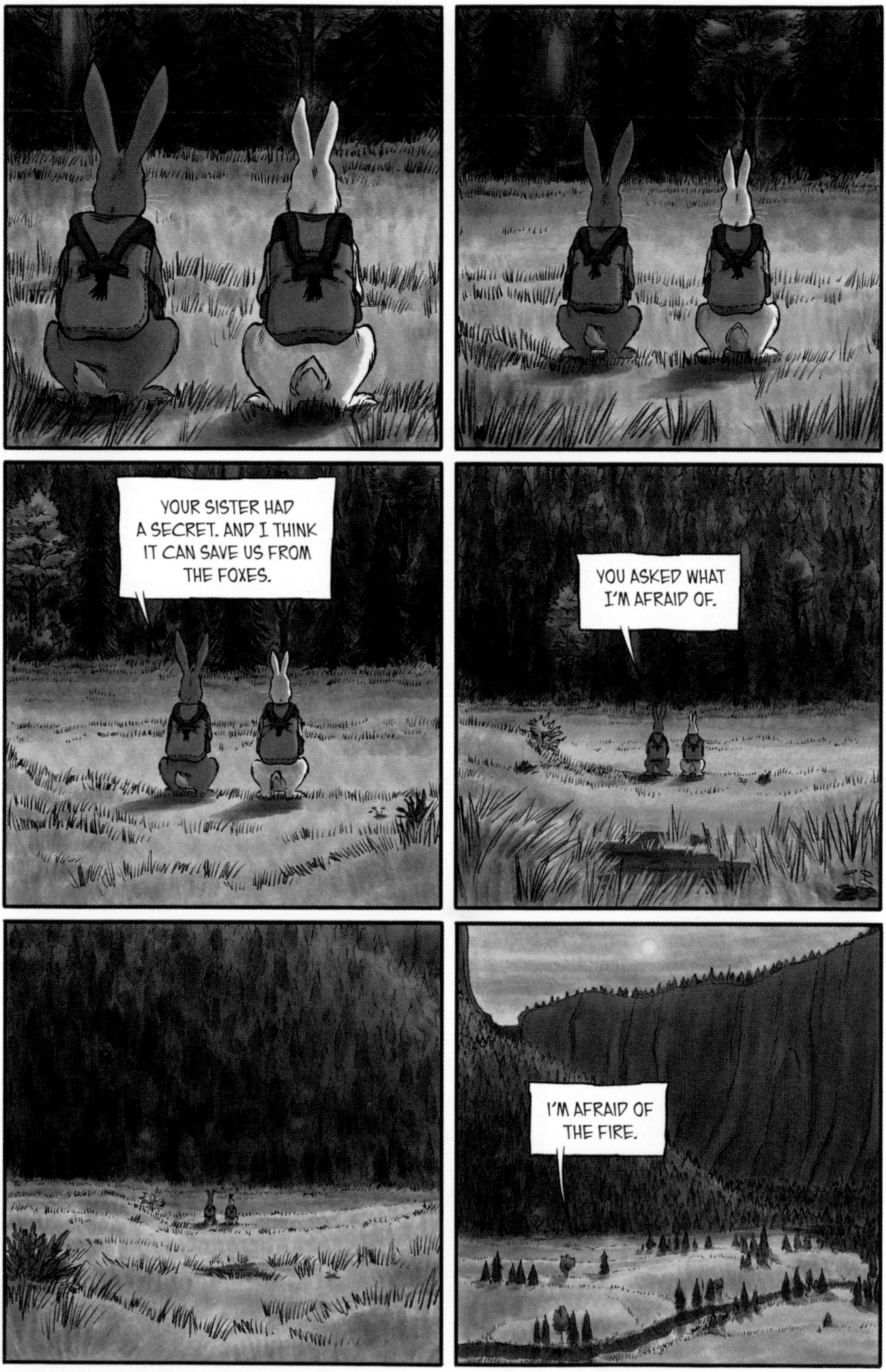
YOUR SISTER HAD A SECRET. AND I THINK IT CAN SAVE US FROM THE FOXES.
YOU ASKED WHAT I'M AFRAID OF.
I'M AFRAID OF THE FIRE.

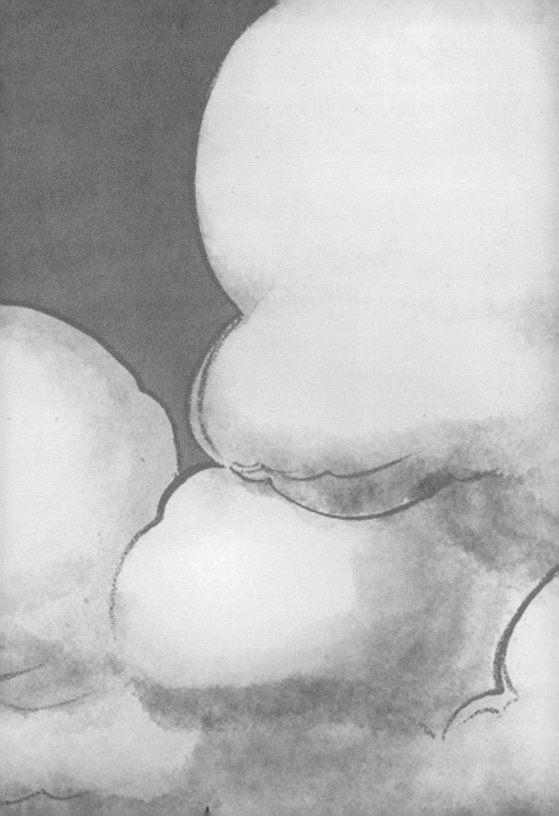

II

"WE WILL ALL BE FREE"

5. _____

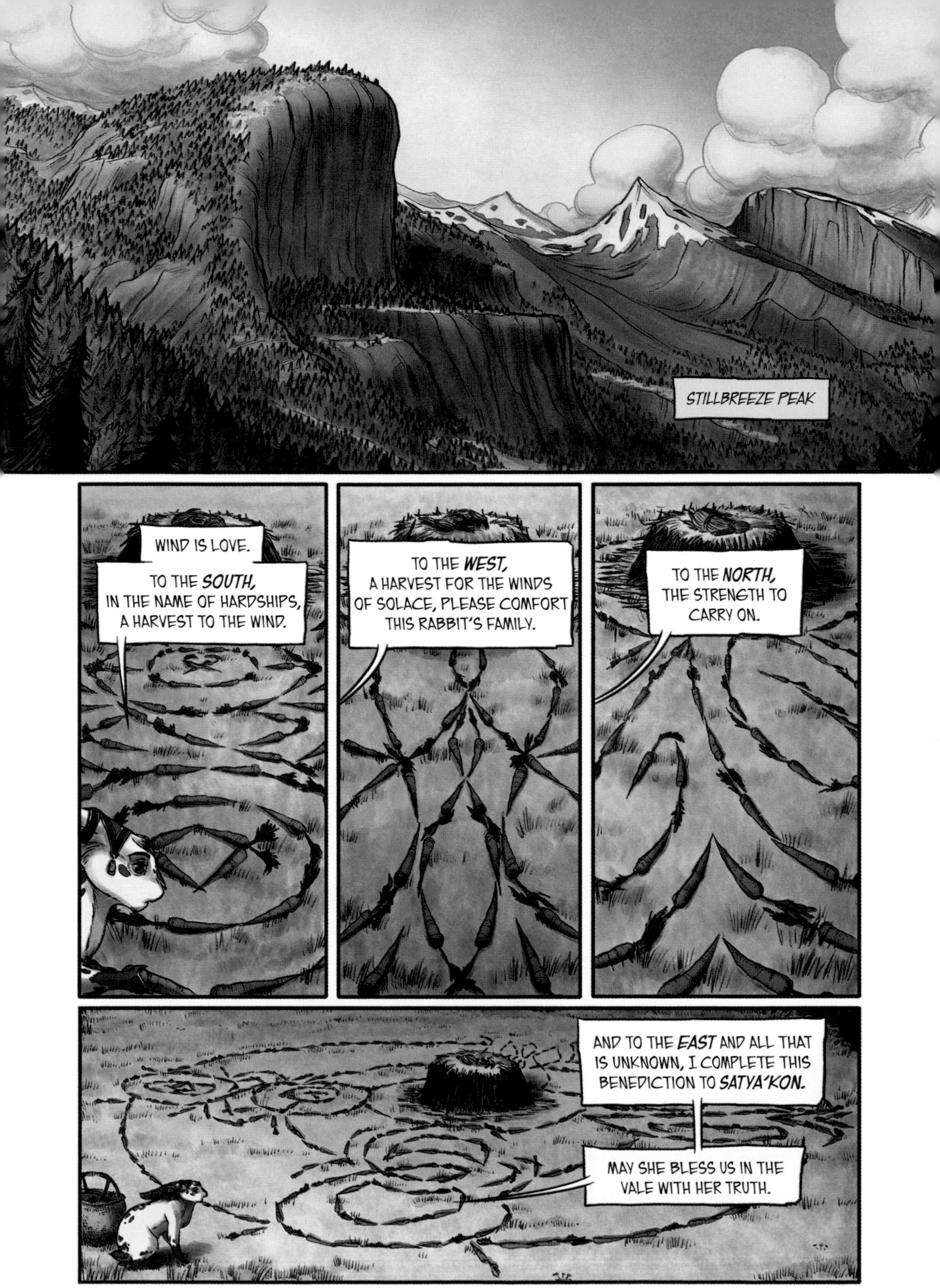
STILLBREEZE PEAK
WIND IS LOVE.
TO THE SOUTH, IN THE NAME OF HARDSHIPS, A HARVEST TO THE WIND.
TO THE WEST, A HARVEST FOR THE WINDS OF SOLACE, PLEASE COMFORT THIS RABBIT'S FAMILY.
TO THE NORTH, THE STRENGTH TO CARRY ON.
AND TO THE EAST AND ALL THAT IS UNKNOWN, I COMPLETE THIS BENEDICTION TO SATYA'KON.
MAY SHE BLESS US IN THE VALE WITH HER TRUTH.

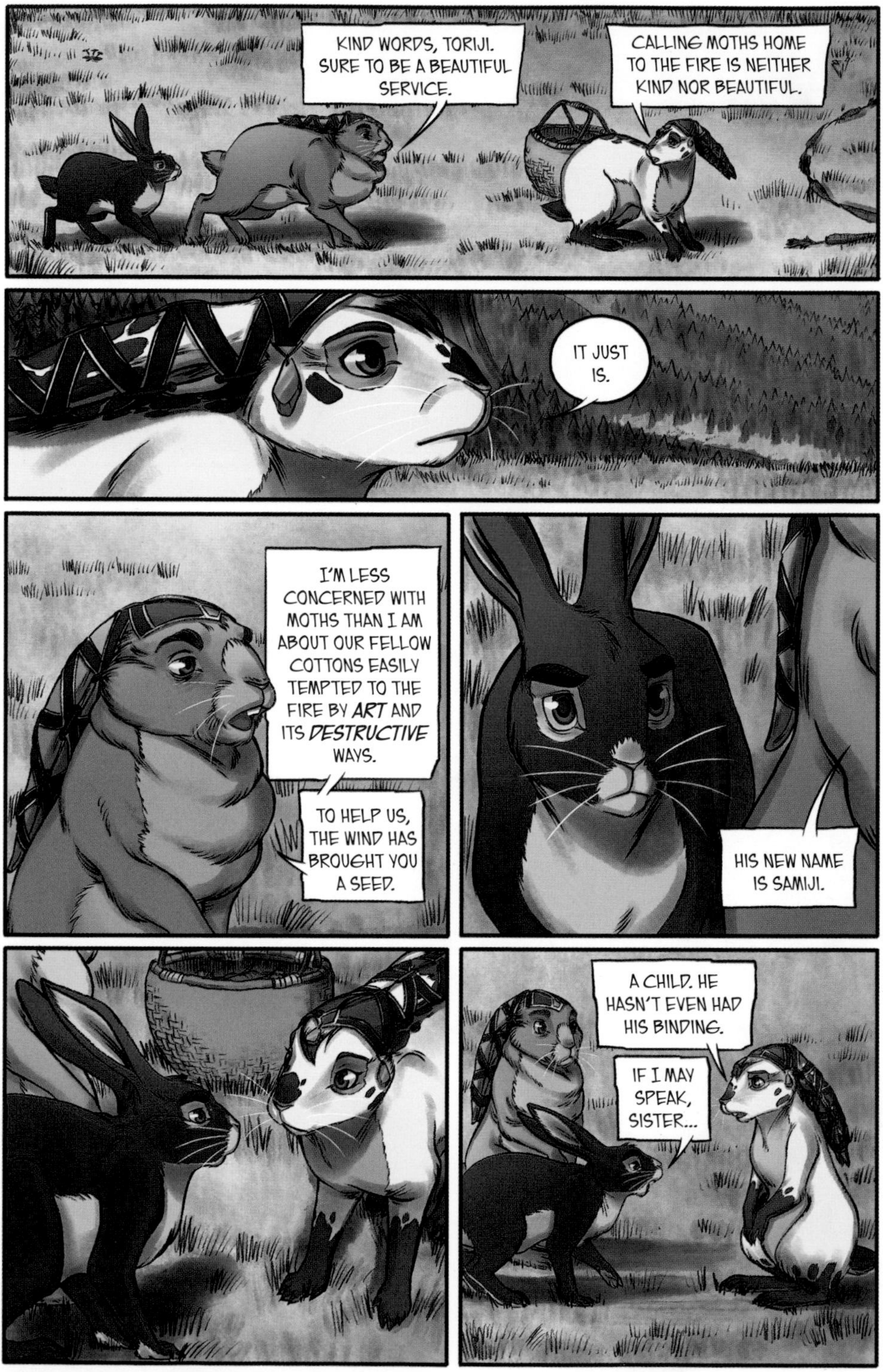
KIND WORDS, TORIJI. SURE TO BE A BEAUTIFUL SERVICE.
CALLING MOTHS HOME TO THE FIRE IS NEITHER KIND NOR BEAUTIFUL.
IT JUST IS.
I'M LESS CONCERNED WITH MOTHS THAN I AM ABOUT OUR FELLOW COTTONS EASILY TEMPTED TO THE FIRE BY *ART* AND ITS *DESTRUCTIVE* WAYS.
TO HELP US, THE WIND HAS BROUGHT YOU A SEED.
HIS NEW NAME IS SAMIJI.
A CHILD. HE HASN'T EVEN HAD HIS BINDING.
IF I MAY SPEAK, SISTER...

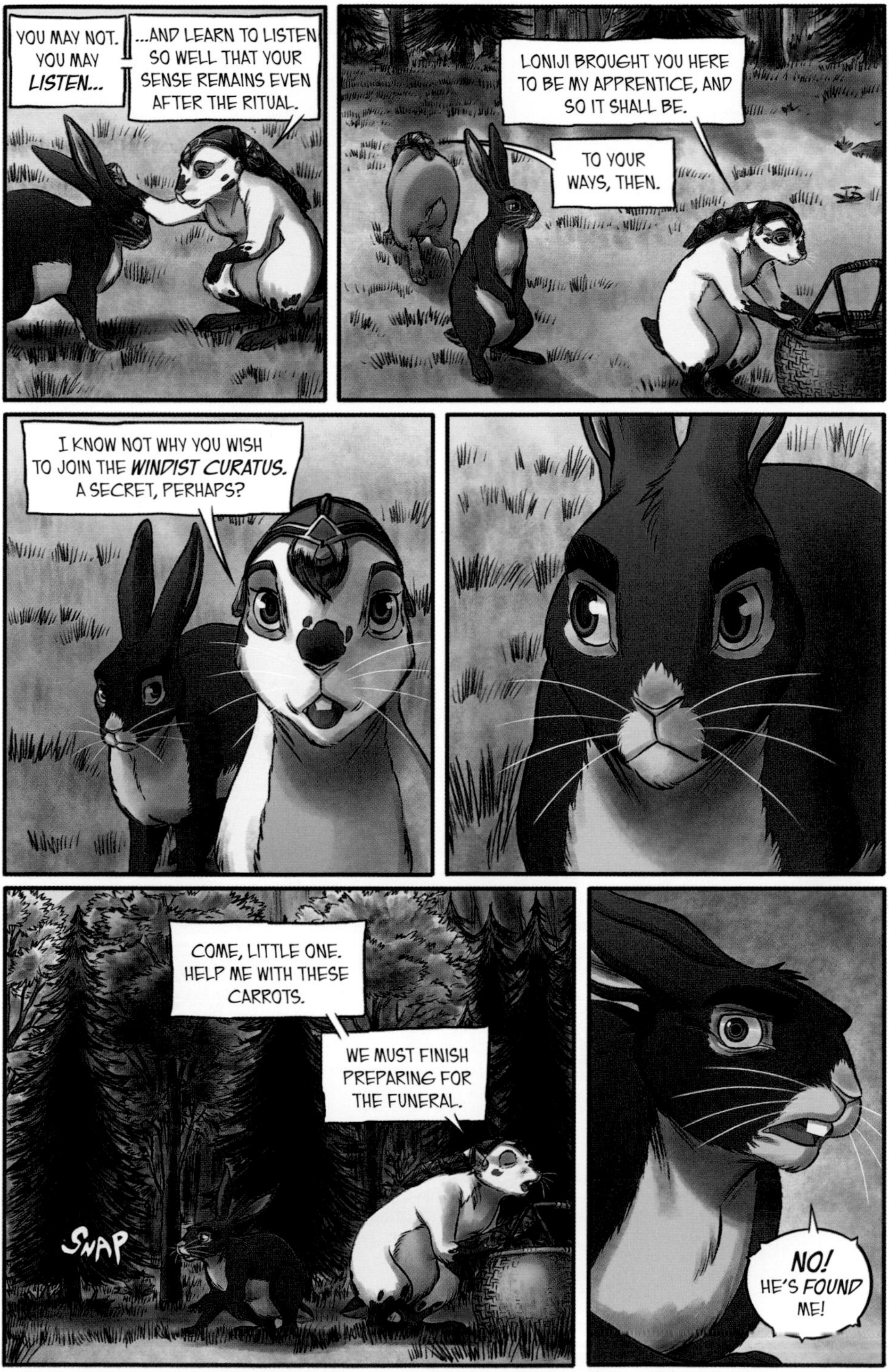
YOU MAY NOT. YOU MAY *LISTEN...*
...AND LEARN TO LISTEN SO WELL THAT YOUR SENSE REMAINS EVEN AFTER THE RITUAL.
LONIJI BROUGHT YOU HERE TO BE MY APPRENTICE, AND SO IT SHALL BE.
TO YOUR WAYS, THEN.
I KNOW NOT WHY YOU WISH TO JOIN THE *WINDIST CURATUS.* A SECRET, PERHAPS?
COME, LITTLE ONE. HELP ME WITH THESE CARROTS.
WE MUST FINISH PREPARING FOR THE FUNERAL.
SNAP
NO! HE'S *FOUND* ME!

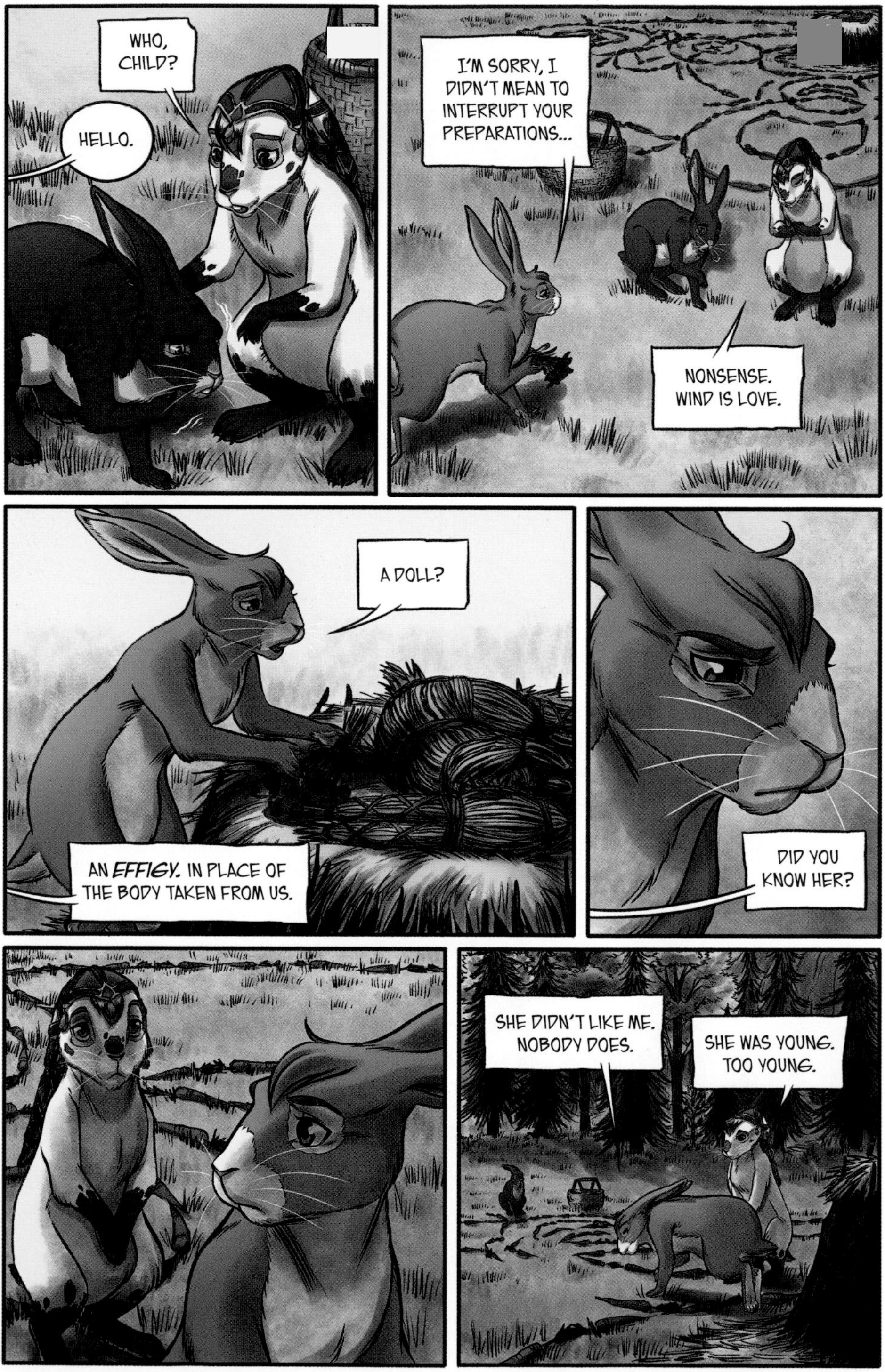
WHO, CHILD?
HELLO.
I'M SORRY, I DIDN'T MEAN TO INTERRUPT YOUR PREPARATIONS...
NONSENSE. WIND IS LOVE.
A DOLL?
AN *EFFIGY.* IN PLACE OF THE BODY TAKEN FROM US.
DID YOU KNOW HER?
SHE DIDN'T LIKE ME. NOBODY DOES.
SHE WAS YOUNG. TOO YOUNG.

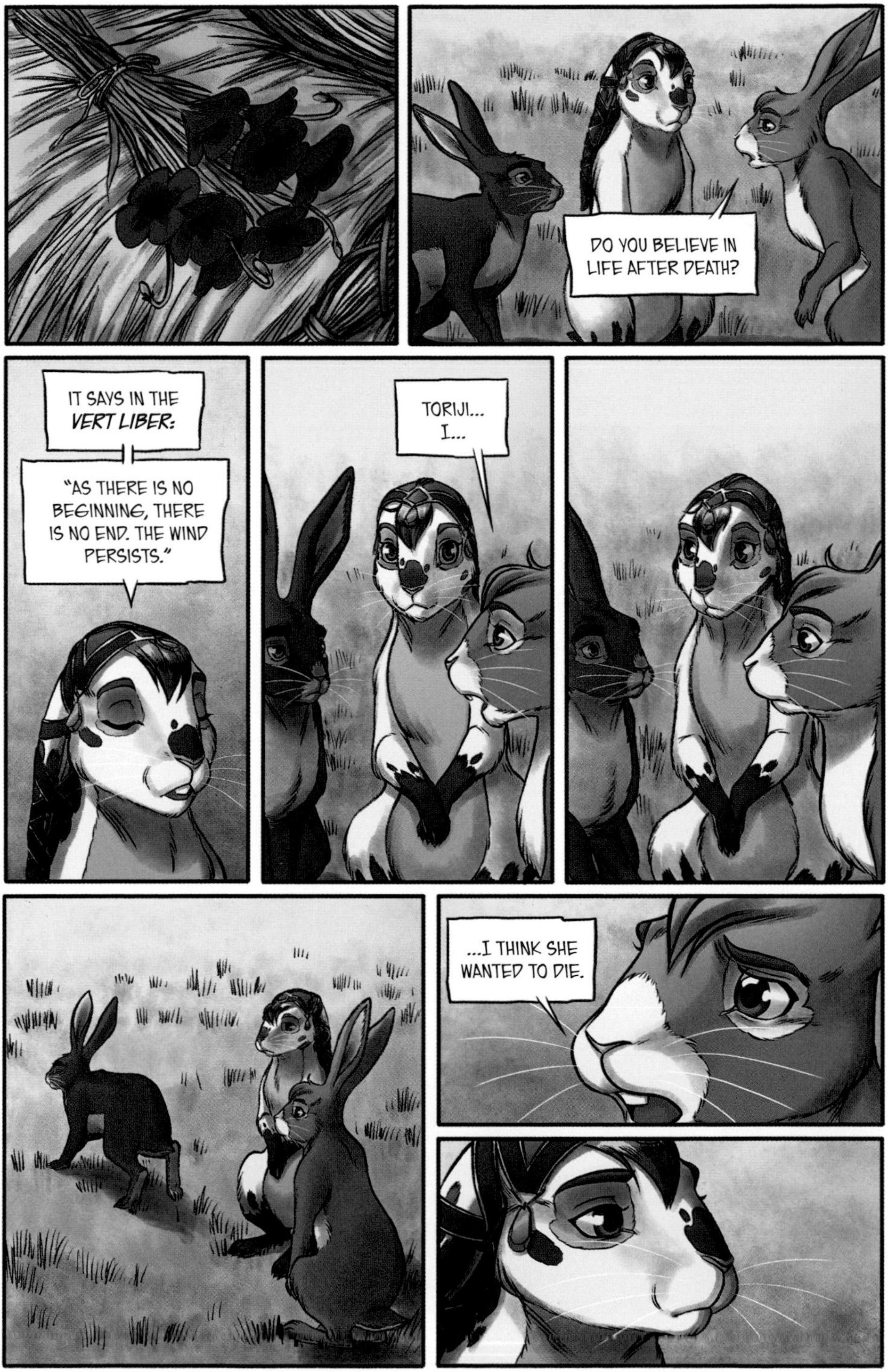
DO YOU BELIEVE IN LIFE AFTER DEATH?
IT SAYS IN THE *VERT LIBER:*
"AS THERE IS NO BEGINNING, THERE IS NO END. THE WIND PERSISTS."
TORIJI... I...
...I THINK SHE WANTED TO DIE.

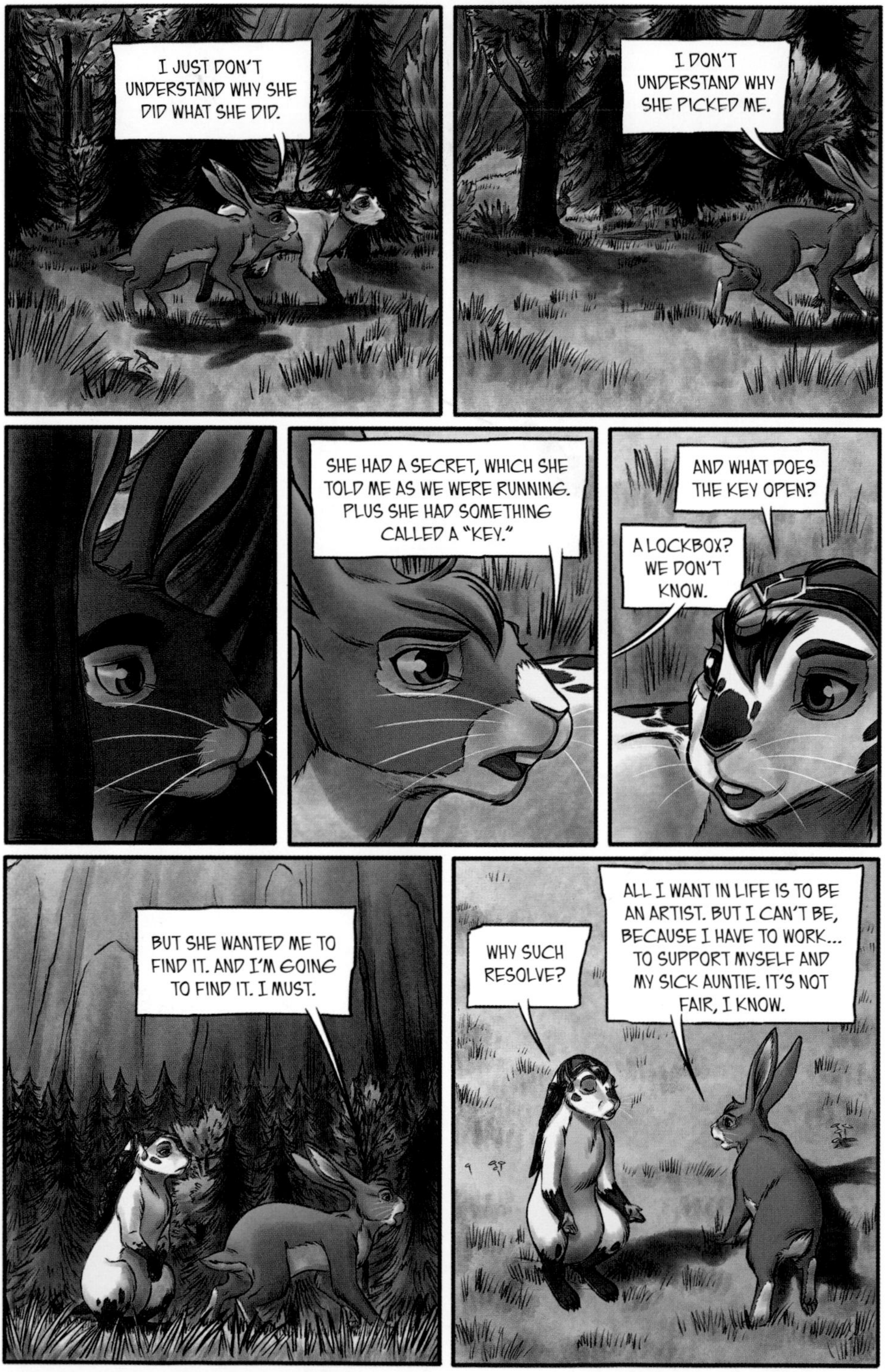
I JUST DON'T UNDERSTAND WHY SHE DID WHAT SHE DID.
I DON'T UNDERSTAND WHY SHE PICKED ME.
SHE HAD A SECRET, WHICH SHE TOLD ME AS WE WERE RUNNING. PLUS SHE HAD SOMETHING CALLED A "KEY."
AND WHAT DOES THE KEY OPEN?
A LOCKBOX? WE DON'T KNOW.
BUT SHE WANTED ME TO FIND IT. AND I'M GOING TO FIND IT. I MUST.
WHY SUCH RESOLVE?
ALL I WANT IN LIFE IS TO BE AN ARTIST. BUT I CAN'T BE, BECAUSE I HAVE TO WORK... TO SUPPORT MYSELF AND MY SICK AUNTIE. IT'S NOT FAIR, I KNOW.

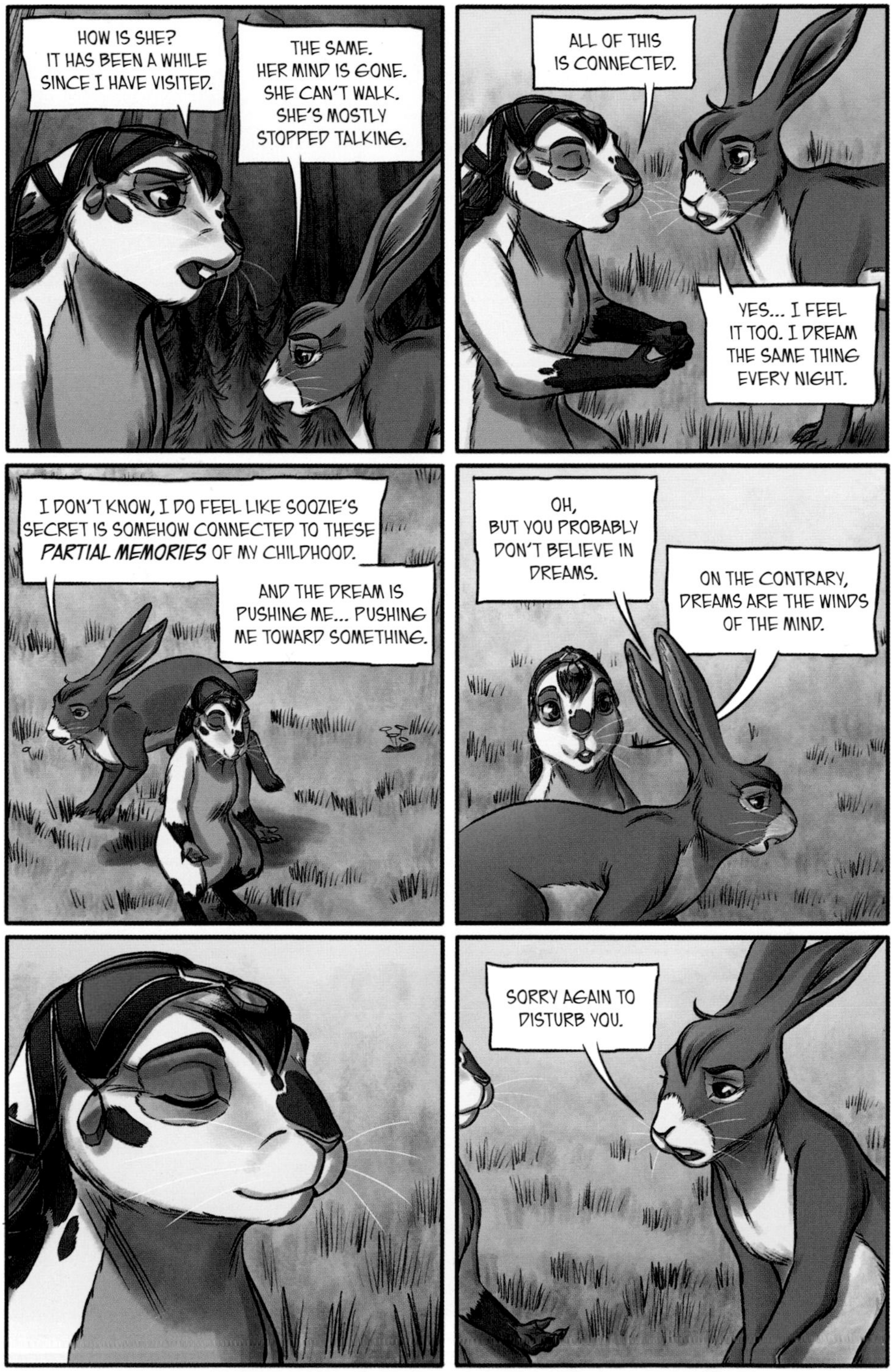
HOW IS SHE? IT HAS BEEN A WHILE SINCE I HAVE VISITED.
THE SAME. HER MIND IS GONE. SHE CAN'T WALK. SHE'S MOSTLY STOPPED TALKING.
ALL OF THIS IS CONNECTED.
YES... I FEEL IT TOO. I DREAM THE SAME THING EVERY NIGHT.
I DON'T KNOW, I DO FEEL LIKE SOOZIE'S SECRET IS SOMEHOW CONNECTED TO THESE *PARTIAL MEMORIES* OF MY CHILDHOOD.
AND THE DREAM IS PUSHING ME... PUSHING ME TOWARD SOMETHING.
OH, BUT YOU PROBABLY DON'T BELIEVE IN DREAMS.
ON THE CONTRARY, DREAMS ARE THE WINDS OF THE MIND.
SORRY AGAIN TO DISTURB YOU.

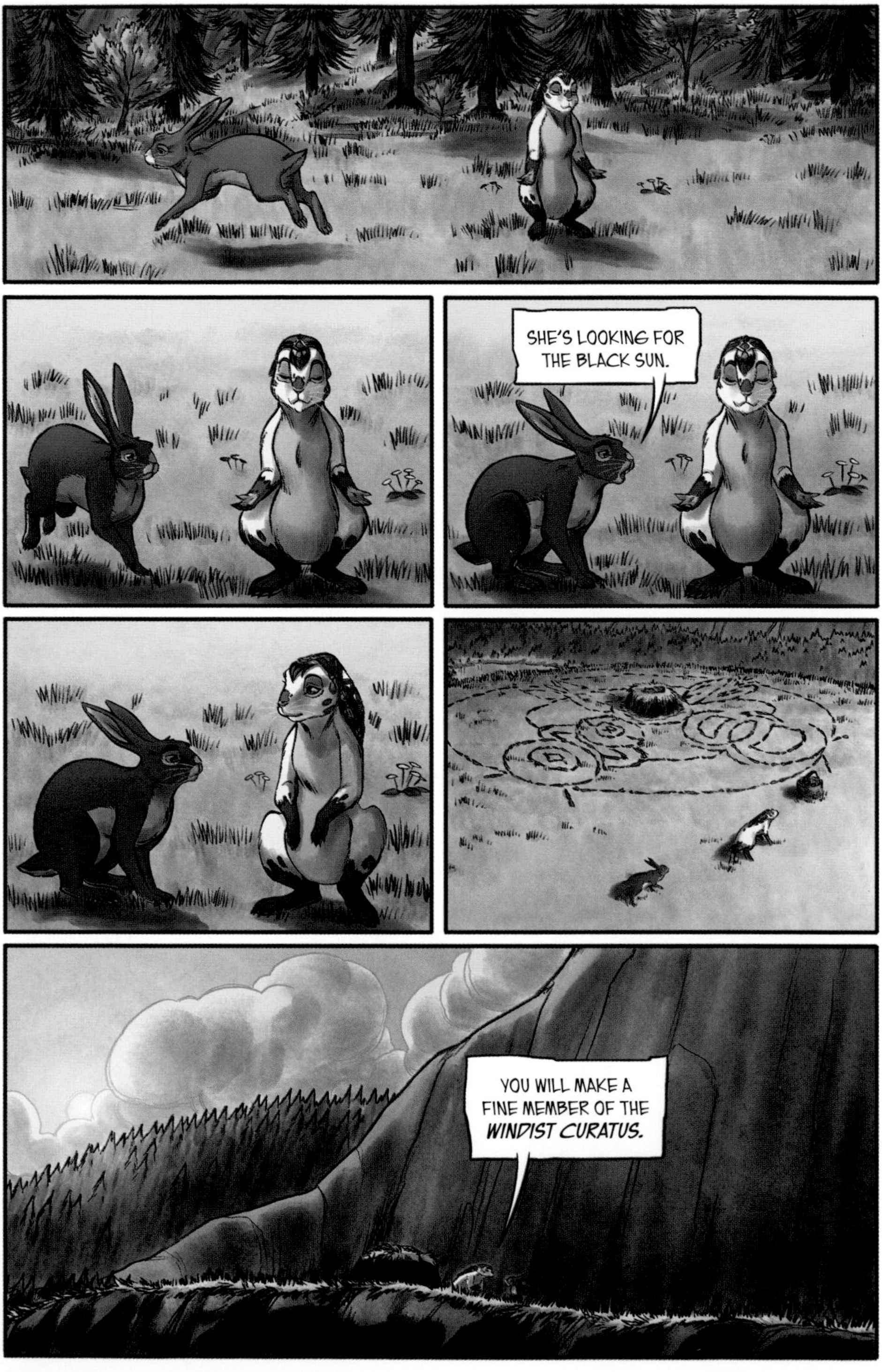
SHE'S LOOKING FOR THE BLACK SUN.
YOU WILL MAKE A FINE MEMBER OF THE *WINDIST CURATUS.*

6. _____

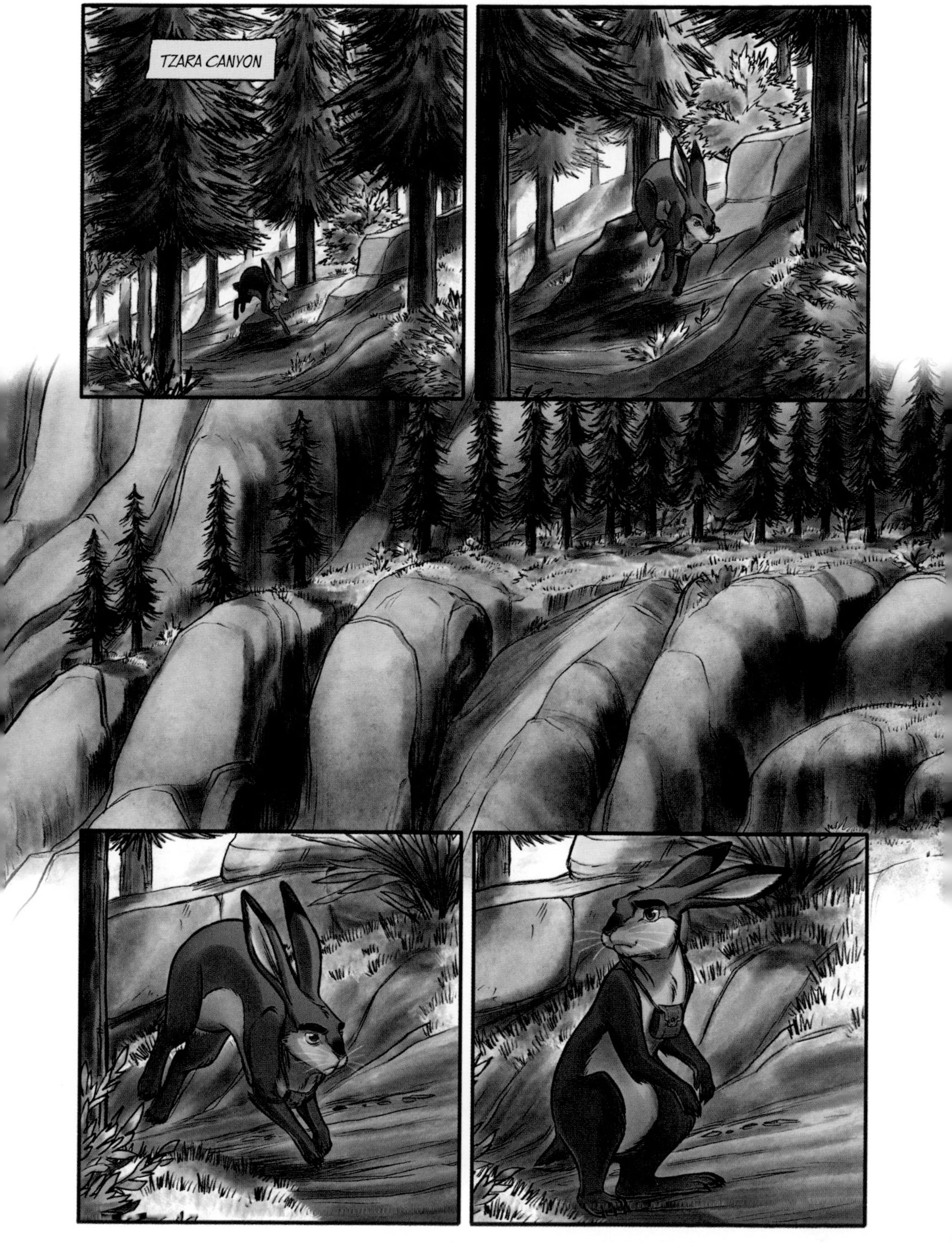
TZARA CANYON

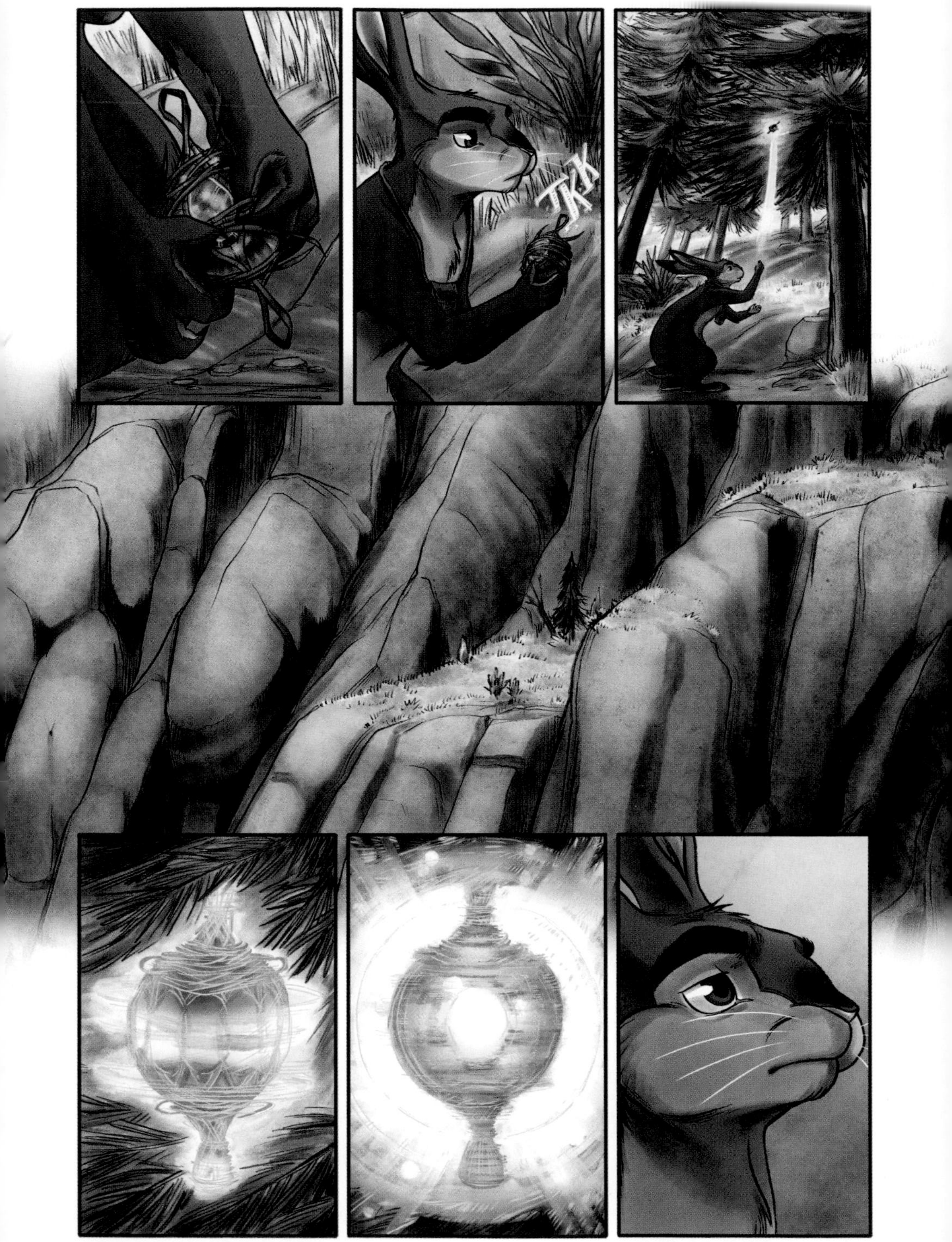
TKK

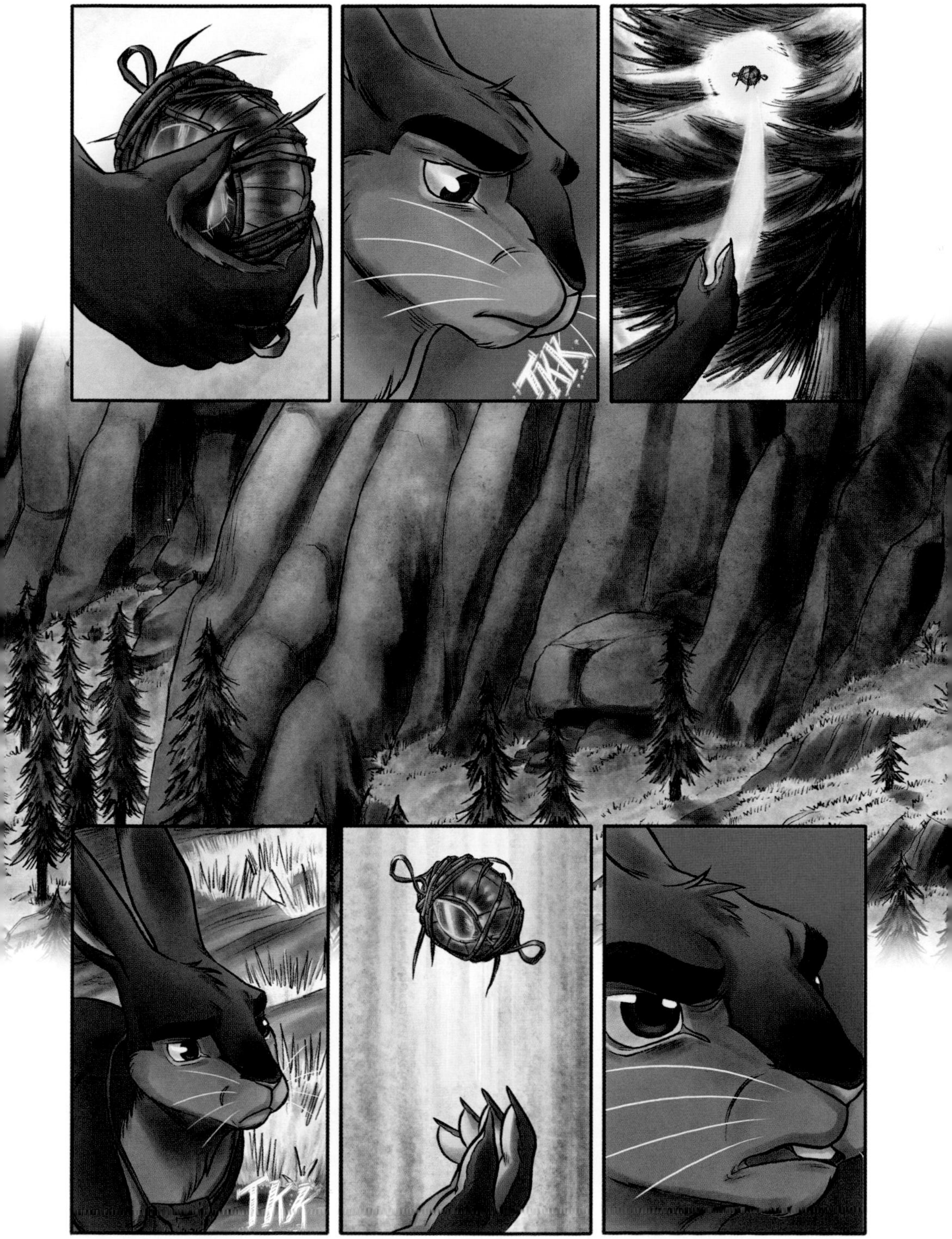
TKK
TKR

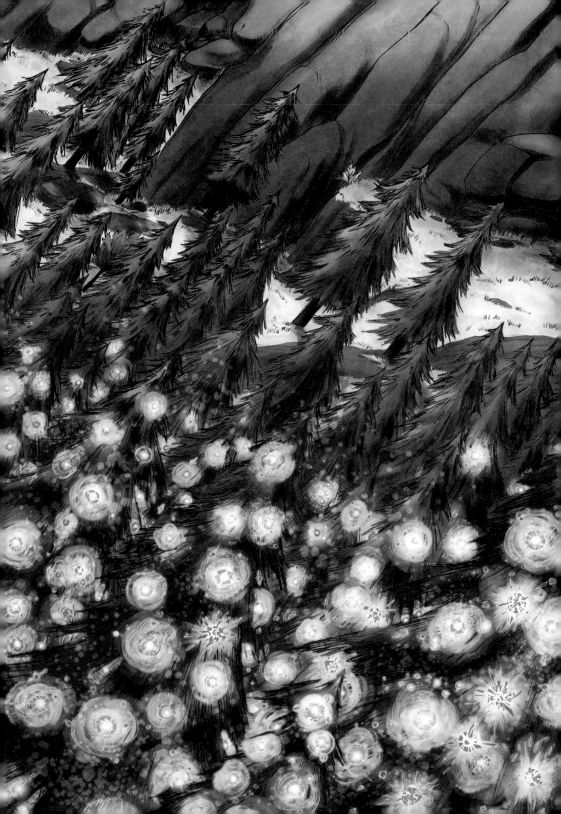

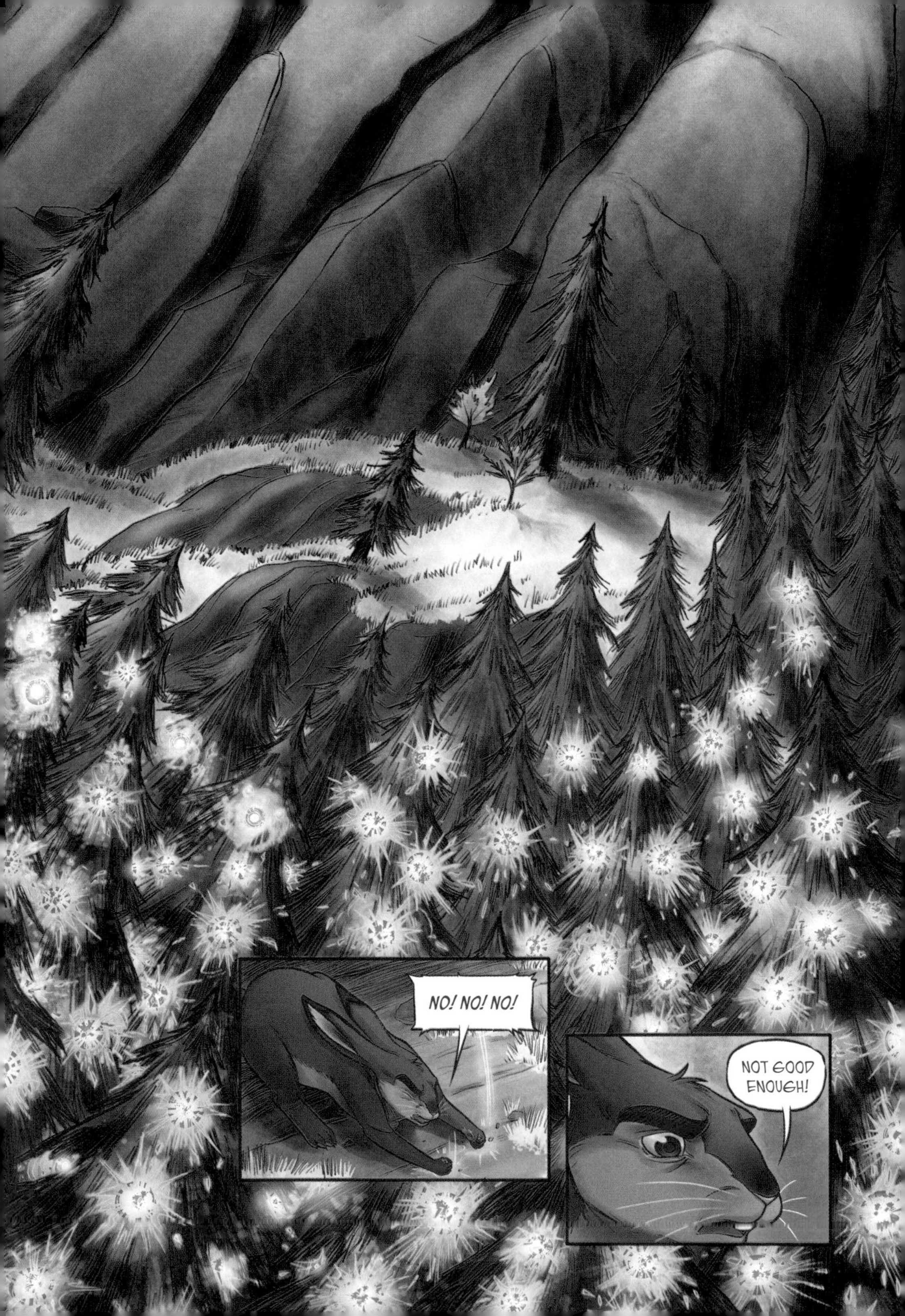
NO! NO! NO!
NOT GOOD ENOUGH!

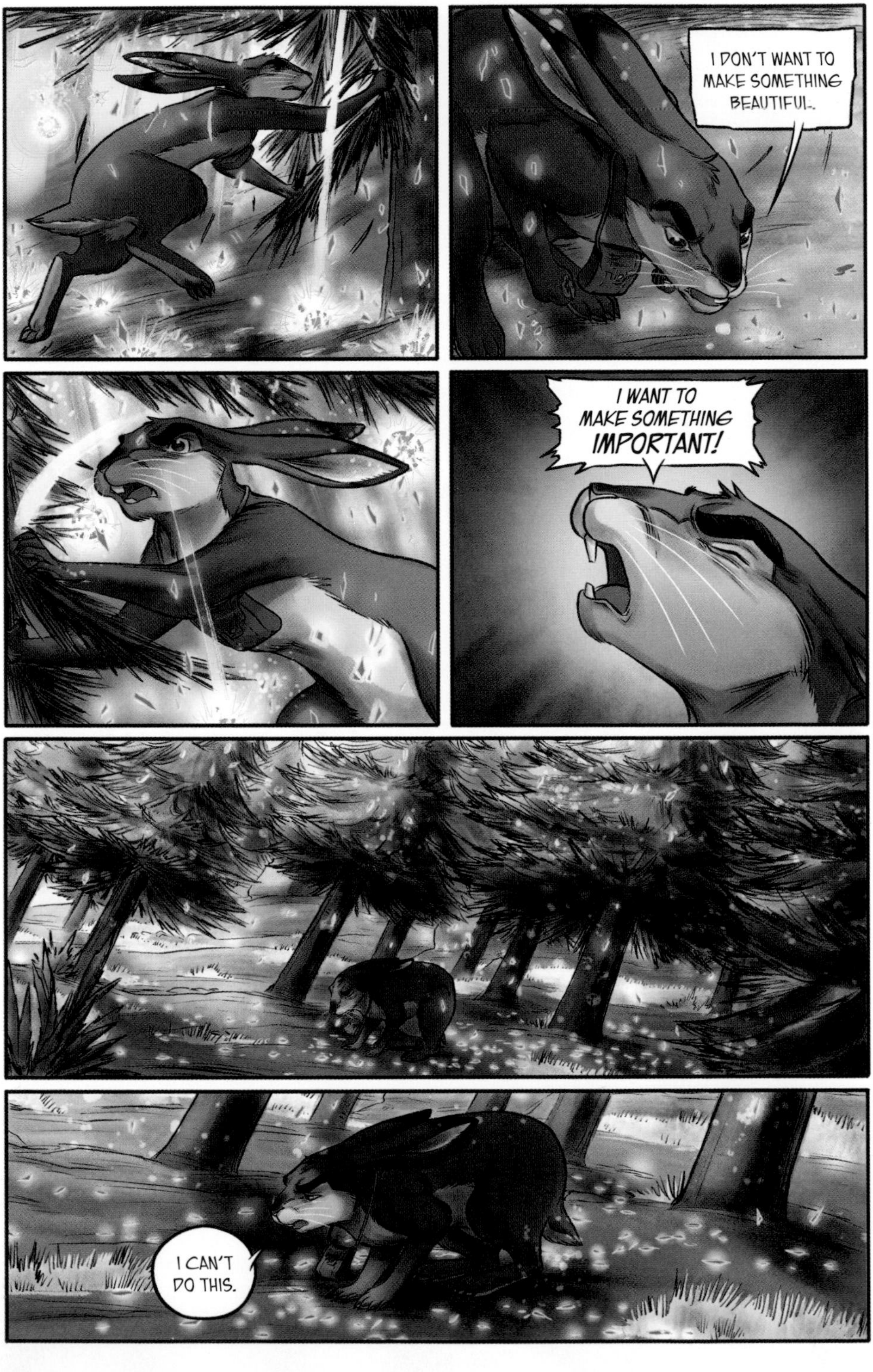

I DON'T WANT TO MAKE SOMETHING BEAUTIFUL..
I WANT TO MAKE SOMETHING IMPORTANT!
I CAN'T DO THIS.

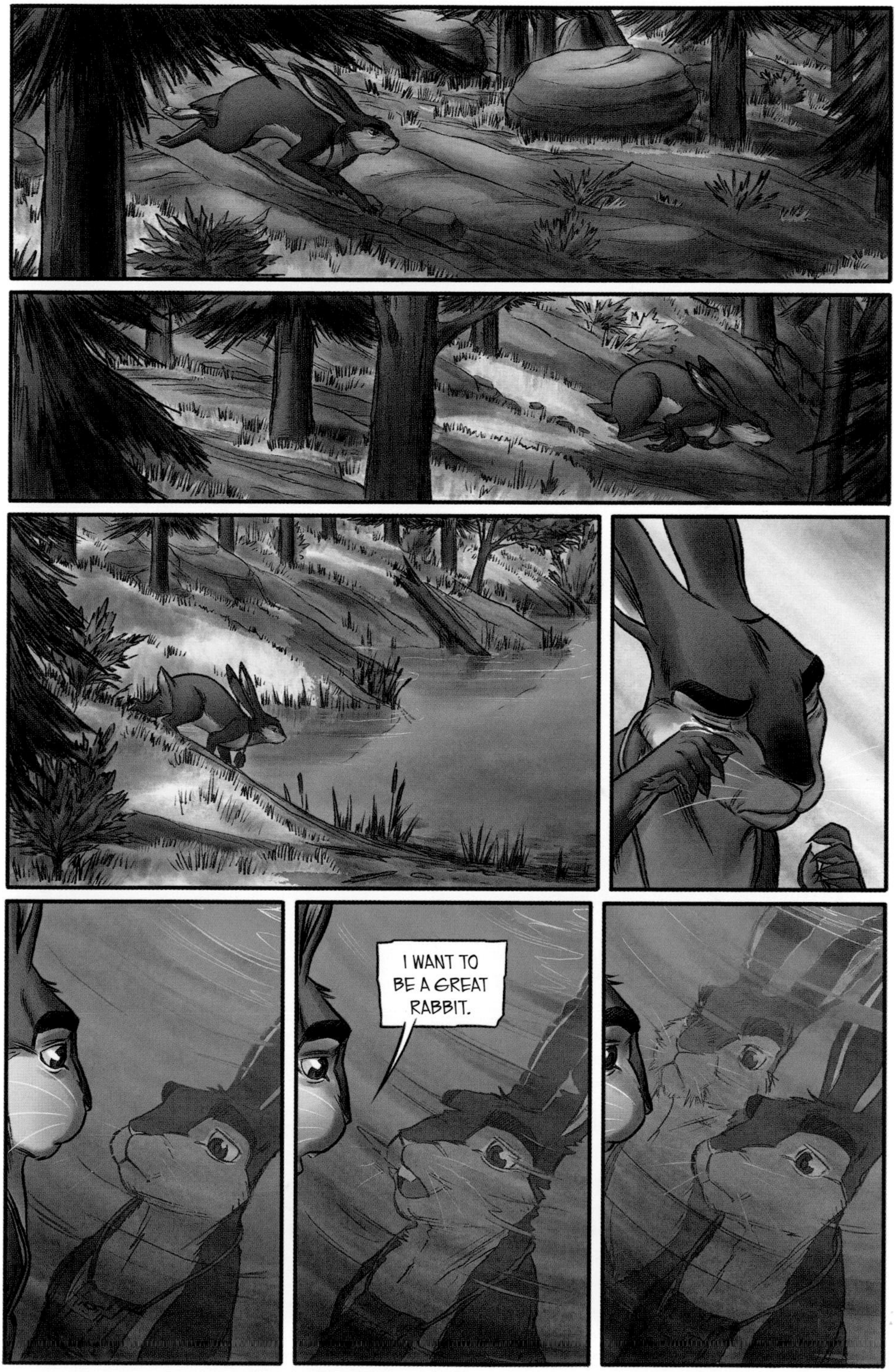
I WANT TO
BE A GREAT
RABBIT.

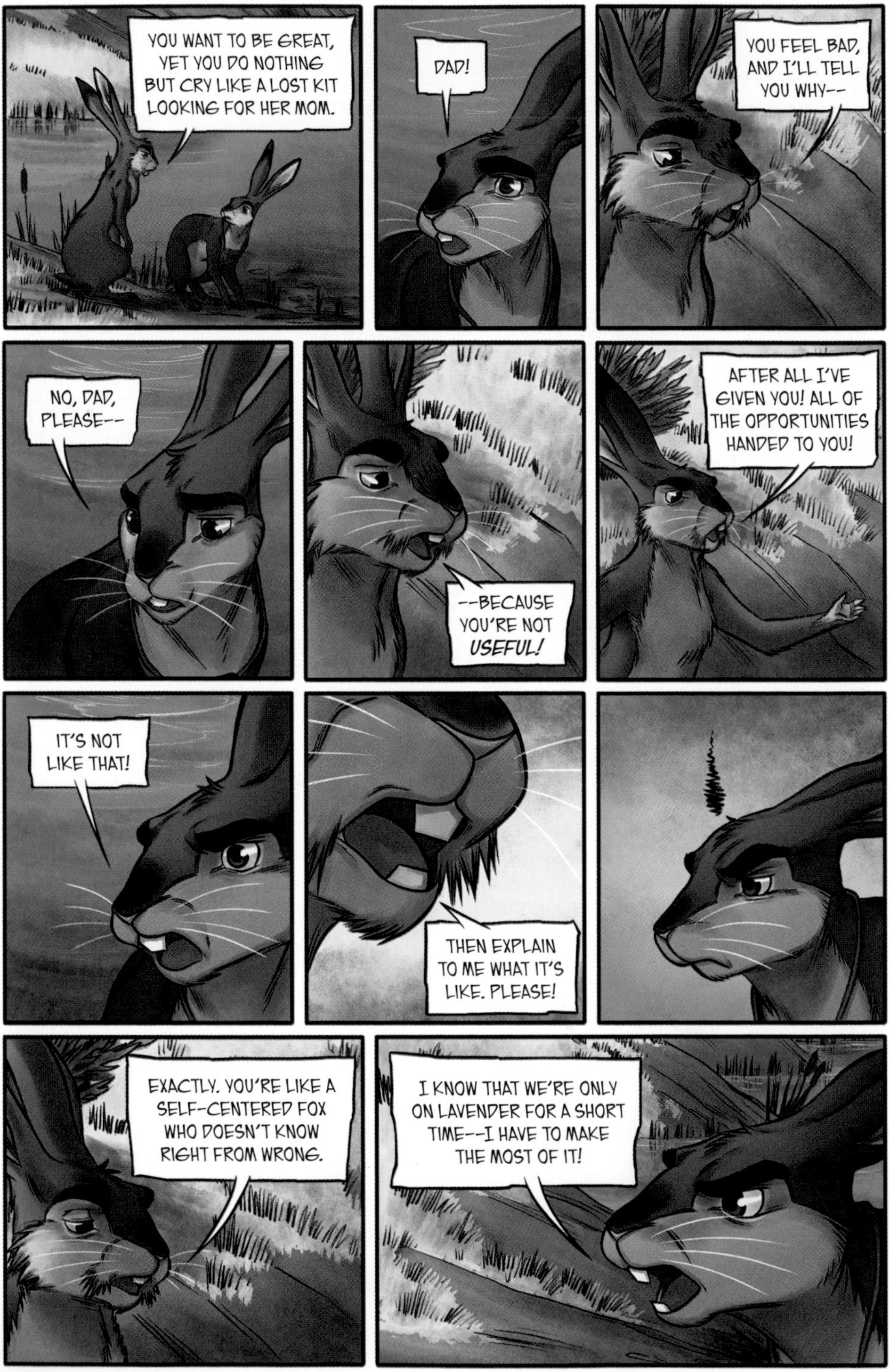
YOU WANT TO BE GREAT, YET YOU DO NOTHING BUT CRY LIKE A LOST KIT LOOKING FOR HER MOM.
DAD!
YOU FEEL BAD, AND I'LL TELL YOU WHY--
NO, DAD, PLEASE--
--BECAUSE YOU'RE NOT *USEFUL!*
AFTER ALL I'VE GIVEN YOU! ALL OF THE OPPORTUNITIES HANDED TO YOU!
IT'S NOT LIKE THAT!
THEN EXPLAIN TO ME WHAT IT'S LIKE. PLEASE!
EXACTLY. YOU'RE LIKE A SELF-CENTERED FOX WHO DOESN'T KNOW RIGHT FROM WRONG.
I KNOW THAT WE'RE ONLY ON LAVENDER FOR A SHORT TIME--I HAVE TO MAKE THE MOST OF IT!

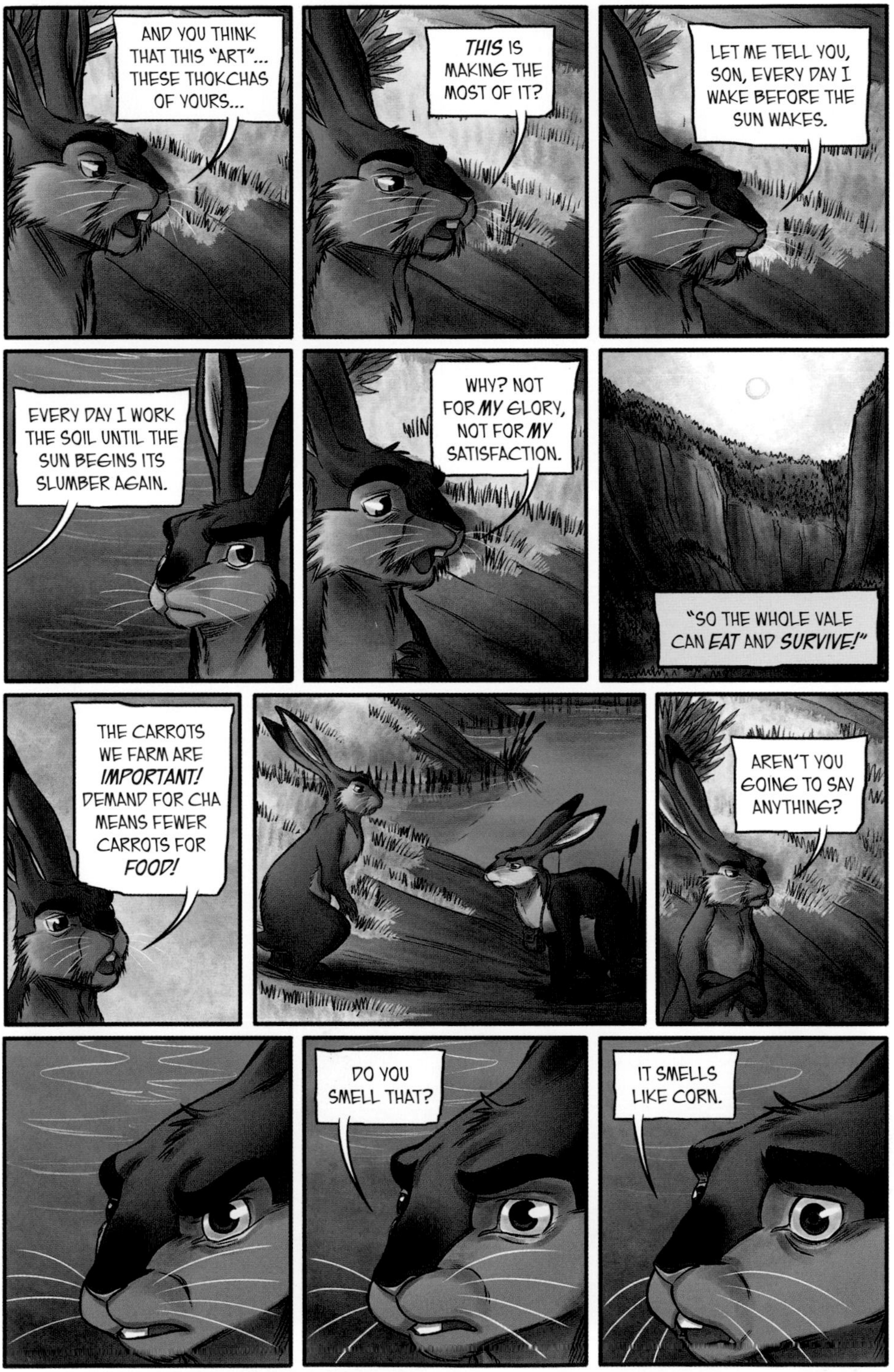
AND YOU THINK THAT THIS "ART"... THESE THOKCHAS OF YOURS...
THIS IS MAKING THE MOST OF IT?
LET ME TELL YOU, SON, EVERY DAY I WAKE BEFORE THE SUN WAKES.
EVERY DAY I WORK THE SOIL UNTIL THE SUN BEGINS ITS SLUMBER AGAIN.
WHY? NOT FOR *MY* GLORY, NOT FOR *MY* SATISFACTION.
"SO THE WHOLE VALE CAN *EAT* AND *SURVIVE!*"
THE CARROTS WE FARM ARE *IMPORTANT!* DEMAND FOR CHA MEANS FEWER CARROTS FOR *FOOD!*
AREN'T YOU GOING TO SAY ANYTHING?
DO YOU SMELL THAT?
IT SMELLS LIKE CORN.

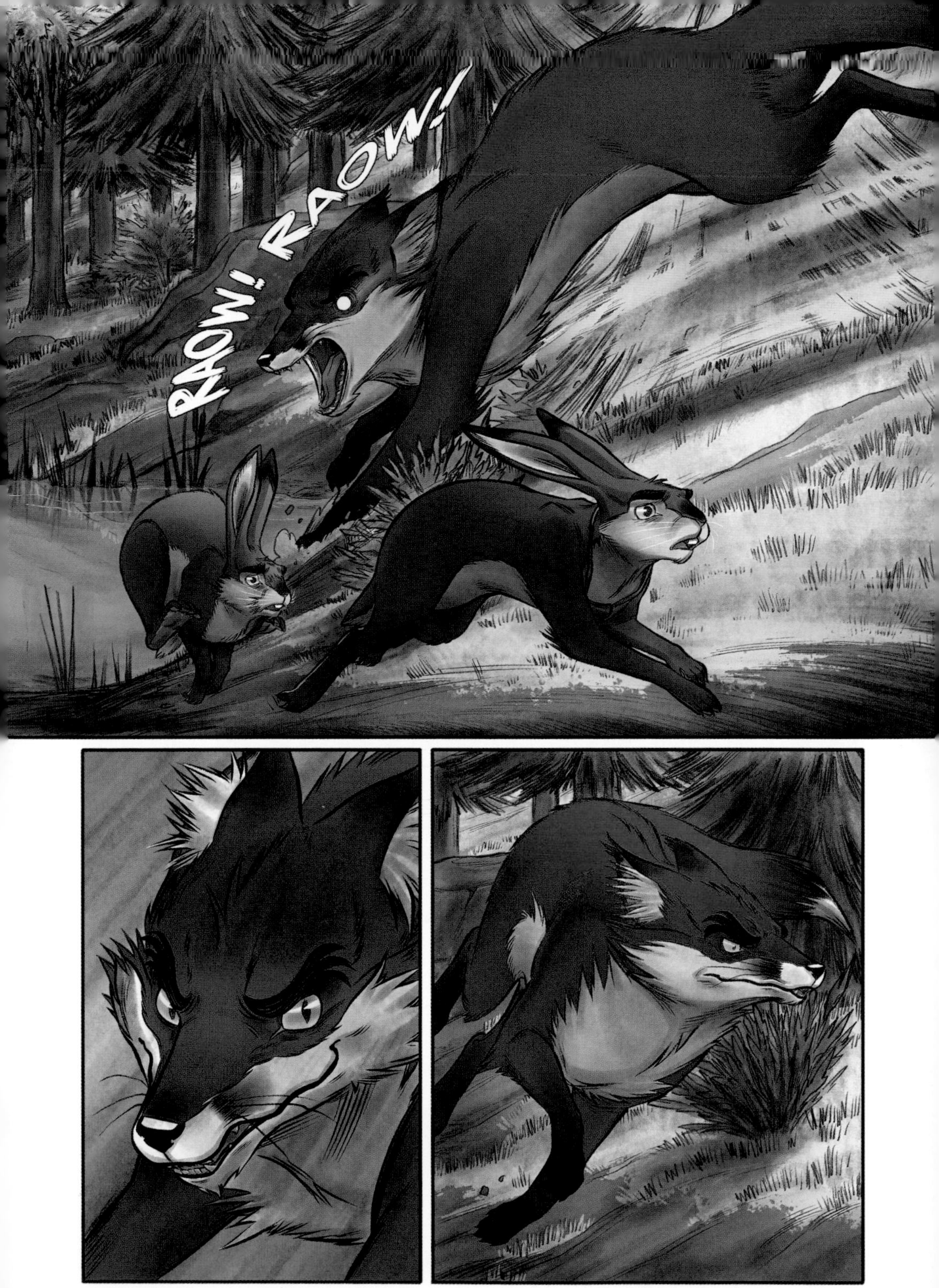
RAOW! RAOW! RAOW!

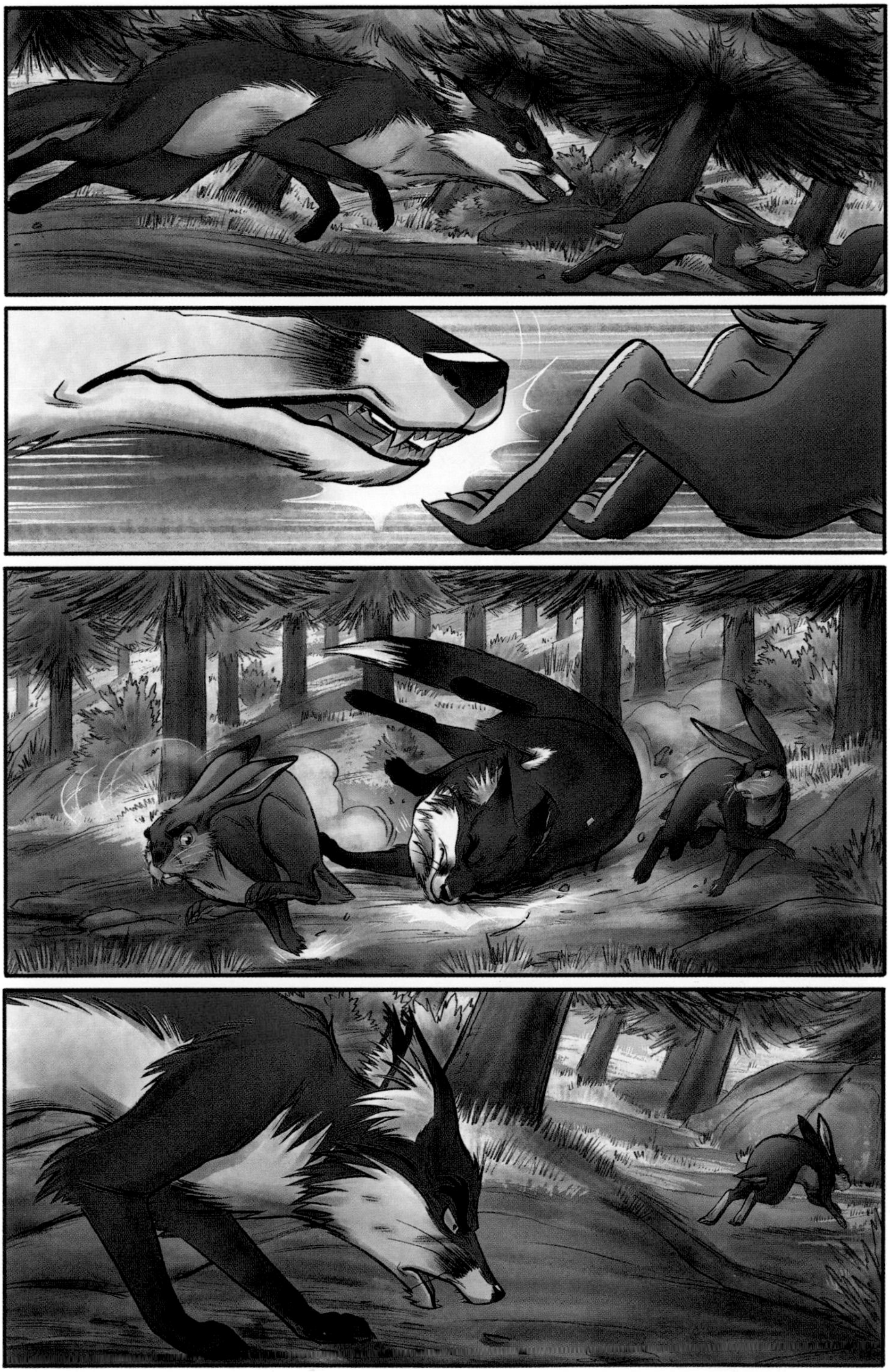

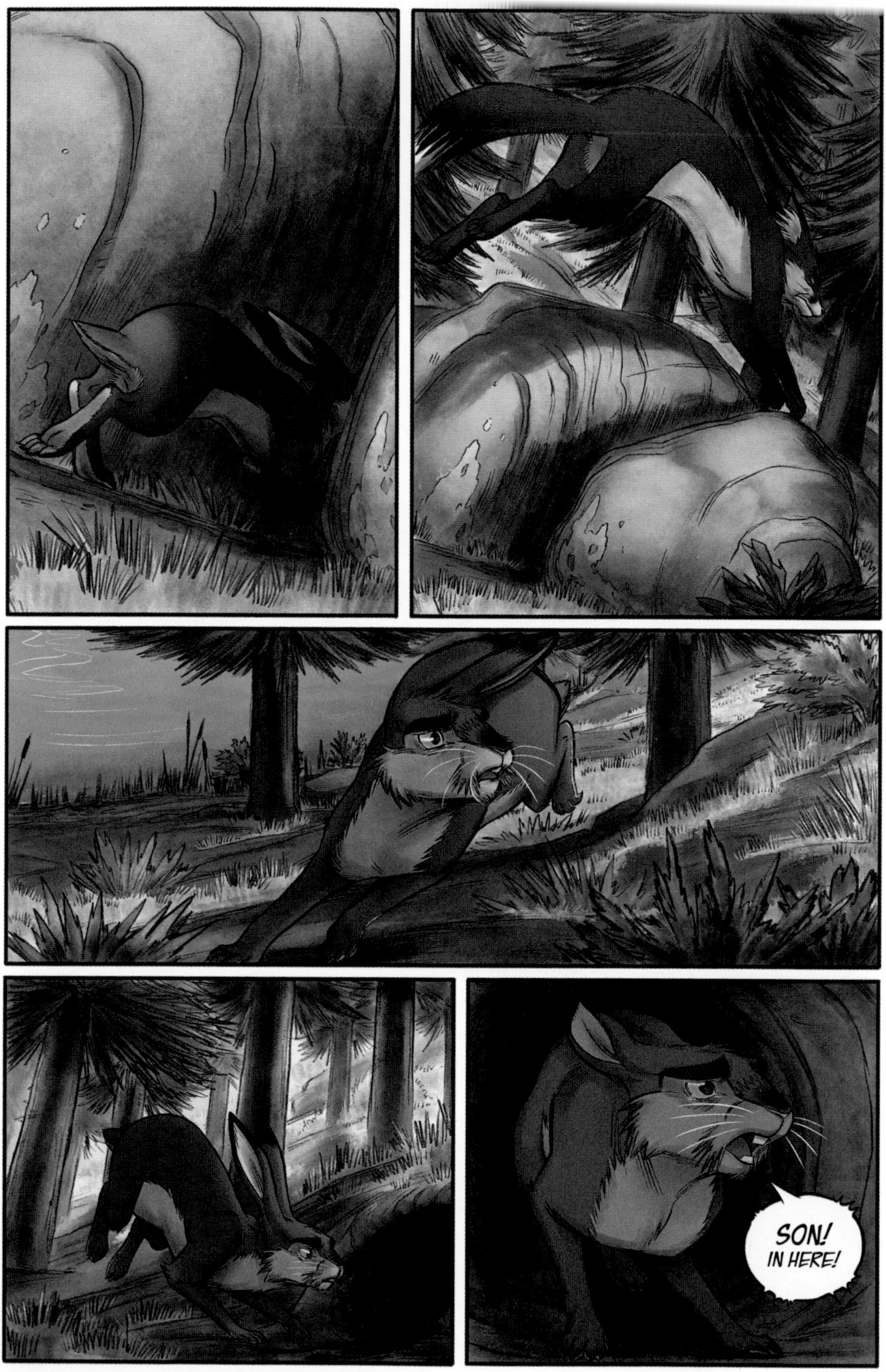
SON! IN HERE!

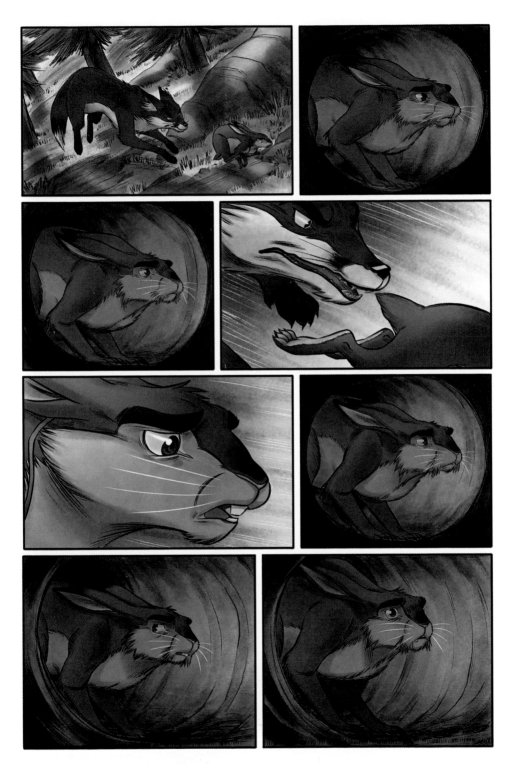

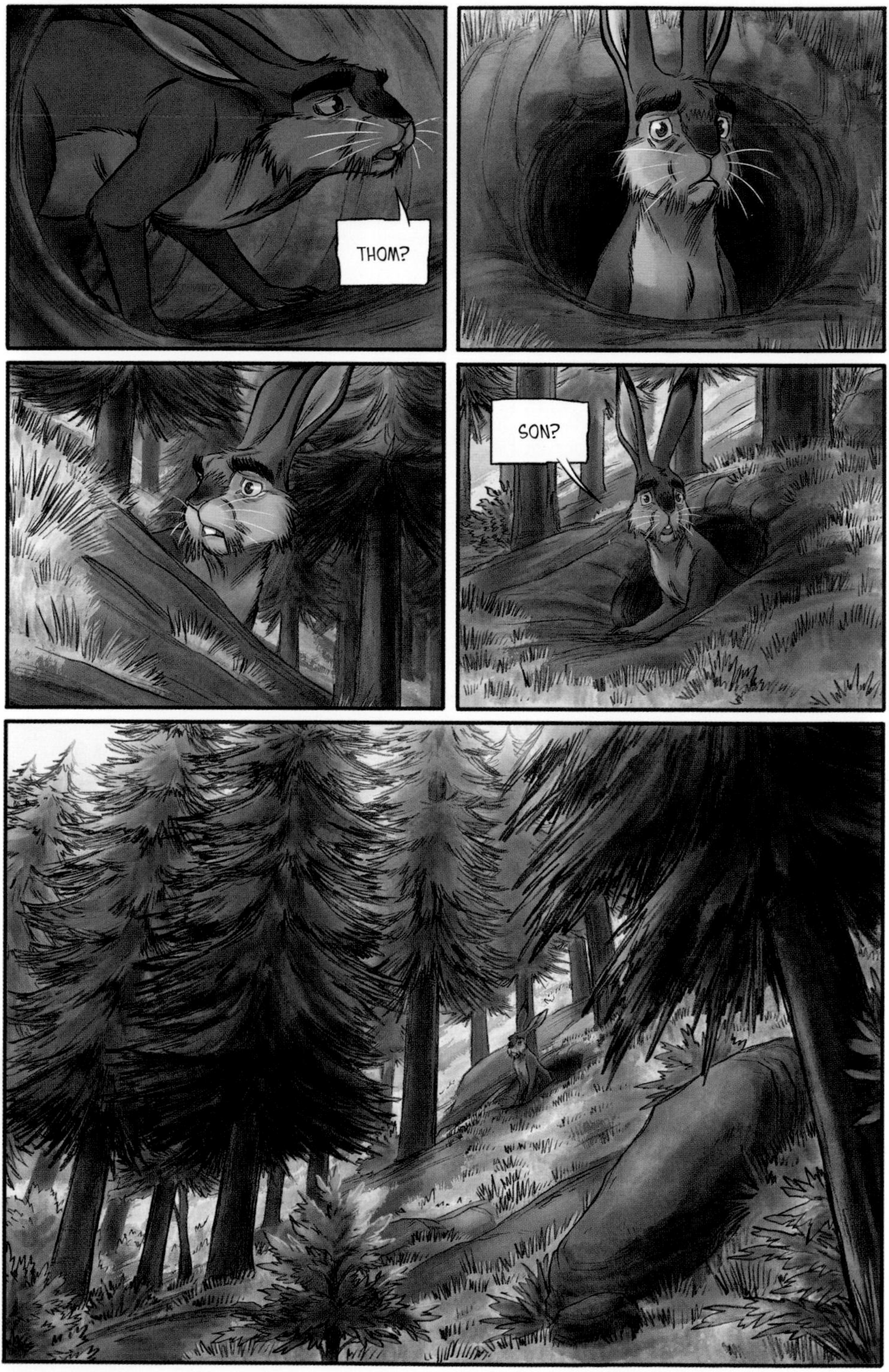
THOM?
SON?

7.

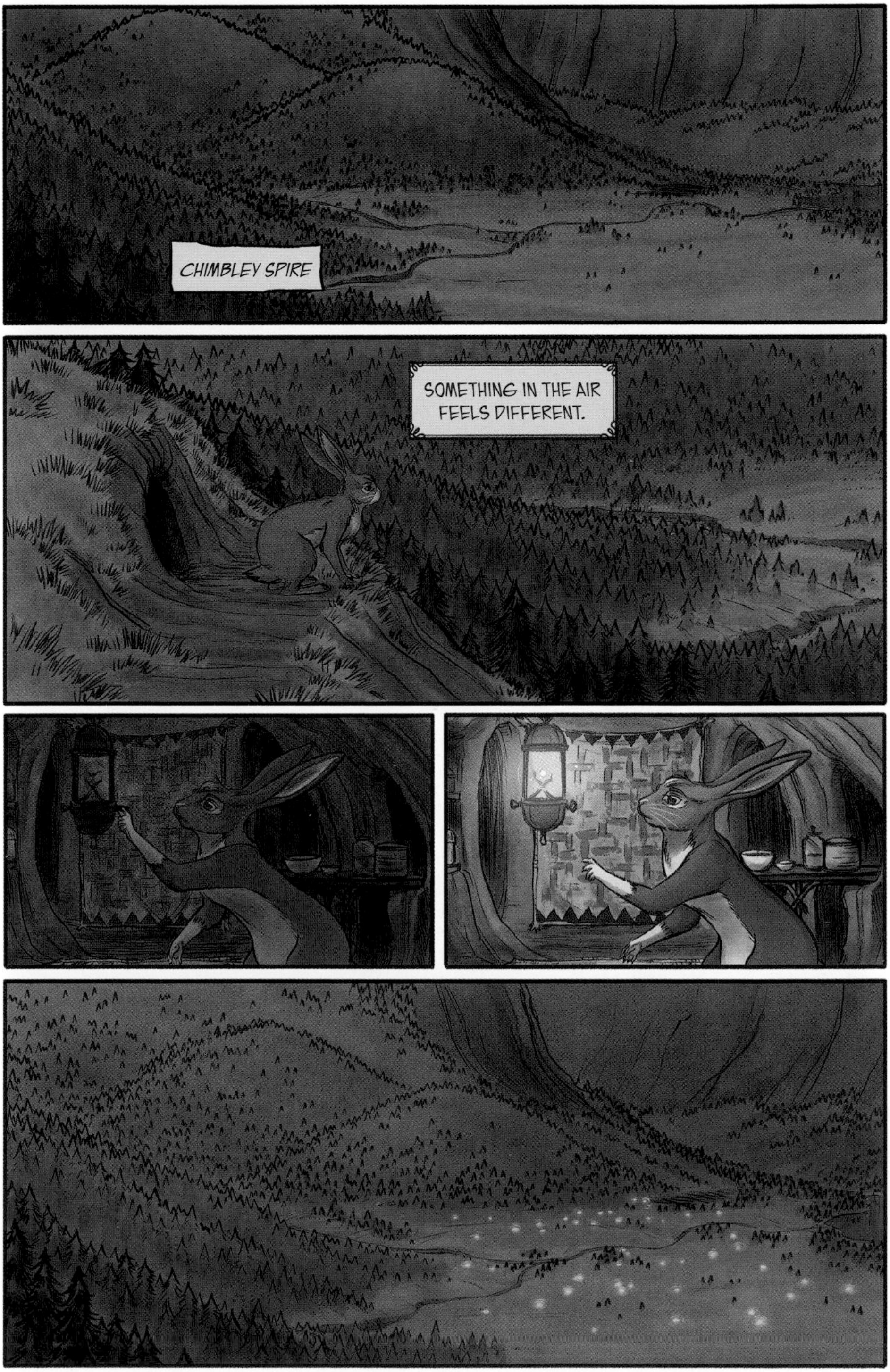
CHIMBLEY SPIRE
SOMETHING IN THE AIR FEELS DIFFERENT.

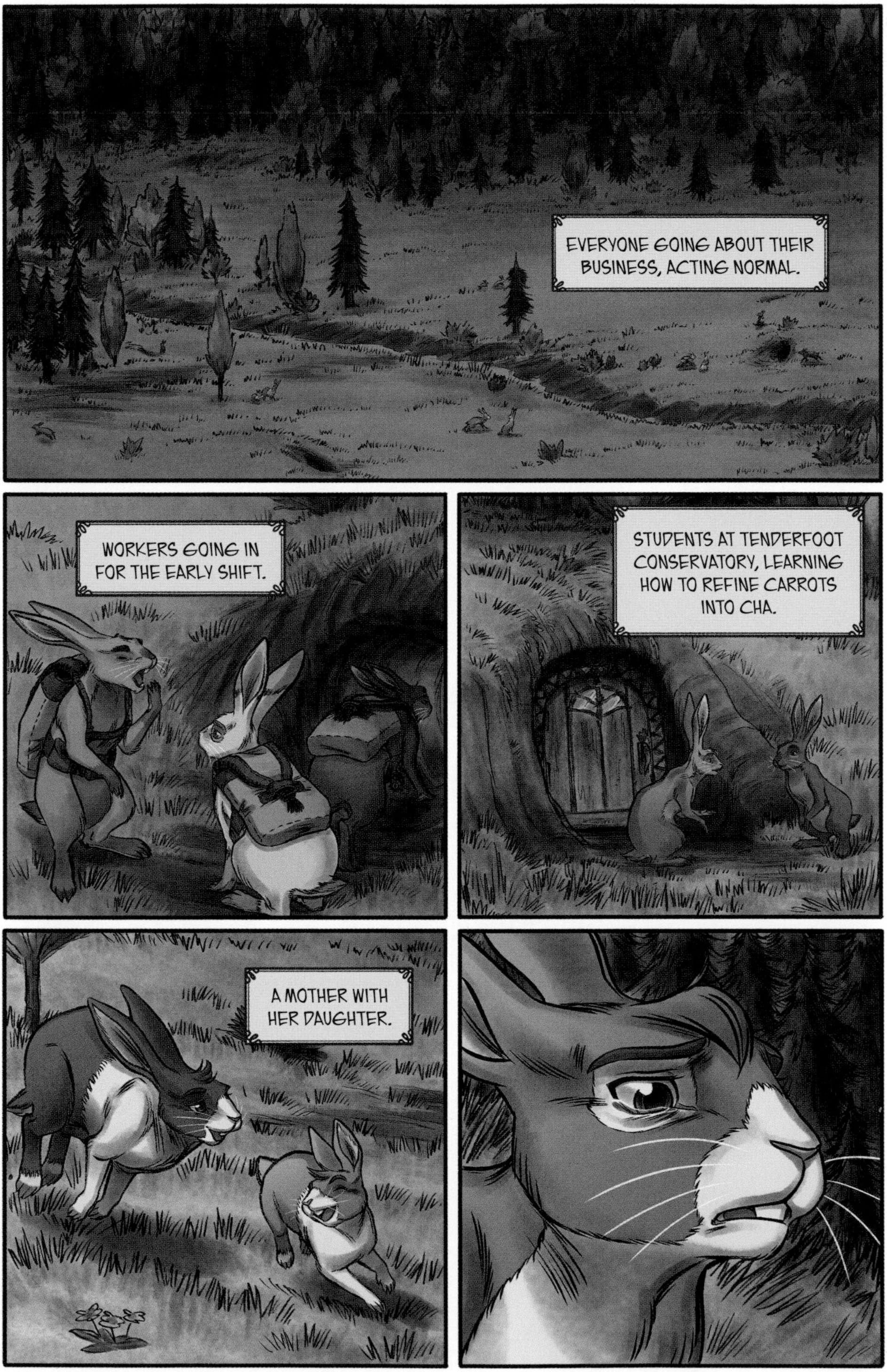
EVERYONE GOING ABOUT THEIR BUSINESS, ACTING NORMAL.
WORKERS GOING IN FOR THE EARLY SHIFT.
STUDENTS AT TENDERFOOT CONSERVATORY, LEARNING HOW TO REFINE CARROTS INTO CHA.
A MOTHER WITH HER DAUGHTER.

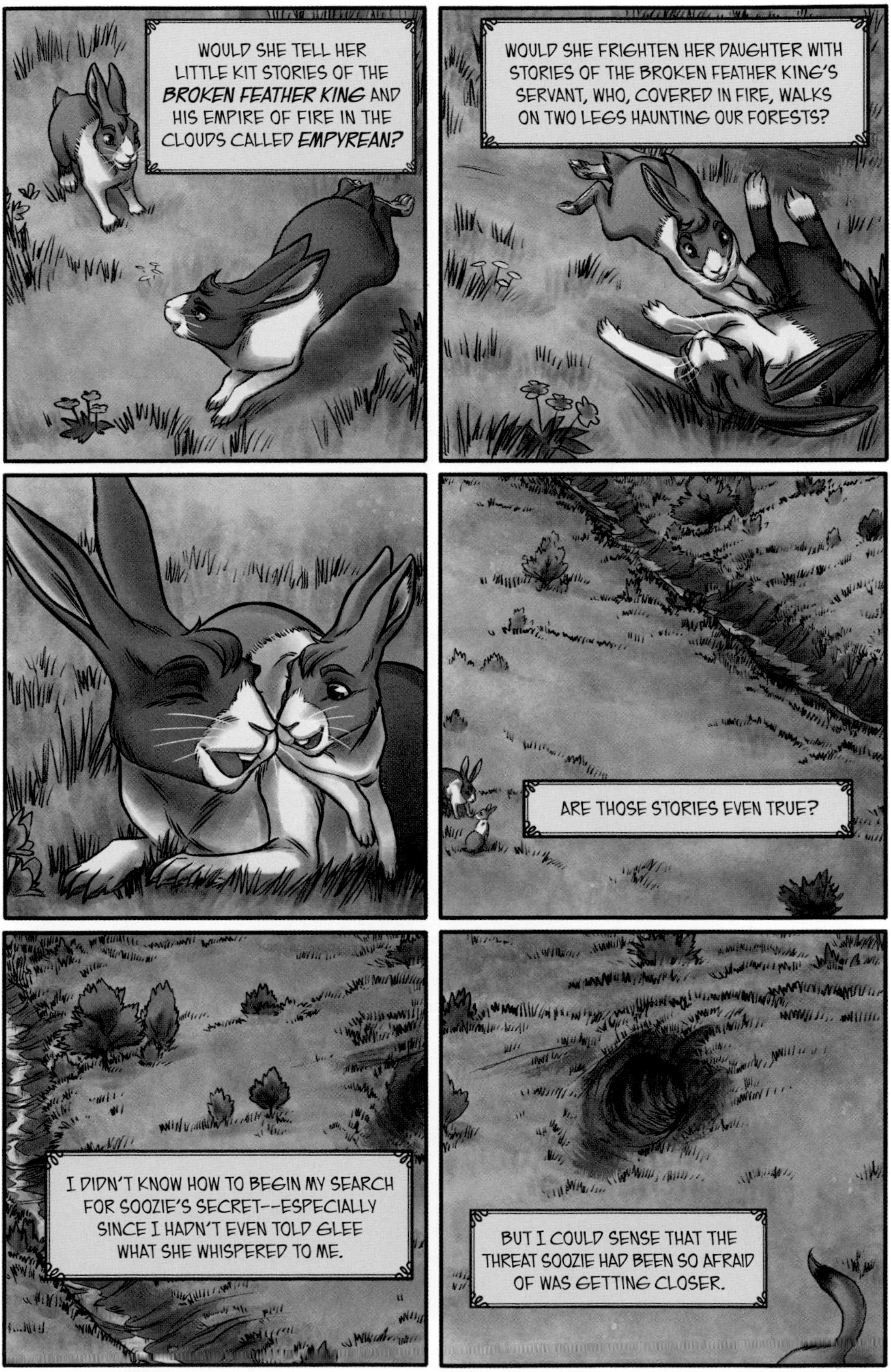
WOULD SHE TELL HER LITTLE KIT STORIES OF THE BROKEN FEATHER KING AND HIS EMPIRE OF FIRE IN THE CLOUDS CALLED EMPYREAN?
WOULD SHE FRIGHTEN HER DAUGHTER WITH STORIES OF THE BROKEN FEATHER KING'S SERVANT, WHO, COVERED IN FIRE, WALKS ON TWO LEGS HAUNTING OUR FORESTS?
ARE THOSE STORIES EVEN TRUE?
I DIDN'T KNOW HOW TO BEGIN MY SEARCH FOR SOOZIE'S SECRET--ESPECIALLY SINCE I HADN'T EVEN TOLD GLEE WHAT SHE WHISPERED TO ME.
BUT I COULD SENSE THAT THE THREAT SOOZIE HAD BEEN SO AFRAID OF WAS GETTING CLOSER.

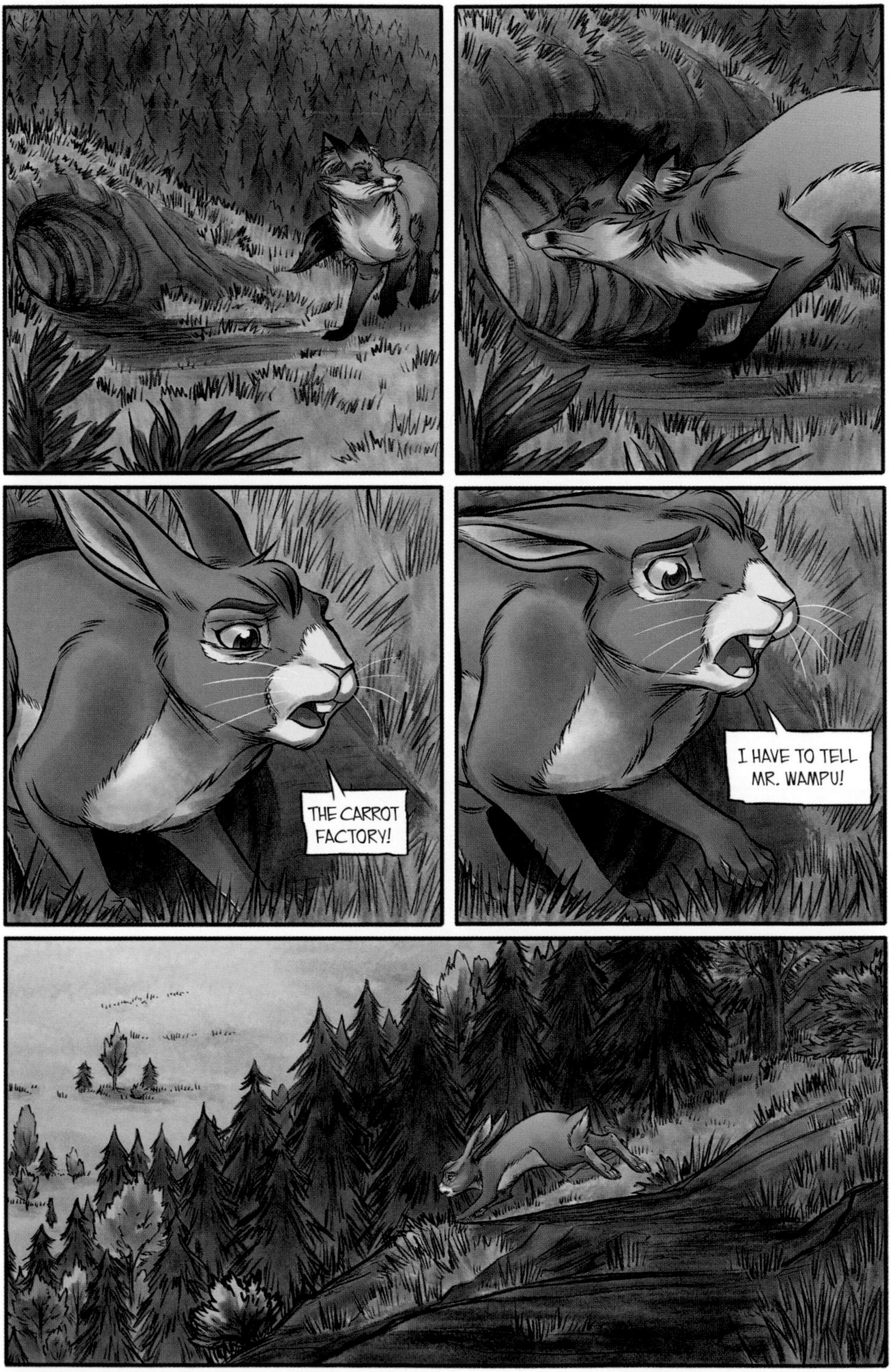
THE CARROT FACTORY!
I HAVE TO TELL MR. WAMPU!

8. _____

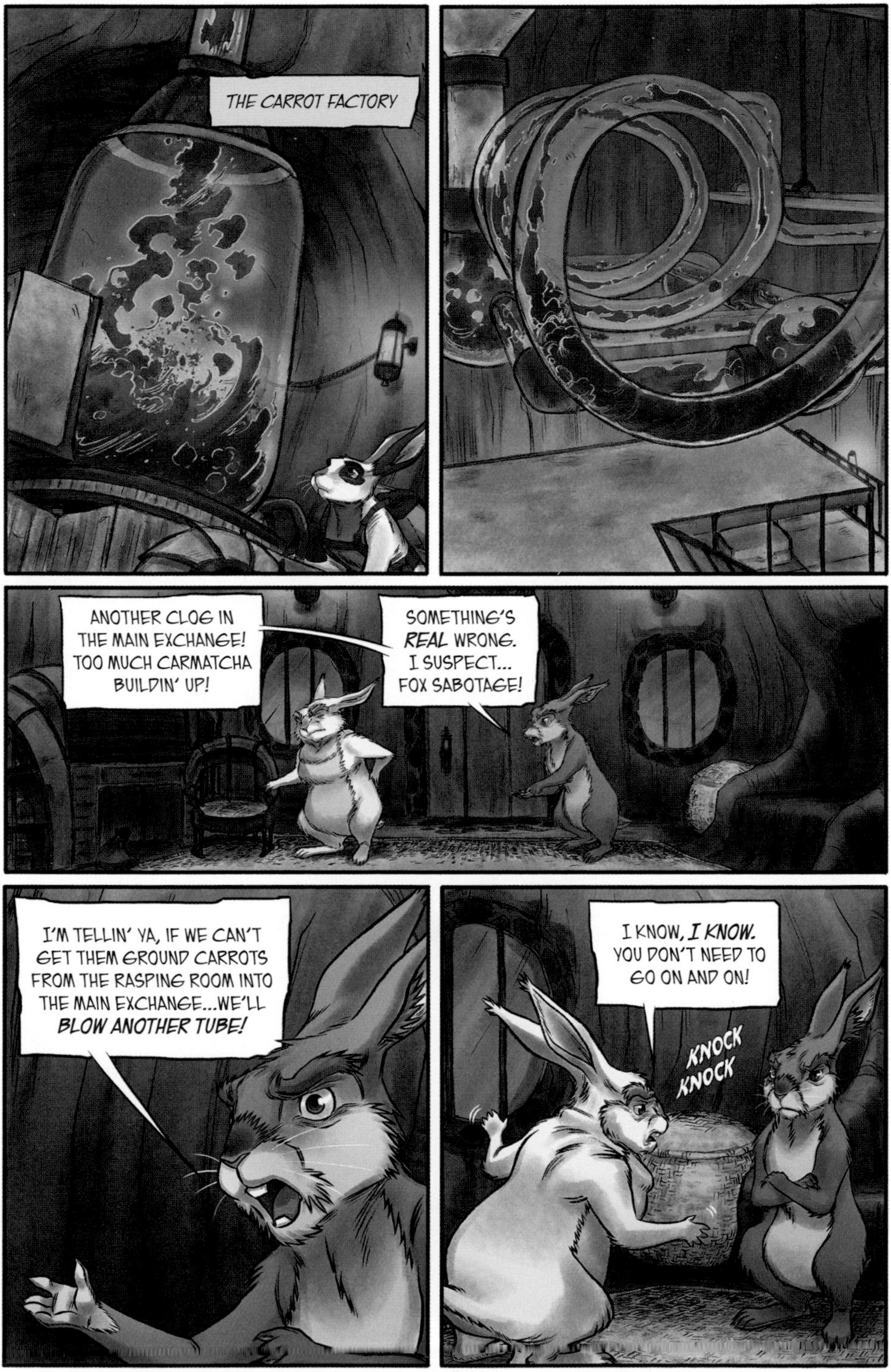
THE CARROT FACTORY
ANOTHER CLOG IN THE MAIN EXCHANGE! TOO MUCH CARMATCHA BUILDIN' UP!
SOMETHING'S *REAL* WRONG. I SUSPECT... FOX SABOTAGE!
I'M TELLIN' YA, IF WE CAN'T GET THEM GROUND CARROTS FROM THE RASPING ROOM INTO THE MAIN EXCHANGE...WE'LL ***BLOW ANOTHER TUBE!***
I KNOW, ***I KNOW.*** YOU DON'T NEED TO GO ON AND ON!
KNOCK KNOCK

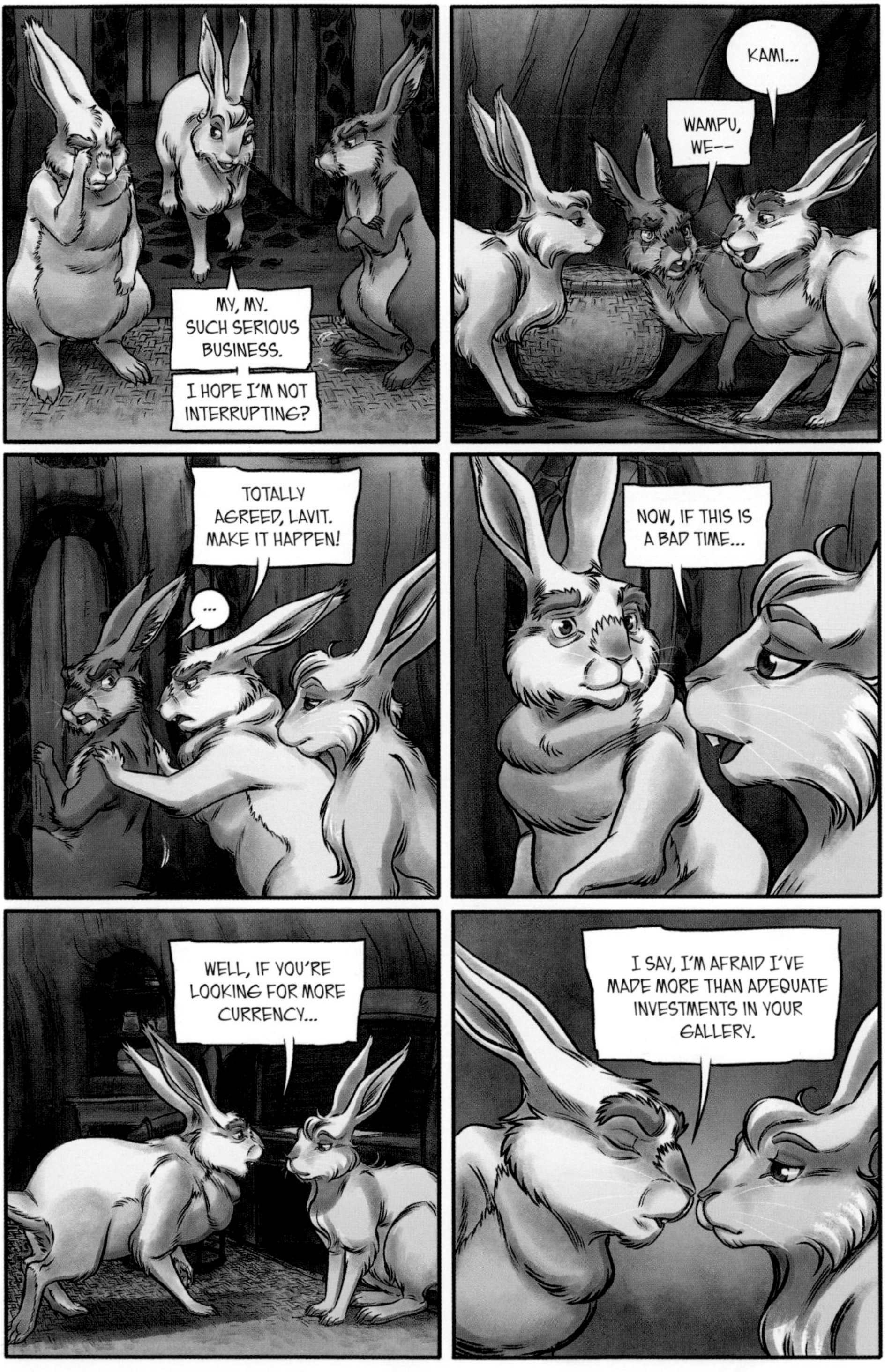
MY, MY. SUCH SERIOUS BUSINESS.
I HOPE I'M NOT INTERRUPTING?
KAMI...
WAMPU, WE--
TOTALLY AGREED, LAVIT. MAKE IT HAPPEN!
...
NOW, IF THIS IS A BAD TIME...
WELL, IF YOU'RE LOOKING FOR MORE CURRENCY...
I SAY, I'M AFRAID I'VE MADE MORE THAN ADEQUATE INVESTMENTS IN YOUR GALLERY.

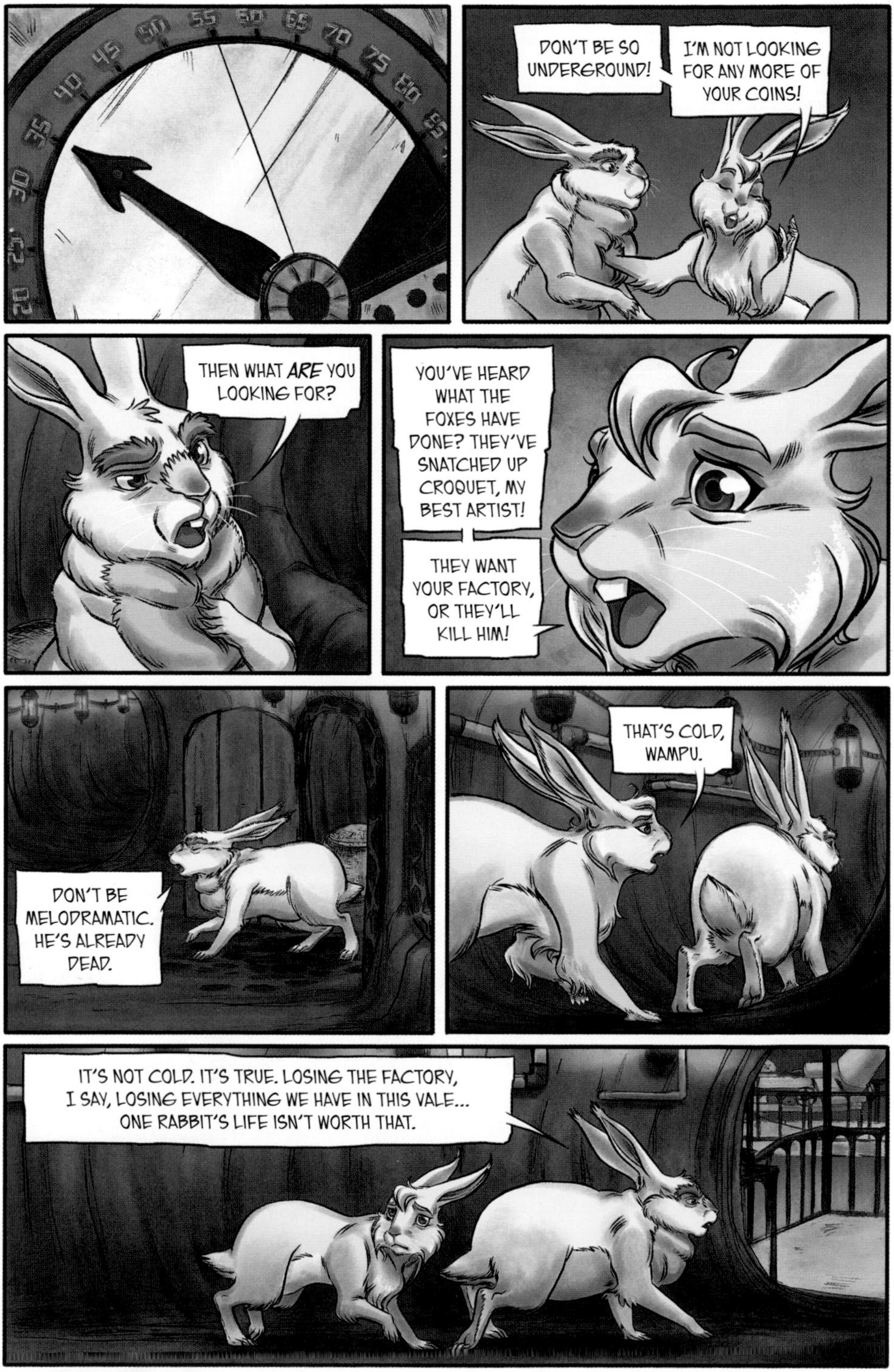

DON'T BE SO UNDERGROUND!
I'M NOT LOOKING FOR ANY MORE OF YOUR COINS!
THEN WHAT ARE YOU LOOKING FOR?
YOU'VE HEARD WHAT THE FOXES HAVE DONE? THEY'VE SNATCHED UP CROQUET, MY BEST ARTIST!
THEY WANT YOUR FACTORY, OR THEY'LL KILL HIM!
DON'T BE MELODRAMATIC. HE'S ALREADY DEAD.
THAT'S COLD, WAMPU.
IT'S NOT COLD. IT'S TRUE. LOSING THE FACTORY, I SAY, LOSING EVERYTHING WE HAVE IN THIS VALE... ONE RABBIT'S LIFE ISN'T WORTH THAT.

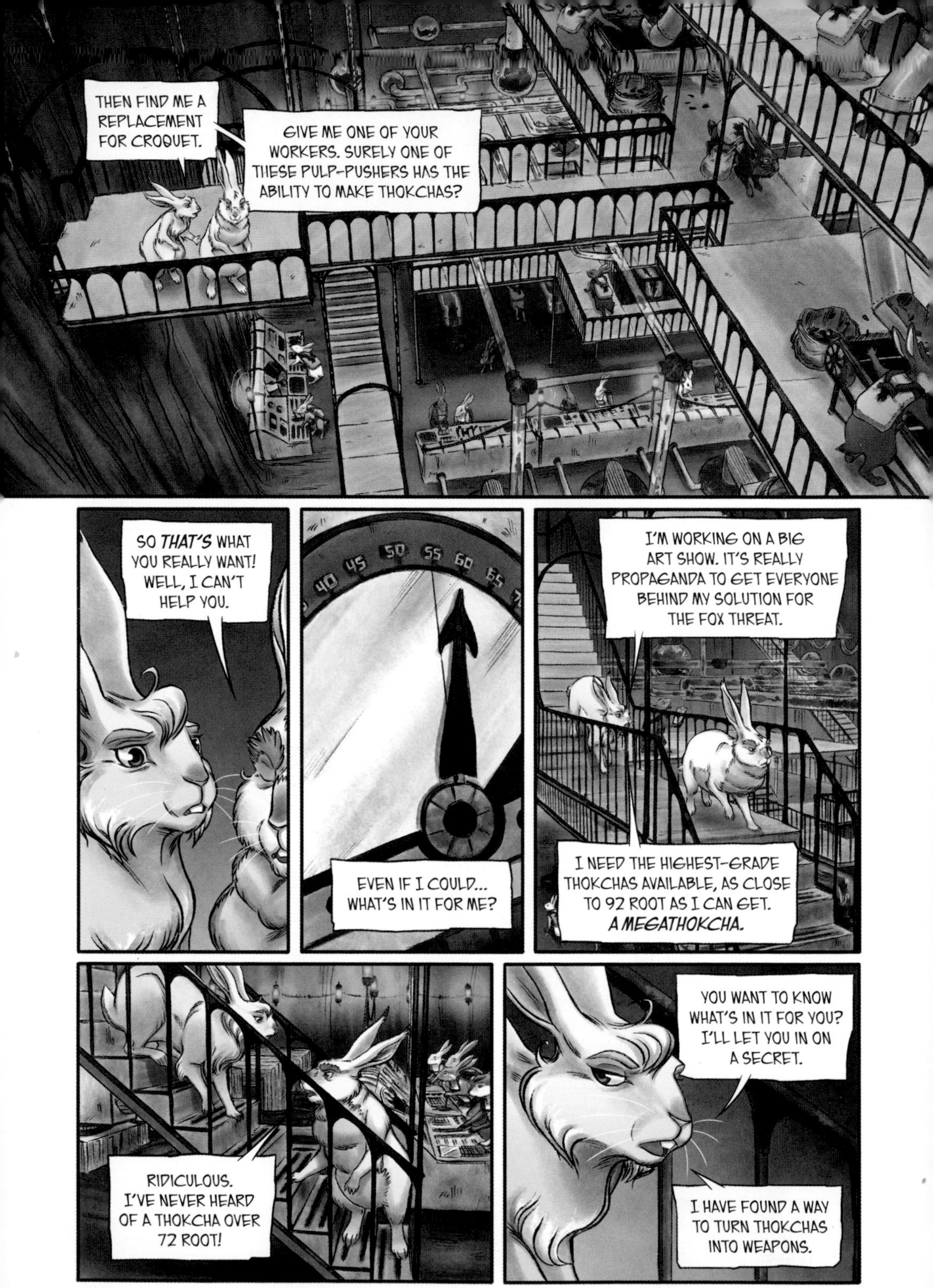
THEN FIND ME A REPLACEMENT FOR CROQUET.
GIVE ME ONE OF YOUR WORKERS. SURELY ONE OF THESE PULP-PUSHERS HAS THE ABILITY TO MAKE THOKCHAS?
SO *THAT'S* WHAT YOU REALLY WANT! WELL, I CAN'T HELP YOU.
40 45 50 55 60 65
EVEN IF I COULD... WHAT'S IN IT FOR ME?
I'M WORKING ON A BIG ART SHOW. IT'S REALLY PROPAGANDA TO GET EVERYONE BEHIND MY SOLUTION FOR THE FOX THREAT.
I NEED THE HIGHEST-GRADE THOKCHAS AVAILABLE, AS CLOSE TO 92 ROOT AS I CAN GET. ***A MEGATHOKCHA.***
RIDICULOUS. I'VE NEVER HEARD OF A THOKCHA OVER 72 ROOT!
YOU WANT TO KNOW WHAT'S IN IT FOR YOU? I'LL LET YOU IN ON A SECRET.
I HAVE FOUND A WAY TO TURN THOKCHAS INTO WEAPONS.

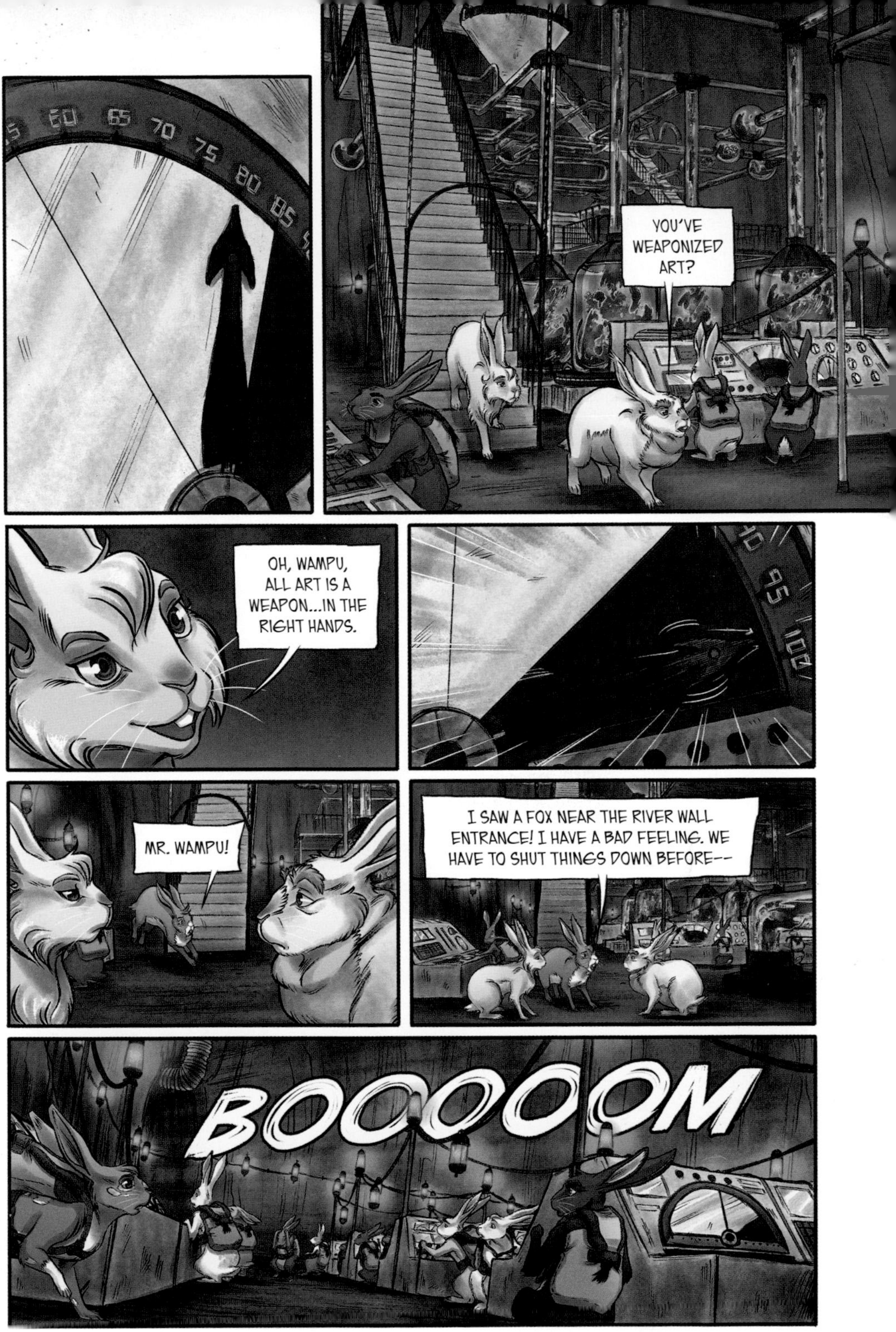
60
65
70
75
80
85
YOU'VE WEAPONIZED ART?
OH, WAMPU, ALL ART IS A WEAPON...IN THE RIGHT HANDS.
95
100
MR. WAMPU!
I SAW A FOX NEAR THE RIVER WALL ENTRANCE! I HAVE A BAD FEELING. WE HAVE TO SHUT THINGS DOWN BEFORE--
BOOOOOM

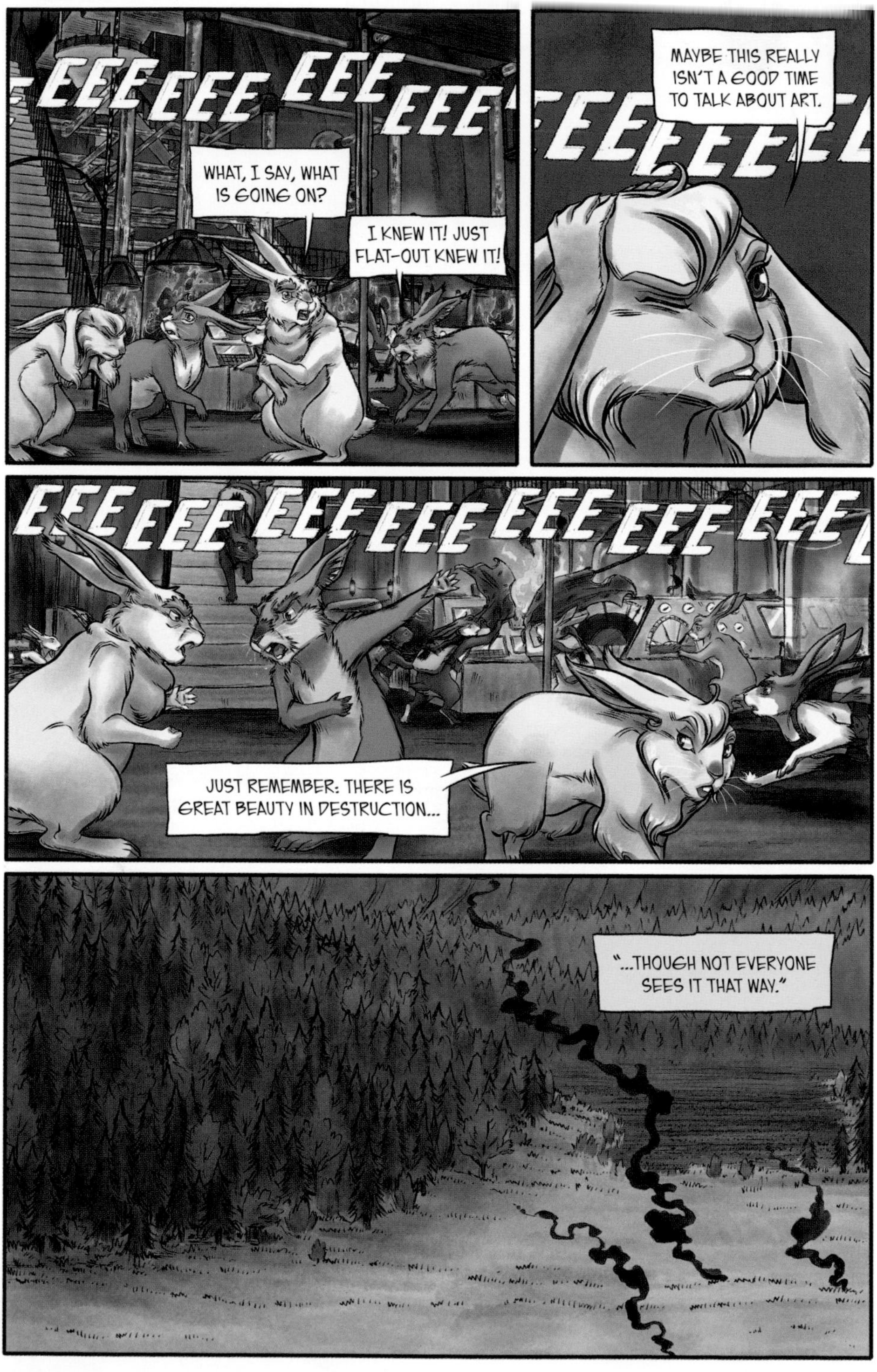
EEEEEEEEEEEE
WHAT, I SAY, WHAT IS GOING ON?
I KNEW IT! JUST FLAT-OUT KNEW IT!
EEEEEEE
MAYBE THIS REALLY ISN'T A GOOD TIME TO TALK ABOUT ART.
EEEEEEEEEEEEEEEEEEEEE
JUST REMEMBER: THERE IS GREAT BEAUTY IN DESTRUCTION...
"...THOUGH NOT EVERYONE SEES IT THAT WAY."

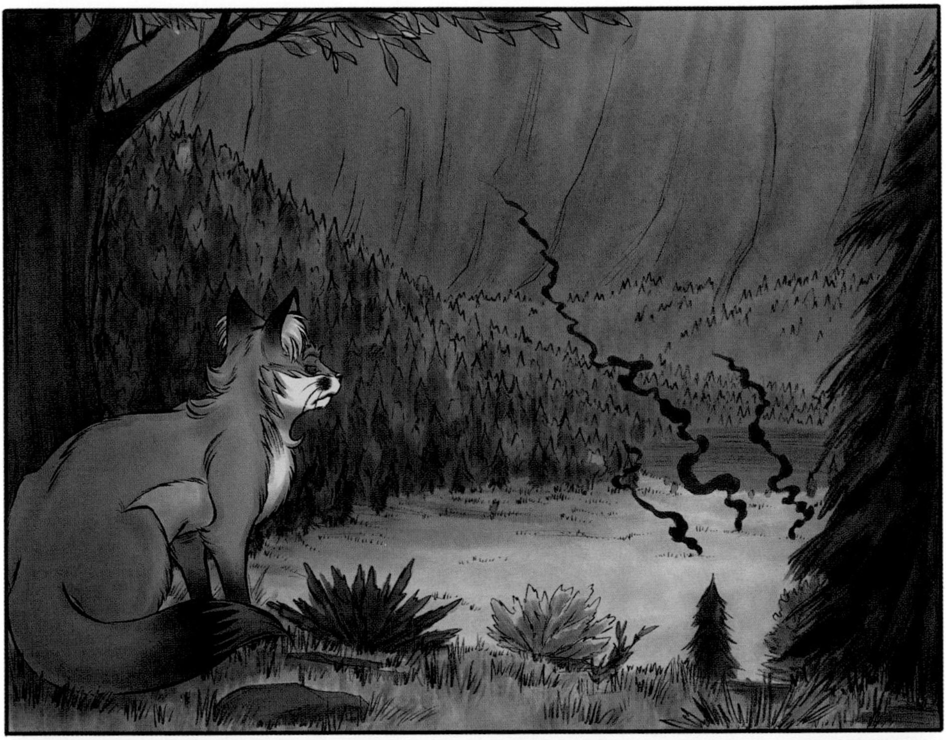

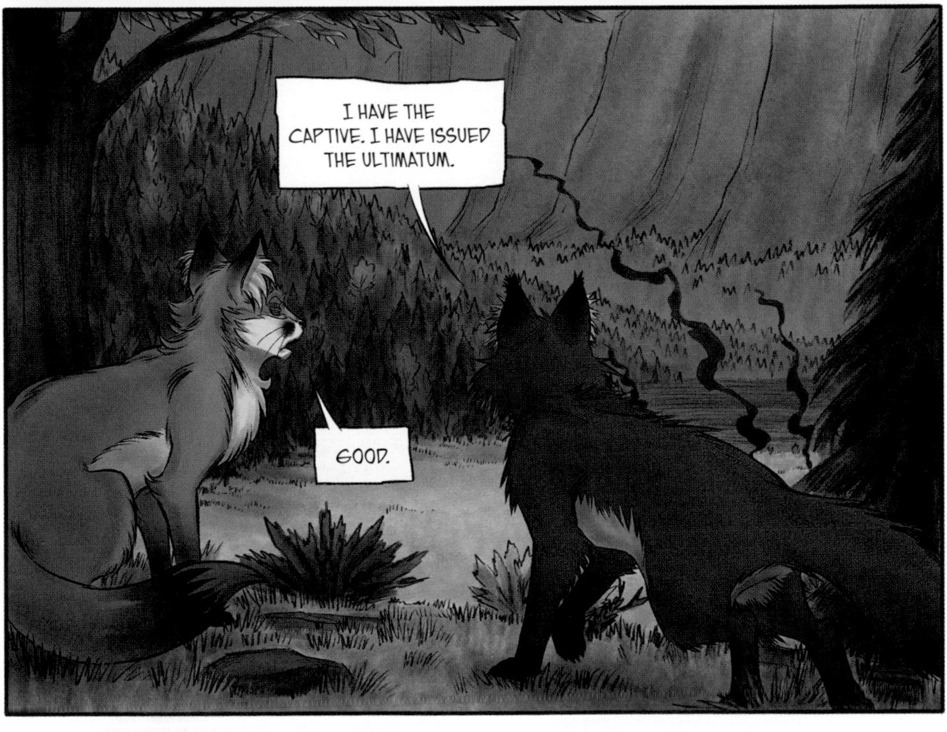
I HAVE THE CAPTIVE. I HAVE ISSUED THE ULTIMATUM.
GOOD.

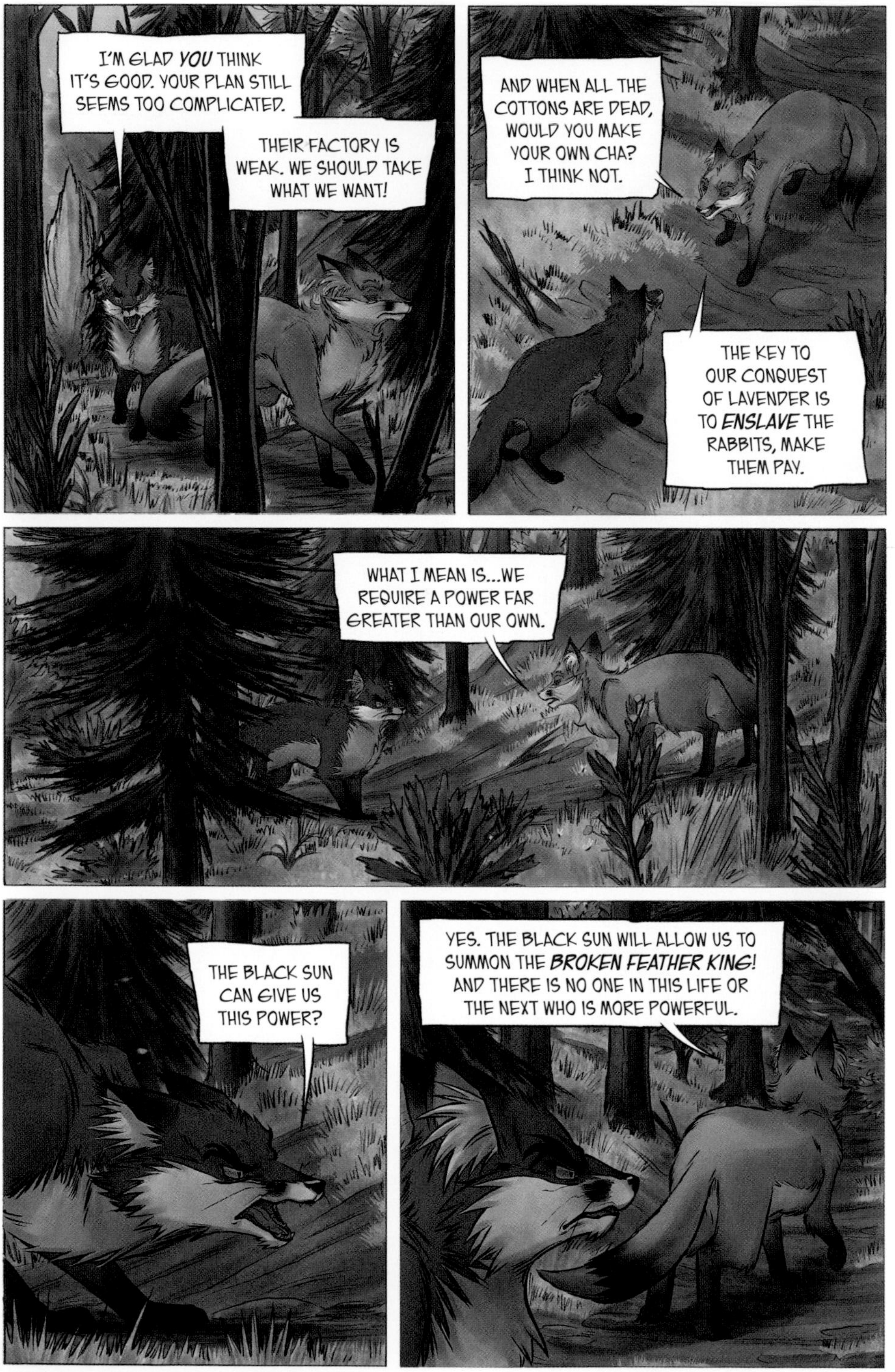
I'M GLAD *YOU* THINK IT'S GOOD. YOUR PLAN STILL SEEMS TOO COMPLICATED.
THEIR FACTORY IS WEAK. WE SHOULD TAKE WHAT WE WANT!
AND WHEN ALL THE COTTONS ARE DEAD, WOULD YOU MAKE YOUR OWN CHA? I THINK NOT.
THE KEY TO OUR CONQUEST OF LAVENDER IS TO *ENSLAVE* THE RABBITS, MAKE THEM PAY.
WHAT I MEAN IS...WE REQUIRE A POWER FAR GREATER THAN OUR OWN.
THE BLACK SUN CAN GIVE US THIS POWER?
YES. THE BLACK SUN WILL ALLOW US TO SUMMON THE *BROKEN FEATHER KING*! AND THERE IS NO ONE IN THIS LIFE OR THE NEXT WHO IS MORE POWERFUL.

9. _____

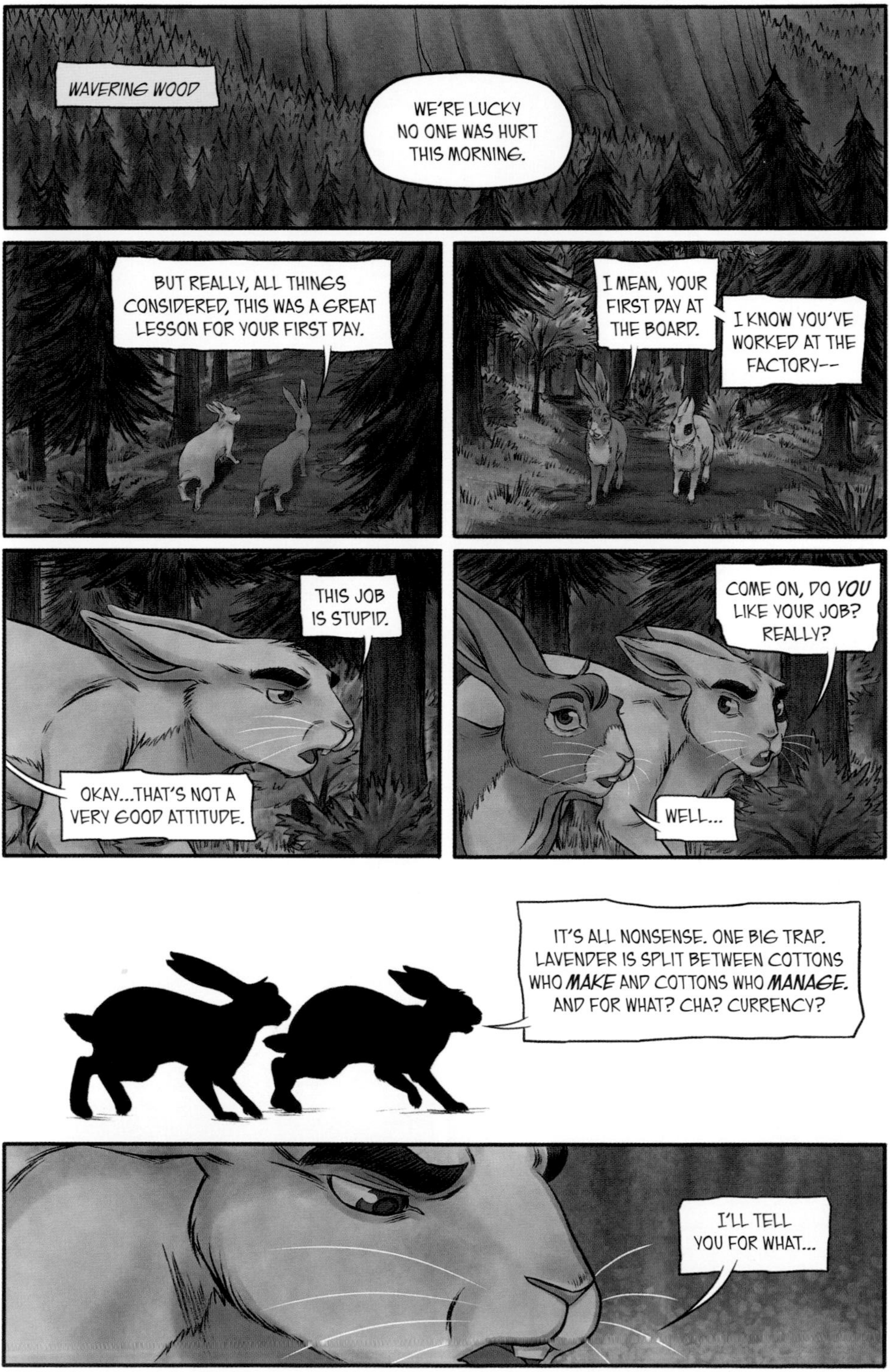
WAVERING WOOD
WE'RE LUCKY NO ONE WAS HURT THIS MORNING.
BUT REALLY, ALL THINGS CONSIDERED, THIS WAS A GREAT LESSON FOR YOUR FIRST DAY.
I MEAN, YOUR FIRST DAY AT THE BOARD.
I KNOW YOU'VE WORKED AT THE FACTORY--
THIS JOB IS STUPID.
OKAY...THAT'S NOT A VERY GOOD ATTITUDE.
COME ON, DO YOU LIKE YOUR JOB? REALLY?
WELL...
IT'S ALL NONSENSE. ONE BIG TRAP. LAVENDER IS SPLIT BETWEEN COTTONS WHO MAKE AND COTTONS WHO MANAGE. AND FOR WHAT? CHA? CURRENCY?
I'LL TELL YOU FOR WHAT...

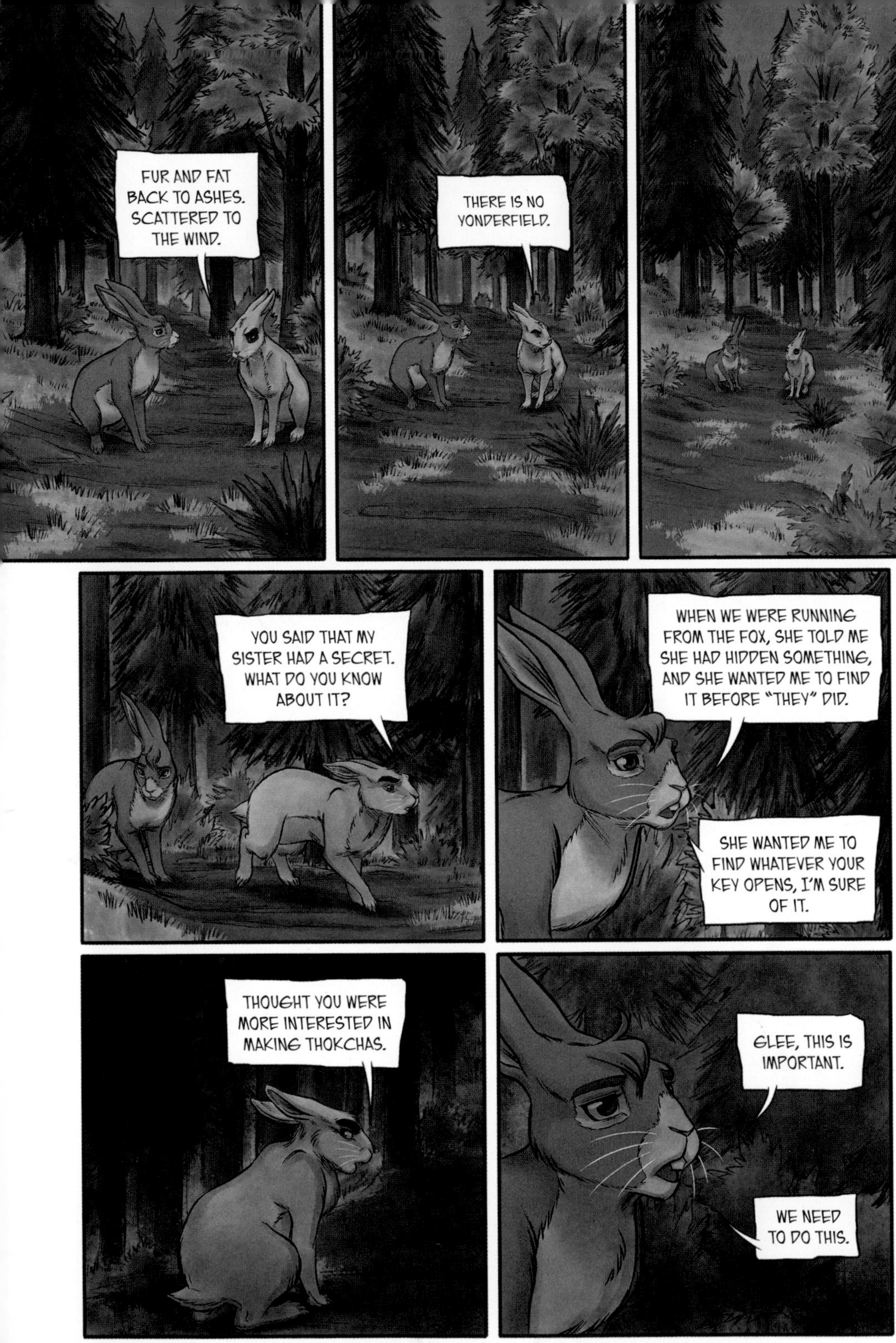
FUR AND FAT BACK TO ASHES. SCATTERED TO THE WIND.
THERE IS NO YONDERFIELD.
YOU SAID THAT MY SISTER HAD A SECRET. WHAT DO YOU KNOW ABOUT IT?
WHEN WE WERE RUNNING FROM THE FOX, SHE TOLD ME SHE HAD HIDDEN SOMETHING, AND SHE WANTED ME TO FIND IT BEFORE "THEY" DID.
SHE WANTED ME TO FIND WHATEVER YOUR KEY OPENS, I'M SURE OF IT.
THOUGHT YOU WERE MORE INTERESTED IN MAKING THOKCHAS.
GLEE, THIS IS IMPORTANT.
WE NEED TO DO THIS.

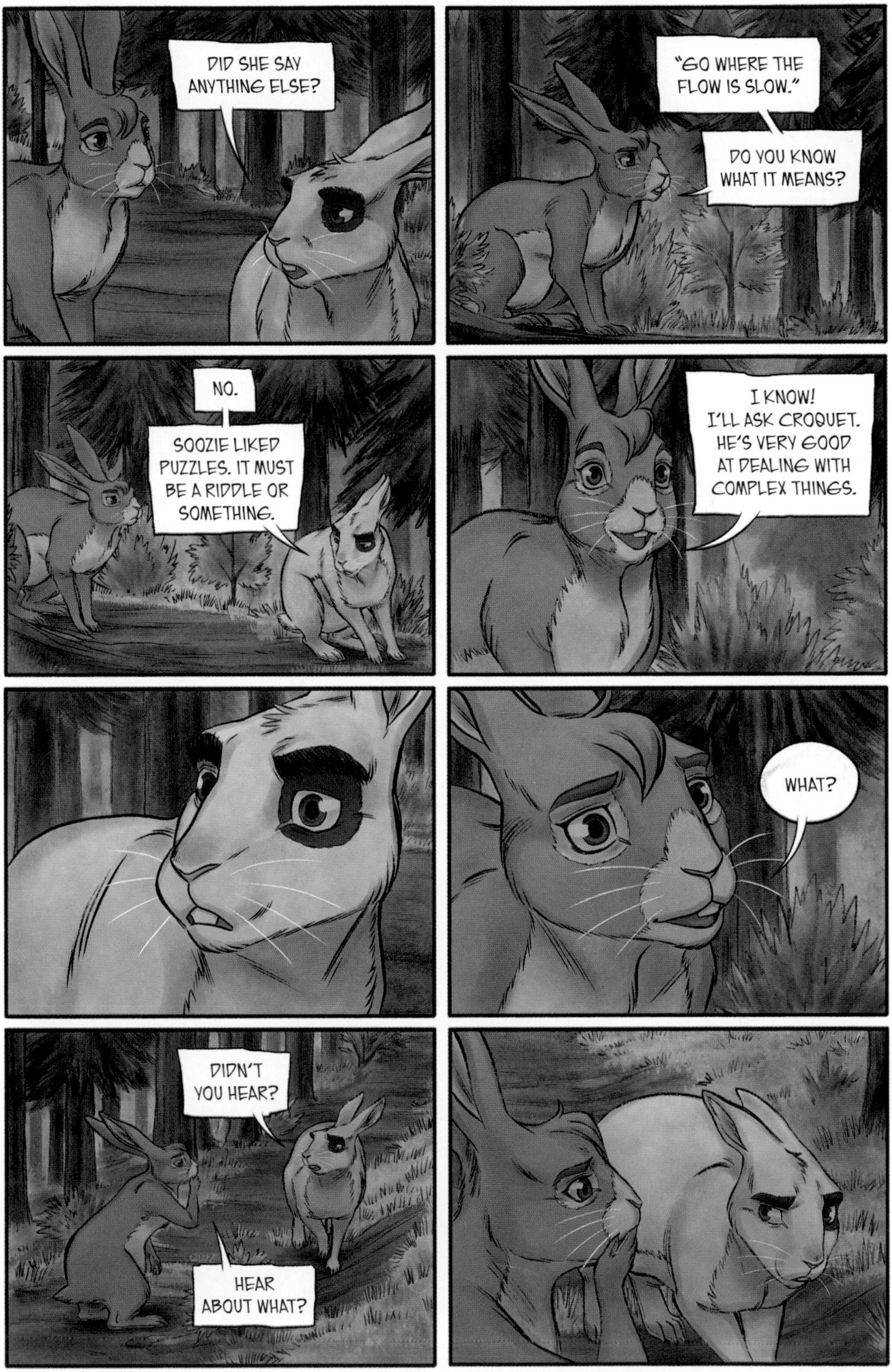
DID SHE SAY ANYTHING ELSE?
"GO WHERE THE FLOW IS SLOW."
DO YOU KNOW WHAT IT MEANS?
NO.
SOOZIE LIKED PUZZLES. IT MUST BE A RIDDLE OR SOMETHING.
I KNOW! I'LL ASK CROQUET. HE'S VERY GOOD AT DEALING WITH COMPLEX THINGS.
WHAT?
DIDN'T YOU HEAR?
HEAR ABOUT WHAT?

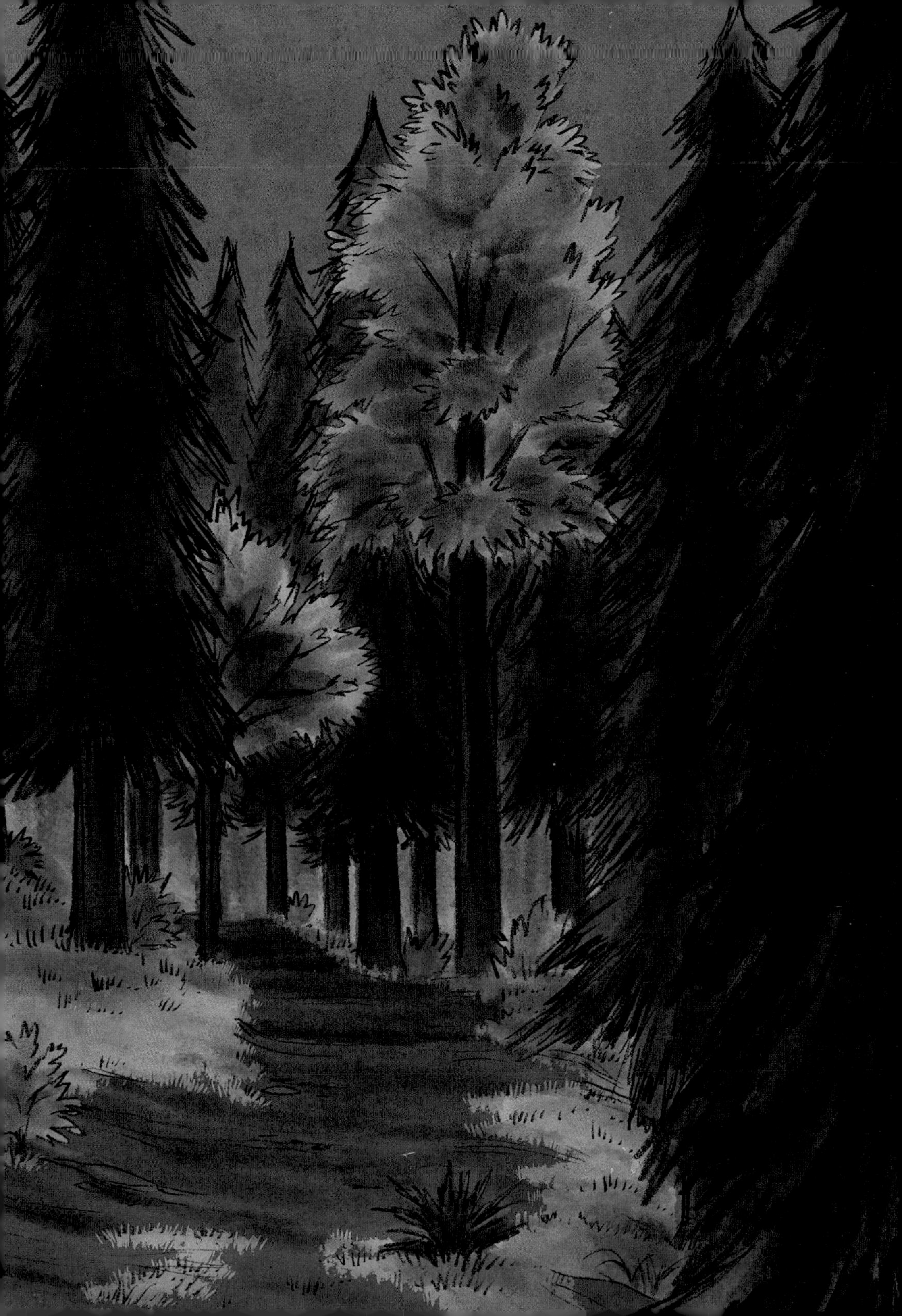

10. _____

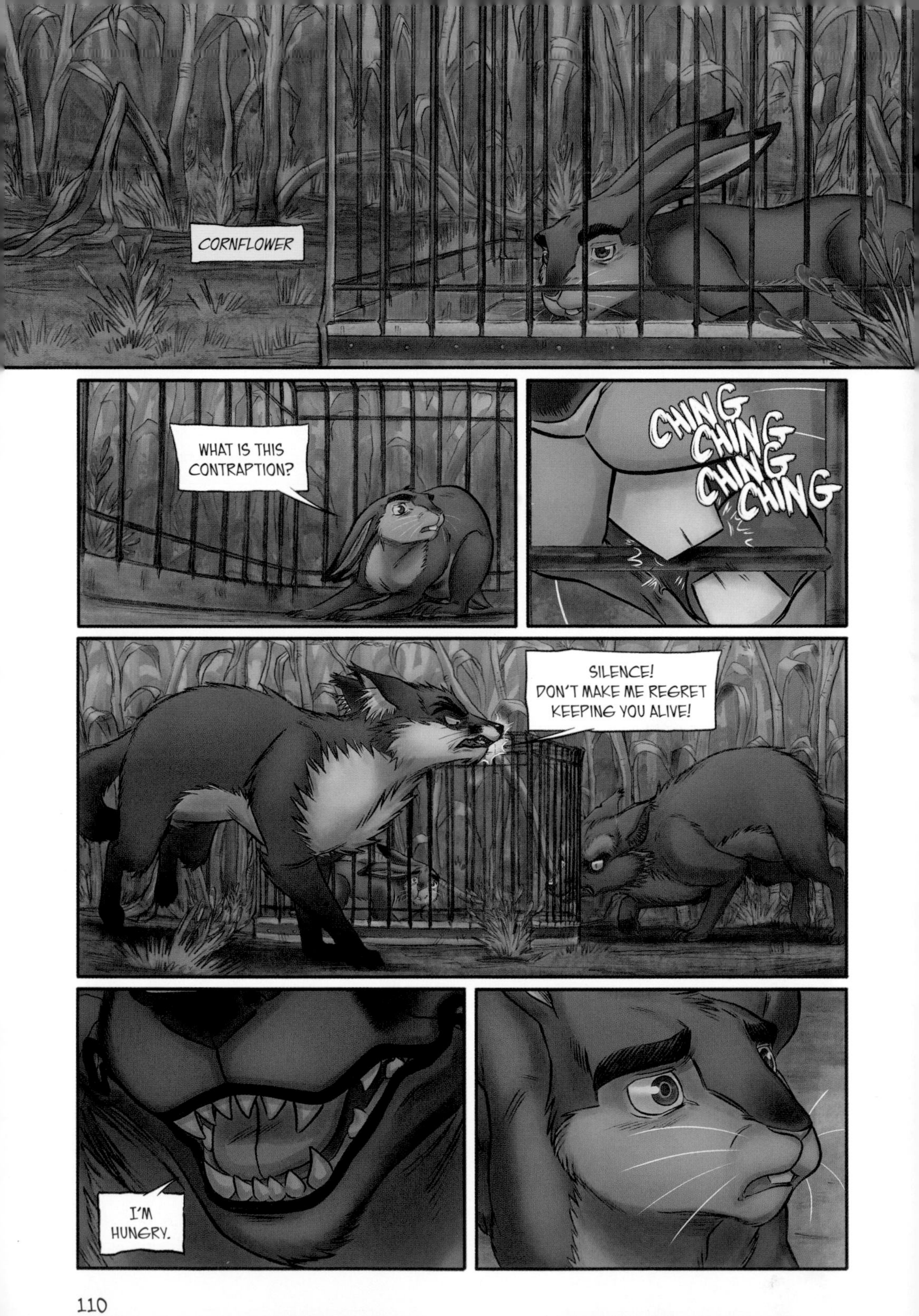

CORNFLOWER
WHAT IS THIS CONTRAPTION?
CHING CHING CHING CHING
SILENCE! DON'T MAKE ME REGRET KEEPING YOU ALIVE!
I'M HUNGRY.

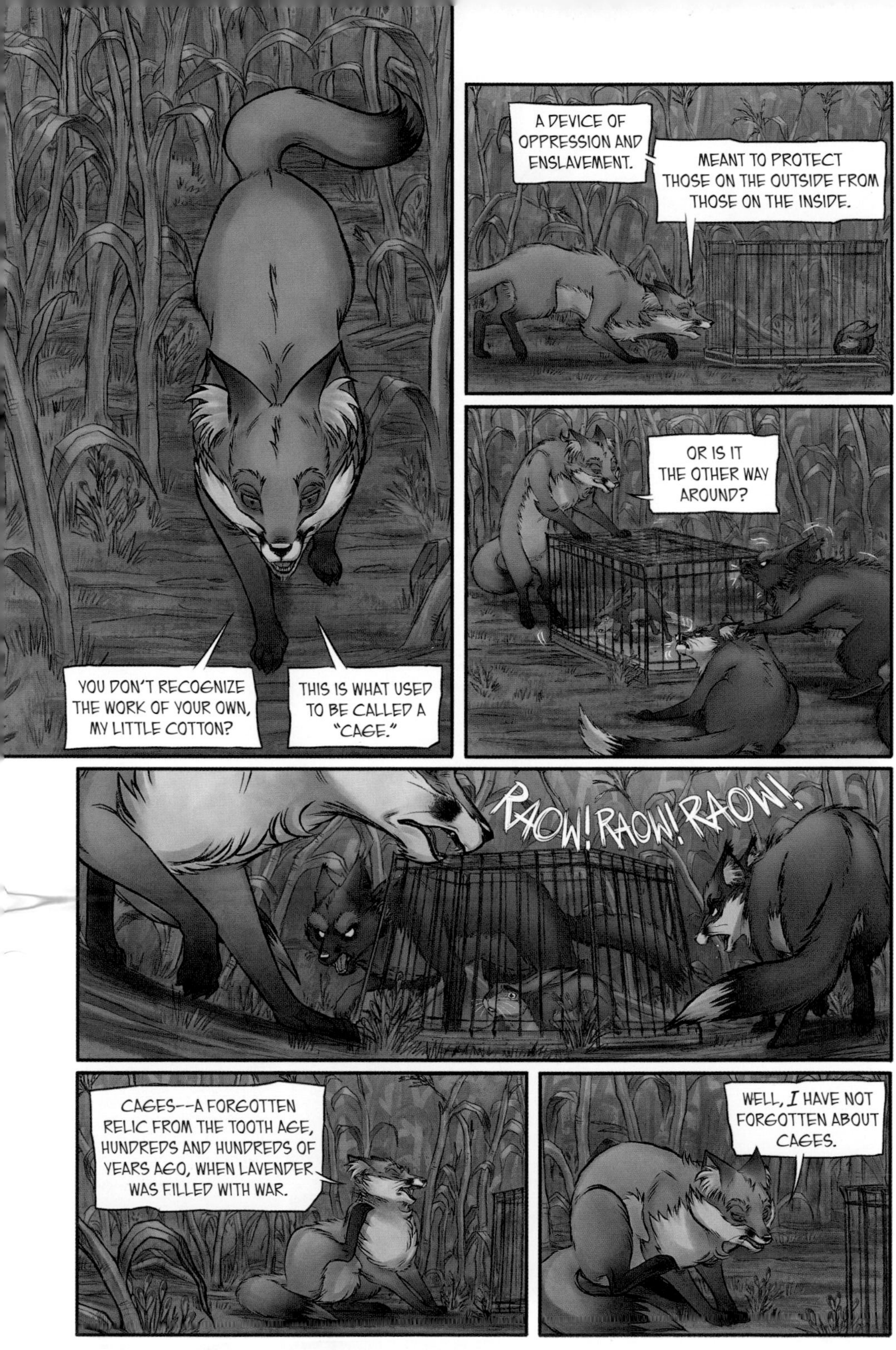
YOU DON'T RECOGNIZE THE WORK OF YOUR OWN, MY LITTLE COTTON?
THIS IS WHAT USED TO BE CALLED A "CAGE."
A DEVICE OF OPPRESSION AND ENSLAVEMENT.
MEANT TO PROTECT THOSE ON THE OUTSIDE FROM THOSE ON THE INSIDE.
OR IS IT THE OTHER WAY AROUND?
RAOW! RAOW! RAOW!
CAGES--A FORGOTTEN RELIC FROM THE TOOTH AGE, HUNDREDS AND HUNDREDS OF YEARS AGO, WHEN LAVENDER WAS FILLED WITH WAR.
WELL, *I* HAVE NOT FORGOTTEN ABOUT CAGES.

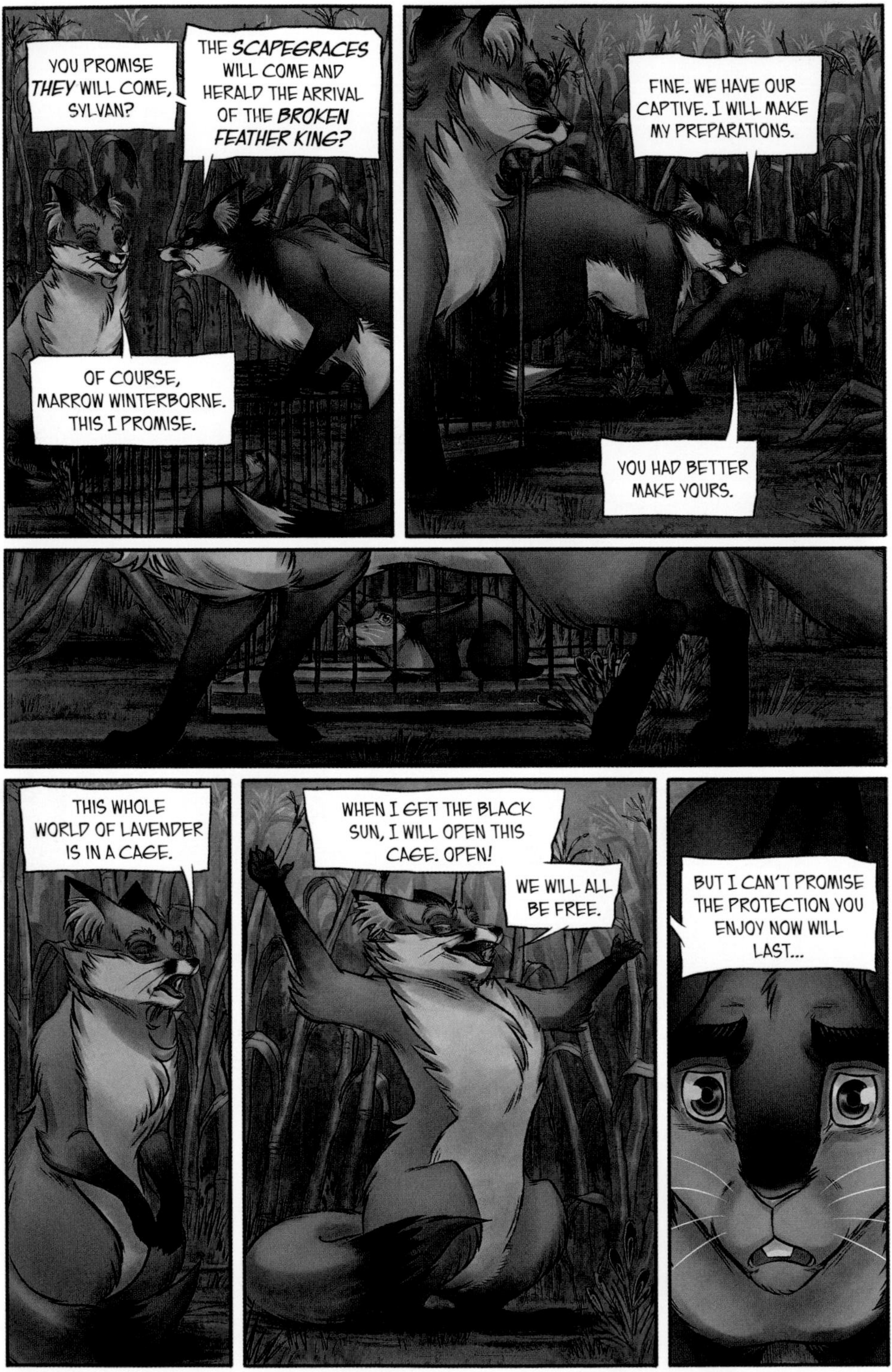
YOU PROMISE THEY WILL COME, SYLVAN?
THE SCAPEGRACES WILL COME AND HERALD THE ARRIVAL OF THE BROKEN FEATHER KING?
OF COURSE, MARROW WINTERBORNE. THIS I PROMISE.
FINE. WE HAVE OUR CAPTIVE. I WILL MAKE MY PREPARATIONS.
YOU HAD BETTER MAKE YOURS.
THIS WHOLE WORLD OF LAVENDER IS IN A CAGE.
WHEN I GET THE BLACK SUN, I WILL OPEN THIS CAGE. OPEN!
WE WILL ALL BE FREE.
BUT I CAN'T PROMISE THE PROTECTION YOU ENJOY NOW WILL LAST...

11.

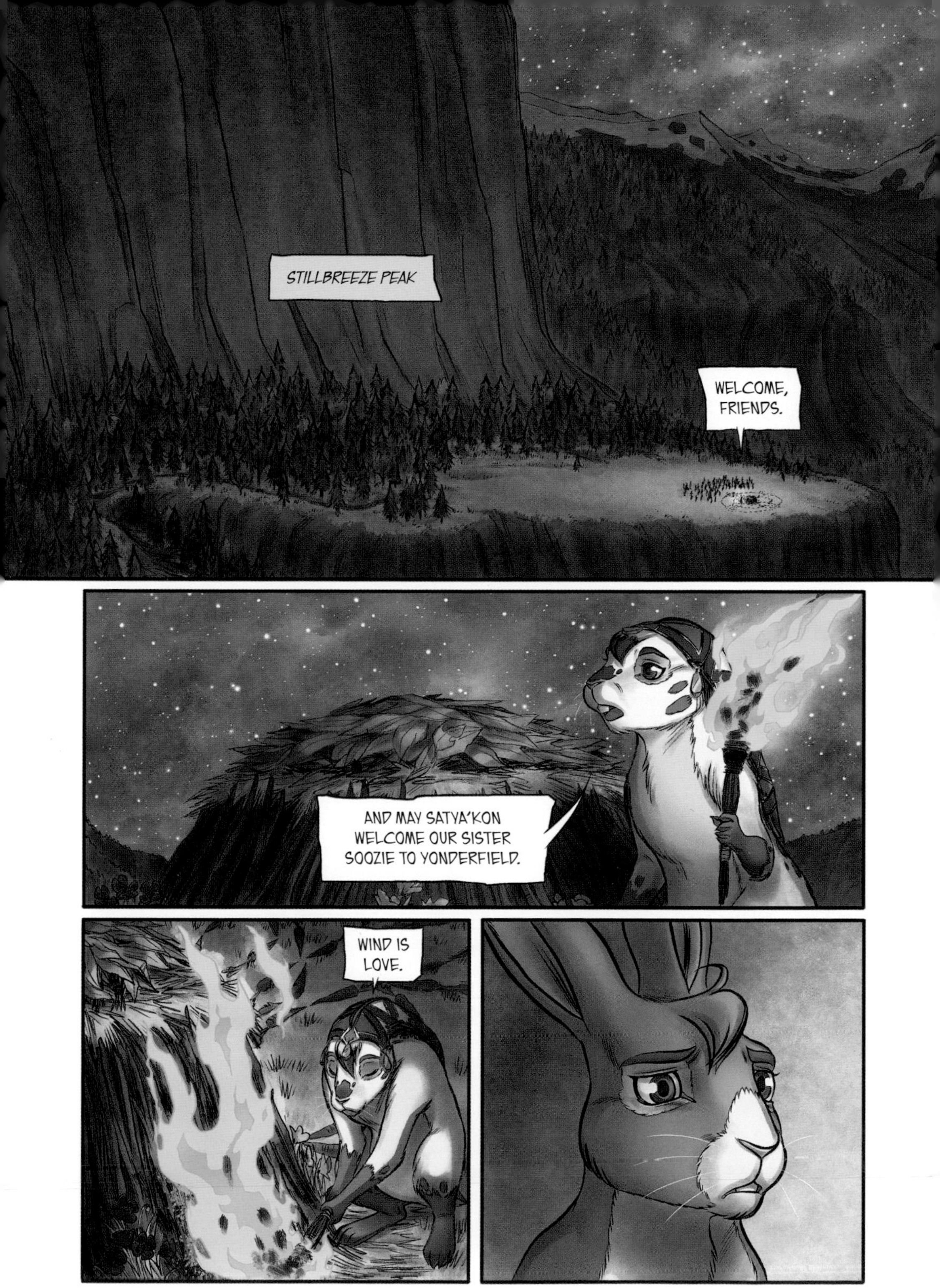
STILLBREEZE PEAK
WELCOME, FRIENDS.
AND MAY SATYA'KON WELCOME OUR SISTER SOOZIE TO YONDERFIELD.
WIND IS LOVE.

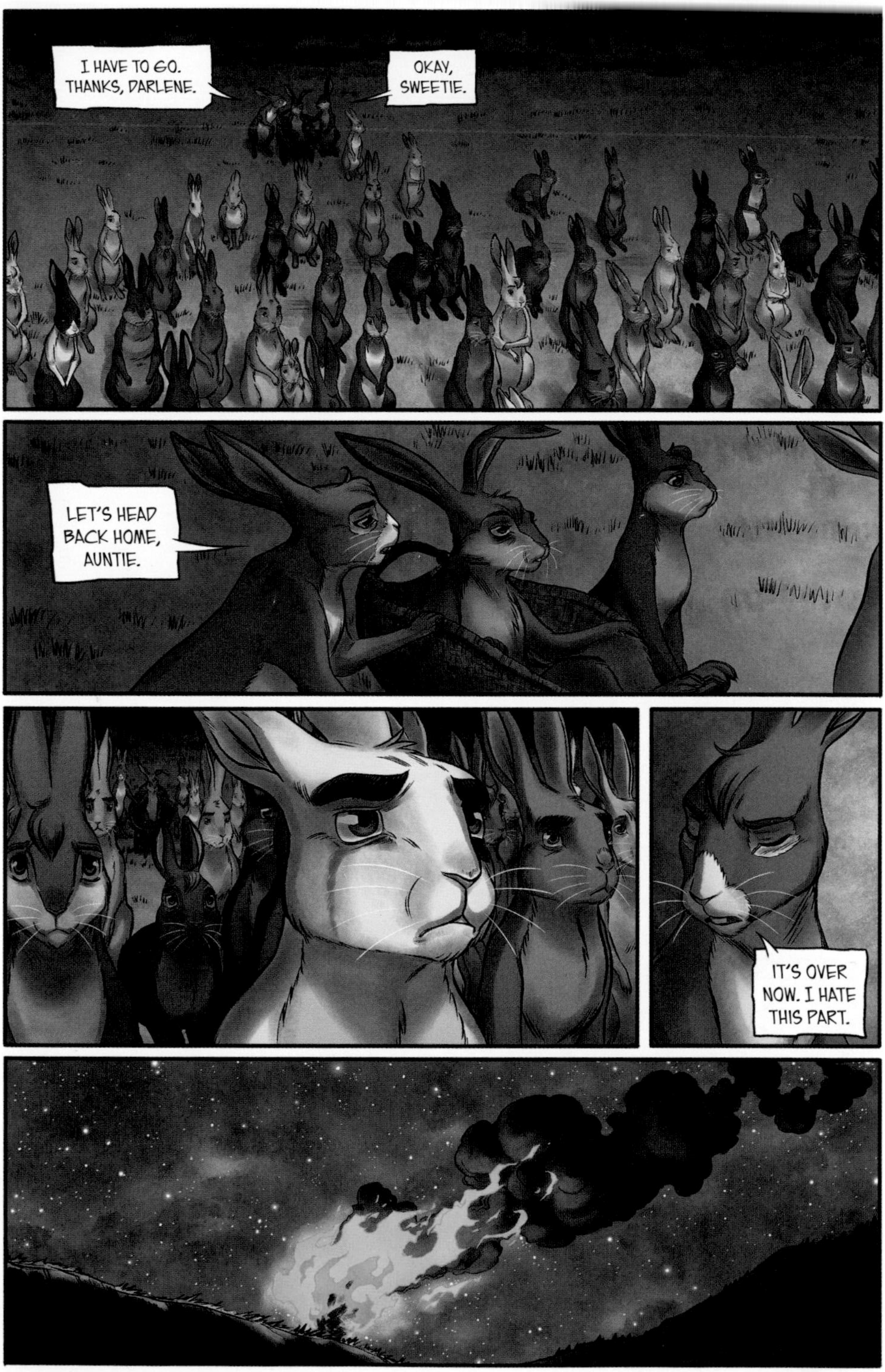
I HAVE TO GO. THANKS, DARLENE.
OKAY, SWEETIE.
LET'S HEAD BACK HOME, AUNTIE.
IT'S OVER NOW. I HATE THIS PART.

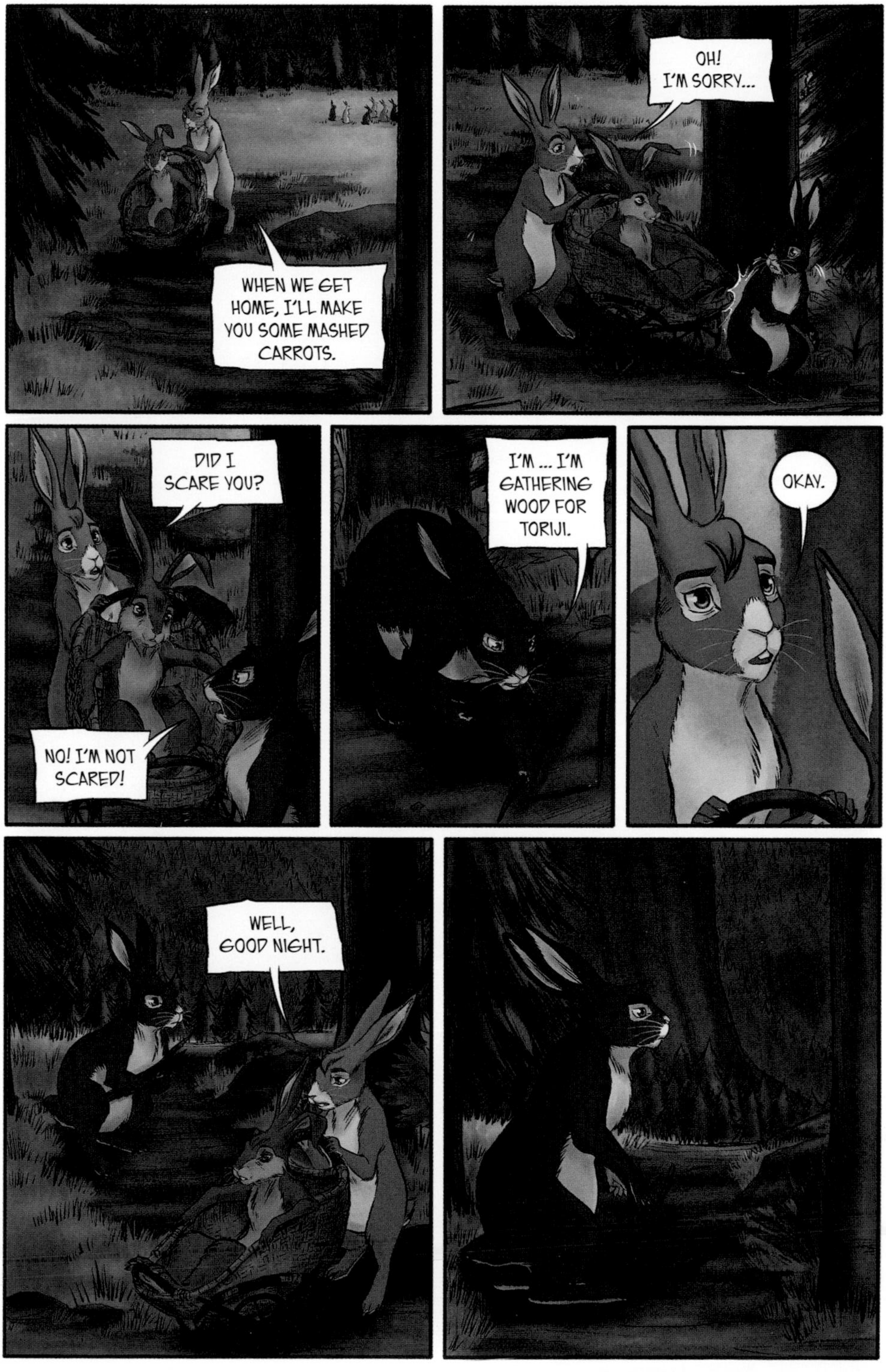
WHEN WE GET HOME, I'LL MAKE YOU SOME MASHED CARROTS.
OH! I'M SORRY...
DID I SCARE YOU?
NO! I'M NOT SCARED!
I'M ... I'M GATHERING WOOD FOR TORIJI.
OKAY.
WELL, GOOD NIGHT.

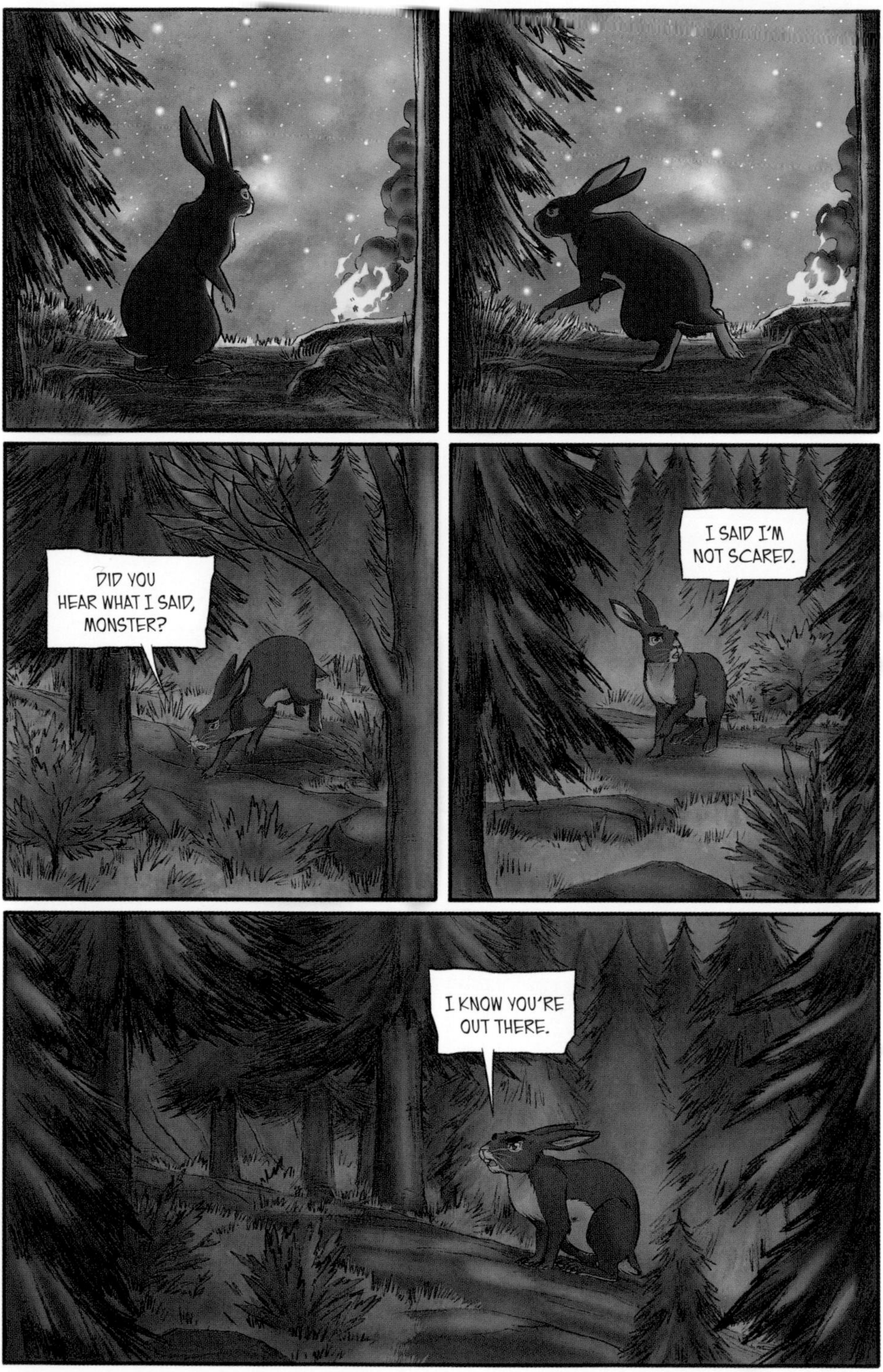
DID YOU HEAR WHAT I SAID, MONSTER?
I SAID I'M NOT SCARED.
I KNOW YOU'RE OUT THERE.

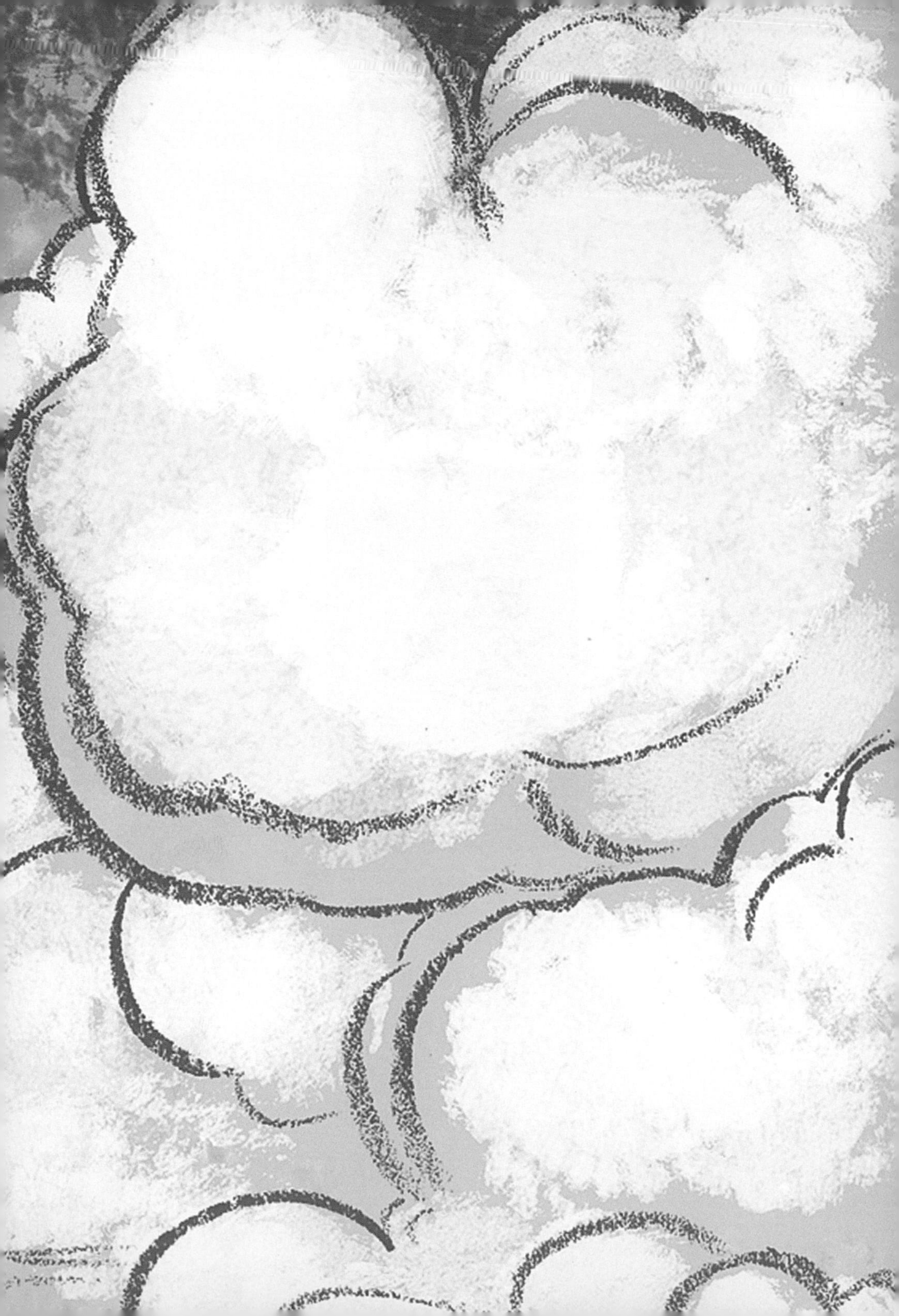

III

" THE TASTE OF GRASS "

12. _____

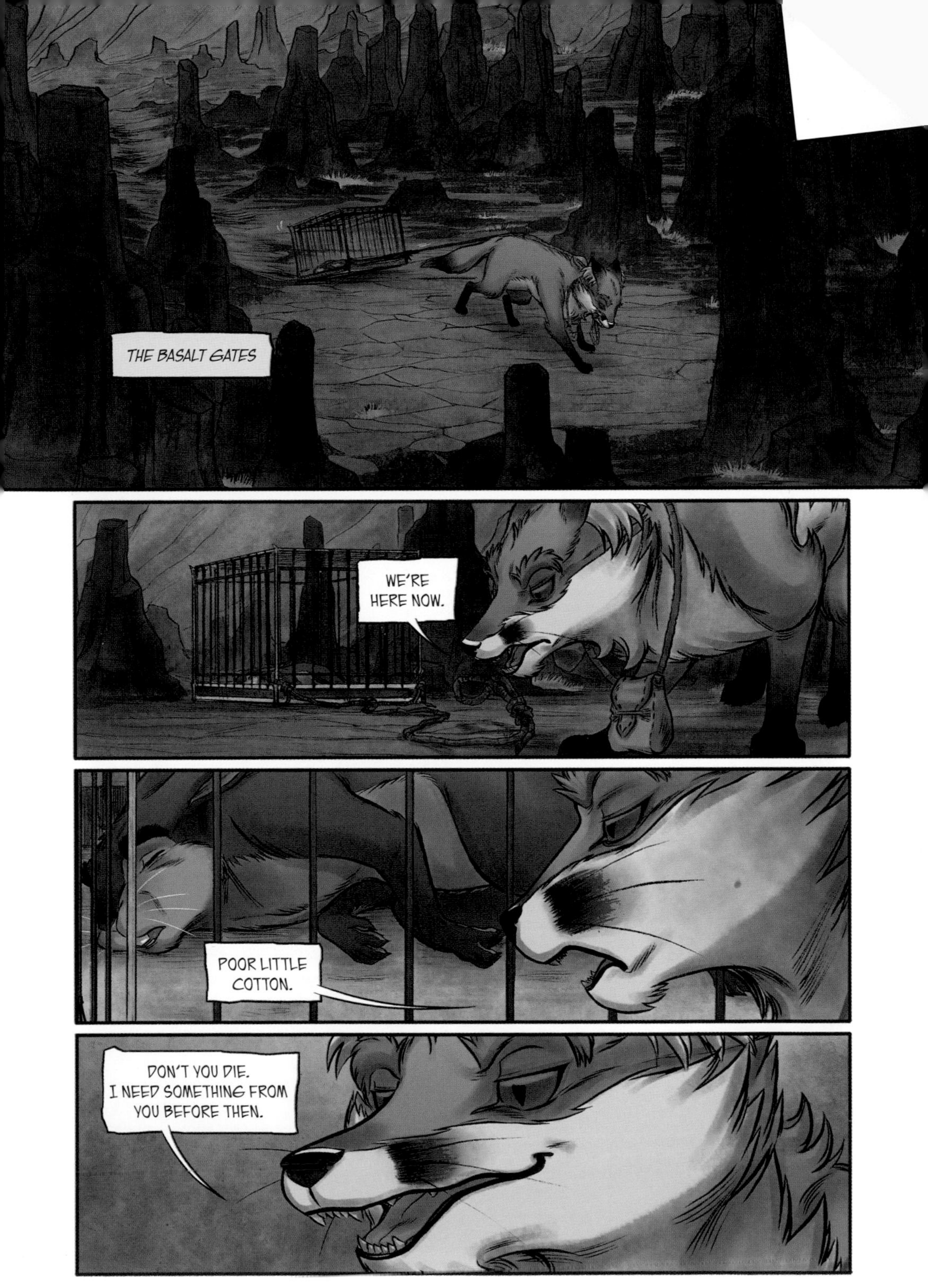
THE BASALT GATES
WE'RE HERE NOW.
POOR LITTLE COTTON.
DON'T YOU DIE. I NEED SOMETHING FROM YOU BEFORE THEN.

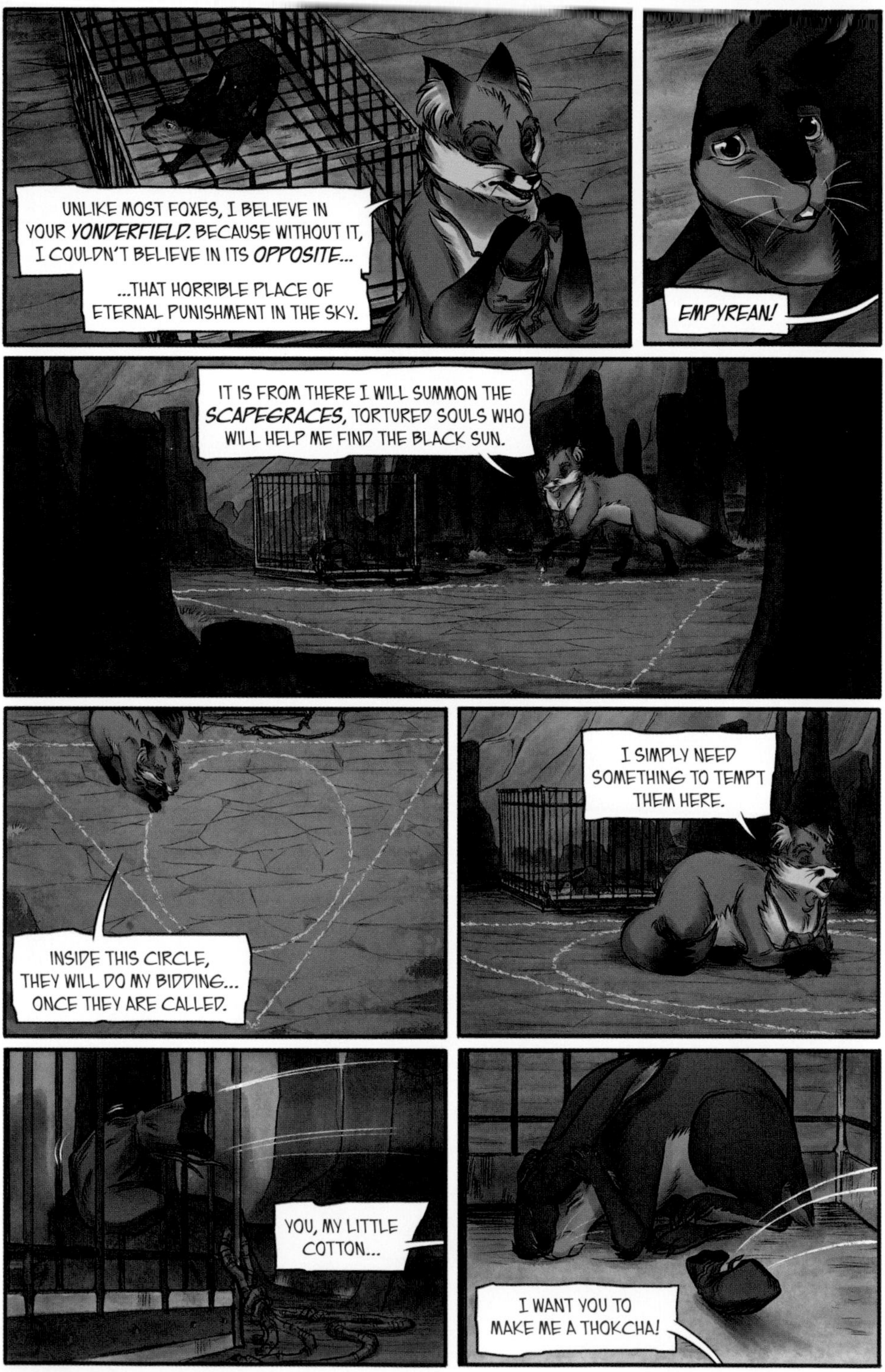
UNLIKE MOST FOXES, I BELIEVE IN YOUR *YONDERFIELD*. BECAUSE WITHOUT IT, I COULDN'T BELIEVE IN ITS *OPPOSITE*...
...THAT HORRIBLE PLACE OF ETERNAL PUNISHMENT IN THE SKY.
EMPYREAN!
IT IS FROM THERE I WILL SUMMON THE *SCAPEGRACES*, TORTURED SOULS WHO WILL HELP ME FIND THE BLACK SUN.
INSIDE THIS CIRCLE, THEY WILL DO MY BIDDING... ONCE THEY ARE CALLED.
I SIMPLY NEED SOMETHING TO TEMPT THEM HERE.
YOU, MY LITTLE COTTON...
I WANT YOU TO MAKE ME A THOKCHA!

13.

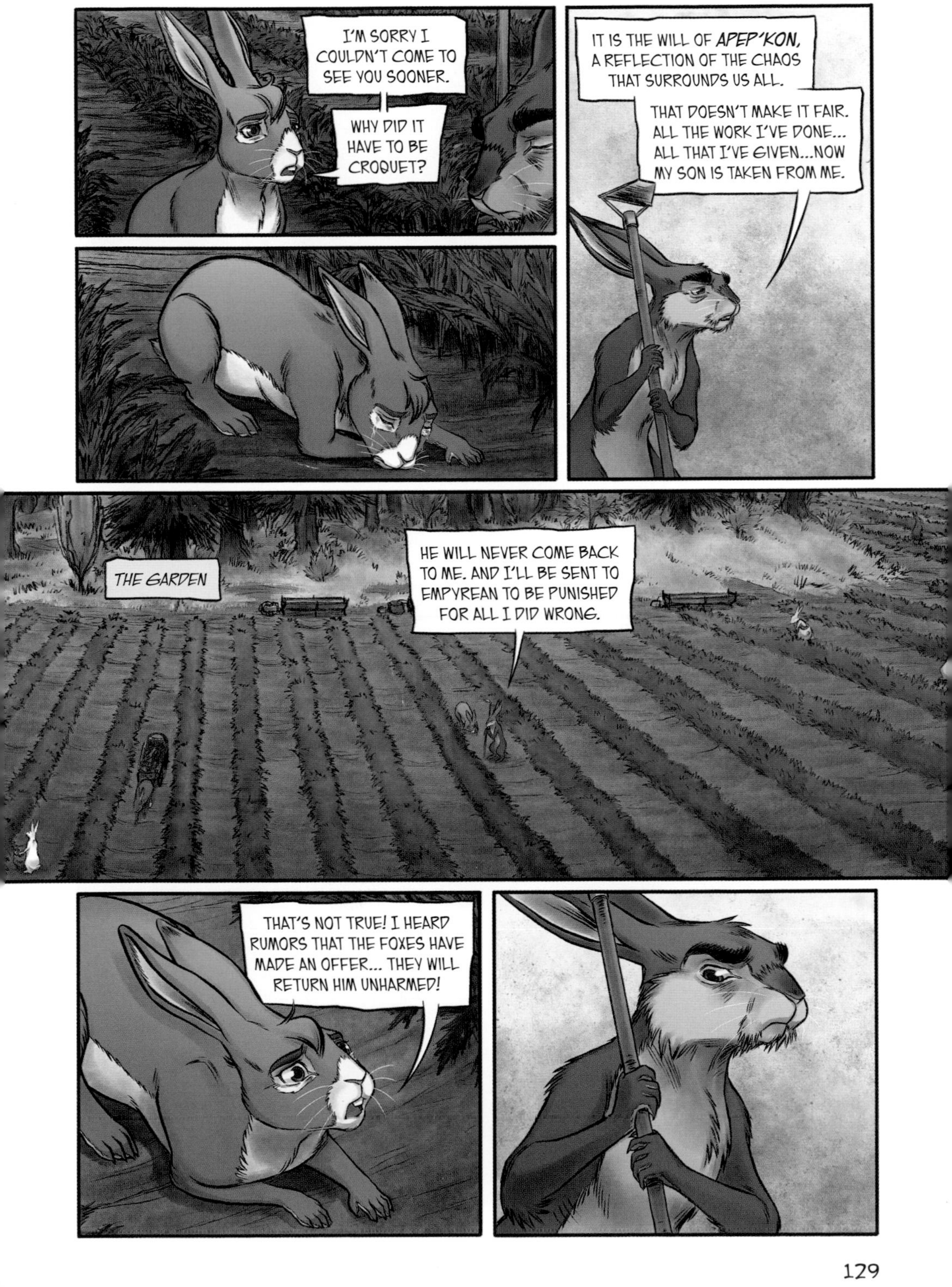

I'M SORRY I COULDN'T COME TO SEE YOU SOONER.
WHY DID IT HAVE TO BE CROQUET?
IT IS THE WILL OF *APEP'KON,* A REFLECTION OF THE CHAOS THAT SURROUNDS US ALL.
THAT DOESN'T MAKE IT FAIR. ALL THE WORK I'VE DONE... ALL THAT I'VE GIVEN...NOW MY SON IS TAKEN FROM ME.
THE GARDEN
HE WILL NEVER COME BACK TO ME. AND I'LL BE SENT TO EMPYREAN TO BE PUNISHED FOR ALL I DID WRONG.
THAT'S NOT TRUE! I HEARD RUMORS THAT THE FOXES HAVE MADE AN OFFER... THEY WILL RETURN HIM UNHARMED!

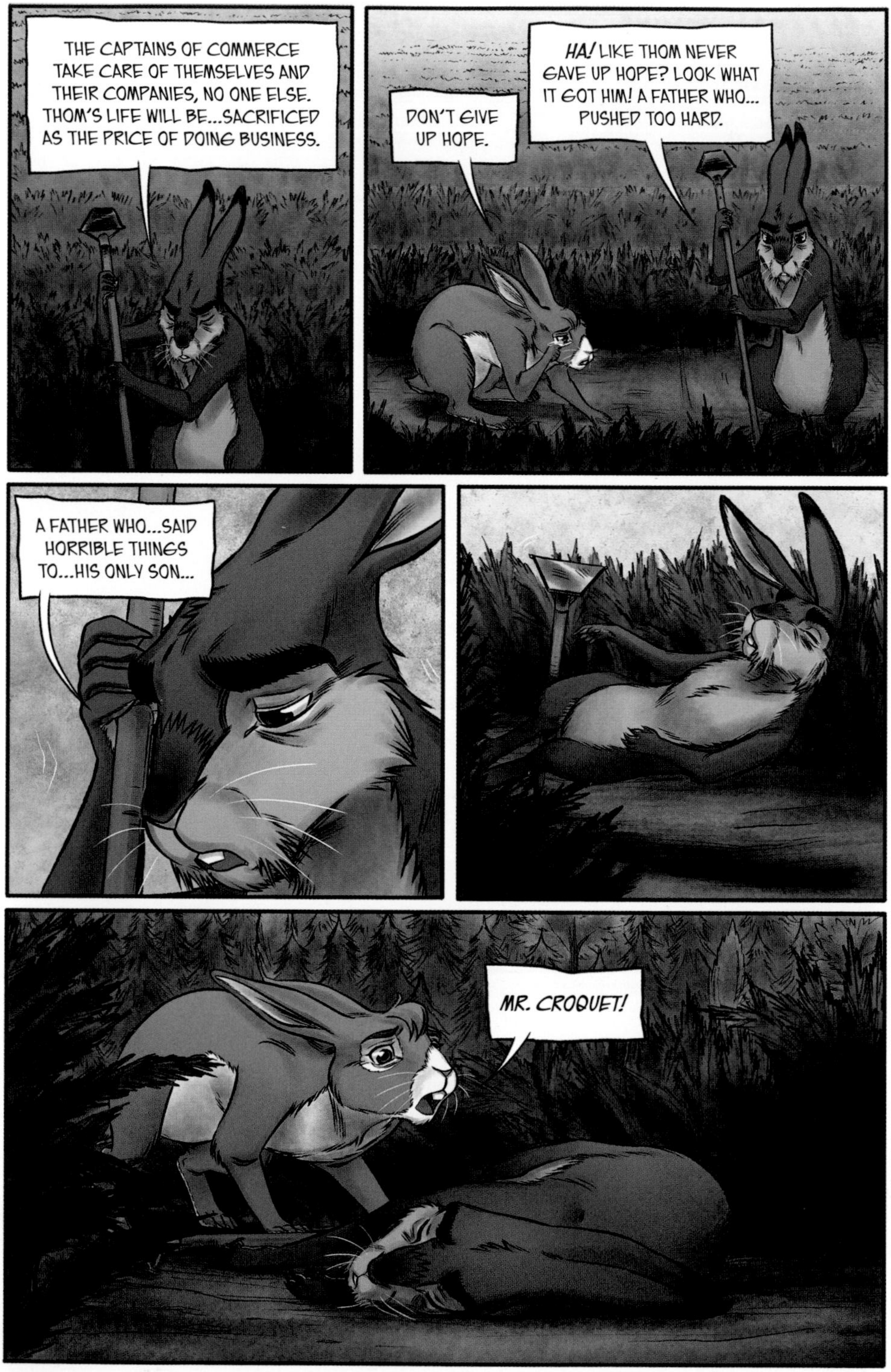
THE CAPTAINS OF COMMERCE TAKE CARE OF THEMSELVES AND THEIR COMPANIES, NO ONE ELSE. THOM'S LIFE WILL BE...SACRIFICED AS THE PRICE OF DOING BUSINESS.
DON'T GIVE UP HOPE.
HA! LIKE THOM NEVER GAVE UP HOPE? LOOK WHAT IT GOT HIM! A FATHER WHO... PUSHED TOO HARD.
A FATHER WHO...SAID HORRIBLE THINGS TO...HIS ONLY SON...
MR. CROQUET!

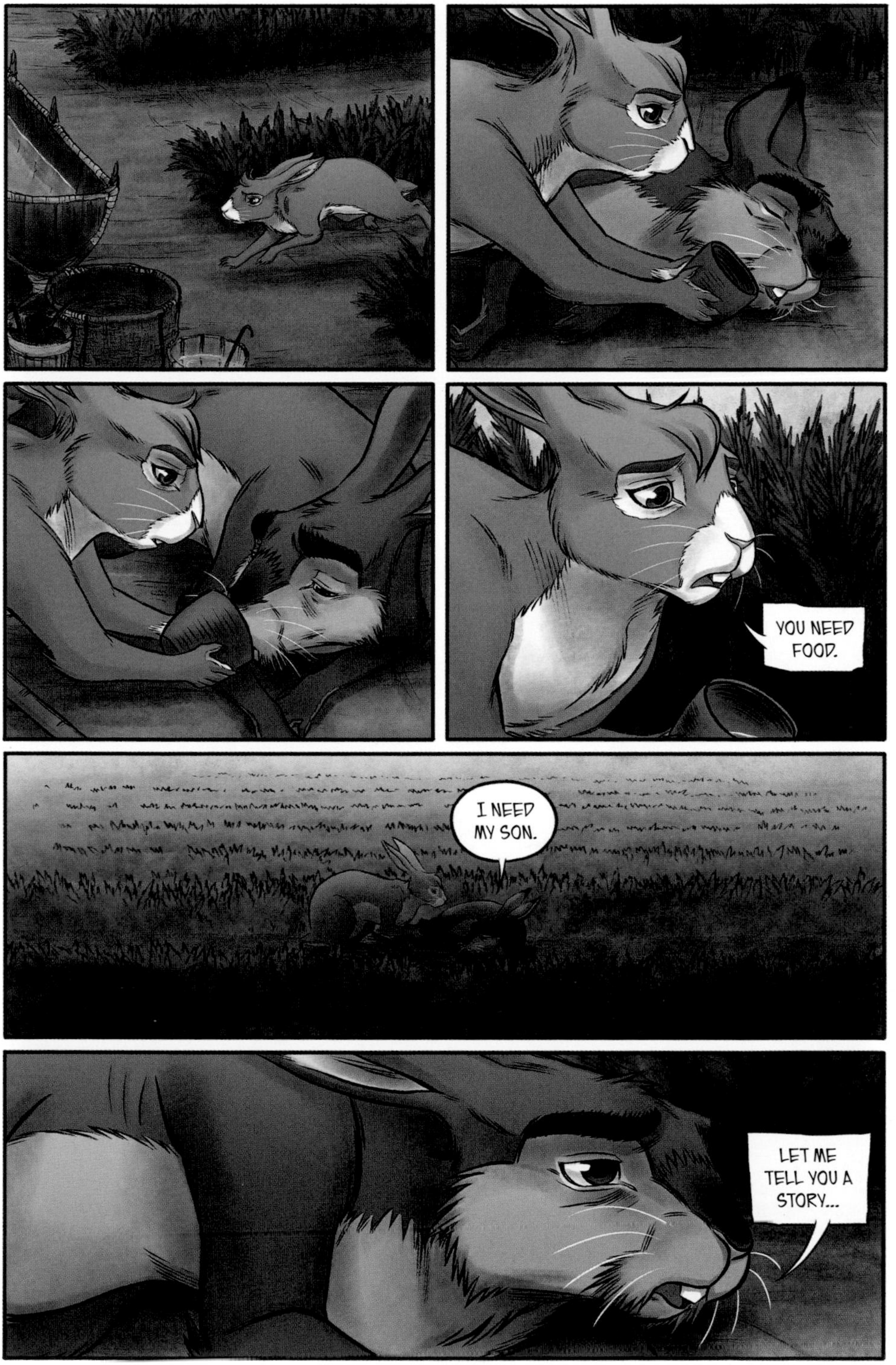
YOU NEED FOOD.
I NEED MY SON.
LET ME TELL YOU A STORY...

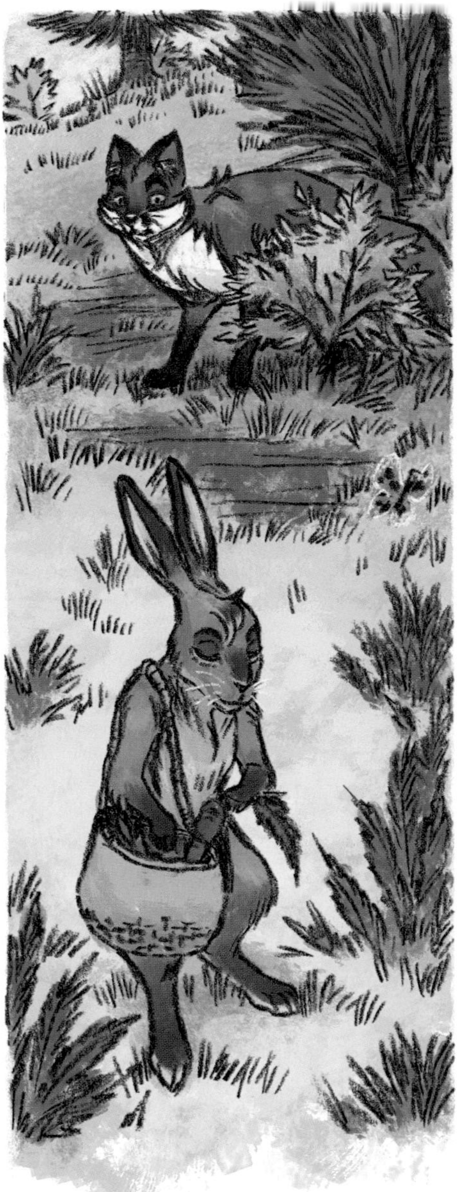

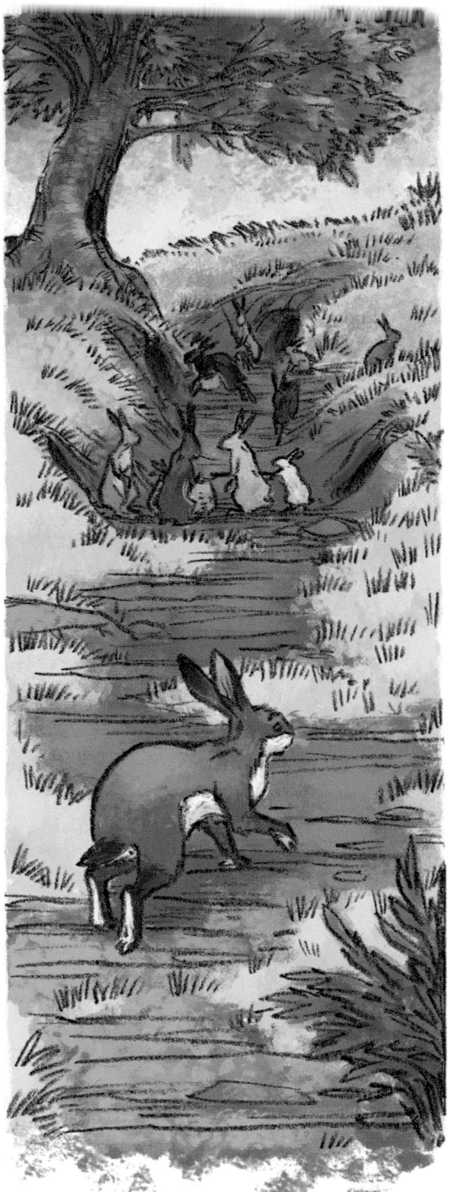

Once upon a time, the King of Foxes saw a rabbit maiden collecting carrots in a field. He had never seen anything or anyone so beautiful. He fell instantly in love.

He knew she would be afraid of his true identity. So he transformed himself into a dashing young rabbit and hopped into the vale, a stranger.

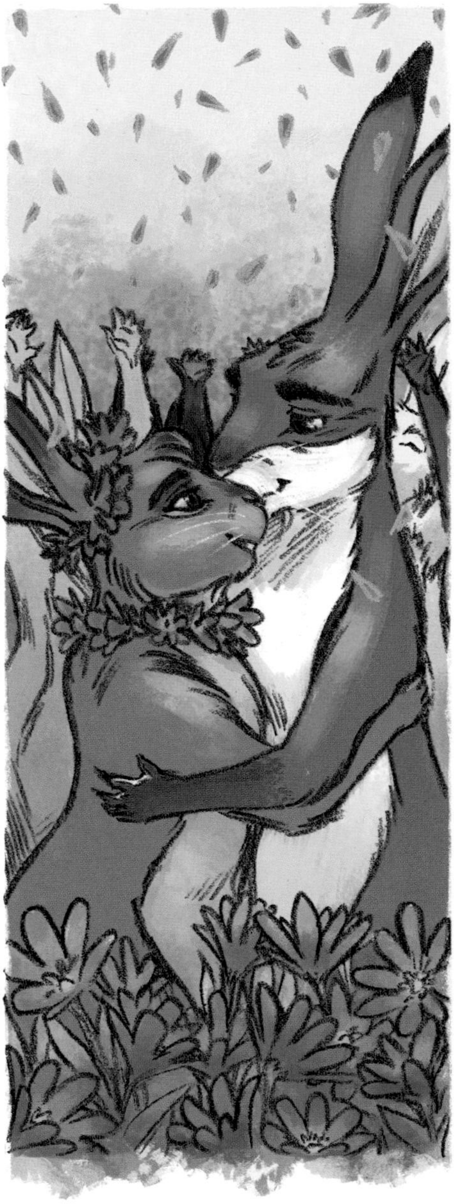

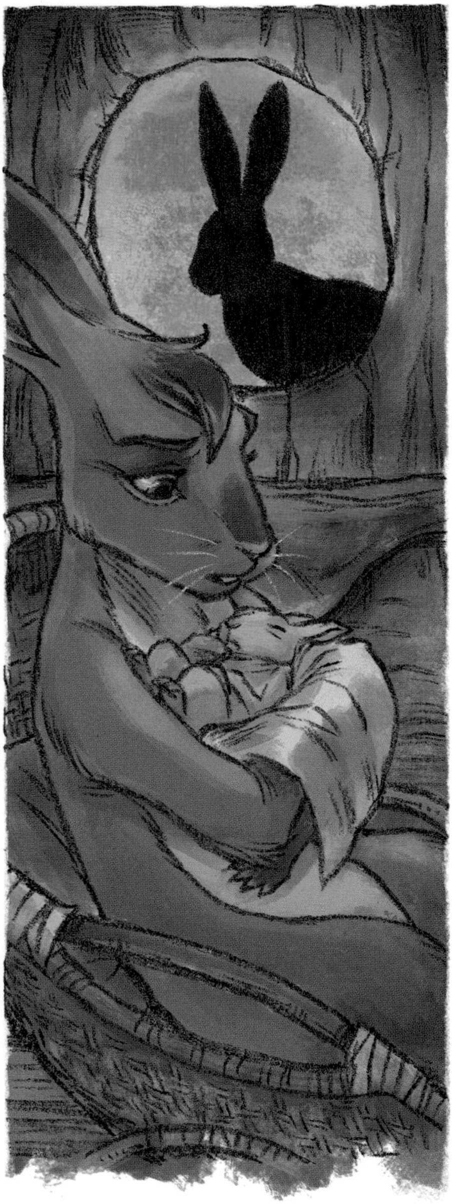

His sly fox ways charmed the locals, and soon he became favored by the rabbit folk. He attracted the attentions of the maiden he loved. They were married and gave birth to a son.

On the boy's belly, the maiden found an inverted triangle, the mark of the foxes. She now knew that her lover was the King of the Foxes. And as everyone understood, rabbits were rabbits, and foxes were foxes.

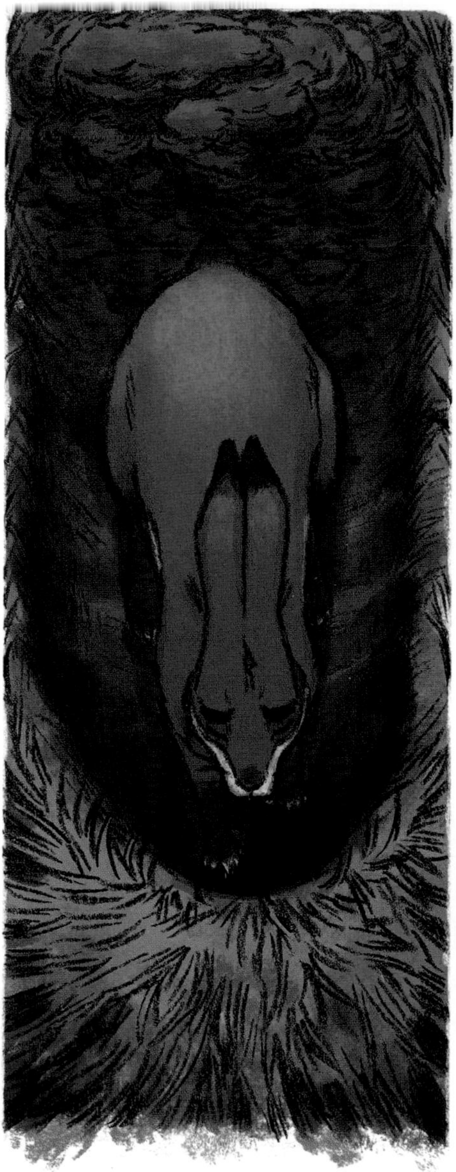

So the King of the Foxes could not stay. Before he left, he dug a burrow for his son, so deep it seemed bottomless. "If you lose your way," he said to his son, "this will take you home."

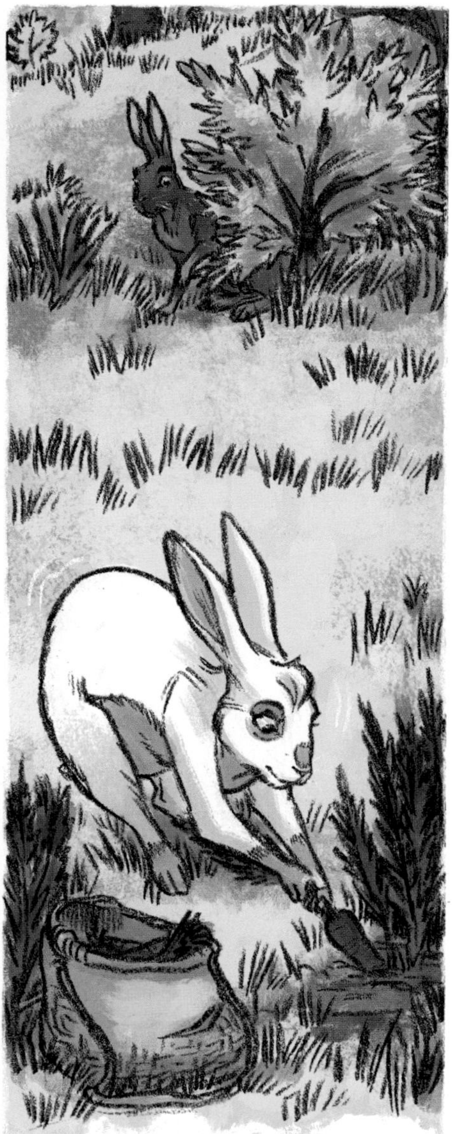

The son grew up an outcast. Shunned by the other rabbits, he lived at the edge of the vale. His one wish was to find big love, like his father had found big love. One day he saw a rabbit maiden collecting carrots in a field.

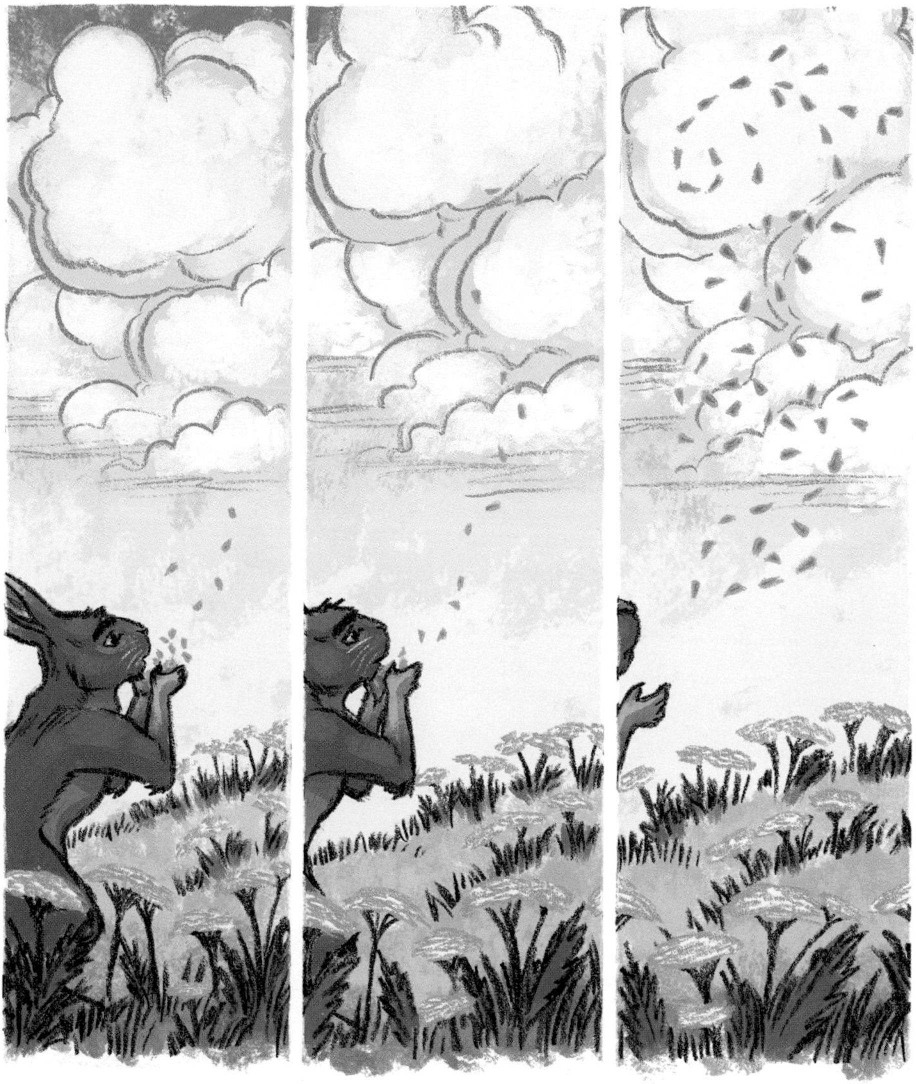

The son sent prayers to the Wind, to Satya'kon, the goddess of truth: What should I do? She said, "Embrace truth; tell her about your inner fox." But when he did so, the maiden was frightened.

The son sent prayers to the Wind, to Apep'kon, the god of chaos: What should I do? He said, "Embrace chaos; tell her anything and everything." But when he did so, the maiden became even more frightened.

The son sent prayers to the Wind, to Crepu'kon, the genderless twilight god of indecision: What should I do? It said, "Embrace indecision; tell her nothing." And so the son did nothing.

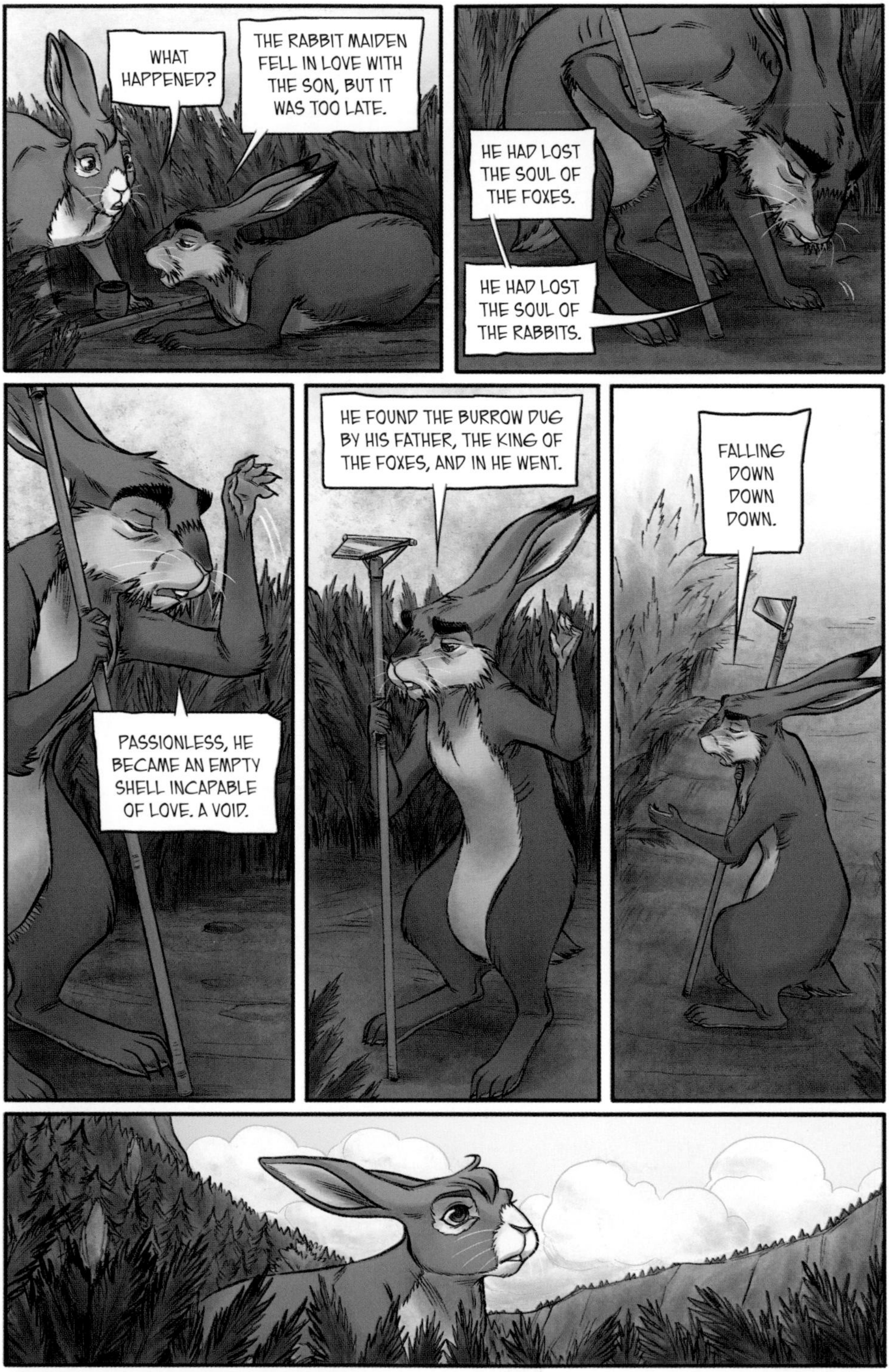
WHAT HAPPENED?
THE RABBIT MAIDEN FELL IN LOVE WITH THE SON, BUT IT WAS TOO LATE.
HE HAD LOST THE SOUL OF THE FOXES.
HE HAD LOST THE SOUL OF THE RABBITS.
PASSIONLESS, HE BECAME AN EMPTY SHELL INCAPABLE OF LOVE. A VOID.
HE FOUND THE BURROW DUG BY HIS FATHER, THE KING OF THE FOXES, AND IN HE WENT.
FALLING DOWN DOWN DOWN.

I FEEL LIKE AN EMPTY SHELL SOMETIMES.

BUT I'M ON A SEARCH FOR A SECRET. I'M GOING TO FIND IT, AND WHEN CROQUET *COMES BACK*, HE'LL SEE THAT I'VE GROWN UP.

THOM WOULDN'T WANT YOU TO DO SOMETHING FOR *HIS* BENEFIT. HE WOULD WANT YOU TO DO WHAT'S IN YOUR *HEART*.

NO.

I COULD NEVER MAKE PEACE WITH THAT.

IT'S A LESSON I HAD TO LEARN THE HARD, PAINFUL WAY.

HE WAS MY LITTLE BOY...

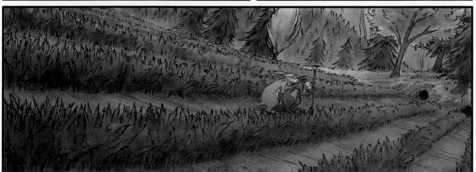

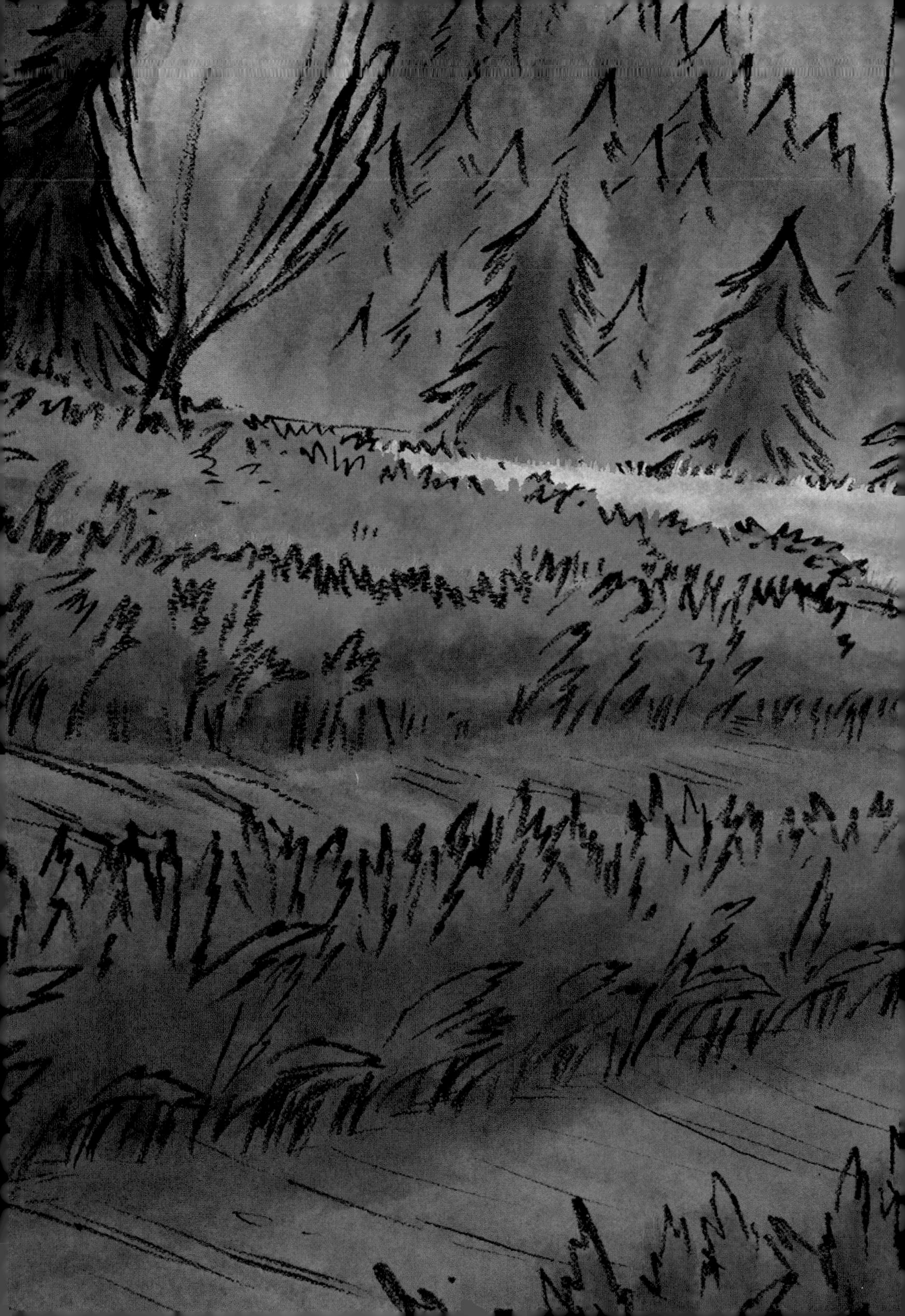

14.

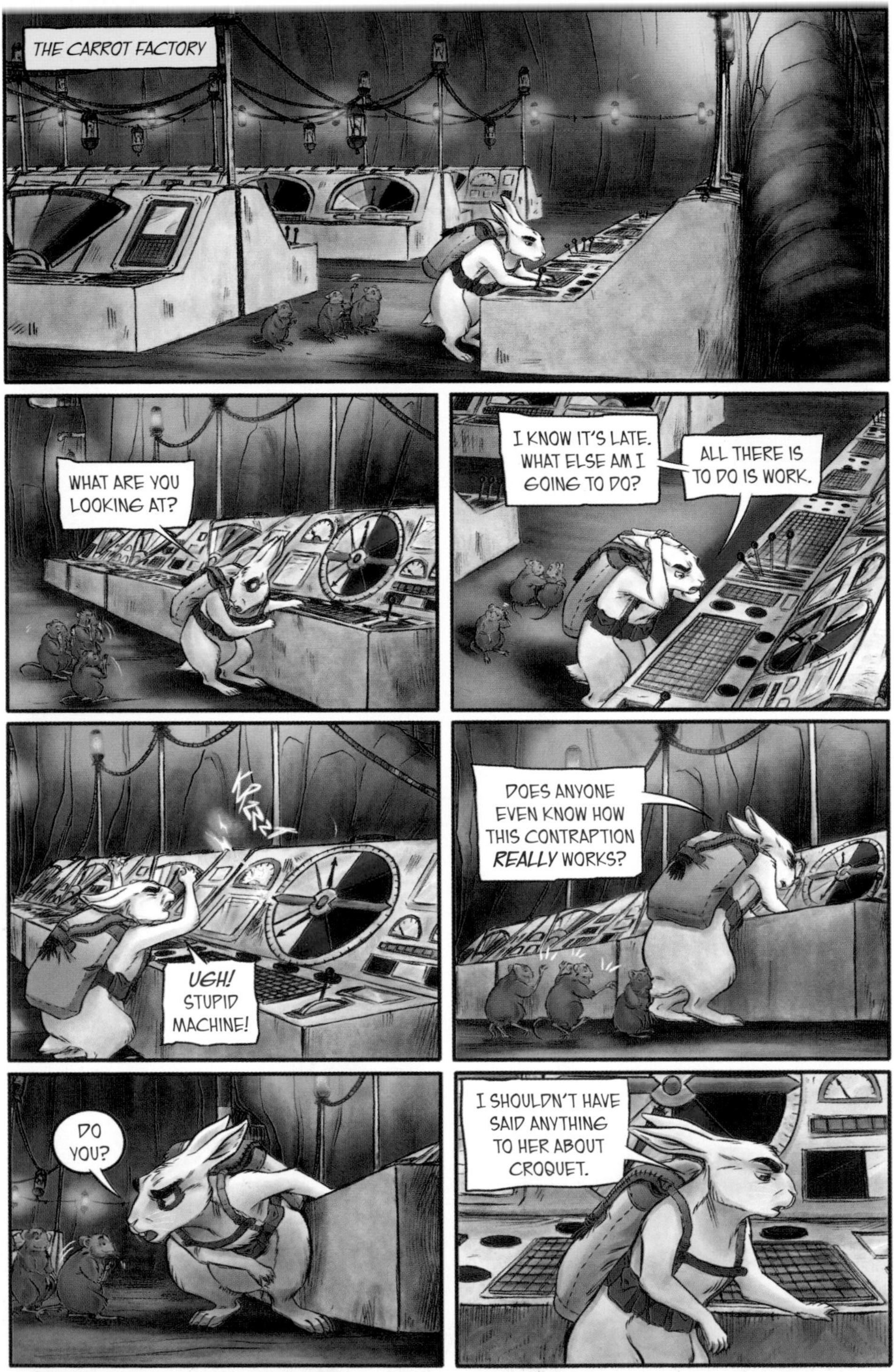
THE CARROT FACTORY
WHAT ARE YOU LOOKING AT?
I KNOW IT'S LATE. WHAT ELSE AM I GOING TO DO?
ALL THERE IS TO DO IS WORK.
KRRNNT
UGH! STUPID MACHINE!
DOES ANYONE EVEN KNOW HOW THIS CONTRAPTION *REALLY* WORKS?
DO YOU?
I SHOULDN'T HAVE SAID ANYTHING TO HER ABOUT CROQUET.

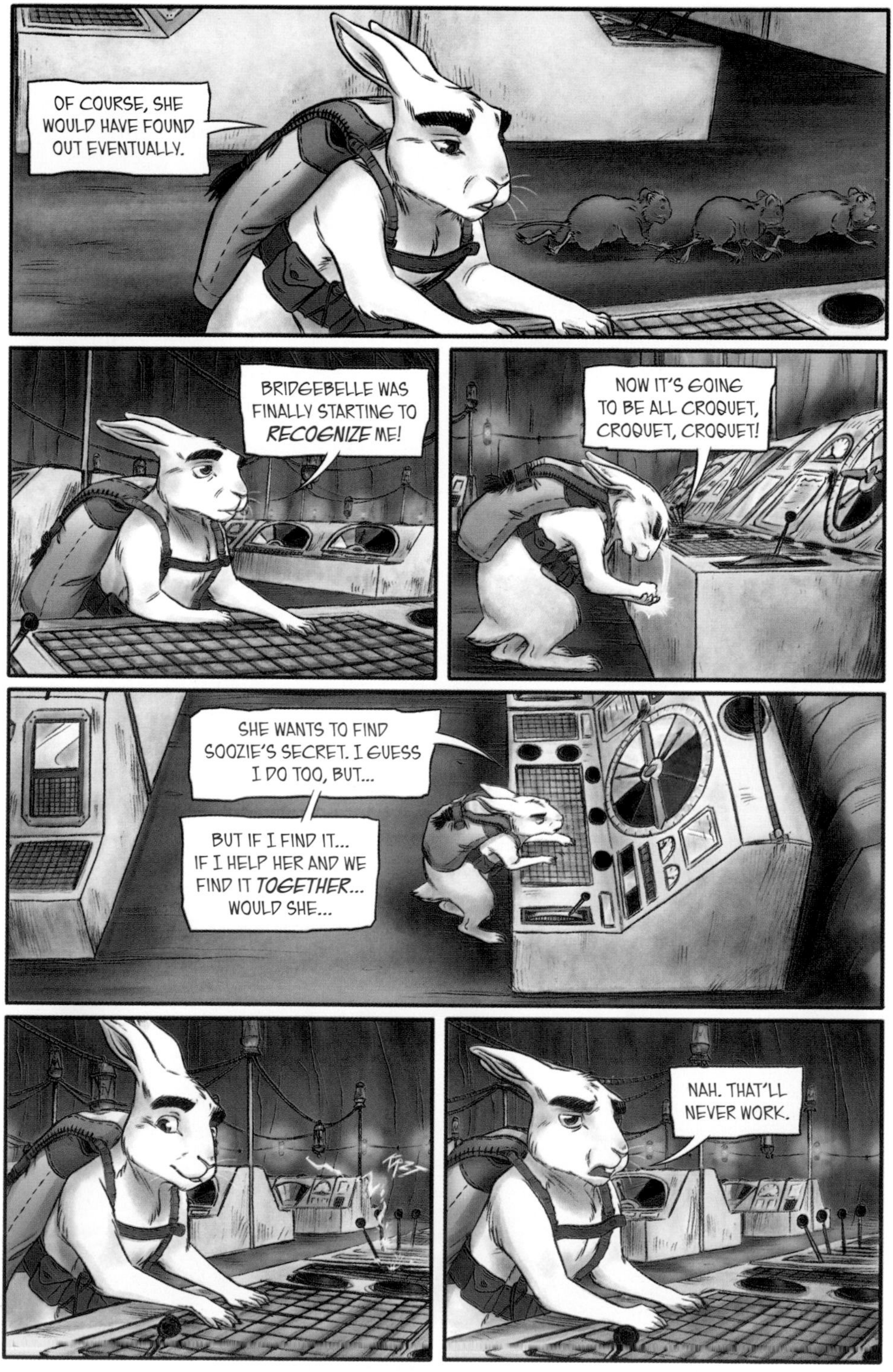
OF COURSE, SHE WOULD HAVE FOUND OUT EVENTUALLY.
BRIDGEBELLE WAS FINALLY STARTING TO *RECOGNIZE* ME!
NOW IT'S GOING TO BE ALL CROQUET, CROQUET, CROQUET!
SHE WANTS TO FIND SOOZIE'S SECRET. I GUESS I DO TOO, BUT...
BUT IF I FIND IT... IF I HELP HER AND WE FIND IT *TOGETHER*... WOULD SHE...
NAH. THAT'LL NEVER WORK.

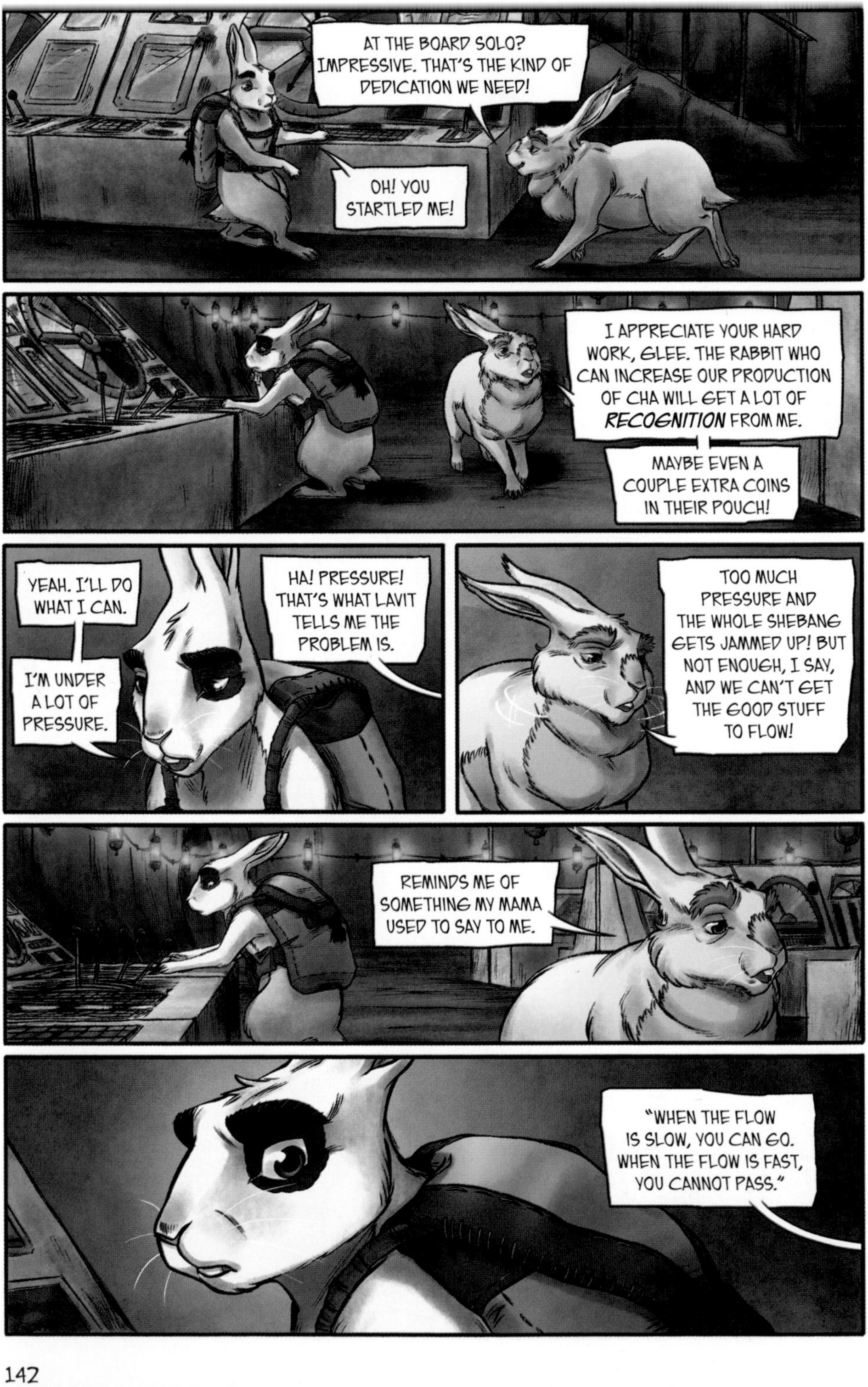
AT THE BOARD SOLO? IMPRESSIVE. THAT'S THE KIND OF DEDICATION WE NEED!
OH! YOU STARTLED ME!
I APPRECIATE YOUR HARD WORK, GLEE. THE RABBIT WHO CAN INCREASE OUR PRODUCTION OF CHA WILL GET A LOT OF *RECOGNITION* FROM ME.
MAYBE EVEN A COUPLE EXTRA COINS IN THEIR POUCH!
YEAH. I'LL DO WHAT I CAN.
I'M UNDER A LOT OF PRESSURE.
HA! PRESSURE! THAT'S WHAT LAVIT TELLS ME THE PROBLEM IS.
TOO MUCH PRESSURE AND THE WHOLE SHEBANG GETS JAMMED UP! BUT NOT ENOUGH, I SAY, AND WE CAN'T GET THE GOOD STUFF TO FLOW!
REMINDS ME OF SOMETHING MY MAMA USED TO SAY TO ME.
"WHEN THE FLOW IS SLOW, YOU CAN GO. WHEN THE FLOW IS FAST, YOU CANNOT PASS."

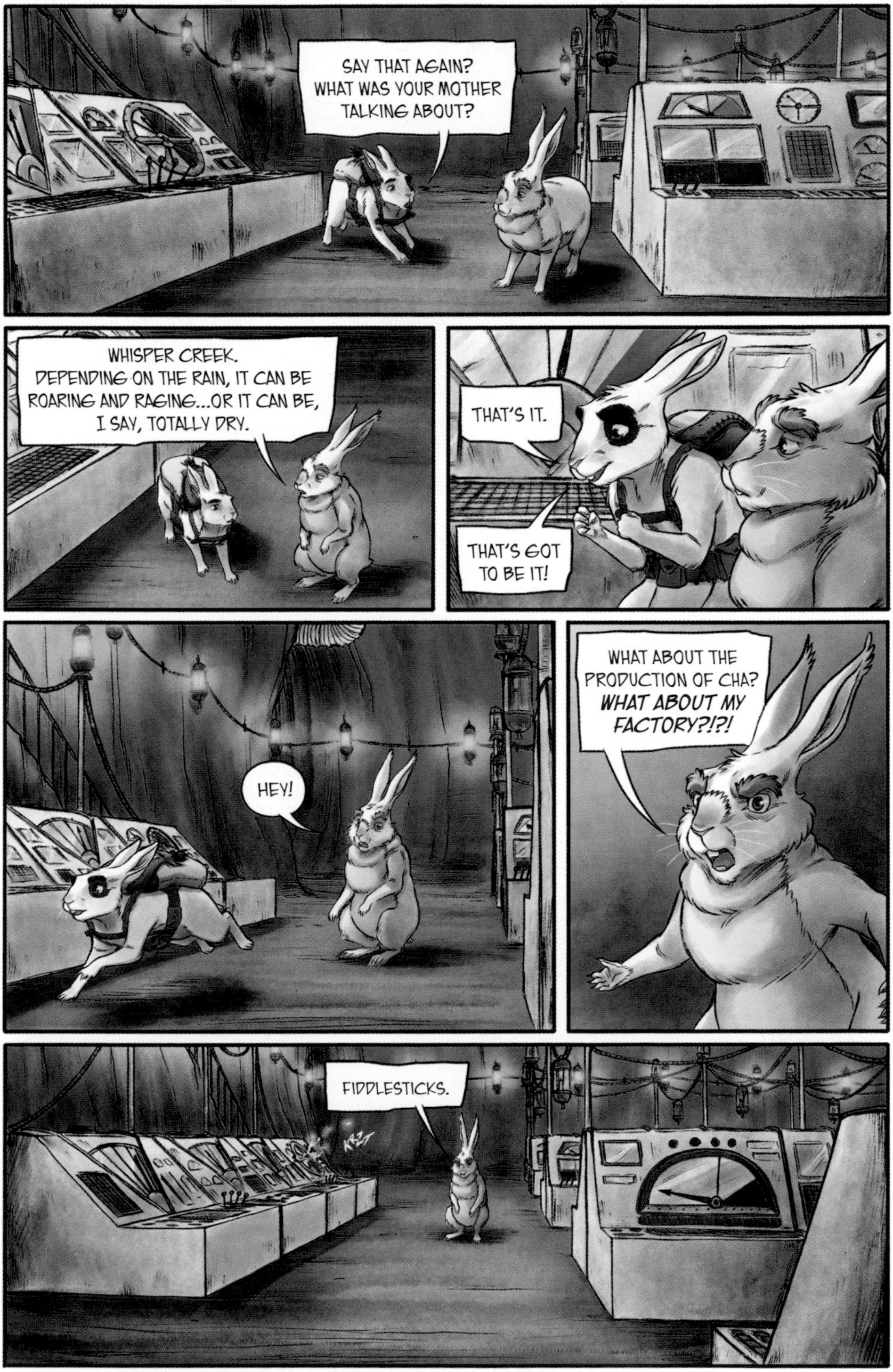
SAY THAT AGAIN? WHAT WAS YOUR MOTHER TALKING ABOUT?
WHISPER CREEK. DEPENDING ON THE RAIN, IT CAN BE ROARING AND RAGING...OR IT CAN BE, I SAY, TOTALLY DRY.
THAT'S IT.
THAT'S GOT TO BE IT!
HEY!
WHAT ABOUT THE PRODUCTION OF CHA? *WHAT ABOUT MY FACTORY?!?!*
FIDDLESTICKS.

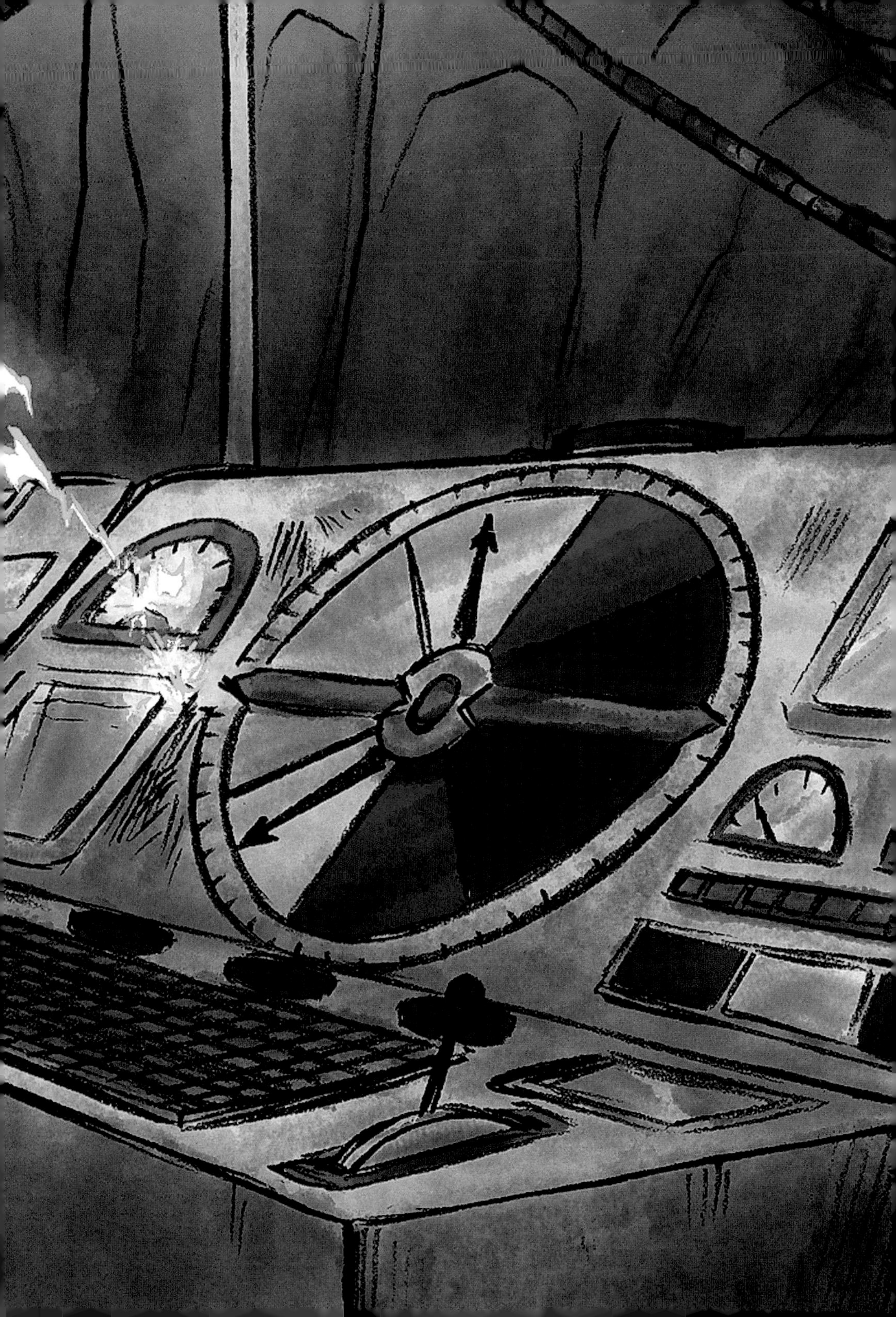

15.

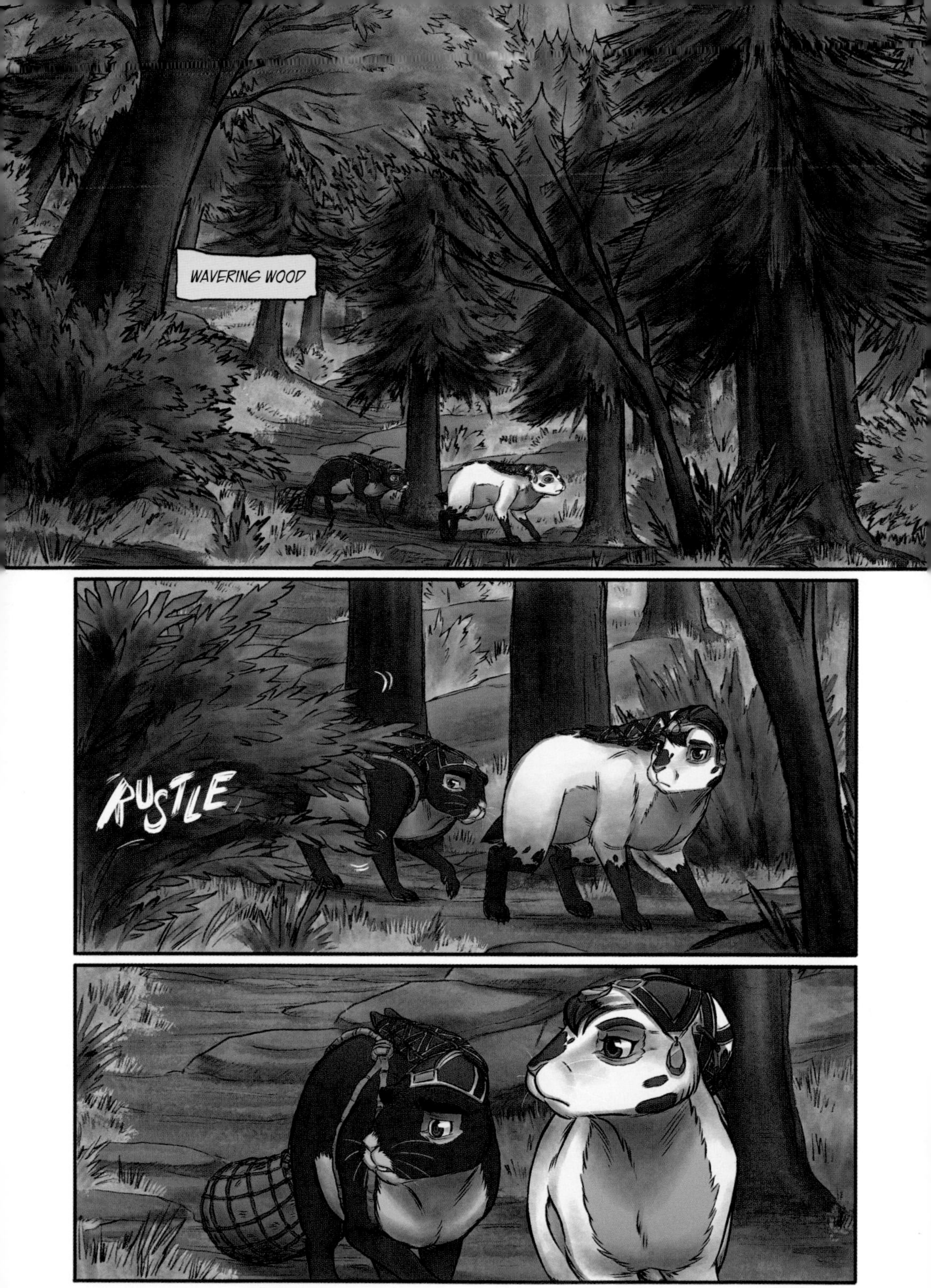
WAVERING WOOD
RUSTLE

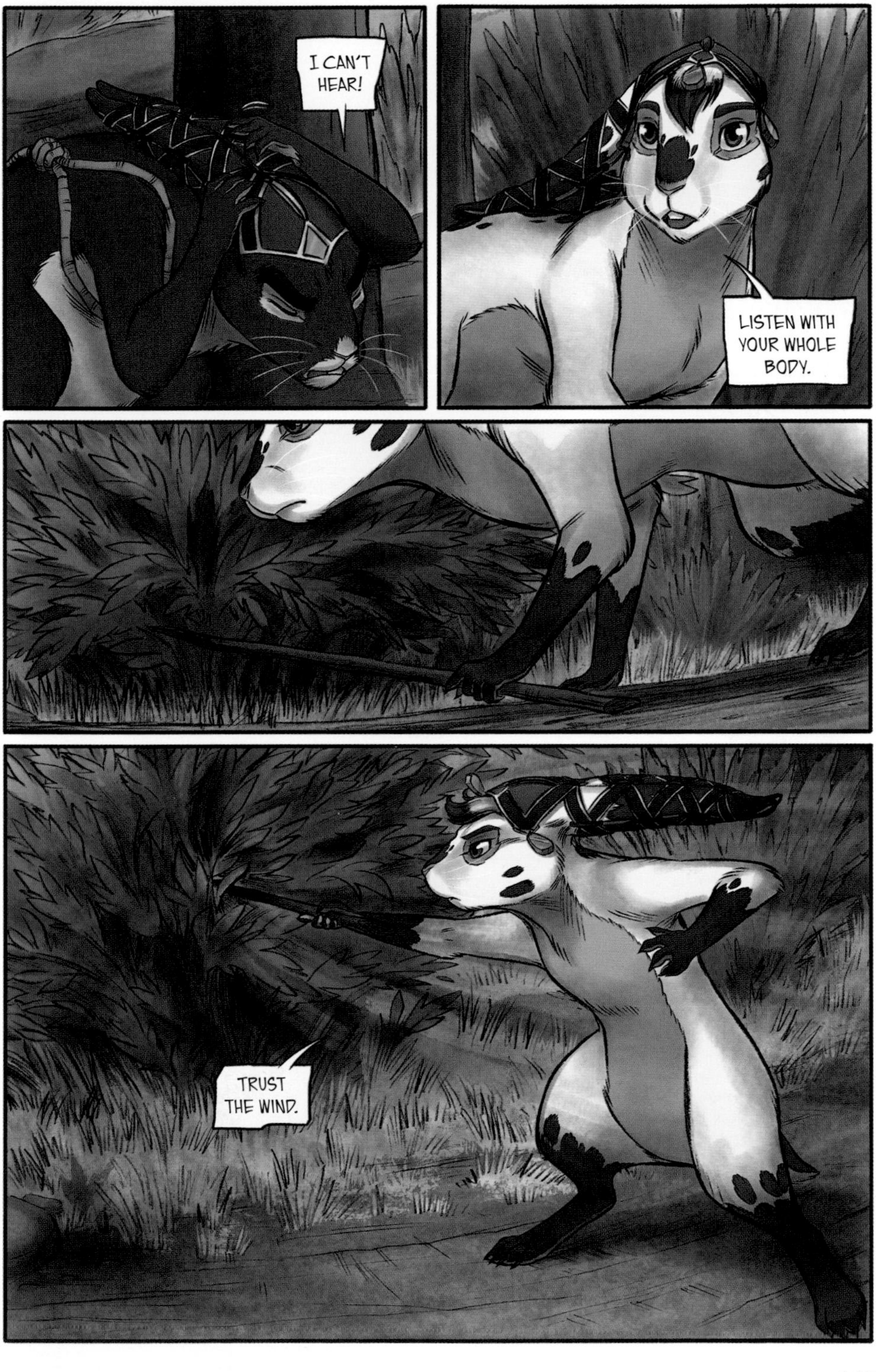
I CAN'T HEAR!
LISTEN WITH YOUR WHOLE BODY.
TRUST THE WIND.

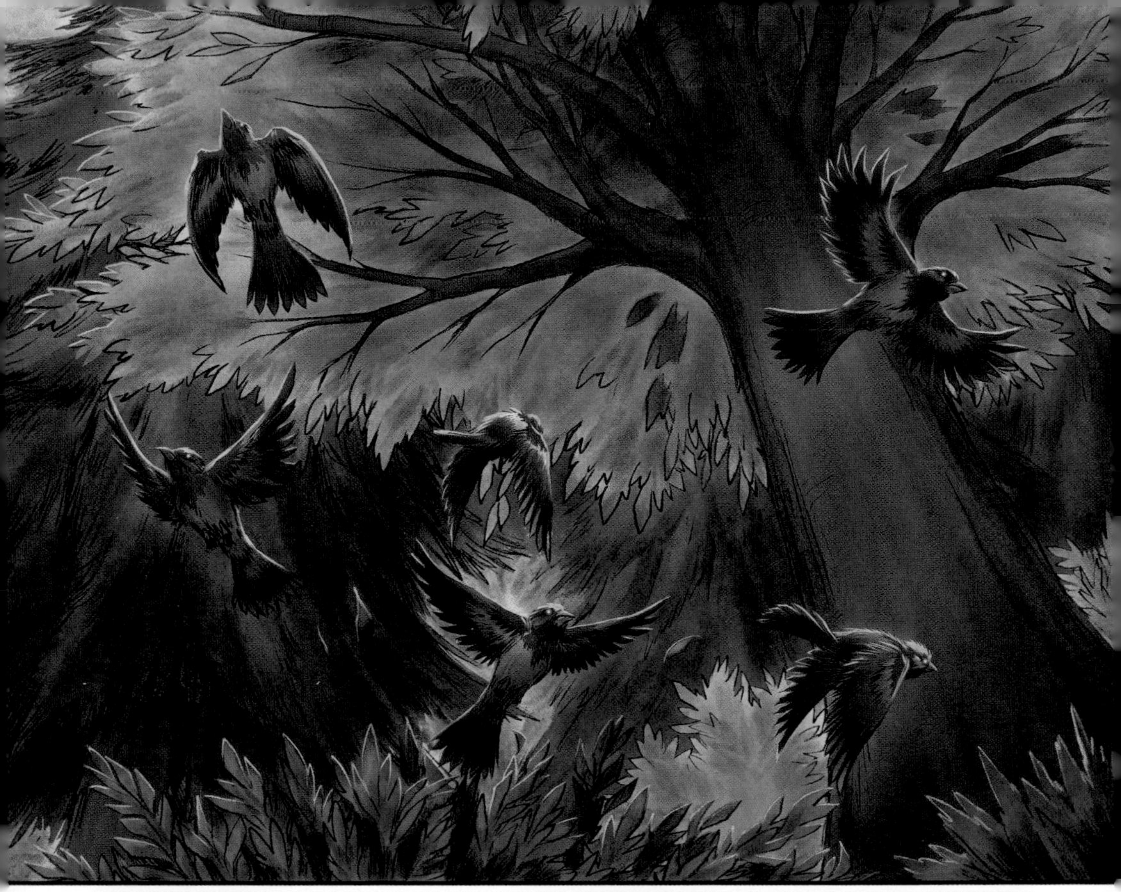

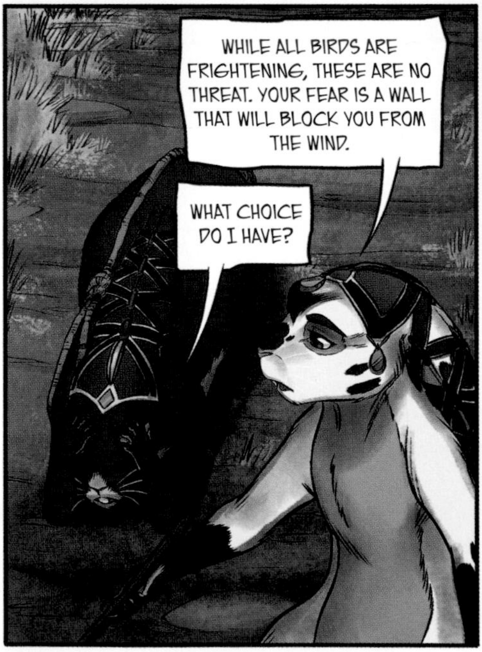
WHILE ALL BIRDS ARE FRIGHTENING, THESE ARE NO THREAT. YOUR FEAR IS A WALL THAT WILL BLOCK YOU FROM THE WIND.
WHAT CHOICE DO I HAVE?

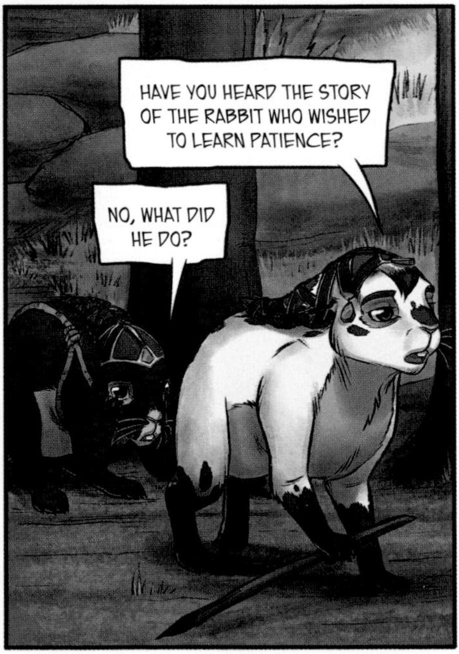
HAVE YOU HEARD THE STORY OF THE RABBIT WHO WISHED TO LEARN PATIENCE?
NO, WHAT DID HE DO?

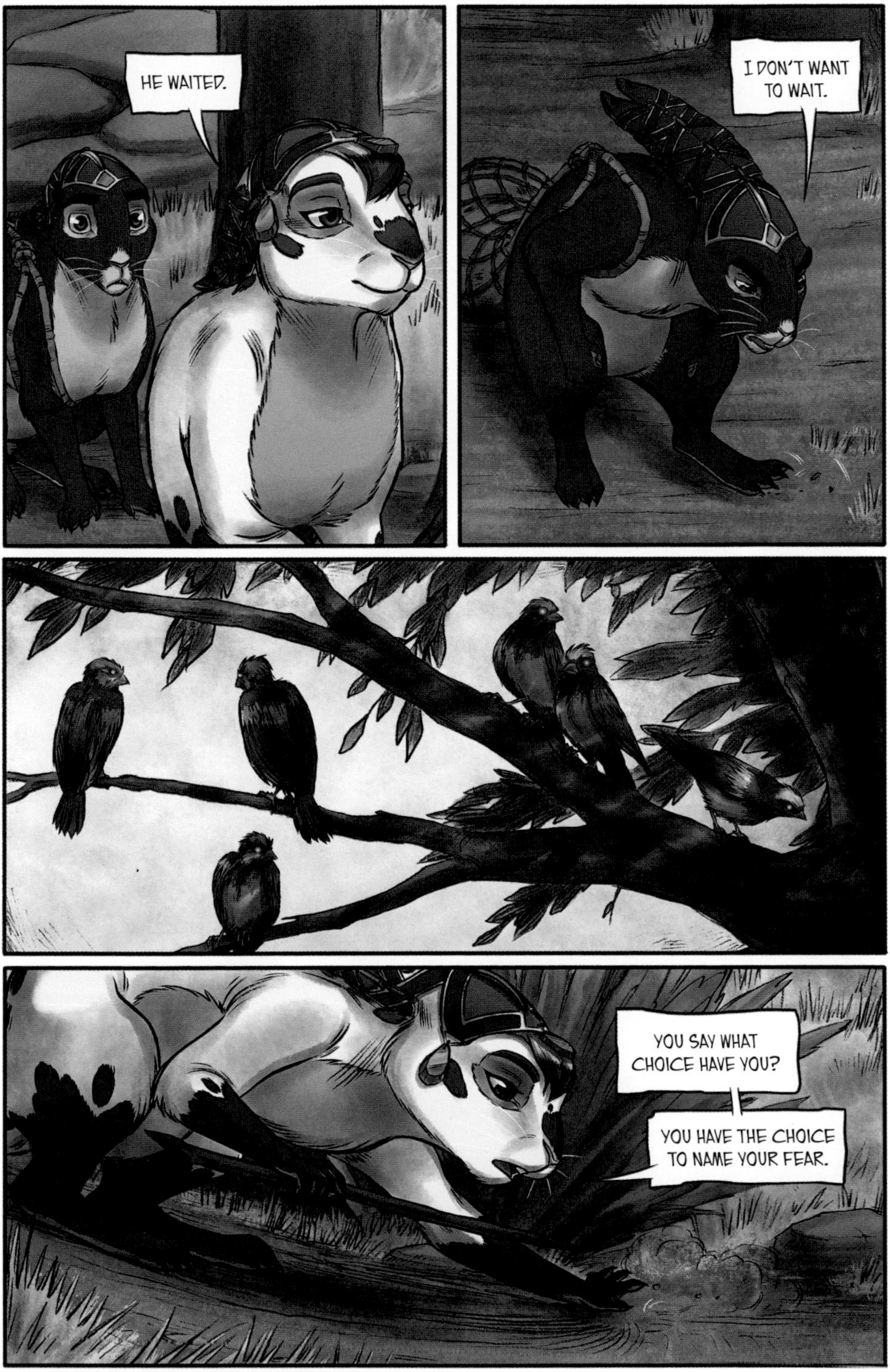
HE WAITED.
I DON'T WANT TO WAIT.
YOU SAY WHAT CHOICE HAVE YOU?
YOU HAVE THE CHOICE TO NAME YOUR FEAR.

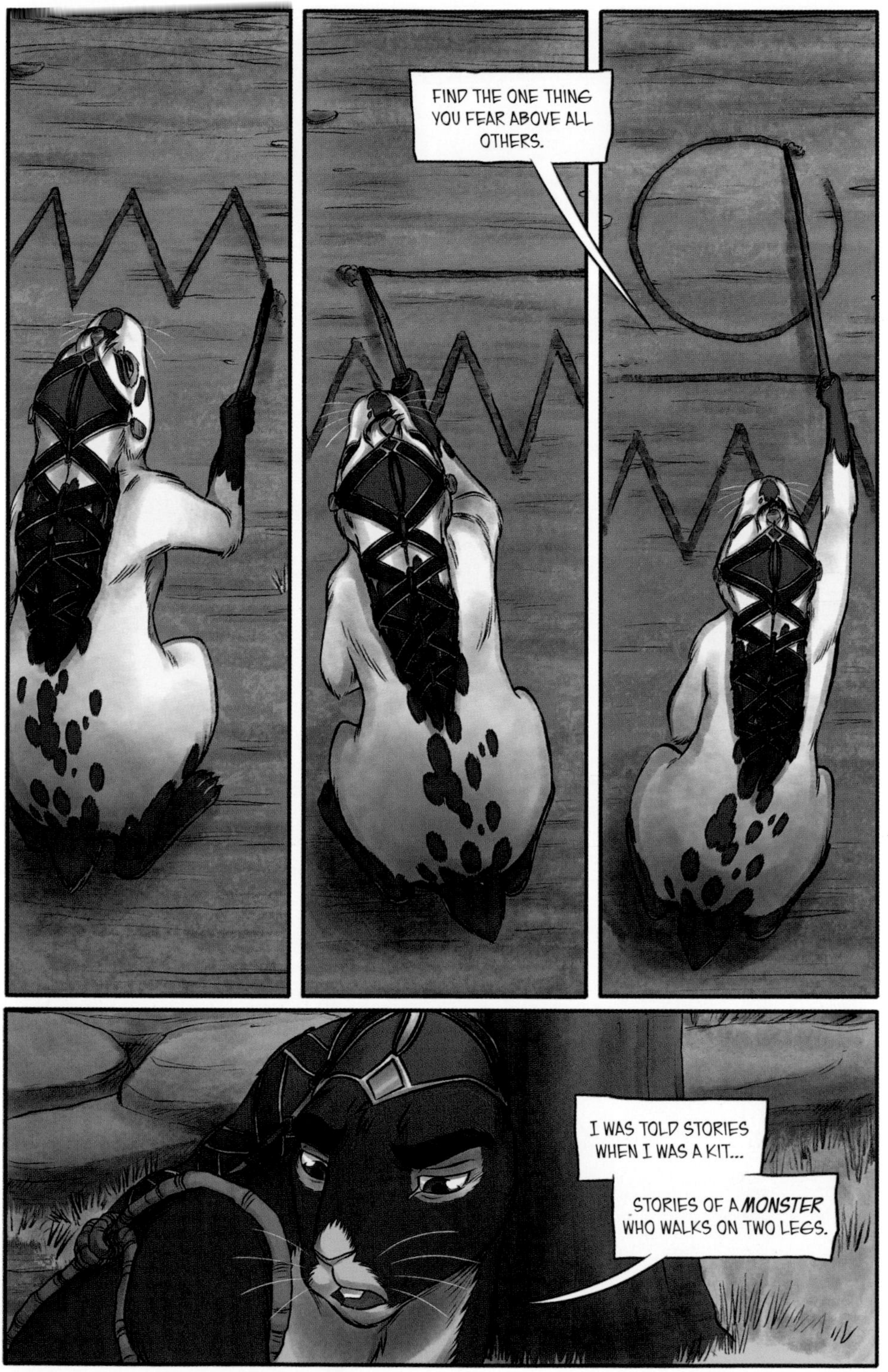
FIND THE ONE THING YOU FEAR ABOVE ALL OTHERS.
I WAS TOLD STORIES WHEN I WAS A KIT...
...STORIES OF A MONSTER WHO WALKS ON TWO LEGS.

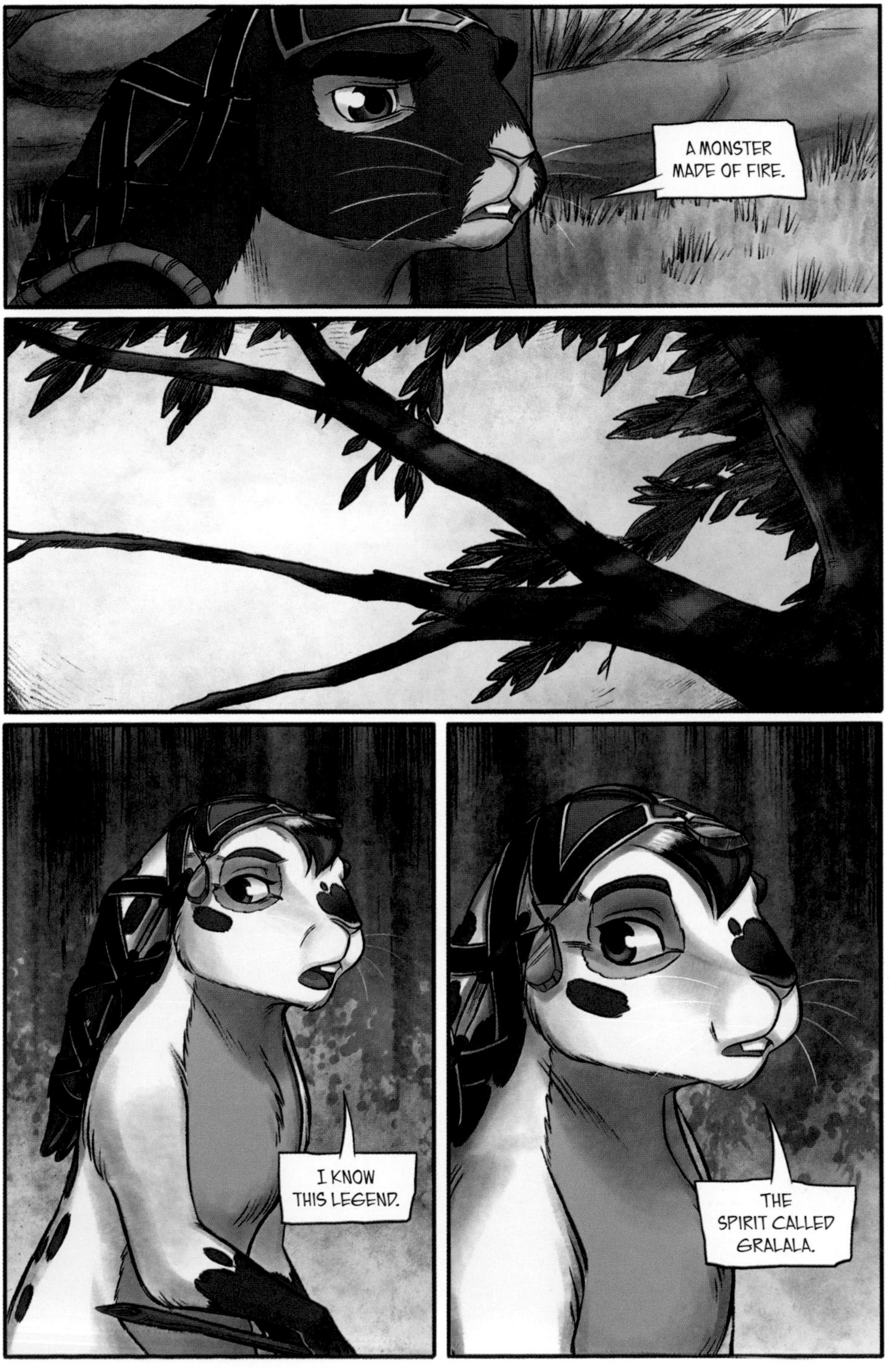
A MONSTER MADE OF FIRE.
I KNOW THIS LEGEND.
THE SPIRIT CALLED GRALALA.

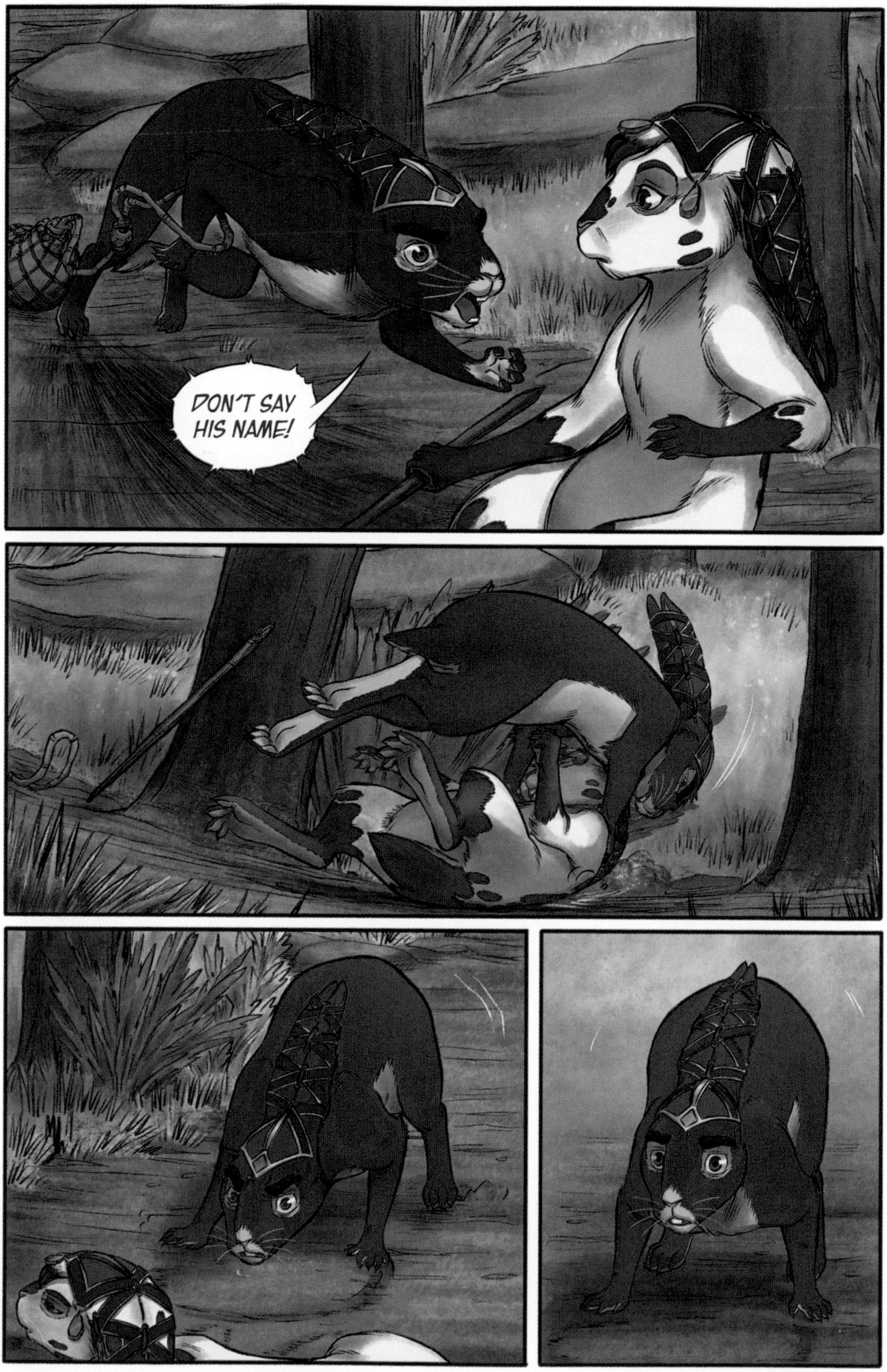
DON'T SAY HIS NAME!

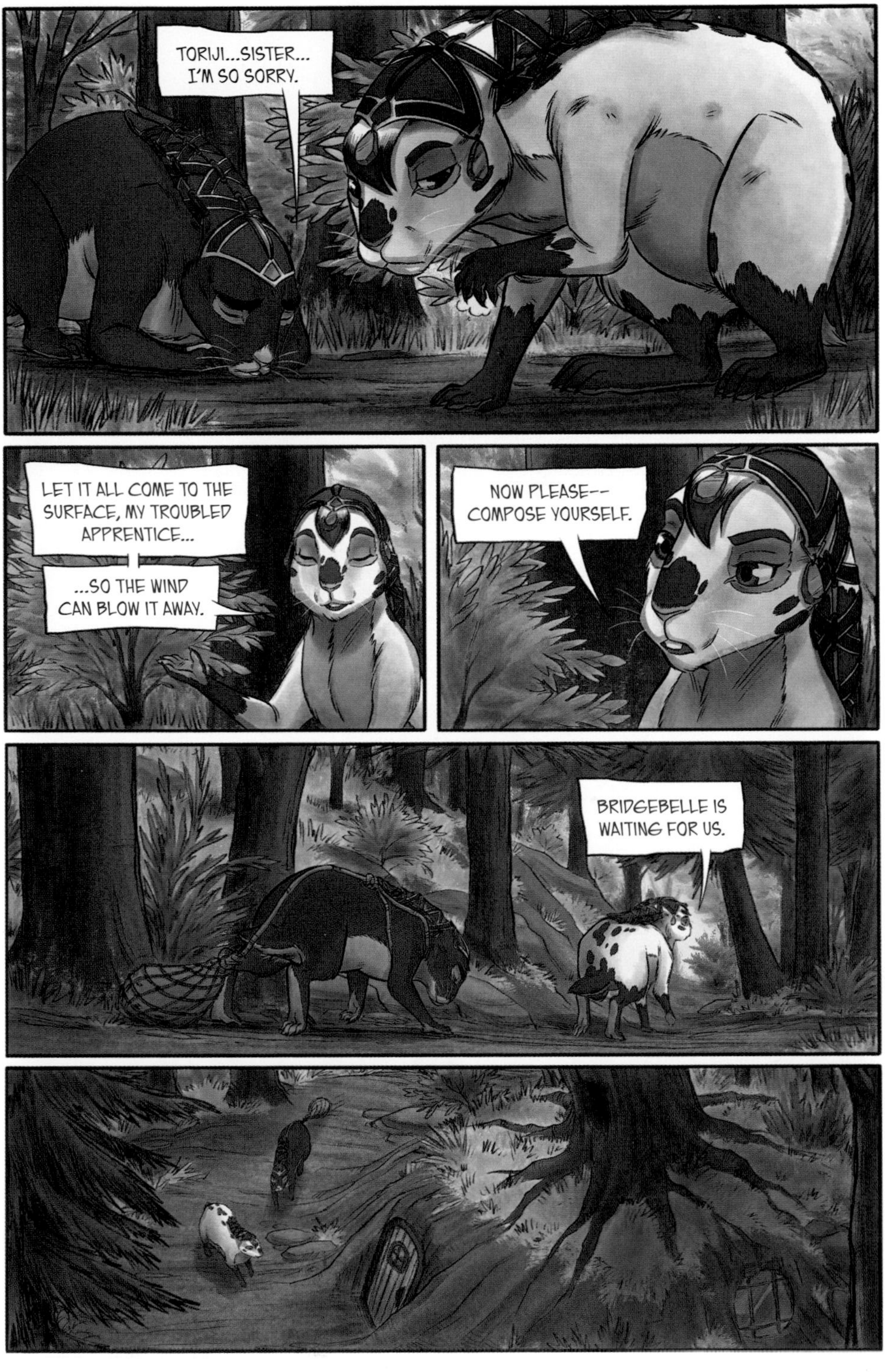
TORIJI...SISTER... I'M SO SORRY.
LET IT ALL COME TO THE SURFACE, MY TROUBLED APPRENTICE...
...SO THE WIND CAN BLOW IT AWAY.
NOW PLEASE-- COMPOSE YOURSELF.
BRIDGEBELLE IS WAITING FOR US.

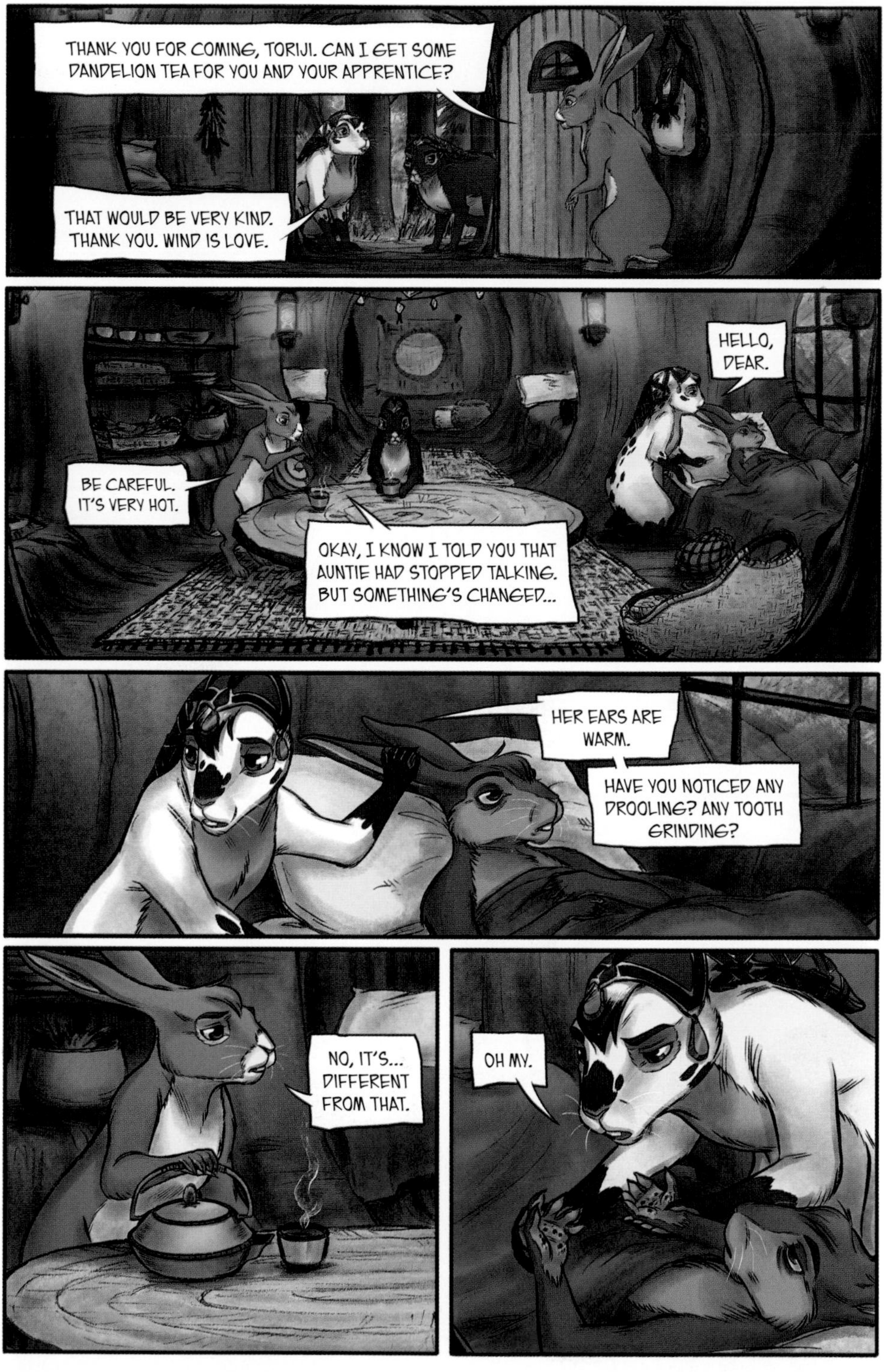
THANK YOU FOR COMING, TORIJI. CAN I GET SOME DANDELION TEA FOR YOU AND YOUR APPRENTICE?
THAT WOULD BE VERY KIND. THANK YOU. WIND IS LOVE.
HELLO, DEAR.
BE CAREFUL. IT'S VERY HOT.
OKAY, I KNOW I TOLD YOU THAT AUNTIE HAD STOPPED TALKING. BUT SOMETHING'S CHANGED...
HER EARS ARE WARM.
HAVE YOU NOTICED ANY DROOLING? ANY TOOTH GRINDING?
NO, IT'S... DIFFERENT FROM THAT.
OH MY.

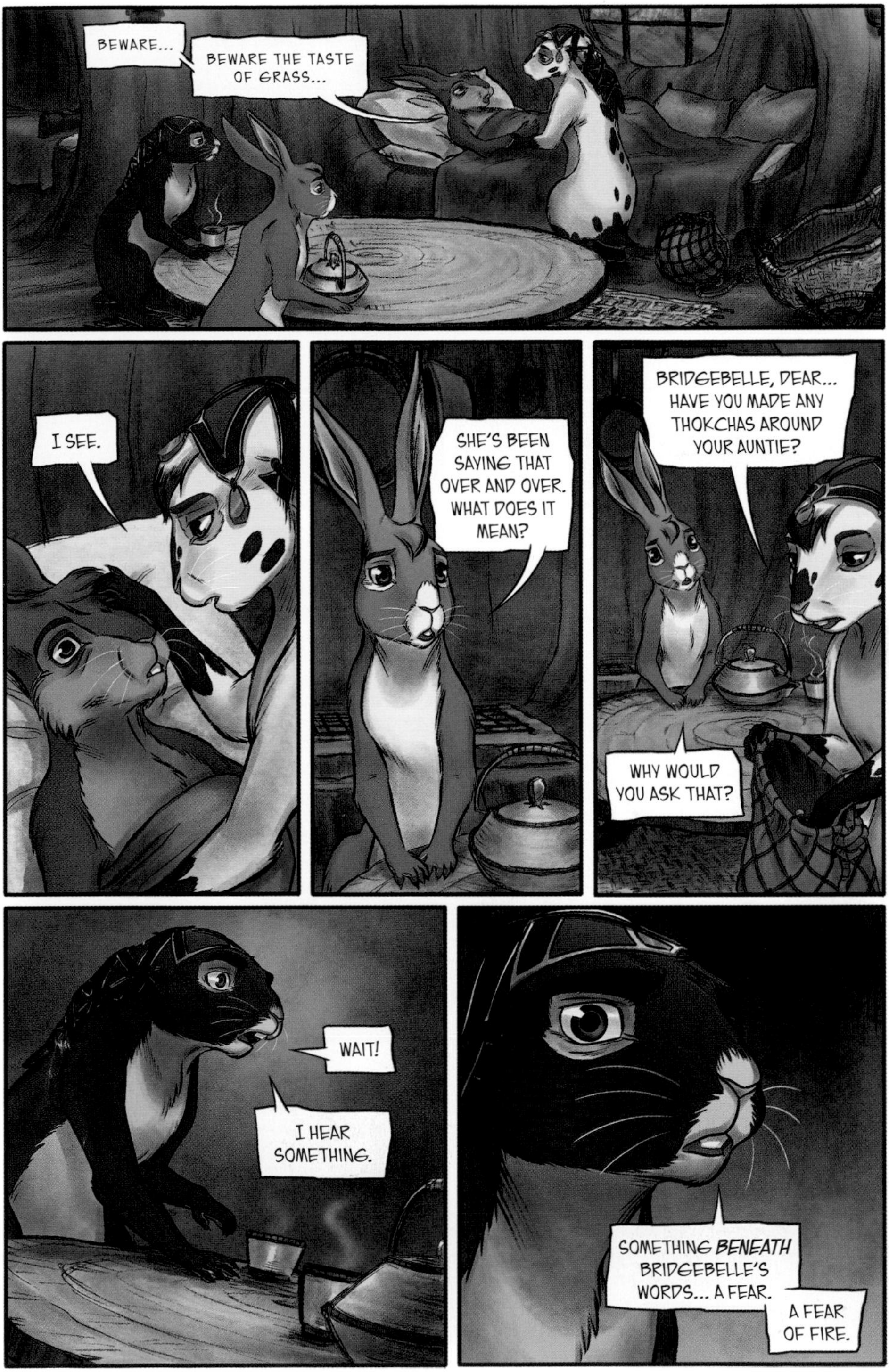
BEWARE...
BEWARE THE TASTE OF GRASS...
I SEE.
SHE'S BEEN SAYING THAT OVER AND OVER. WHAT DOES IT MEAN?
BRIDGEBELLE, DEAR... HAVE YOU MADE ANY THOKCHAS AROUND YOUR AUNTIE?
WHY WOULD YOU ASK THAT?
WAIT!
I HEAR SOMETHING.
SOMETHING *BENEATH* BRIDGEBELLE'S WORDS... A FEAR.
A FEAR OF FIRE.

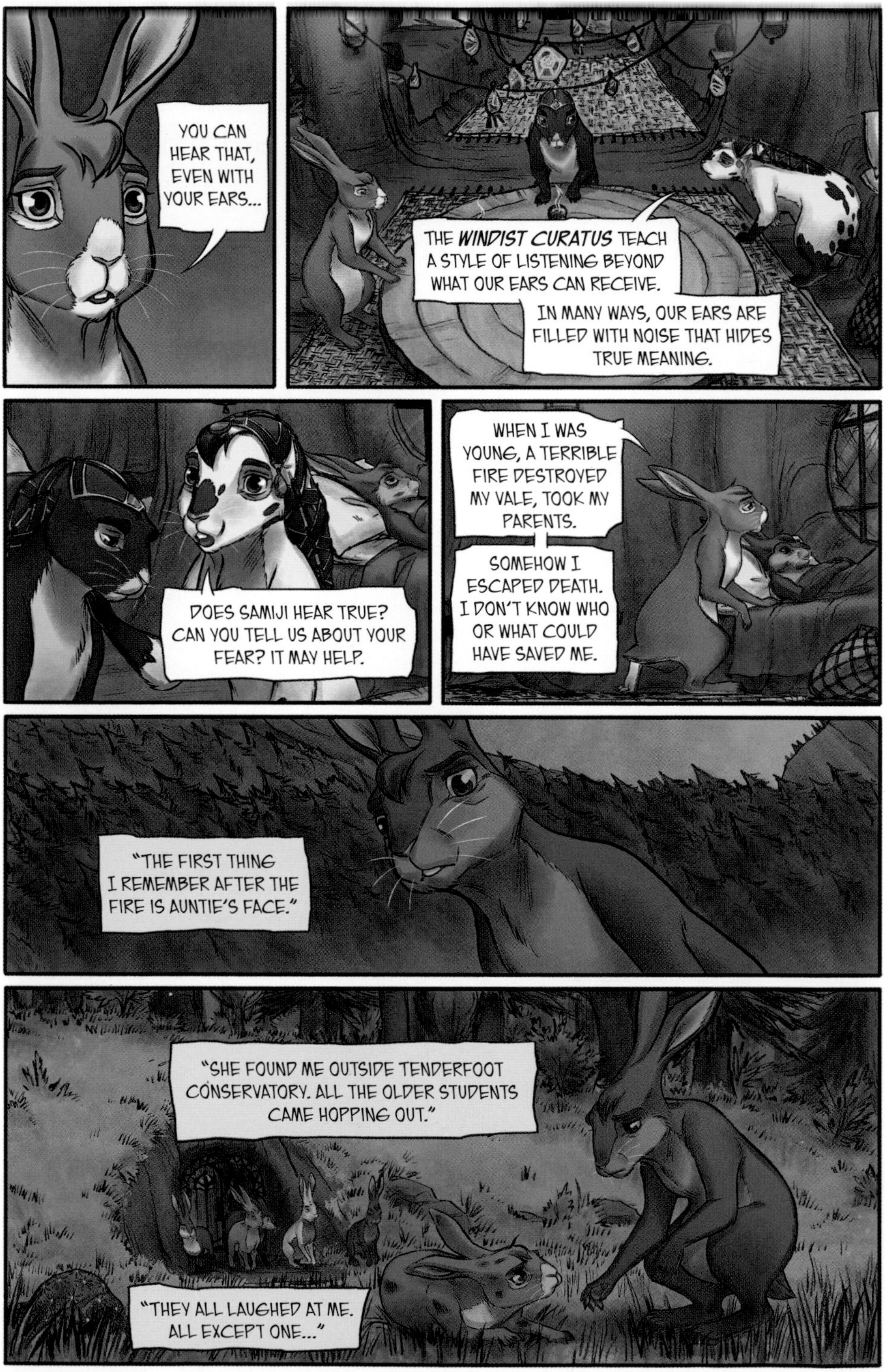
YOU CAN HEAR THAT, EVEN WITH YOUR EARS...
THE *WINDIST CURATUS* TEACH A STYLE OF LISTENING BEYOND WHAT OUR EARS CAN RECEIVE.
IN MANY WAYS, OUR EARS ARE FILLED WITH NOISE THAT HIDES TRUE MEANING.
DOES SAMIJI HEAR TRUE? CAN YOU TELL US ABOUT YOUR FEAR? IT MAY HELP.
WHEN I WAS YOUNG, A TERRIBLE FIRE DESTROYED MY VALE, TOOK MY PARENTS.
SOMEHOW I ESCAPED DEATH. I DON'T KNOW WHO OR WHAT COULD HAVE SAVED ME.
"THE FIRST THING I REMEMBER AFTER THE FIRE IS AUNTIE'S FACE."
"SHE FOUND ME OUTSIDE TENDERFOOT CONSERVATORY. ALL THE OLDER STUDENTS CAME HOPPING OUT."
"THEY ALL LAUGHED AT ME. ALL EXCEPT ONE..."

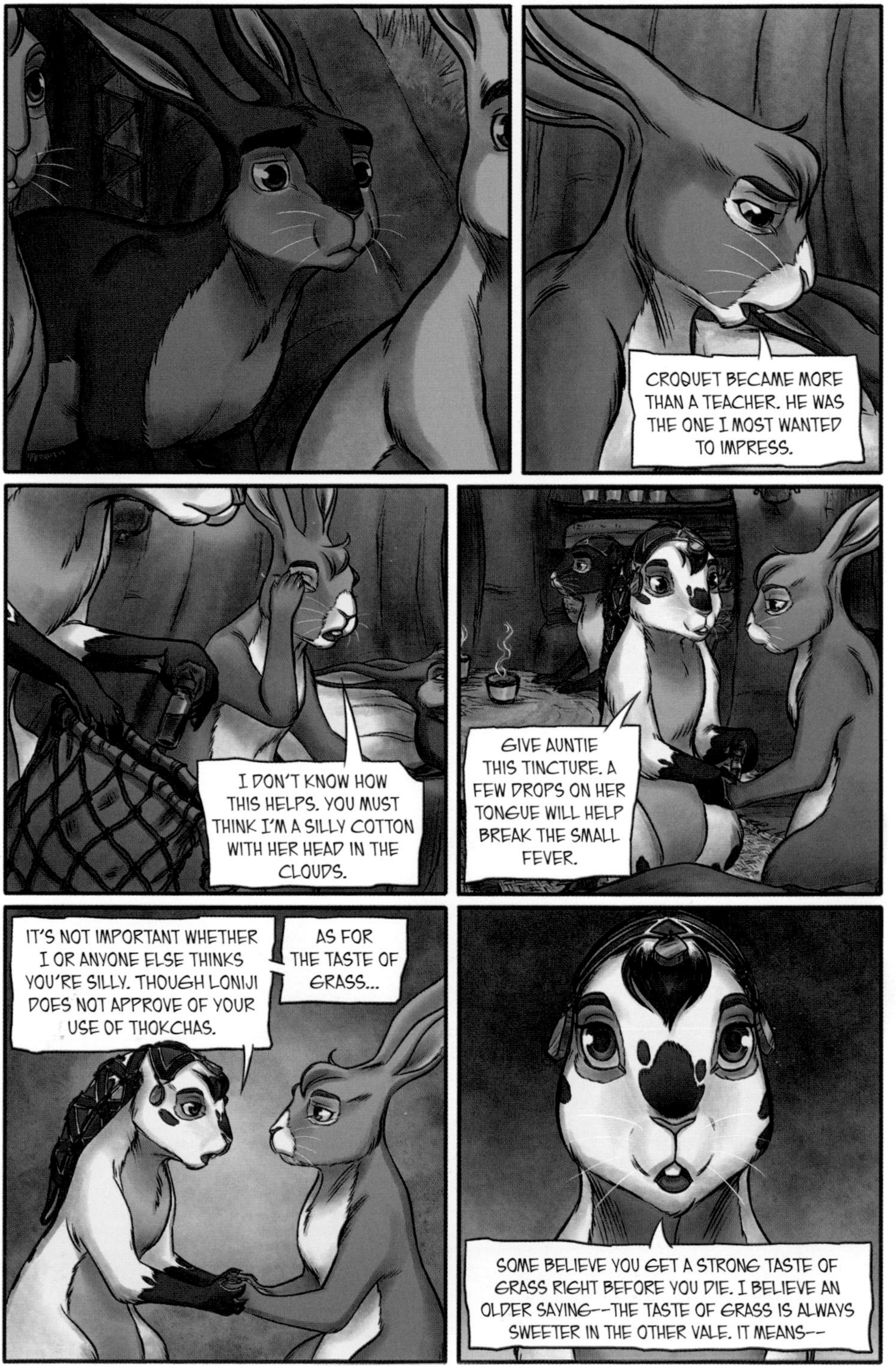
CROQUET BECAME MORE THAN A TEACHER. HE WAS THE ONE I MOST WANTED TO IMPRESS.
I DON'T KNOW HOW THIS HELPS. YOU MUST THINK I'M A SILLY COTTON WITH HER HEAD IN THE CLOUDS.
GIVE AUNTIE THIS TINCTURE. A FEW DROPS ON HER TONGUE WILL HELP BREAK THE SMALL FEVER.
IT'S NOT IMPORTANT WHETHER I OR ANYONE ELSE THINKS YOU'RE SILLY. THOUGH LONIJI DOES NOT APPROVE OF YOUR USE OF THOKCHAS.
AS FOR THE TASTE OF GRASS...
SOME BELIEVE YOU GET A STRONG TASTE OF GRASS RIGHT BEFORE YOU DIE. I BELIEVE AN OLDER SAYING--THE TASTE OF GRASS IS ALWAYS SWEETER IN THE OTHER VALE. IT MEANS--

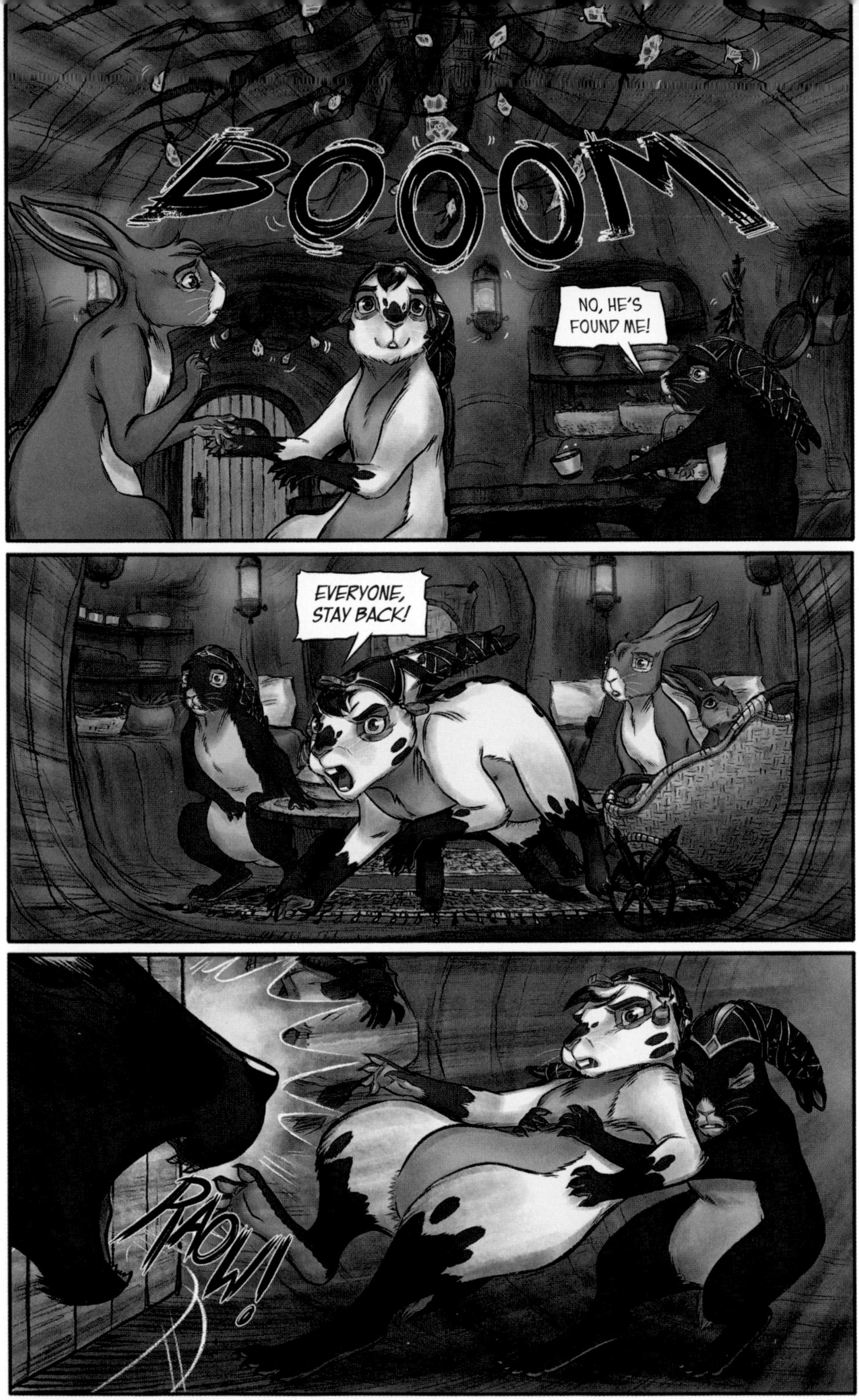
BOOOM
NO, HE'S FOUND ME!
EVERYONE, STAY BACK!
RAOW!

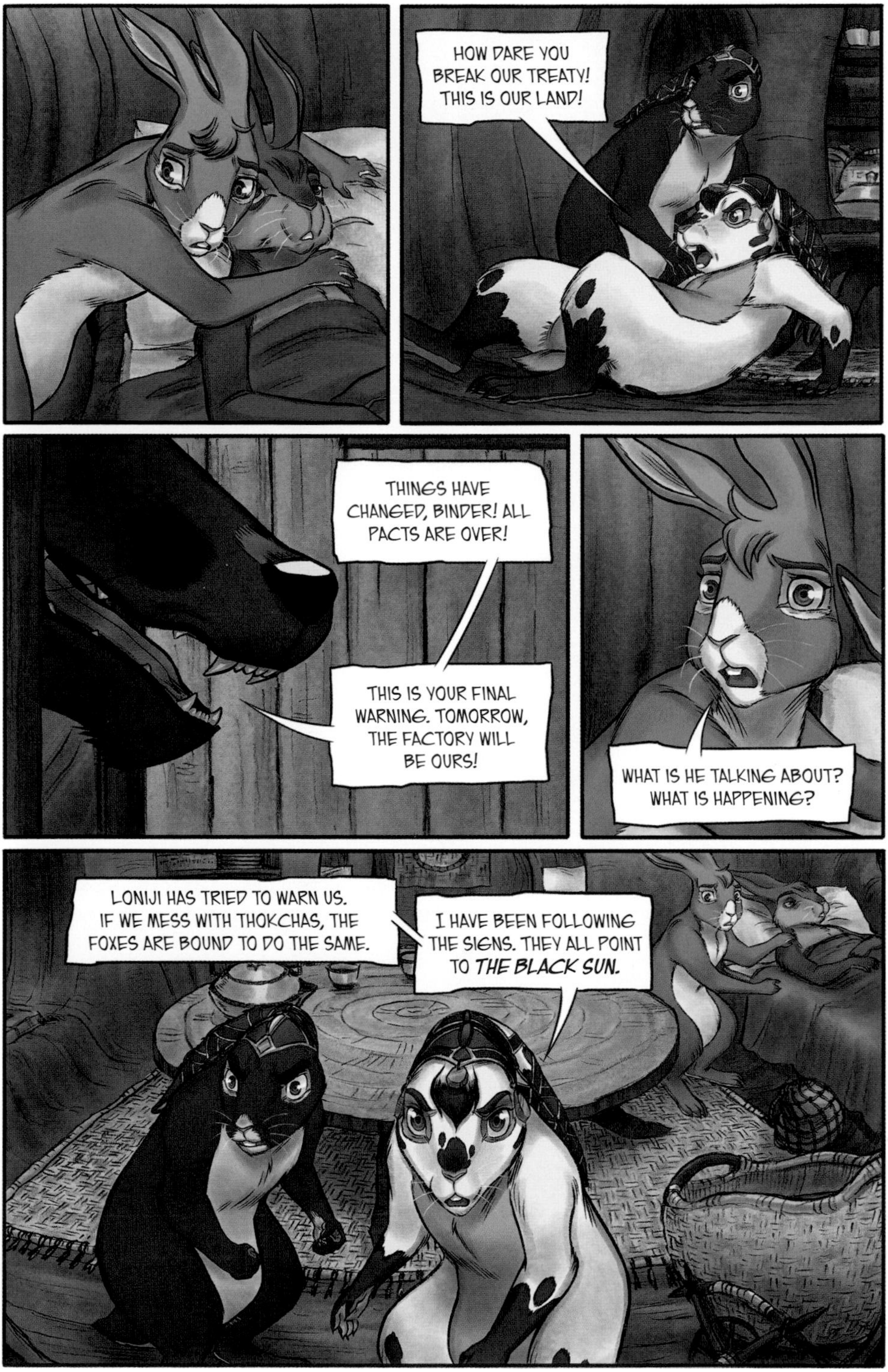
HOW DARE YOU BREAK OUR TREATY! THIS IS OUR LAND!
THINGS HAVE CHANGED, BINDER! ALL PACTS ARE OVER!
THIS IS YOUR FINAL WARNING. TOMORROW, THE FACTORY WILL BE OURS!
WHAT IS HE TALKING ABOUT? WHAT IS HAPPENING?
LONIJI HAS TRIED TO WARN US. IF WE MESS WITH THOKCHAS, THE FOXES ARE BOUND TO DO THE SAME.
I HAVE BEEN FOLLOWING THE SIGNS. THEY ALL POINT TO *THE BLACK SUN.*

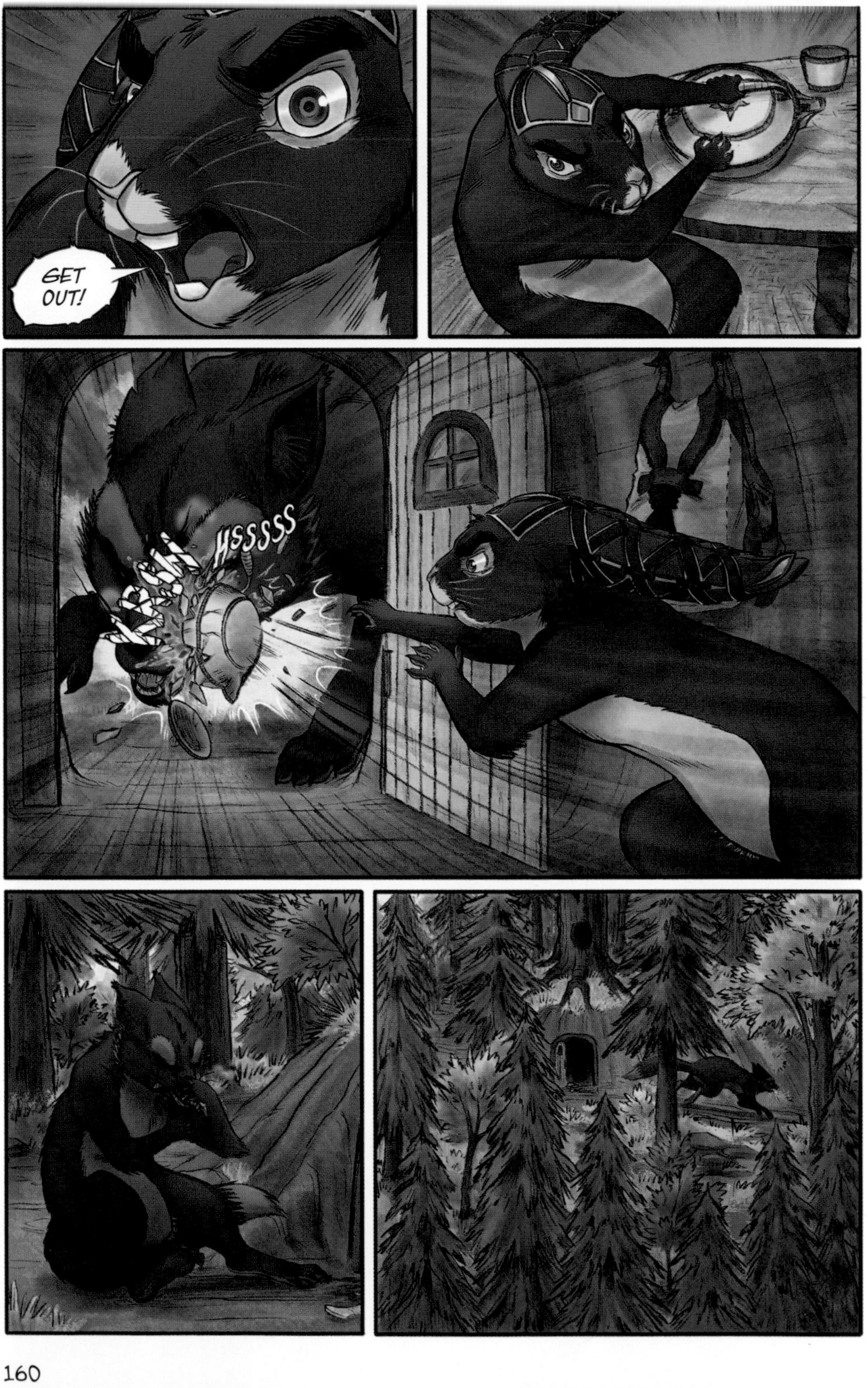
GET OUT!
HSSSSS

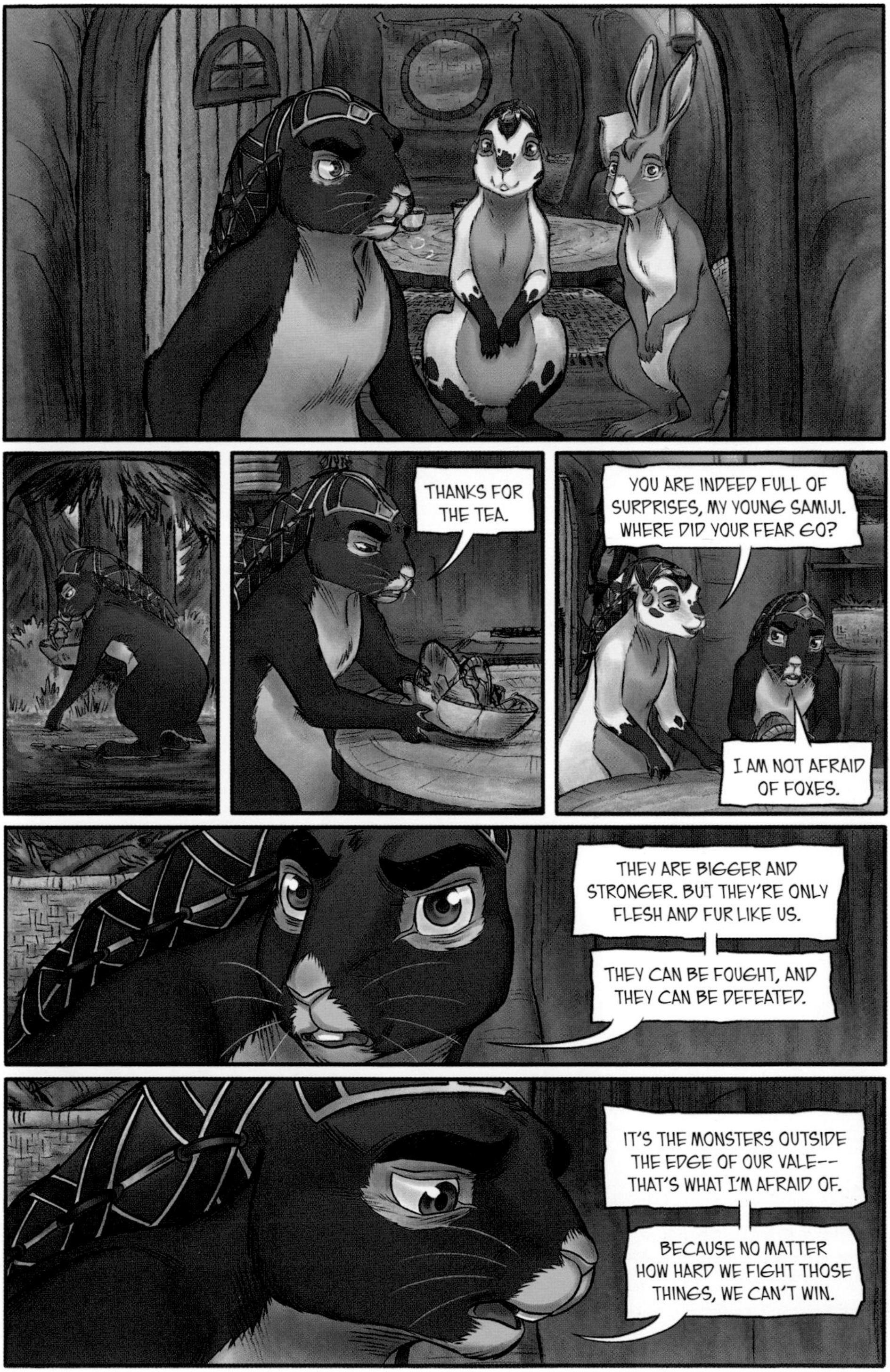
THANKS FOR THE TEA.
YOU ARE INDEED FULL OF SURPRISES, MY YOUNG SAMIJI. WHERE DID YOUR FEAR GO?
I AM NOT AFRAID OF FOXES.
THEY ARE BIGGER AND STRONGER. BUT THEY'RE ONLY FLESH AND FUR LIKE US.
THEY CAN BE FOUGHT, AND THEY CAN BE DEFEATED.
IT'S THE MONSTERS OUTSIDE THE EDGE OF OUR VALE-- THAT'S WHAT I'M AFRAID OF.
BECAUSE NO MATTER HOW HARD WE FIGHT THOSE THINGS, WE CAN'T WIN.

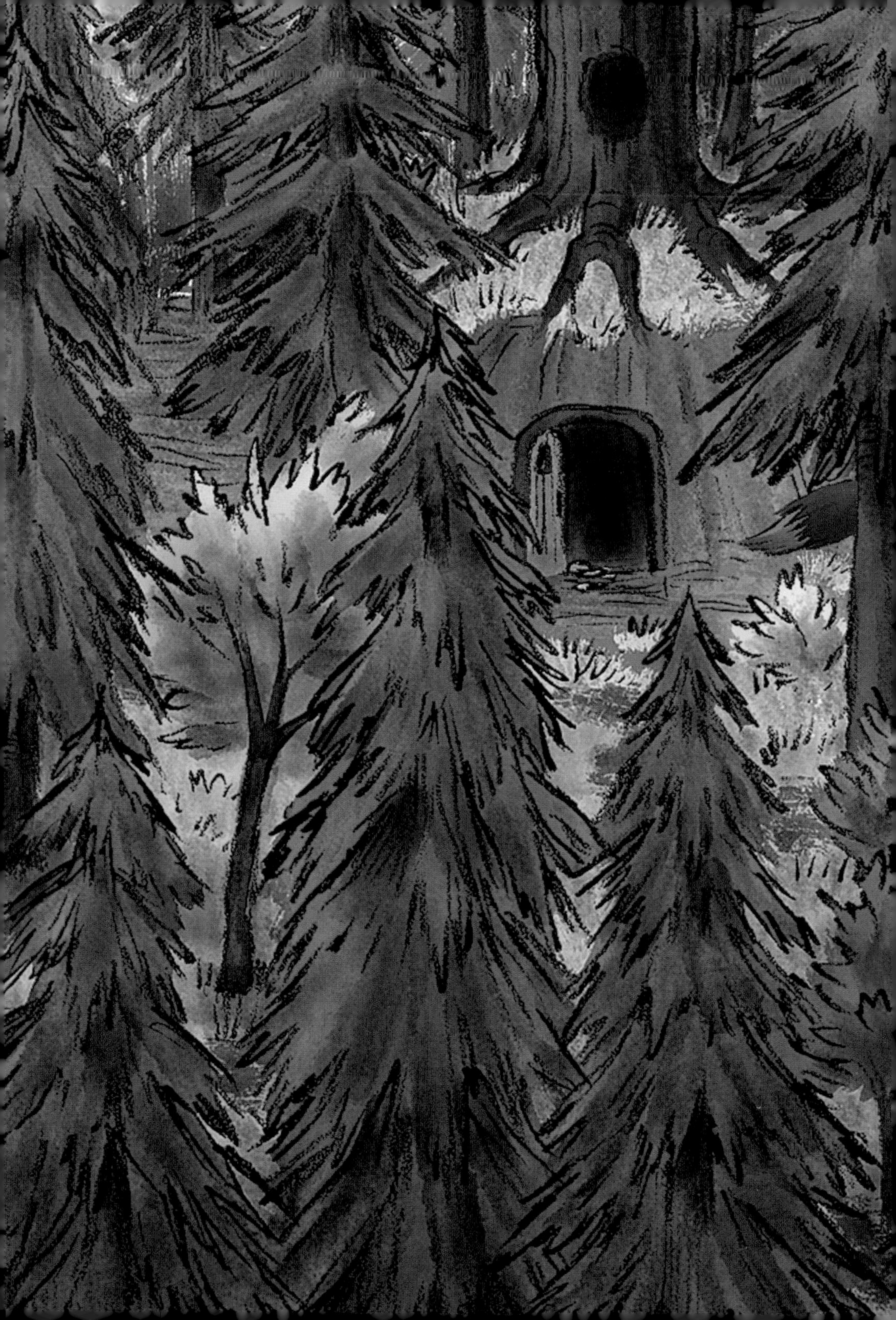

16.

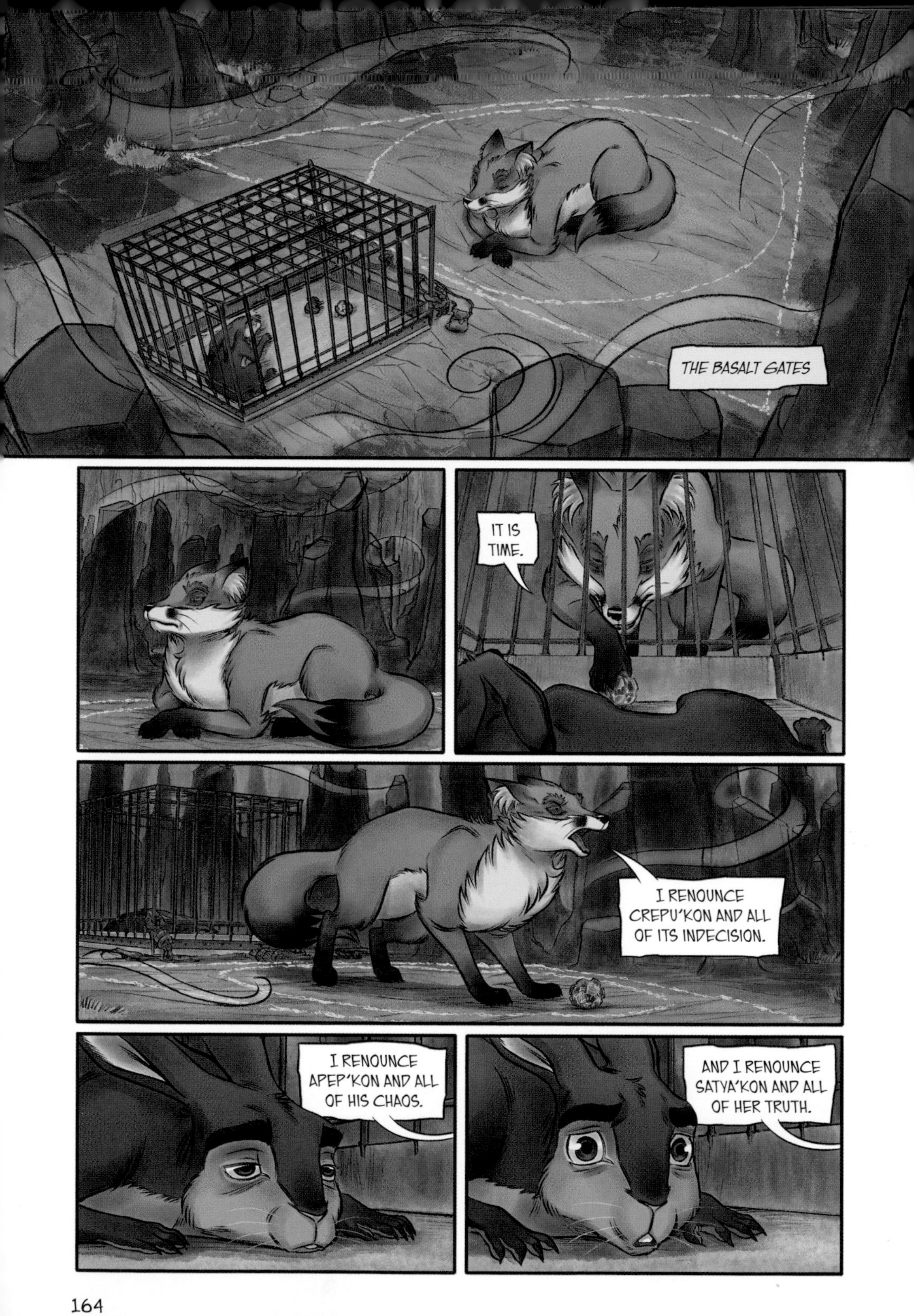

THE BASALT GATES
IT IS TIME.
I RENOUNCE CREPU'KON AND ALL OF ITS INDECISION.
I RENOUNCE APEP'KON AND ALL OF HIS CHAOS.
AND I RENOUNCE SATYA'KON AND ALL OF HER TRUTH.

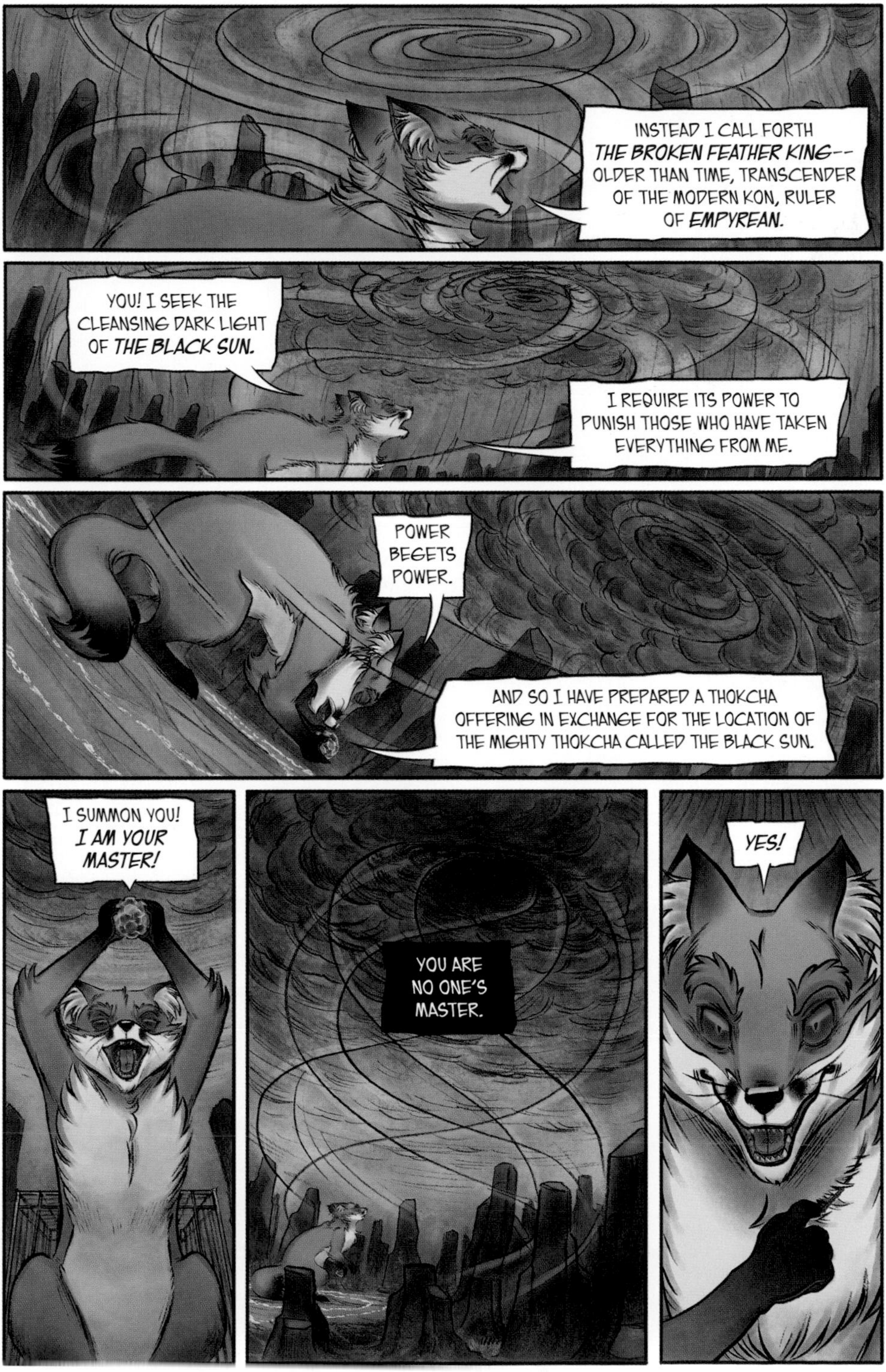

INSTEAD I CALL FORTH THE BROKEN FEATHER KING-- OLDER THAN TIME, TRANSCENDER OF THE MODERN KON, RULER OF EMPYREAN.
YOU! I SEEK THE CLEANSING DARK LIGHT OF THE BLACK SUN.
I REQUIRE ITS POWER TO PUNISH THOSE WHO HAVE TAKEN EVERYTHING FROM ME.
POWER BEGETS POWER.
AND SO I HAVE PREPARED A THOKCHA OFFERING IN EXCHANGE FOR THE LOCATION OF THE MIGHTY THOKCHA CALLED THE BLACK SUN.
I SUMMON YOU! I AM YOUR MASTER!
YOU ARE NO ONE'S MASTER.
YES!

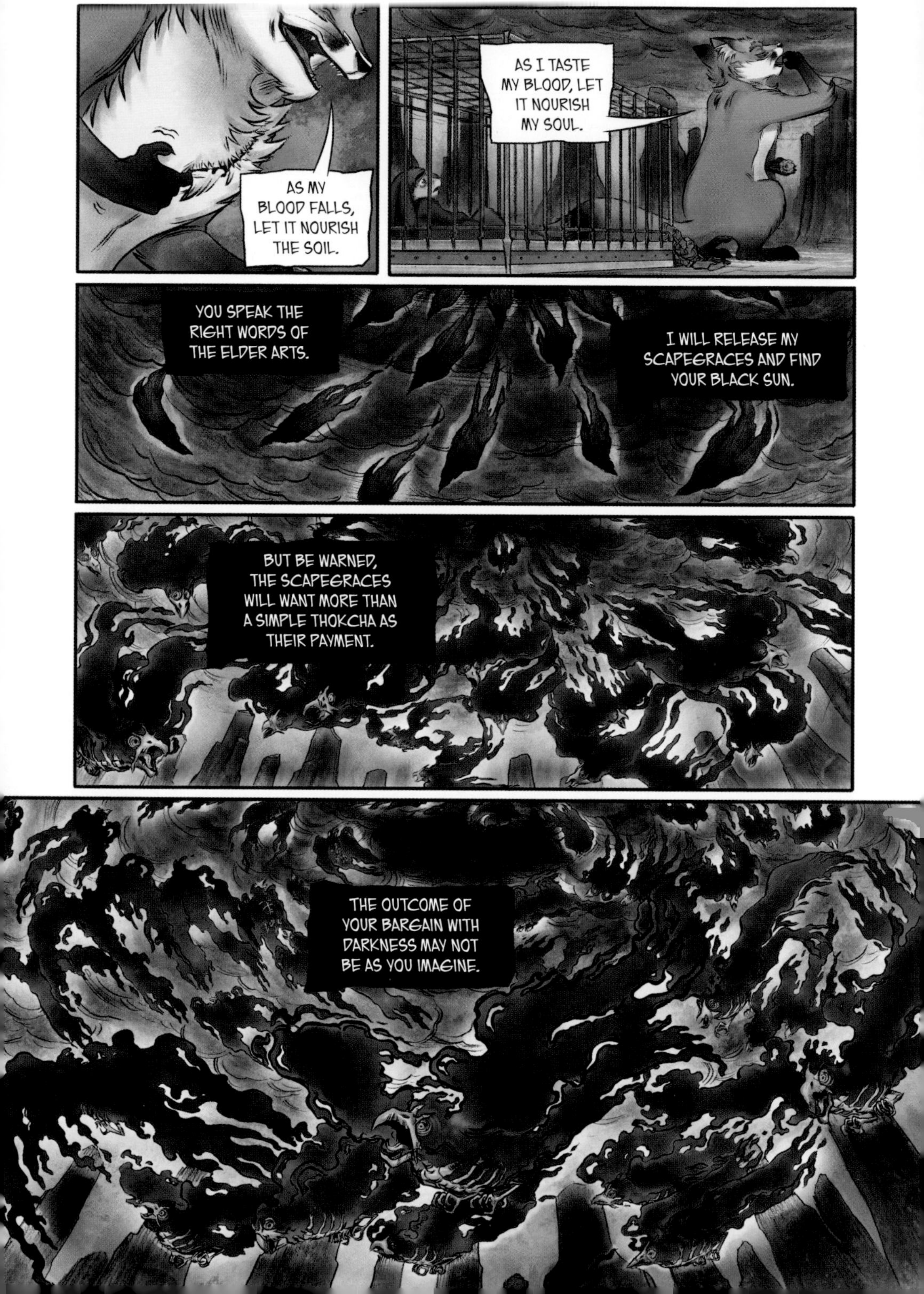
AS MY BLOOD FALLS, LET IT NOURISH THE SOIL.
AS I TASTE MY BLOOD, LET IT NOURISH MY SOUL.
YOU SPEAK THE RIGHT WORDS OF THE ELDER ARTS.
I WILL RELEASE MY SCAPEGRACES AND FIND YOUR BLACK SUN.
BUT BE WARNED, THE SCAPEGRACES WILL WANT MORE THAN A SIMPLE THOKCHA AS THEIR PAYMENT.
THE OUTCOME OF YOUR BARGAIN WITH DARKNESS MAY NOT BE AS YOU IMAGINE.

17.

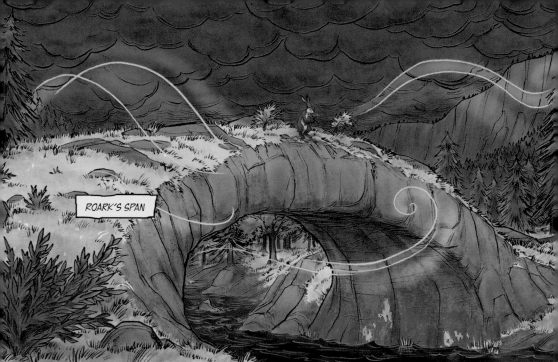

ROARK'S SPAN

OH, SON...
I LOVE YOU
SO MUCH...

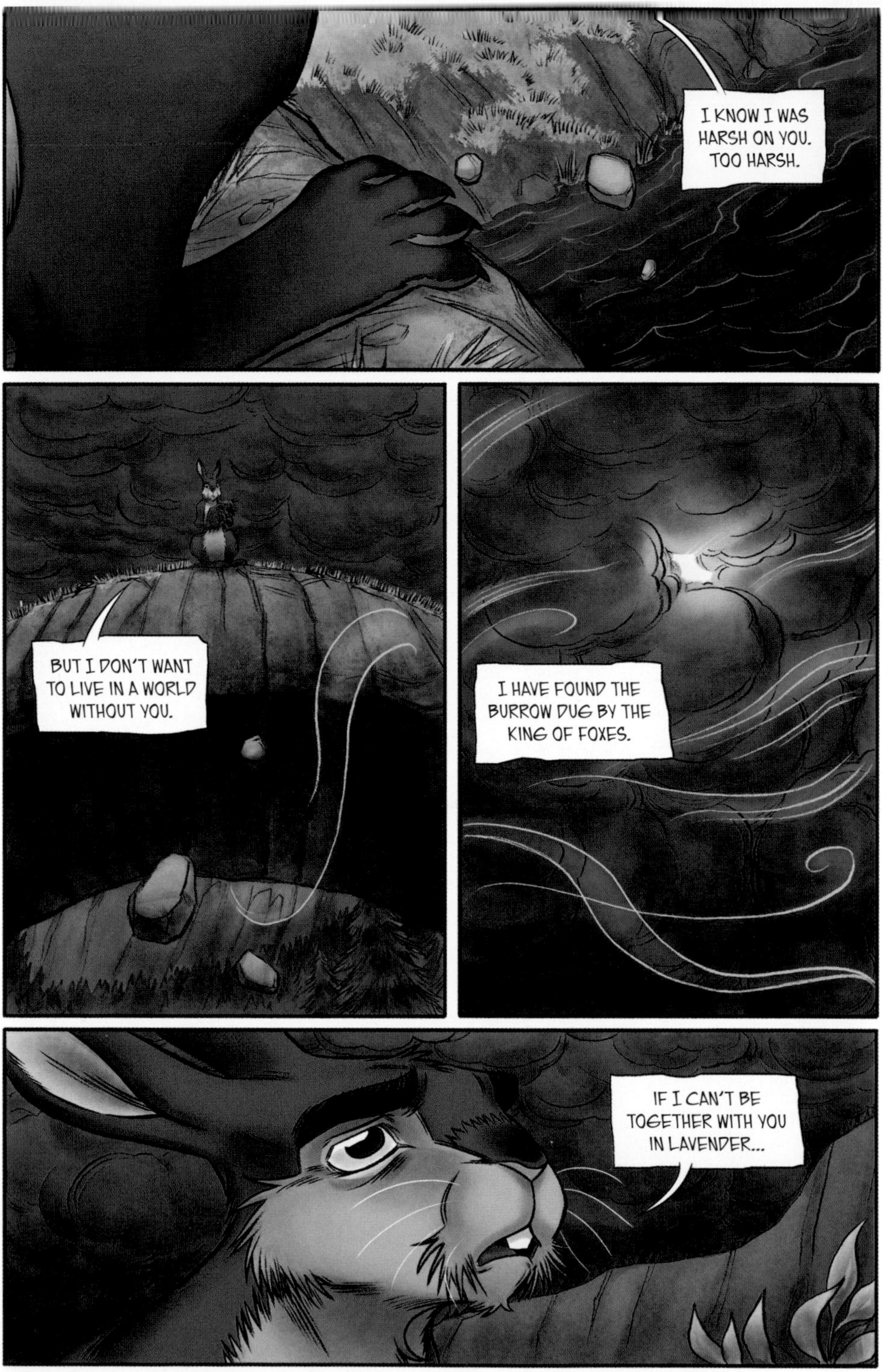
I KNOW I WAS HARSH ON YOU. TOO HARSH.
BUT I DON'T WANT TO LIVE IN A WORLD WITHOUT YOU.
I HAVE FOUND THE BURROW DUG BY THE KING OF FOXES.
IF I CAN'T BE TOGETHER WITH YOU IN LAVENDER...

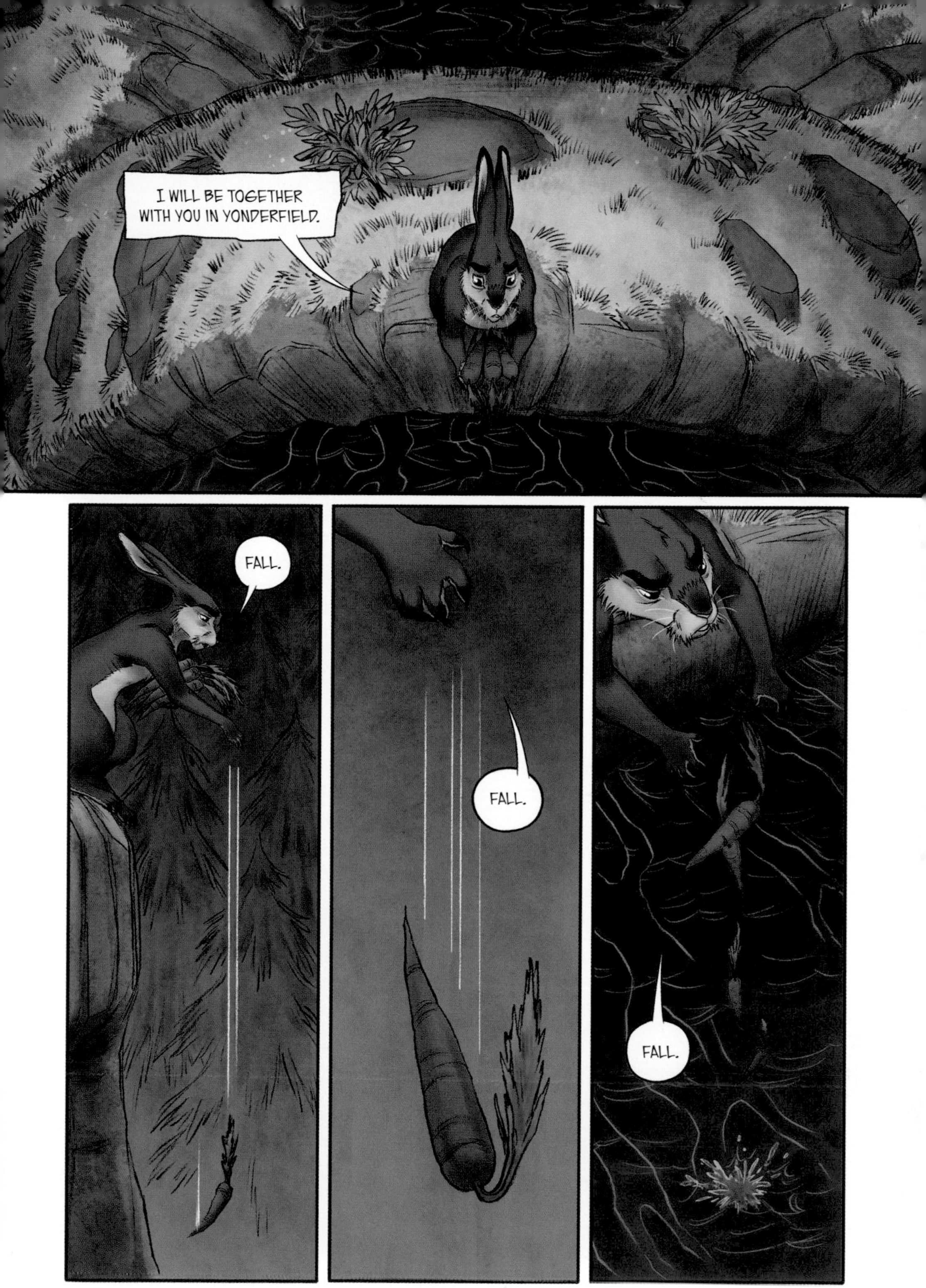
I WILL BE TOGETHER WITH YOU IN YONDERFIELD.
FALL.
FALL.
FALL.

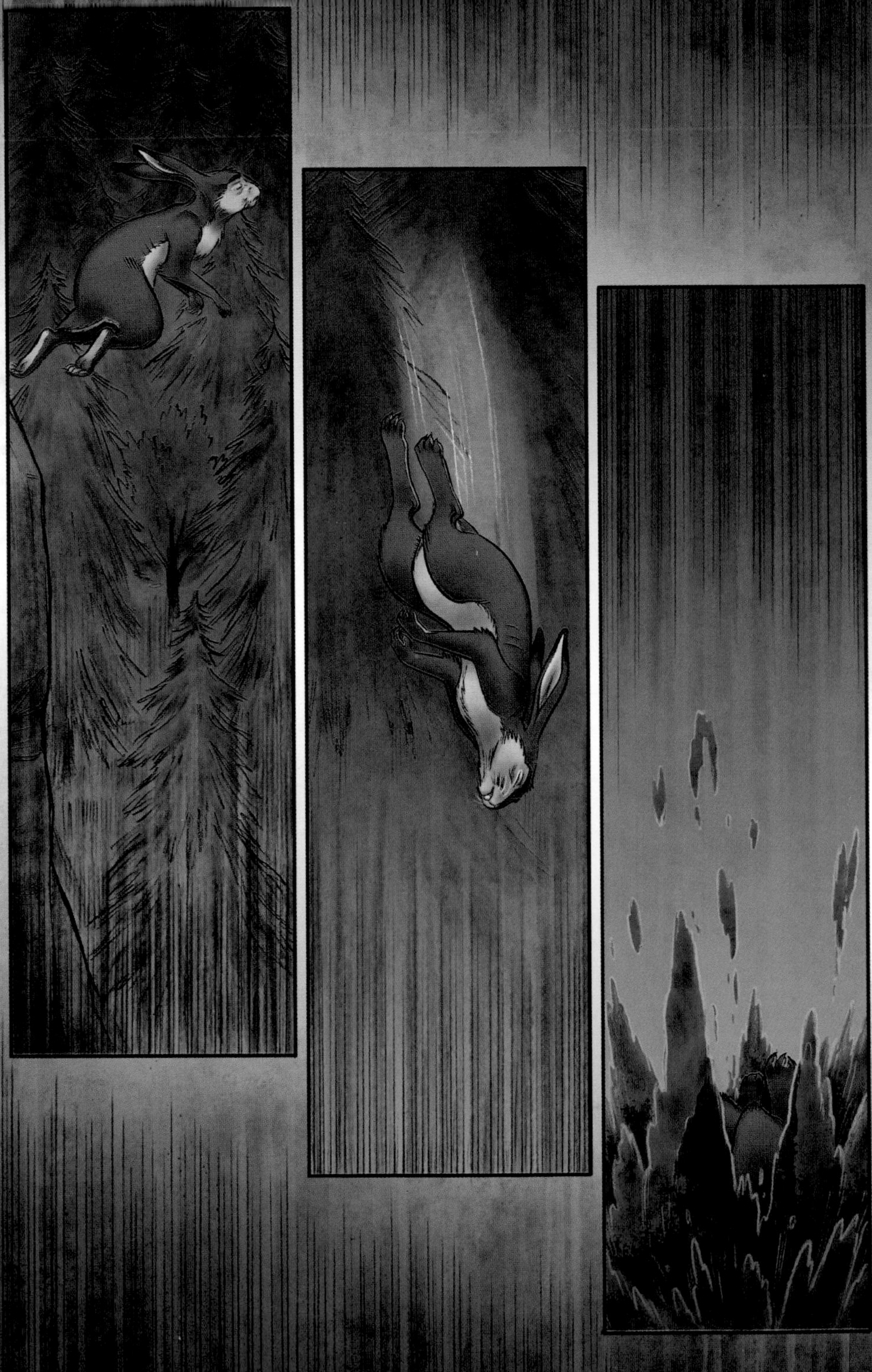

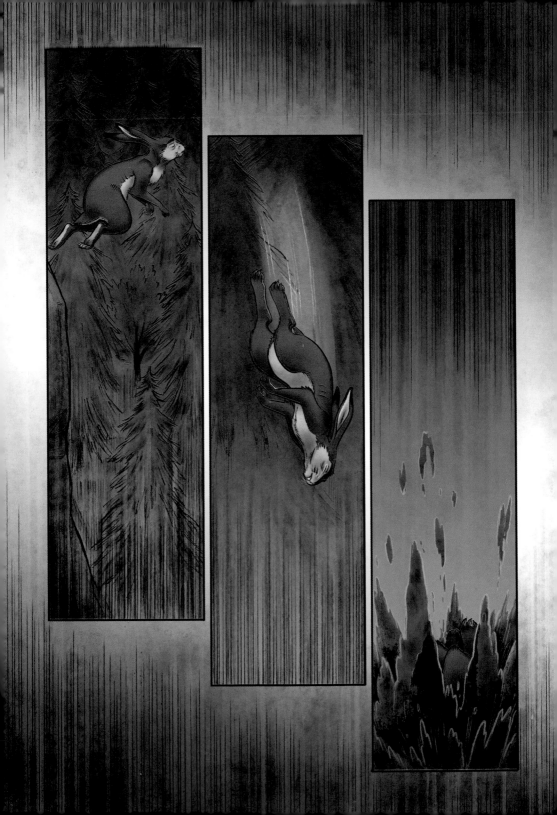

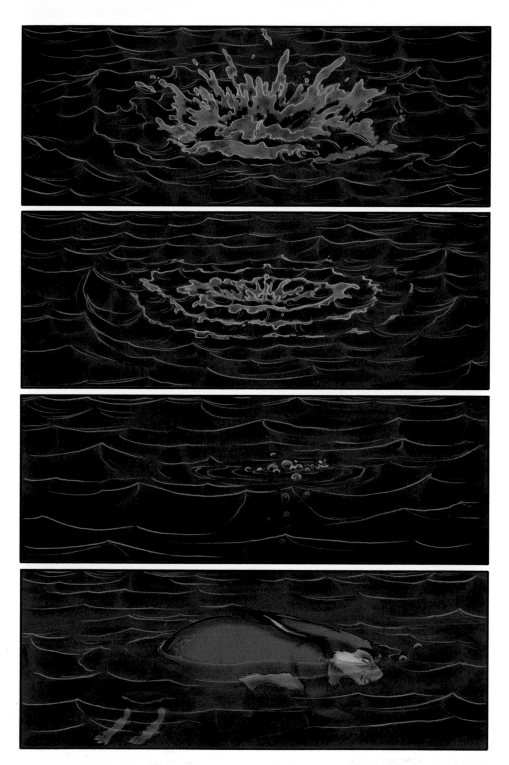

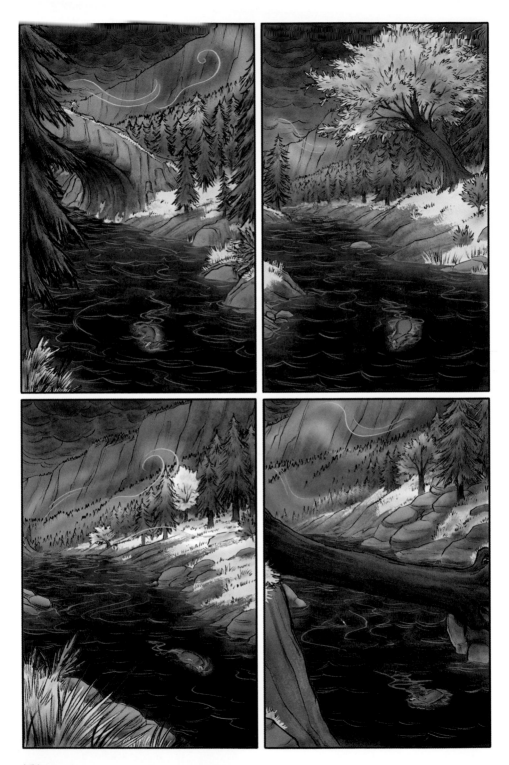

174

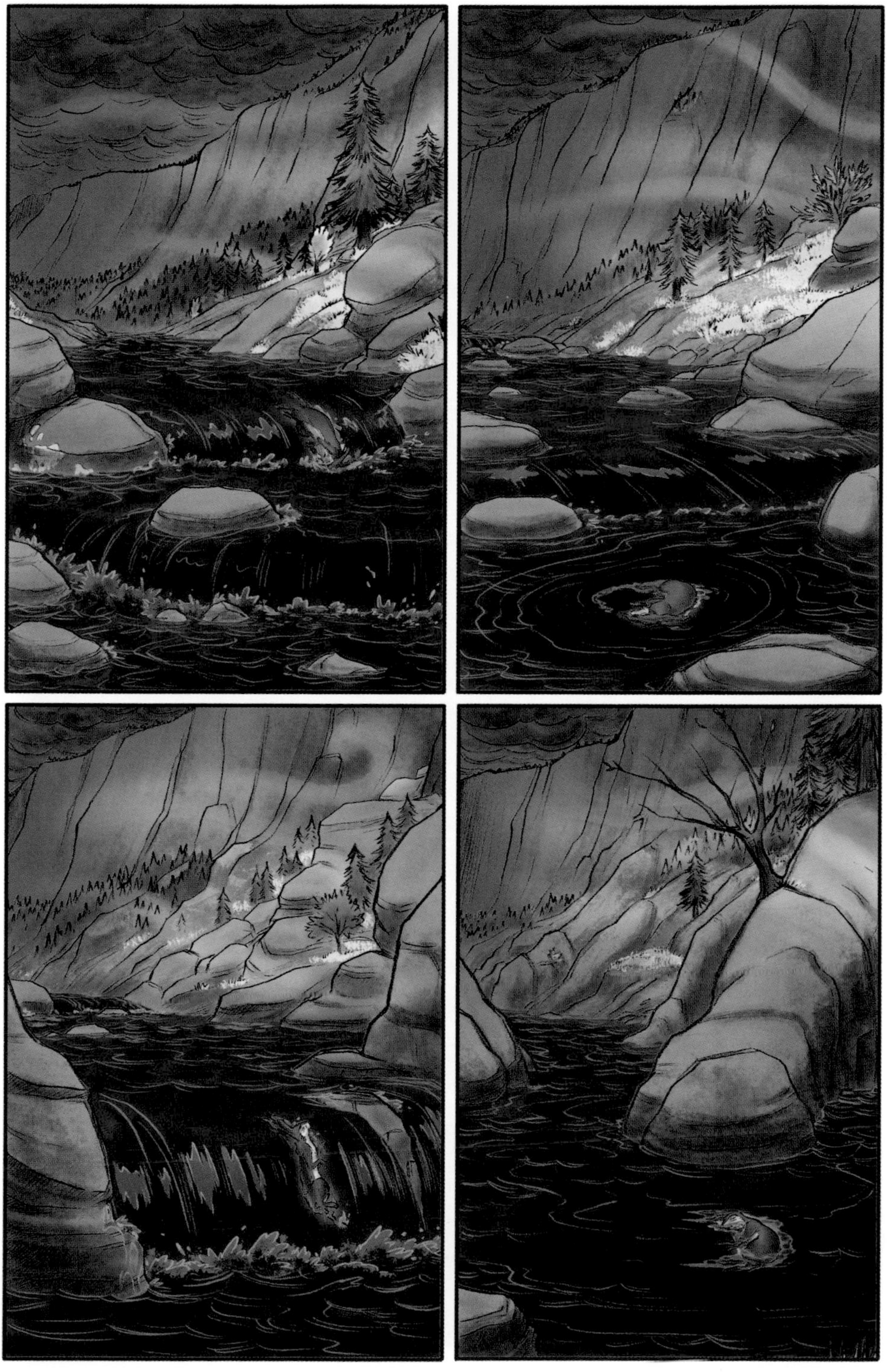

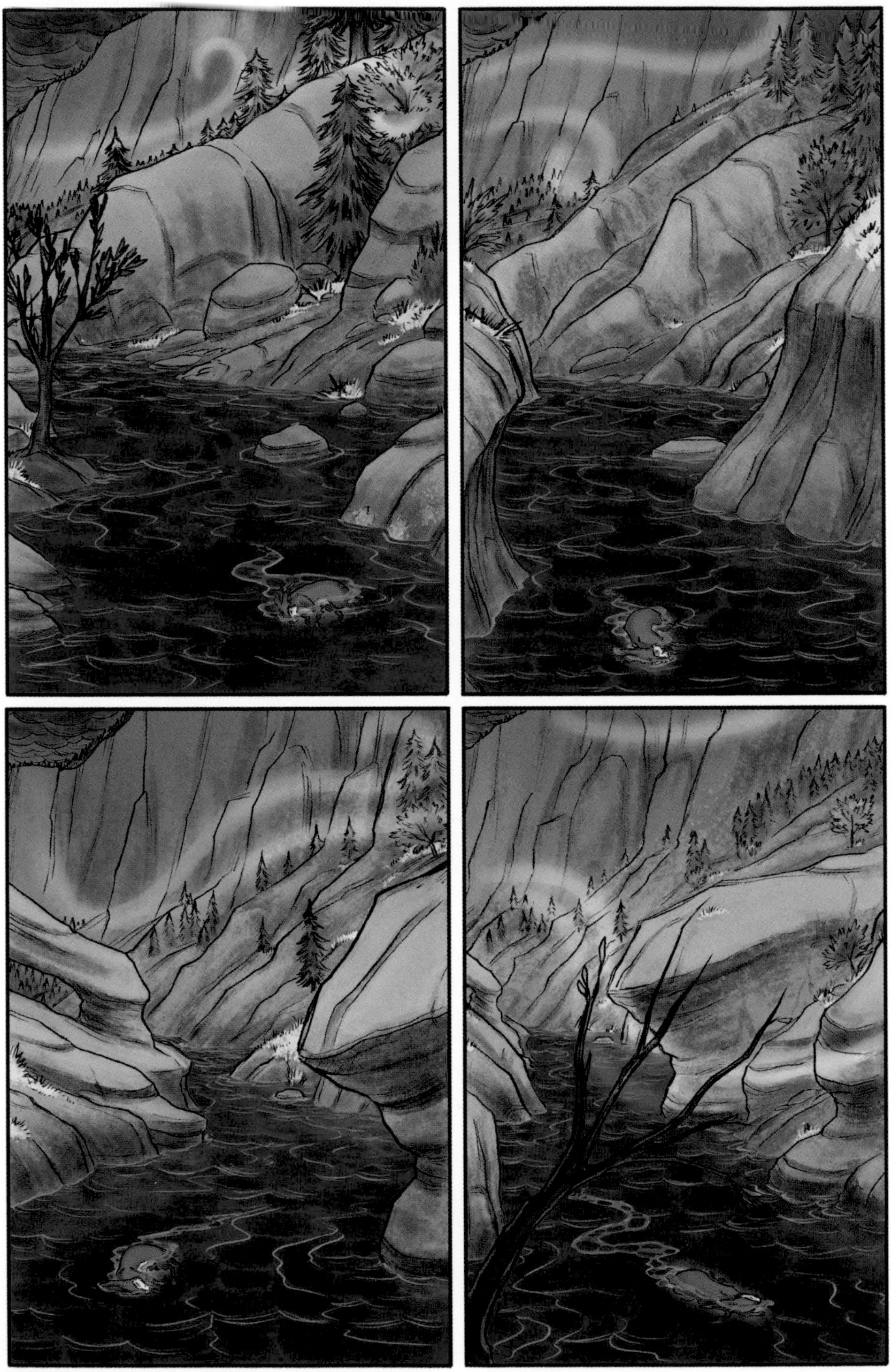

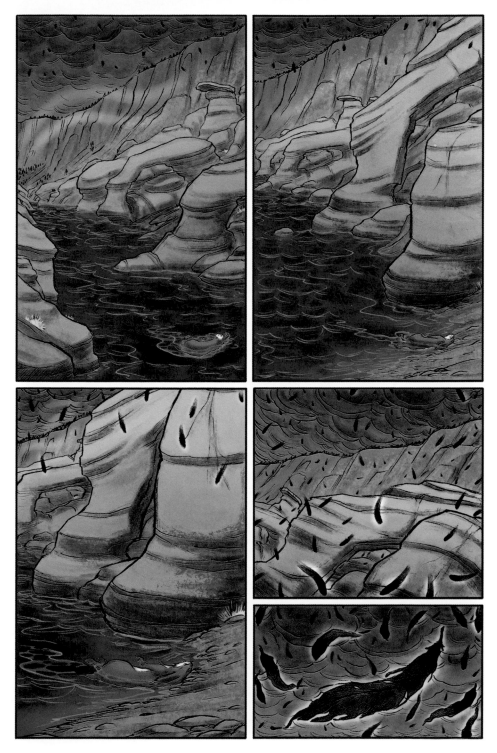

177

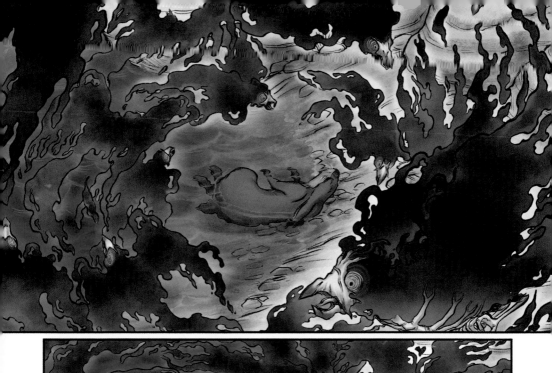

EMPYREAN!

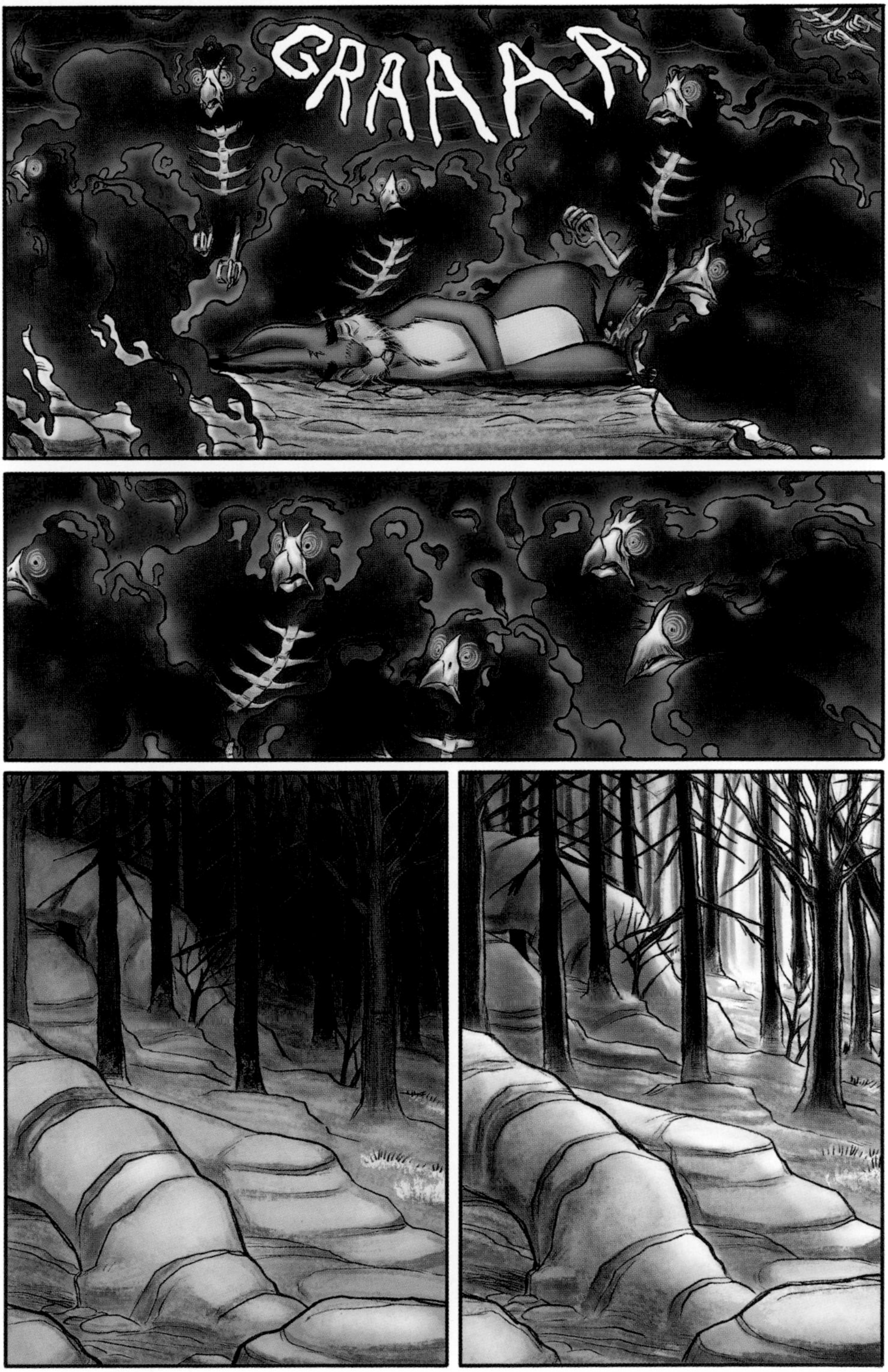
GRAAAR

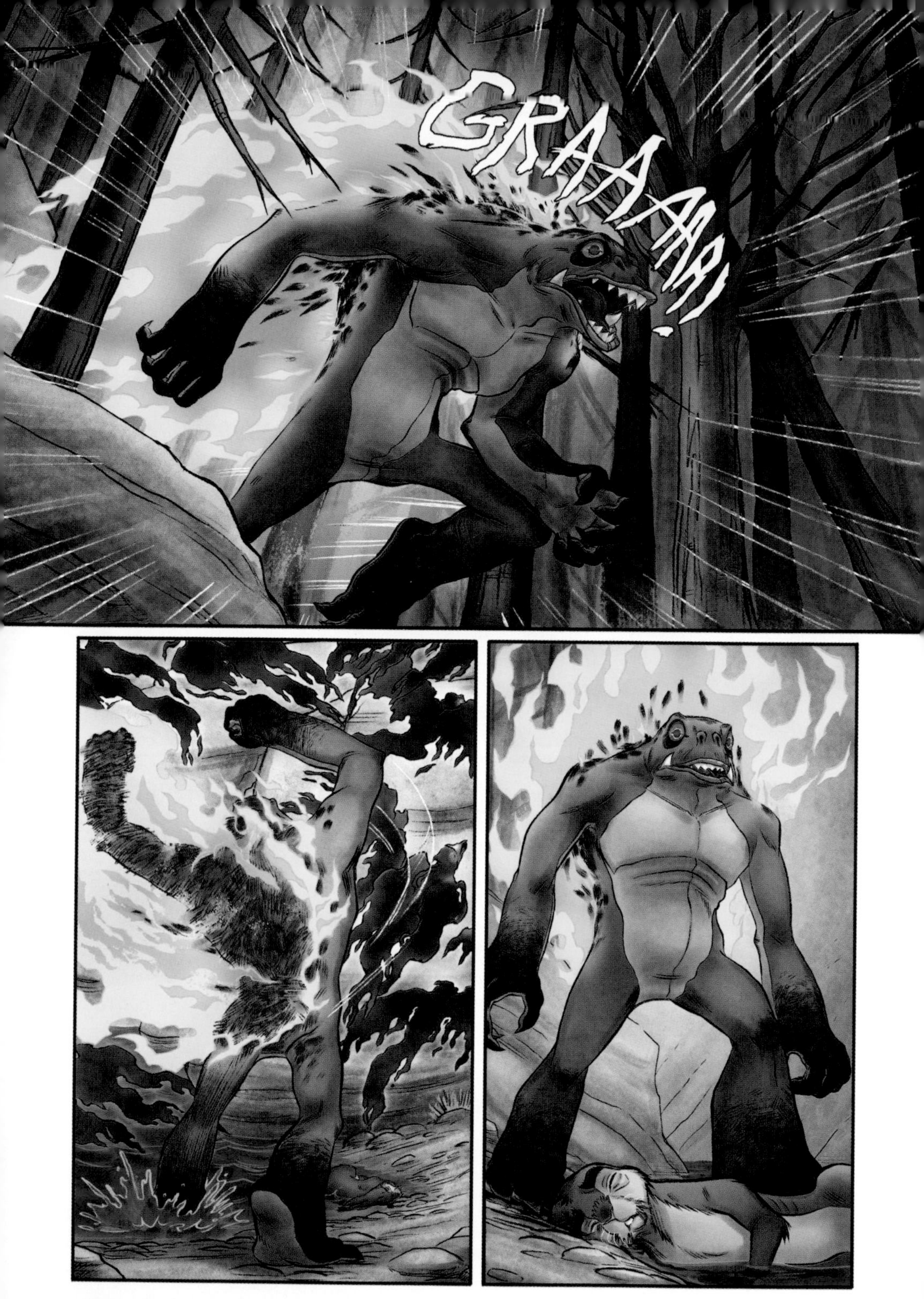
GRAAAAR!

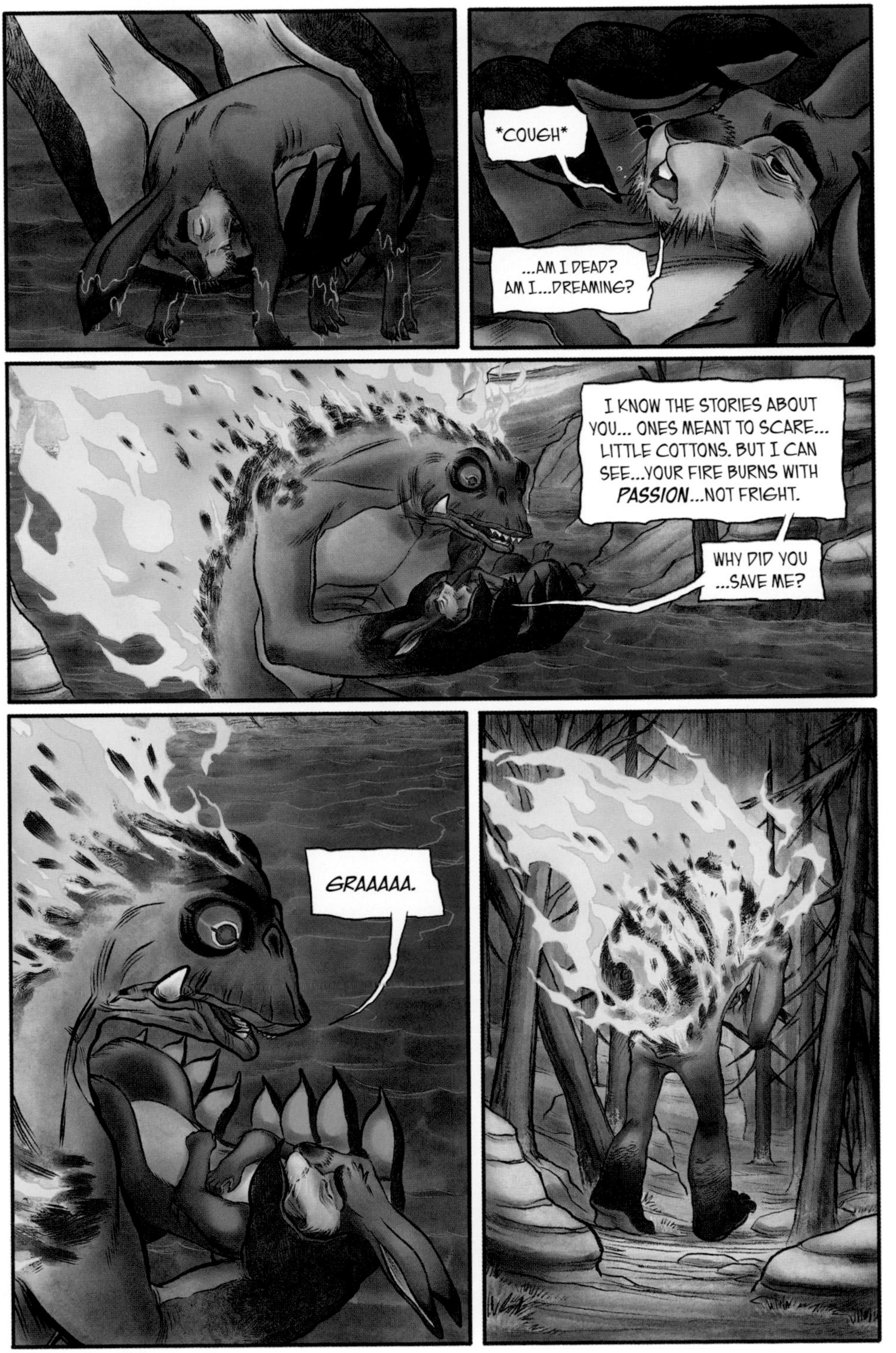
COUGH
...AM I DEAD? AM I...DREAMING?
I KNOW THE STORIES ABOUT YOU... ONES MEANT TO SCARE... LITTLE COTTONS. BUT I CAN SEE...YOUR FIRE BURNS WITH PASSION...NOT FRIGHT.
WHY DID YOU ...SAVE ME?
GRAAAAA.

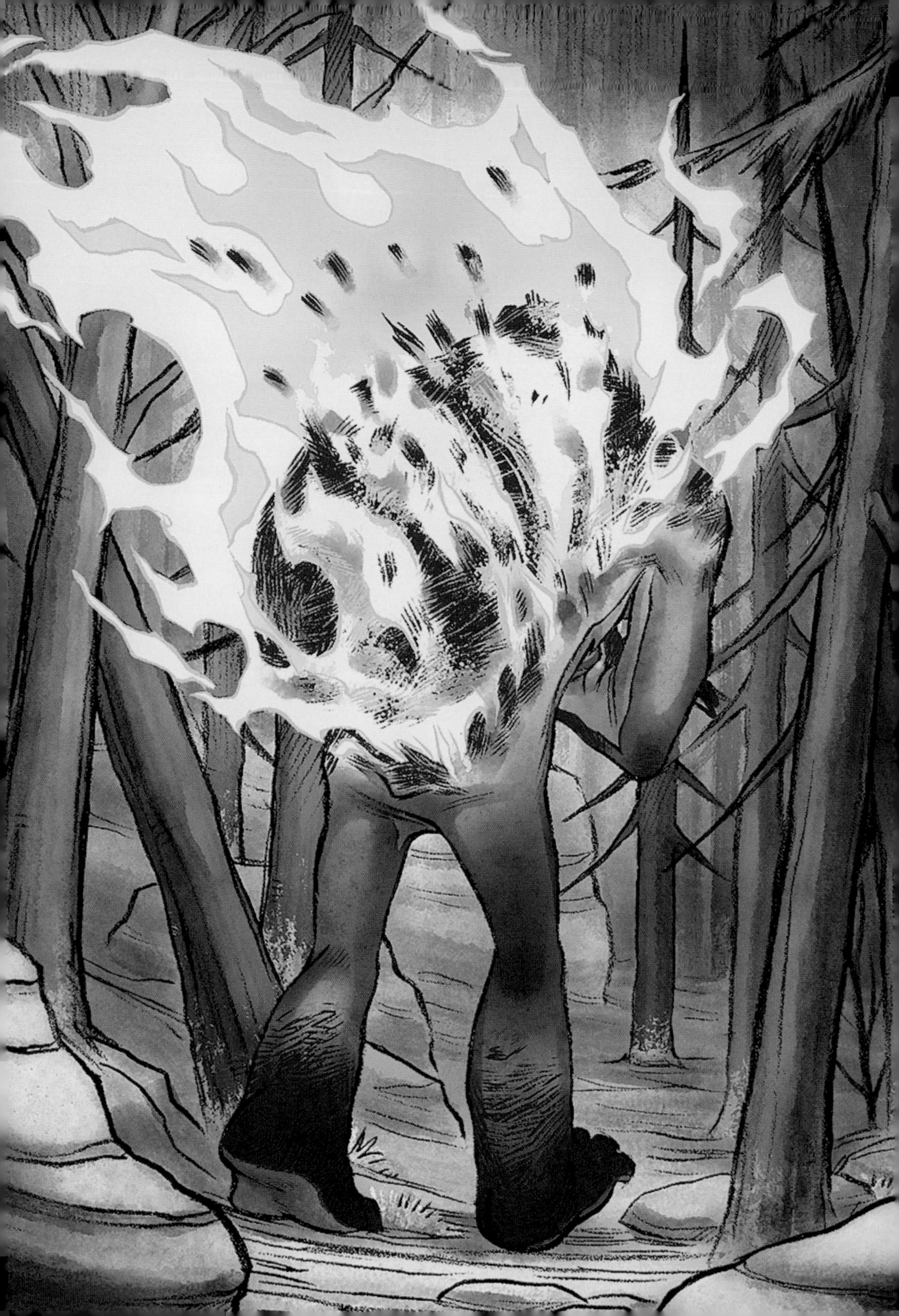

18.

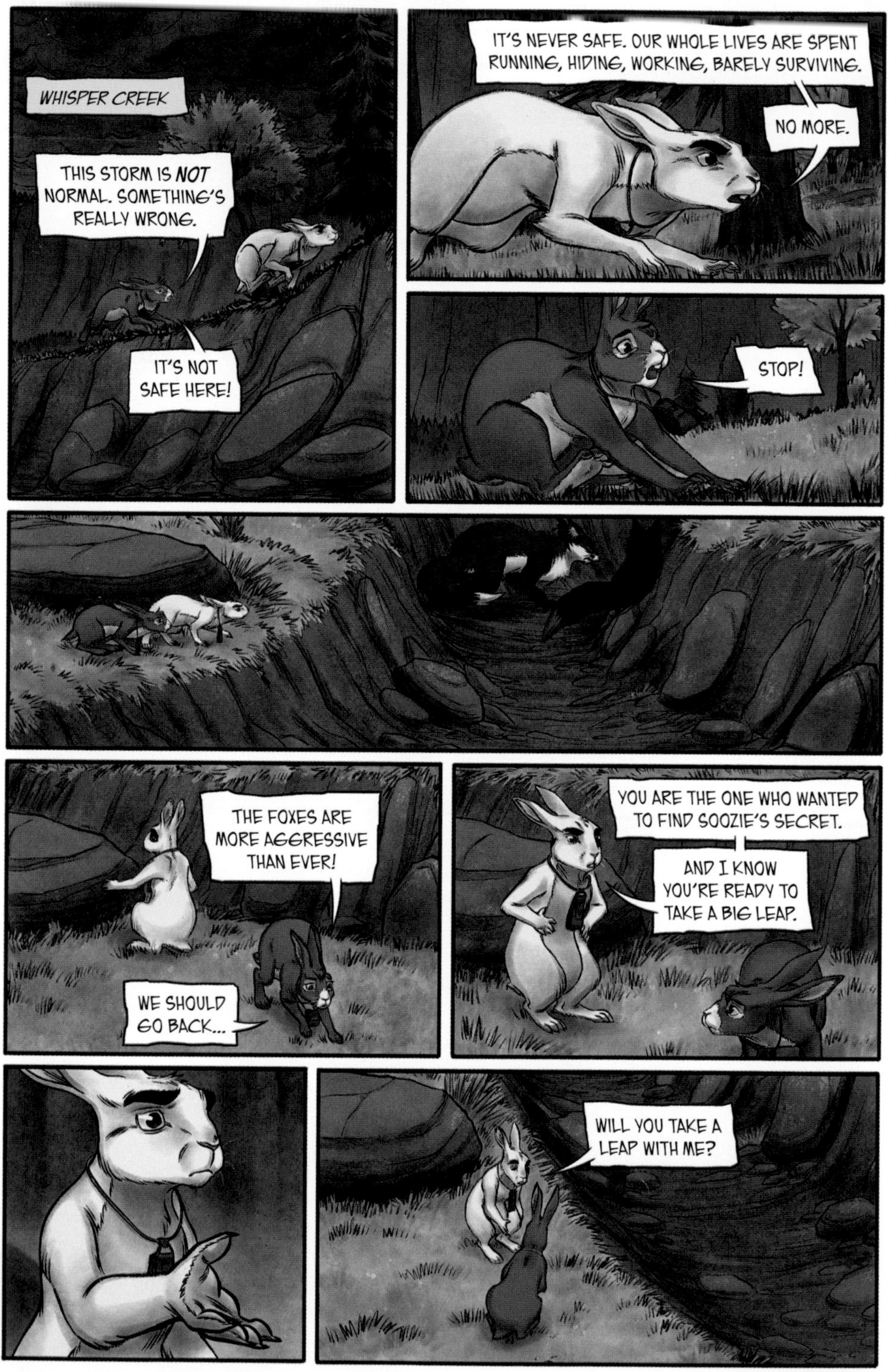
WHISPER CREEK
THIS STORM IS *NOT* NORMAL. SOMETHING'S REALLY WRONG.
IT'S NOT SAFE HERE!
IT'S NEVER SAFE. OUR WHOLE LIVES ARE SPENT RUNNING, HIDING, WORKING, BARELY SURVIVING.
NO MORE.
STOP!
THE FOXES ARE MORE AGGRESSIVE THAN EVER!
WE SHOULD GO BACK...
YOU ARE THE ONE WHO WANTED TO FIND SOOZIE'S SECRET.
AND I KNOW YOU'RE READY TO TAKE A BIG LEAP.
WILL YOU TAKE A LEAP WITH ME?

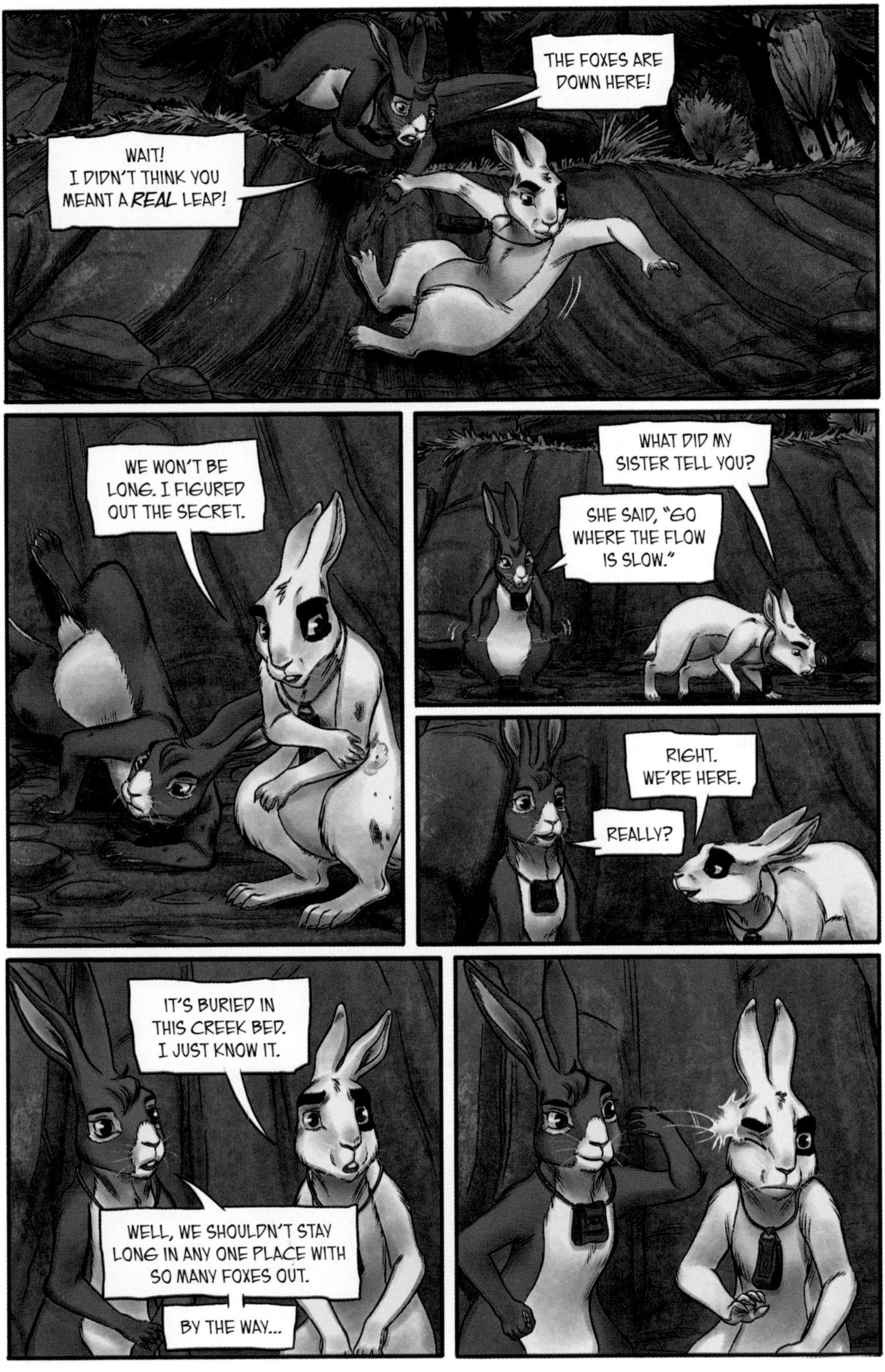
THE FOXES ARE DOWN HERE!
WAIT! I DIDN'T THINK YOU MEANT A *REAL* LEAP!
WE WON'T BE LONG. I FIGURED OUT THE SECRET.
WHAT DID MY SISTER TELL YOU?
SHE SAID, "GO WHERE THE FLOW IS SLOW."
RIGHT. WE'RE HERE.
REALLY?
IT'S BURIED IN THIS CREEK BED. I JUST KNOW IT.
WELL, WE SHOULDN'T STAY LONG IN ANY ONE PLACE WITH SO MANY FOXES OUT.
BY THE WAY...

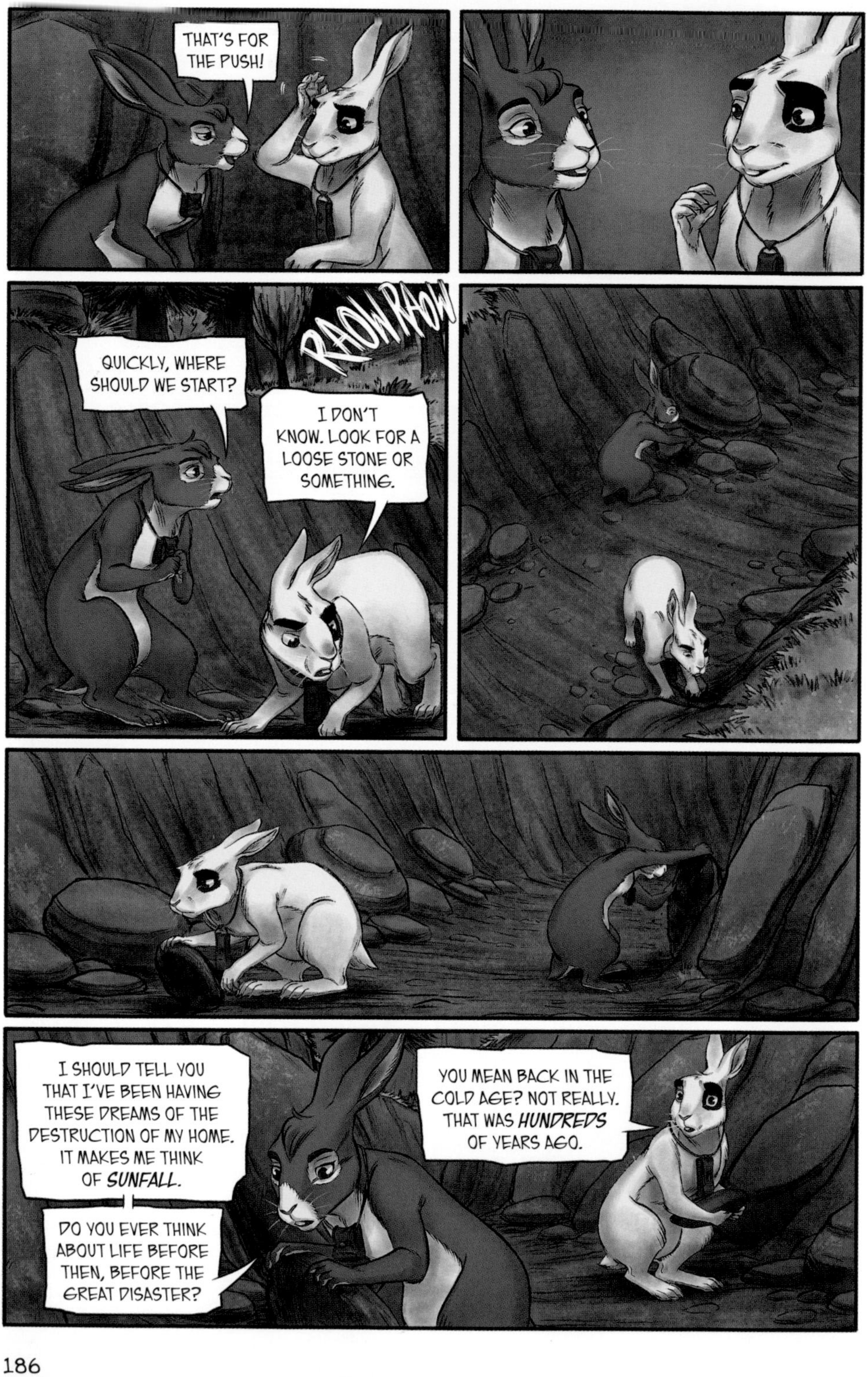
THAT'S FOR THE PUSH!
RAOW RAOW
QUICKLY, WHERE SHOULD WE START?
I DON'T KNOW. LOOK FOR A LOOSE STONE OR SOMETHING.
I SHOULD TELL YOU THAT I'VE BEEN HAVING THESE DREAMS OF THE DESTRUCTION OF MY HOME. IT MAKES ME THINK OF SUNFALL.
DO YOU EVER THINK ABOUT LIFE BEFORE THEN, BEFORE THE GREAT DISASTER?
YOU MEAN BACK IN THE COLD AGE? NOT REALLY. THAT WAS HUNDREDS OF YEARS AGO.

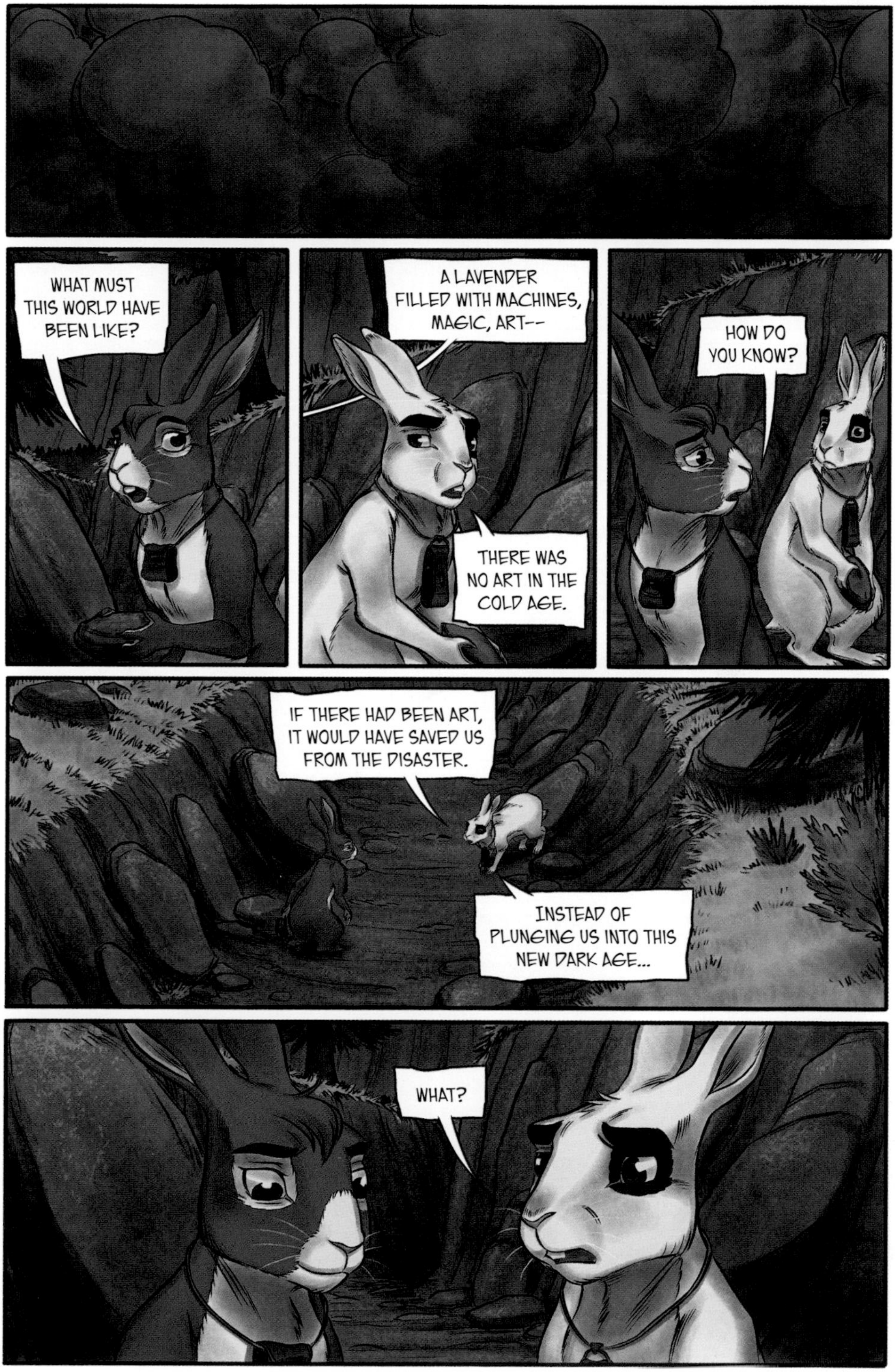
WHAT MUST THIS WORLD HAVE BEEN LIKE?
A LAVENDER FILLED WITH MACHINES, MAGIC, ART--
THERE WAS NO ART IN THE COLD AGE.
HOW DO YOU KNOW?
IF THERE HAD BEEN ART, IT WOULD HAVE SAVED US FROM THE DISASTER.
INSTEAD OF PLUNGING US INTO THIS NEW DARK AGE...
WHAT?

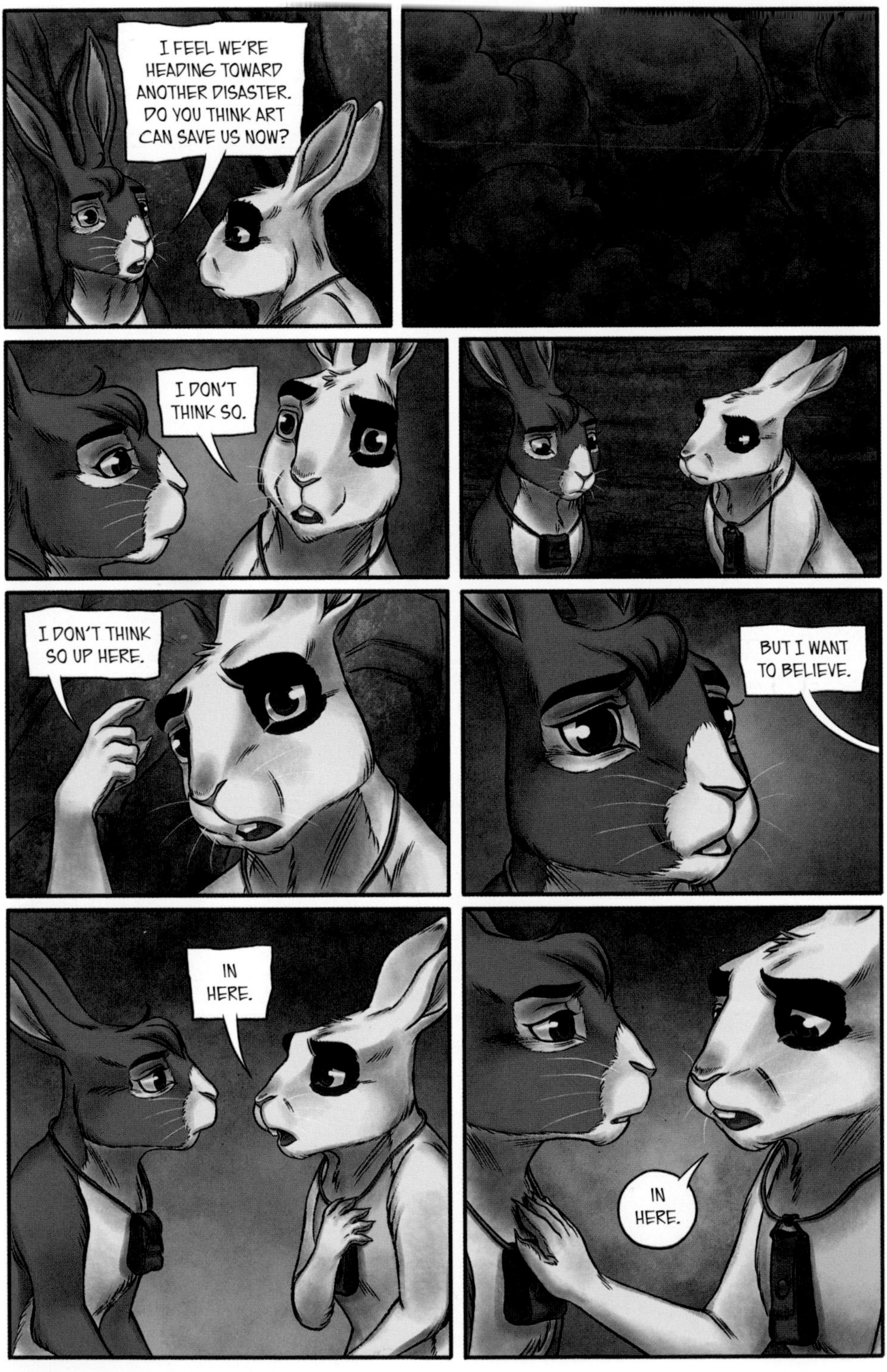
I FEEL WE'RE HEADING TOWARD ANOTHER DISASTER. DO YOU THINK ART CAN SAVE US NOW?
I DON'T THINK SO.
I DON'T THINK SO UP HERE.
BUT I WANT TO BELIEVE.
IN HERE.
IN HERE.

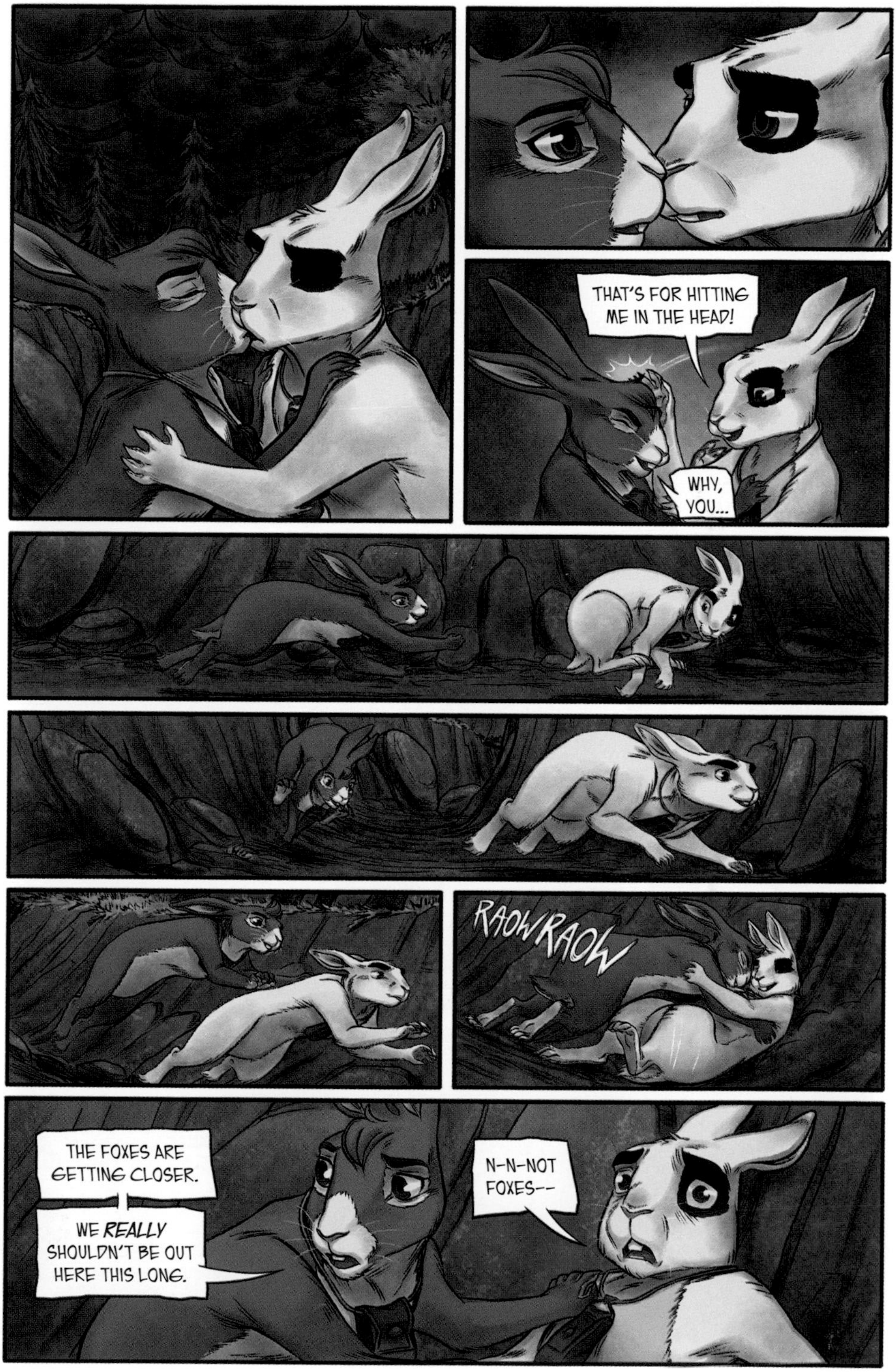
THAT'S FOR HITTING ME IN THE HEAD!
WHY, YOU...
RAOW RAOW
THE FOXES ARE GETTING CLOSER.
WE *REALLY* SHOULDN'T BE OUT HERE THIS LONG.
N-N-NOT FOXES--

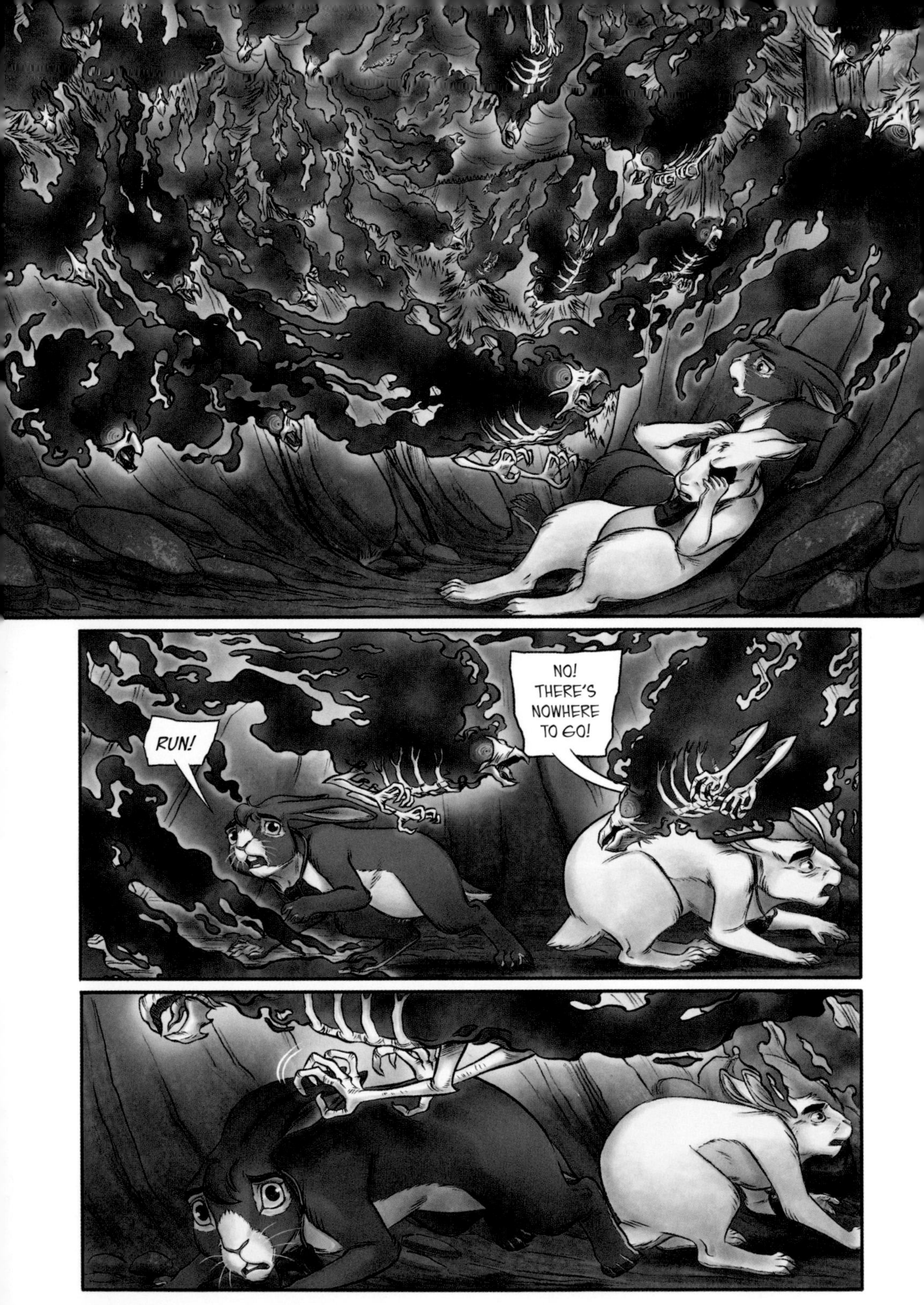
RUN!
NO! THERE'S NOWHERE TO GO!

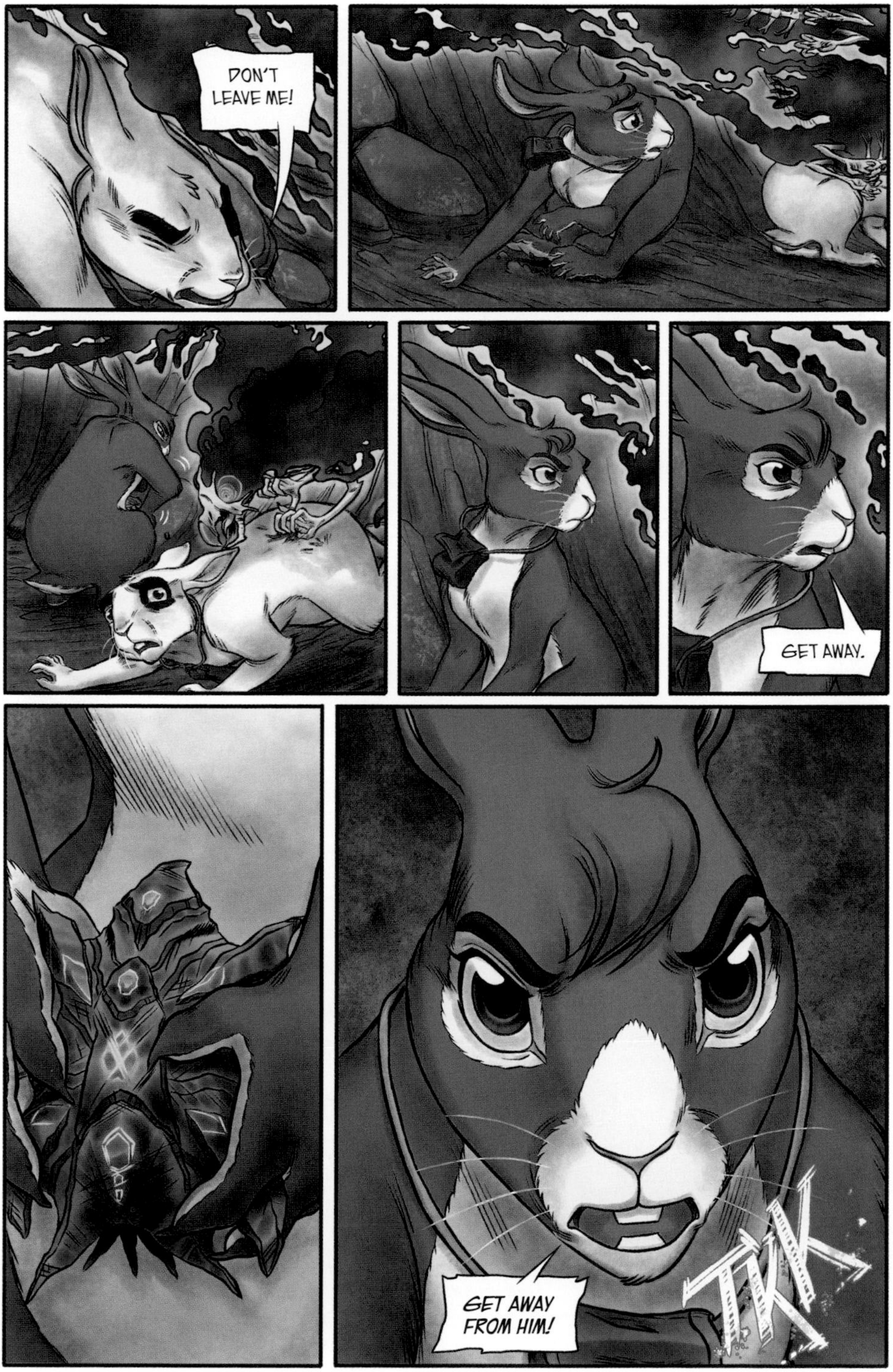
DON'T LEAVE ME!
GET AWAY.
GET AWAY FROM HIM!
TWK

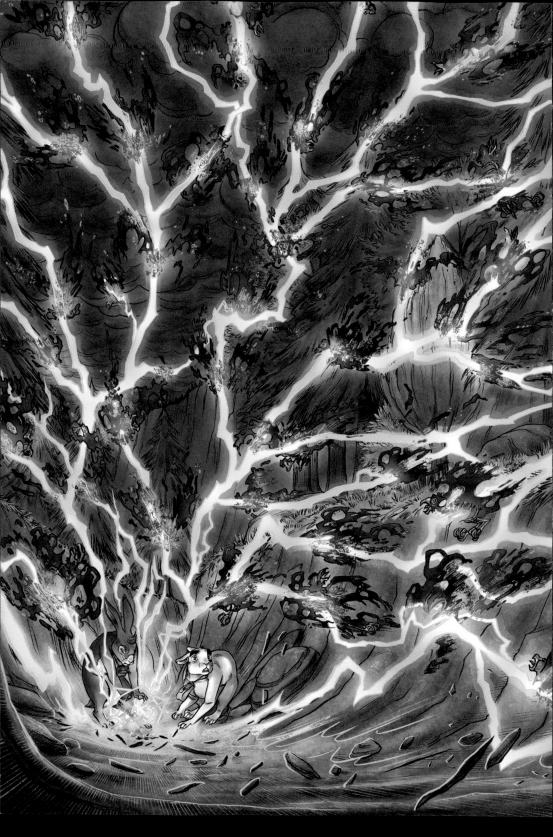

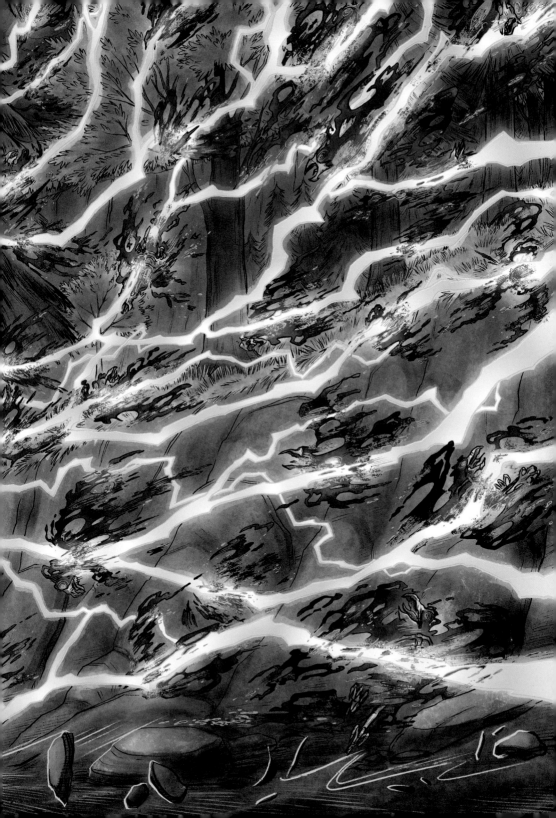

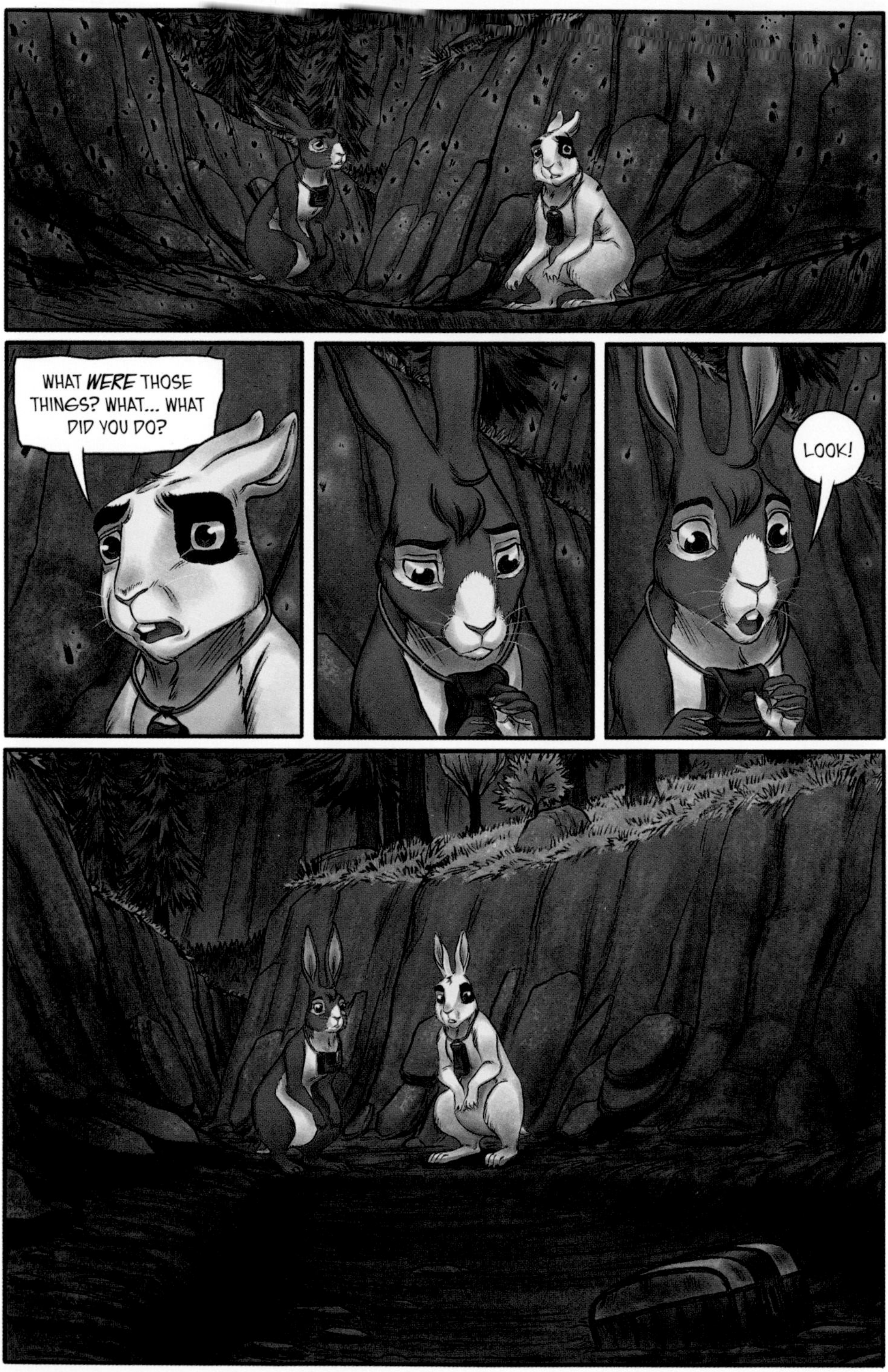
WHAT WERE THOSE THINGS? WHAT... WHAT DID YOU DO?
LOOK!

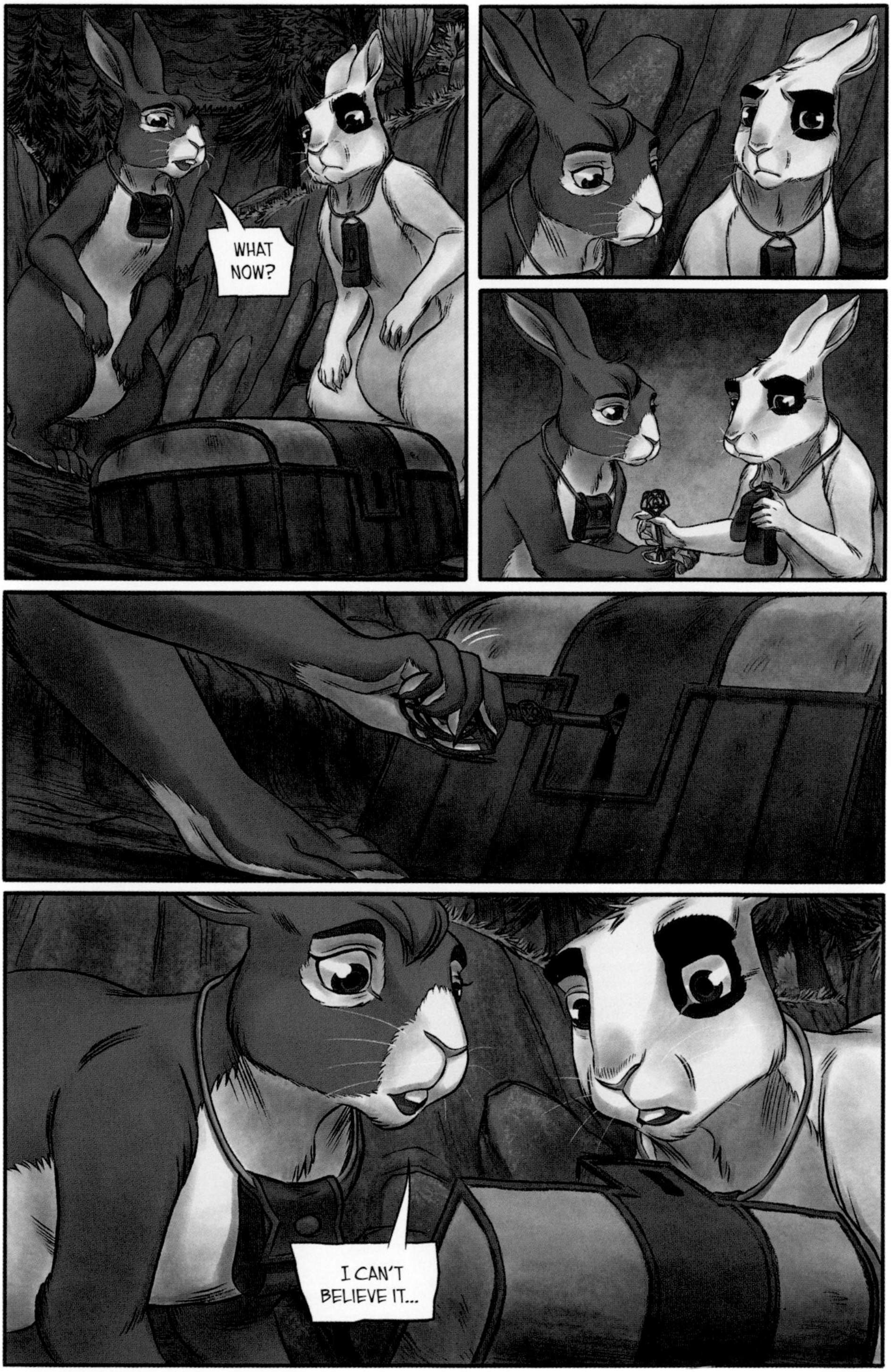
WHAT NOW?
I CAN'T BELIEVE IT...

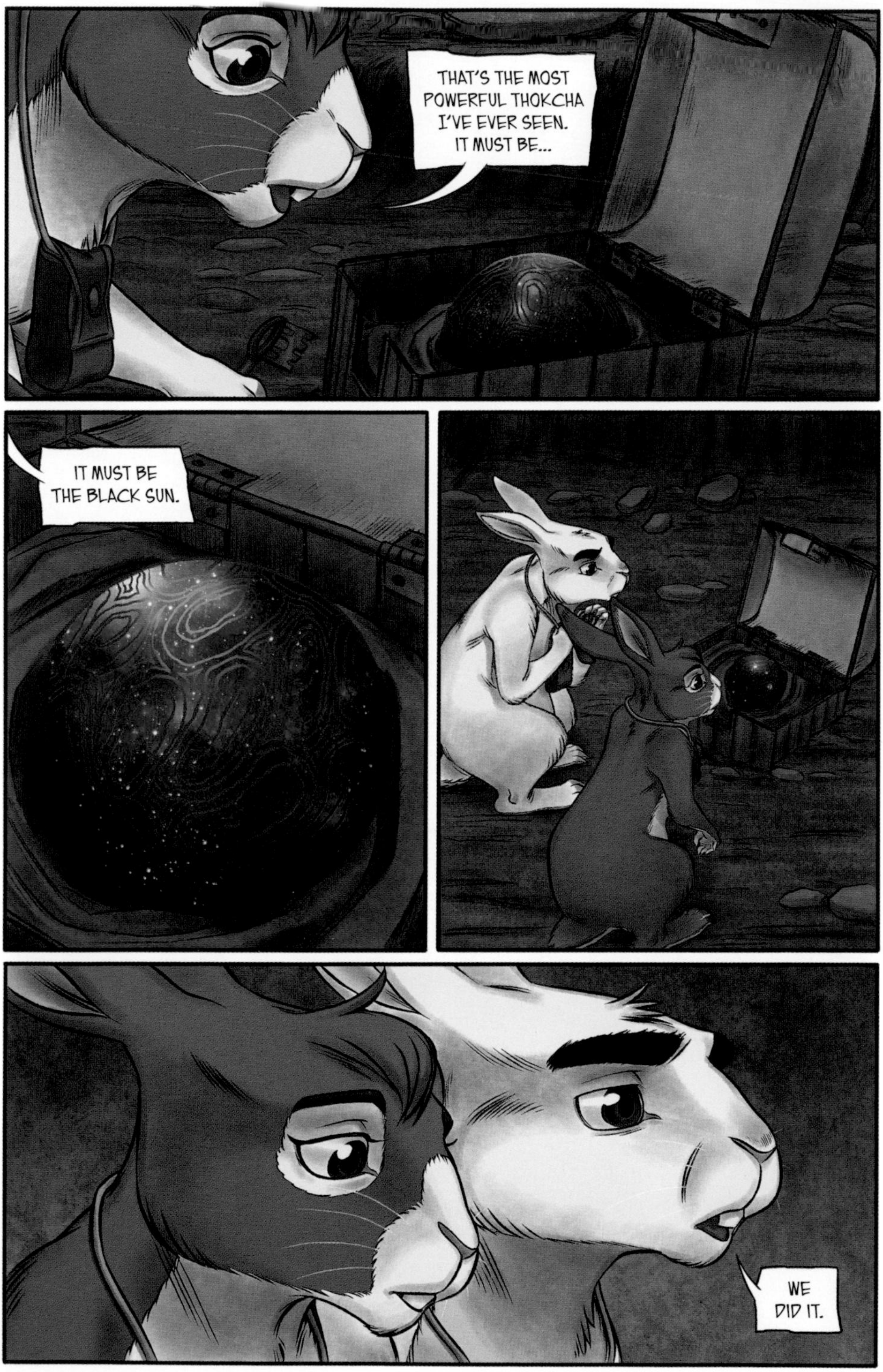
THAT'S THE MOST POWERFUL THOKCHA I'VE EVER SEEN. IT MUST BE...
IT MUST BE THE BLACK SUN.
WE DID IT.

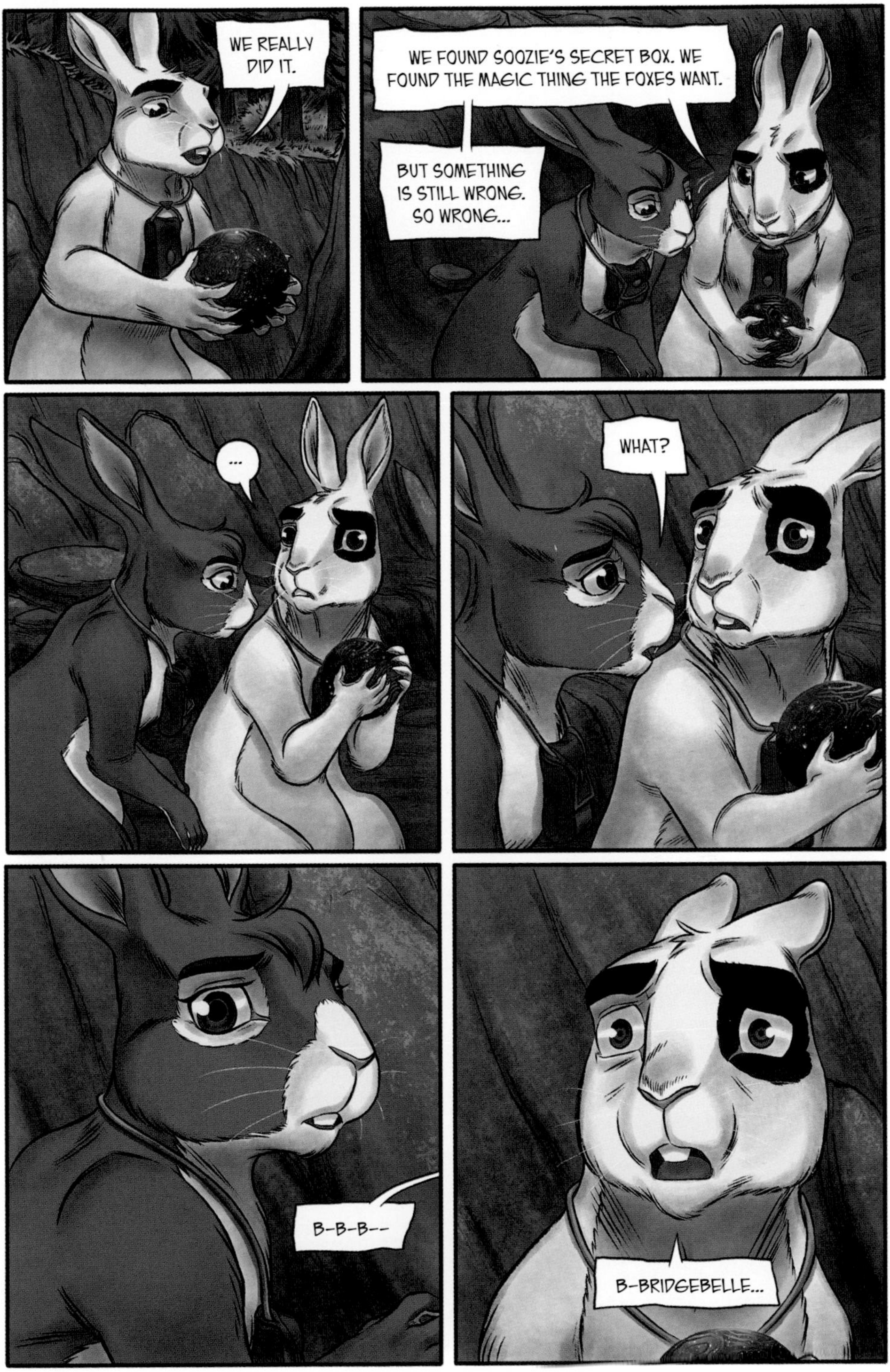
WE REALLY DID IT.
WE FOUND SOOZIE'S SECRET BOX. WE FOUND THE MAGIC THING THE FOXES WANT.
BUT SOMETHING IS STILL WRONG. SO WRONG...
...
WHAT?
B-B-B--
B-BRIDGEBELLE...

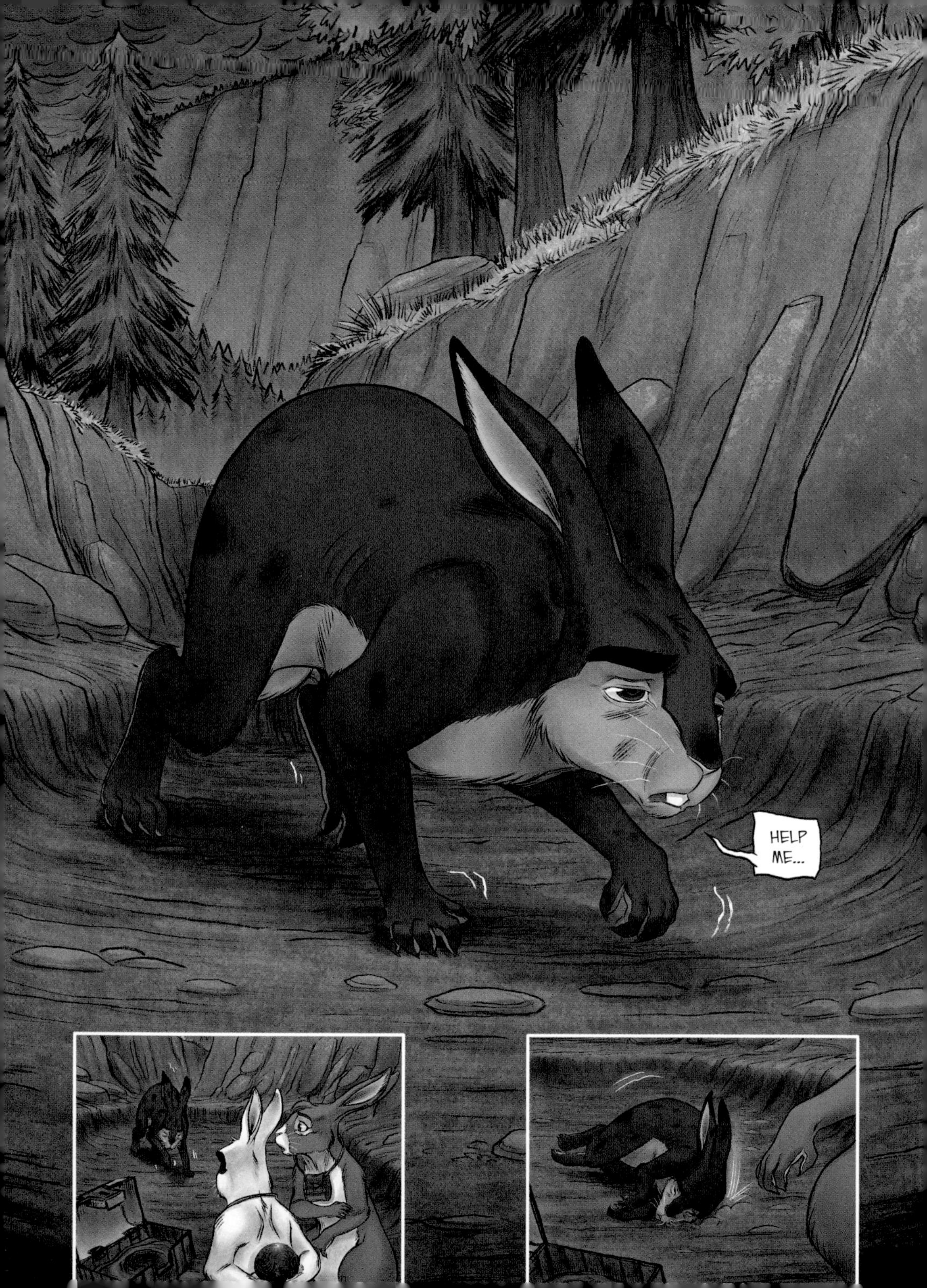
HELP ME...

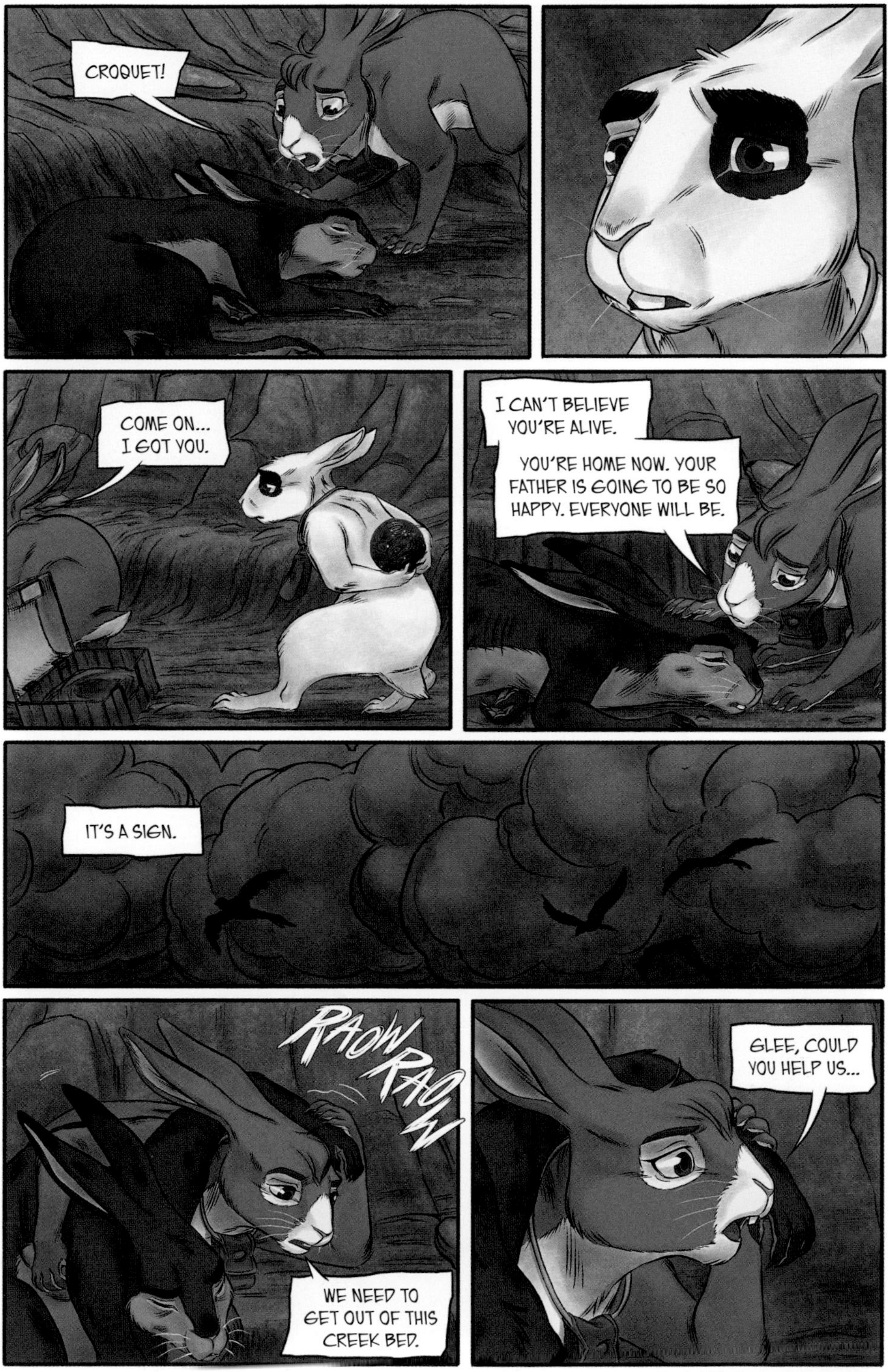

CROQUET!
COME ON... I GOT YOU.
I CAN'T BELIEVE YOU'RE ALIVE.
YOU'RE HOME NOW. YOUR FATHER IS GOING TO BE SO HAPPY. EVERYONE WILL BE.
IT'S A SIGN.
RAOW RAOW
WE NEED TO GET OUT OF THIS CREEK BED.
GLEE, COULD YOU HELP US...

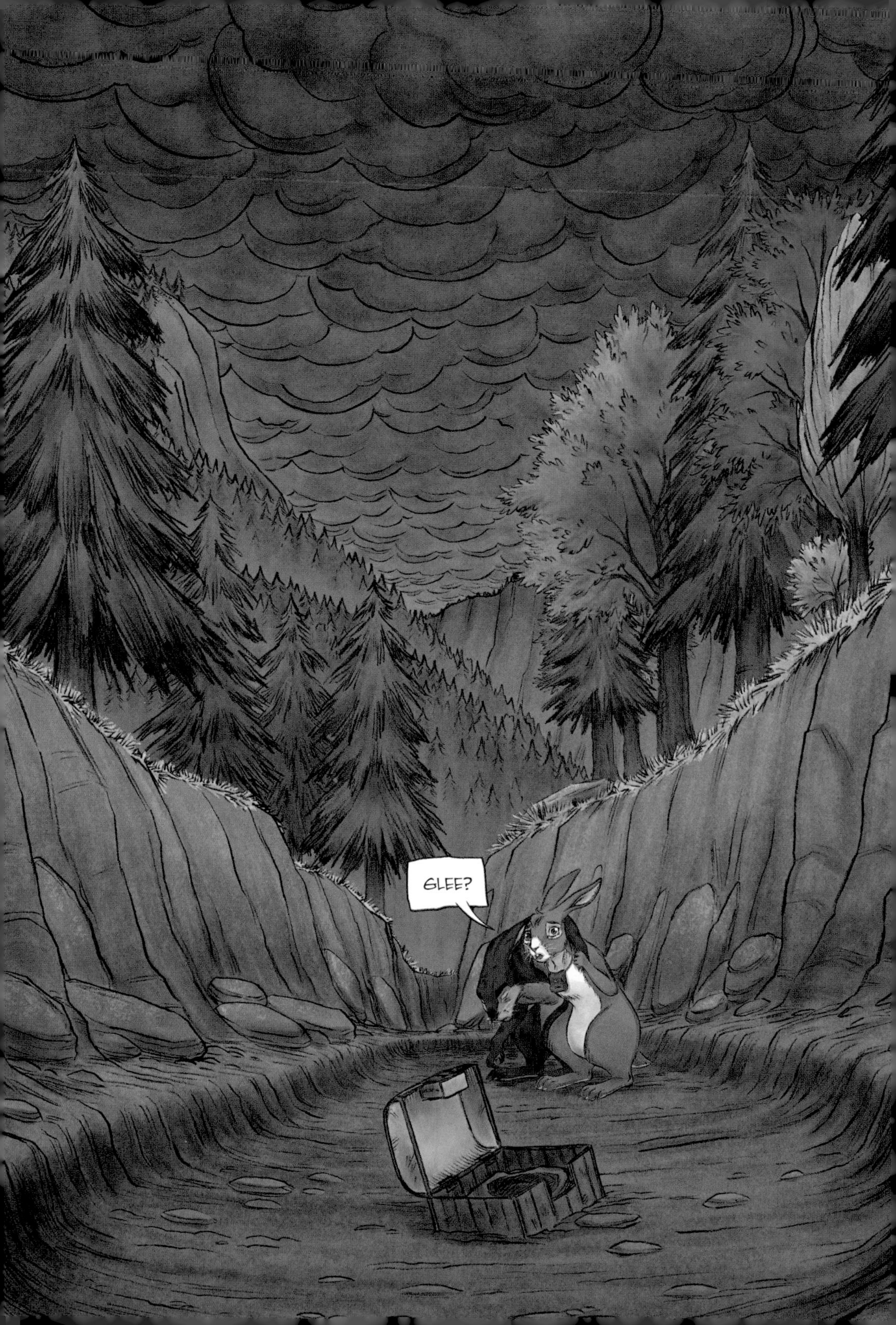
GLEE?

19.

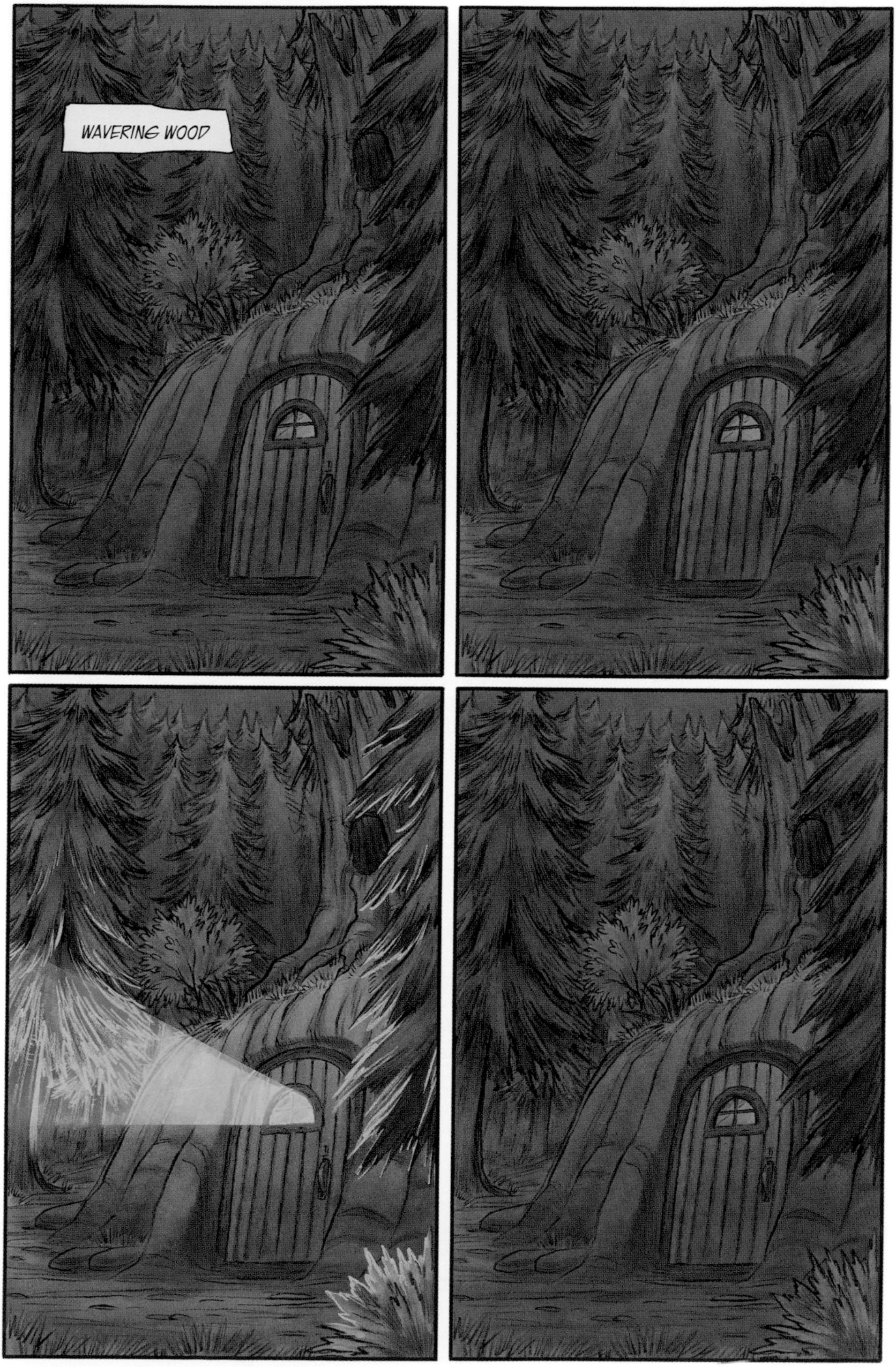
WAVERING WOOD

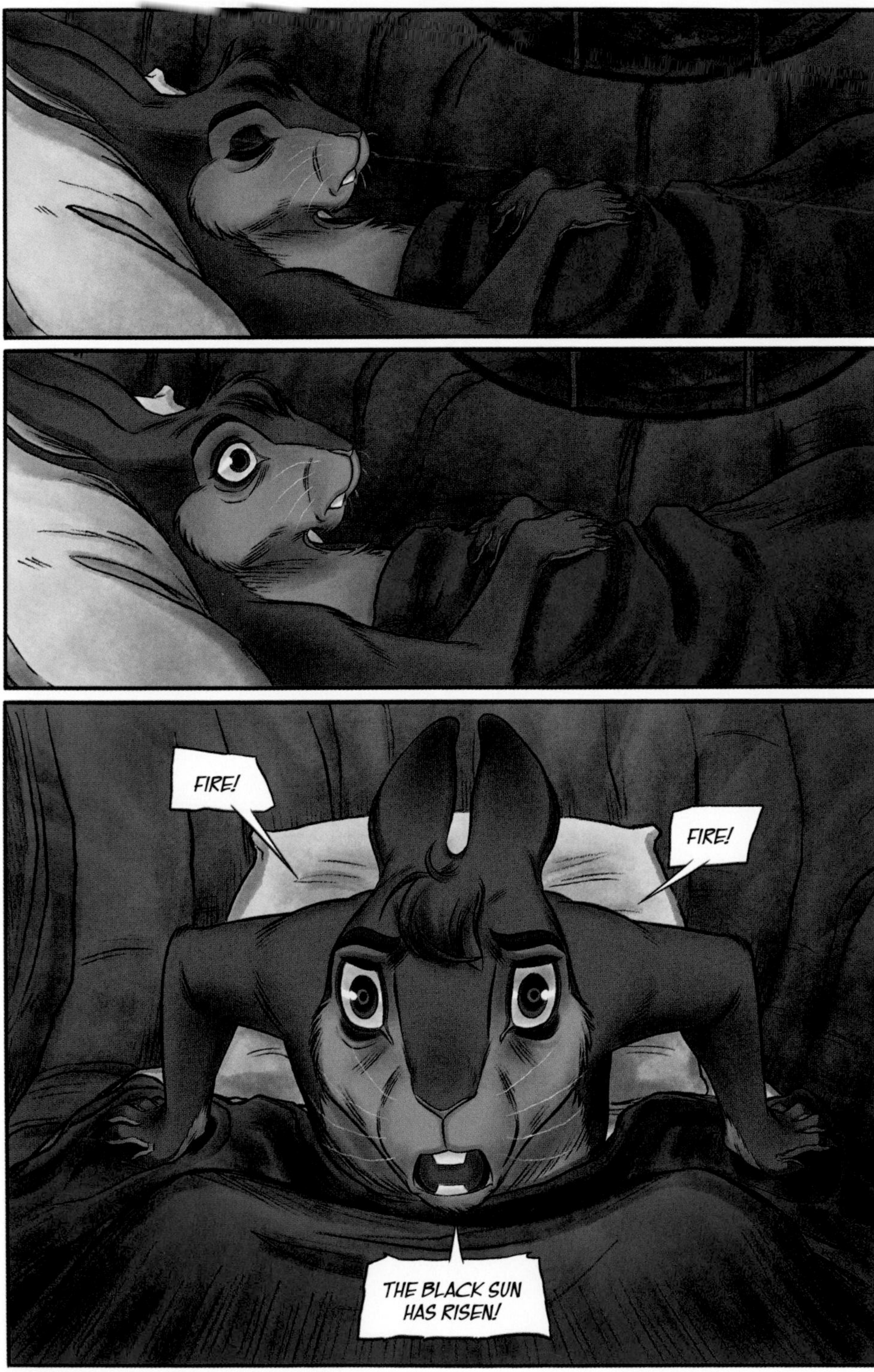
FIRE!
FIRE!
THE BLACK SUN HAS RISEN!

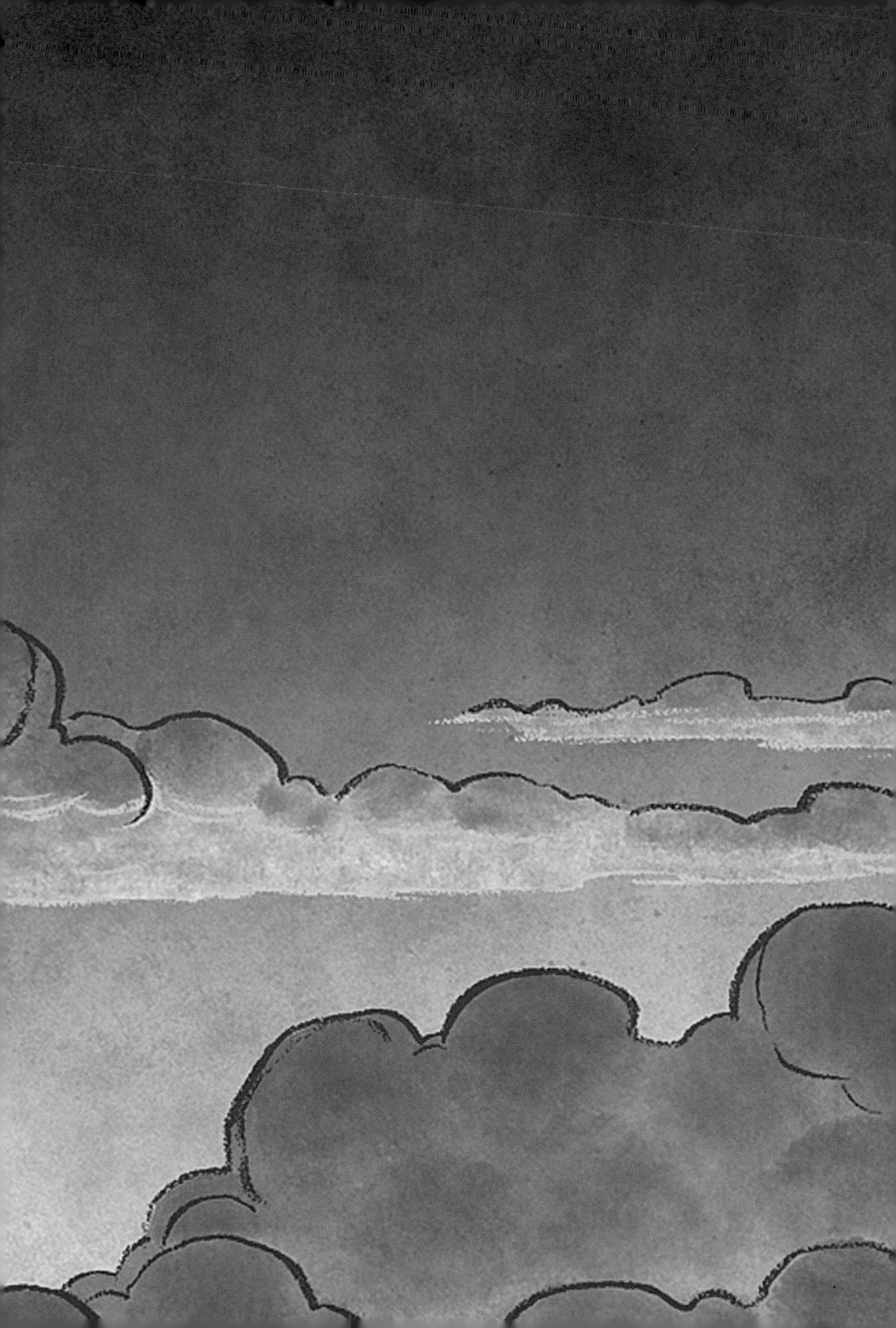

IV

"*THE FIRE, THE SECRET, THE WIND*"

20. _____

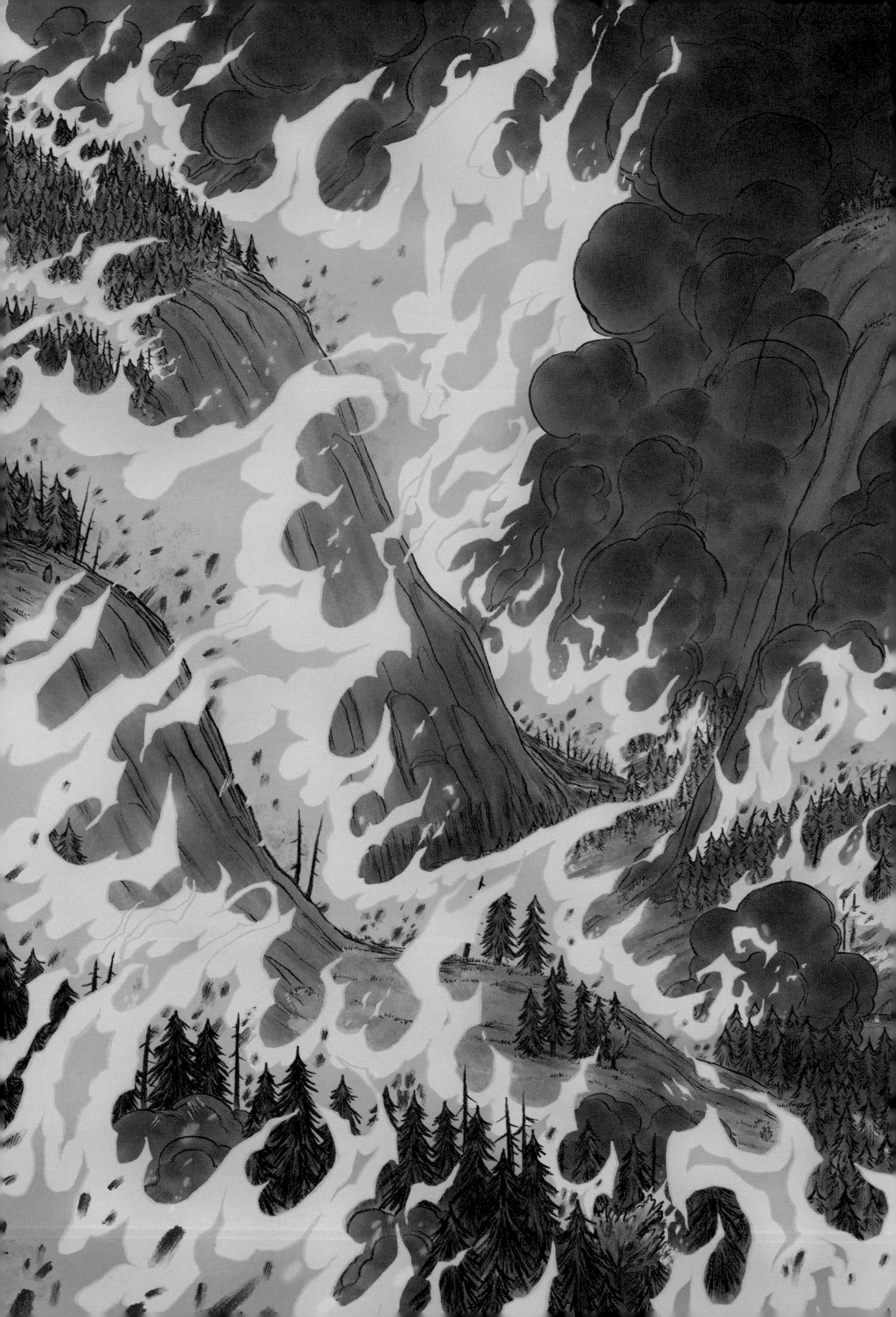

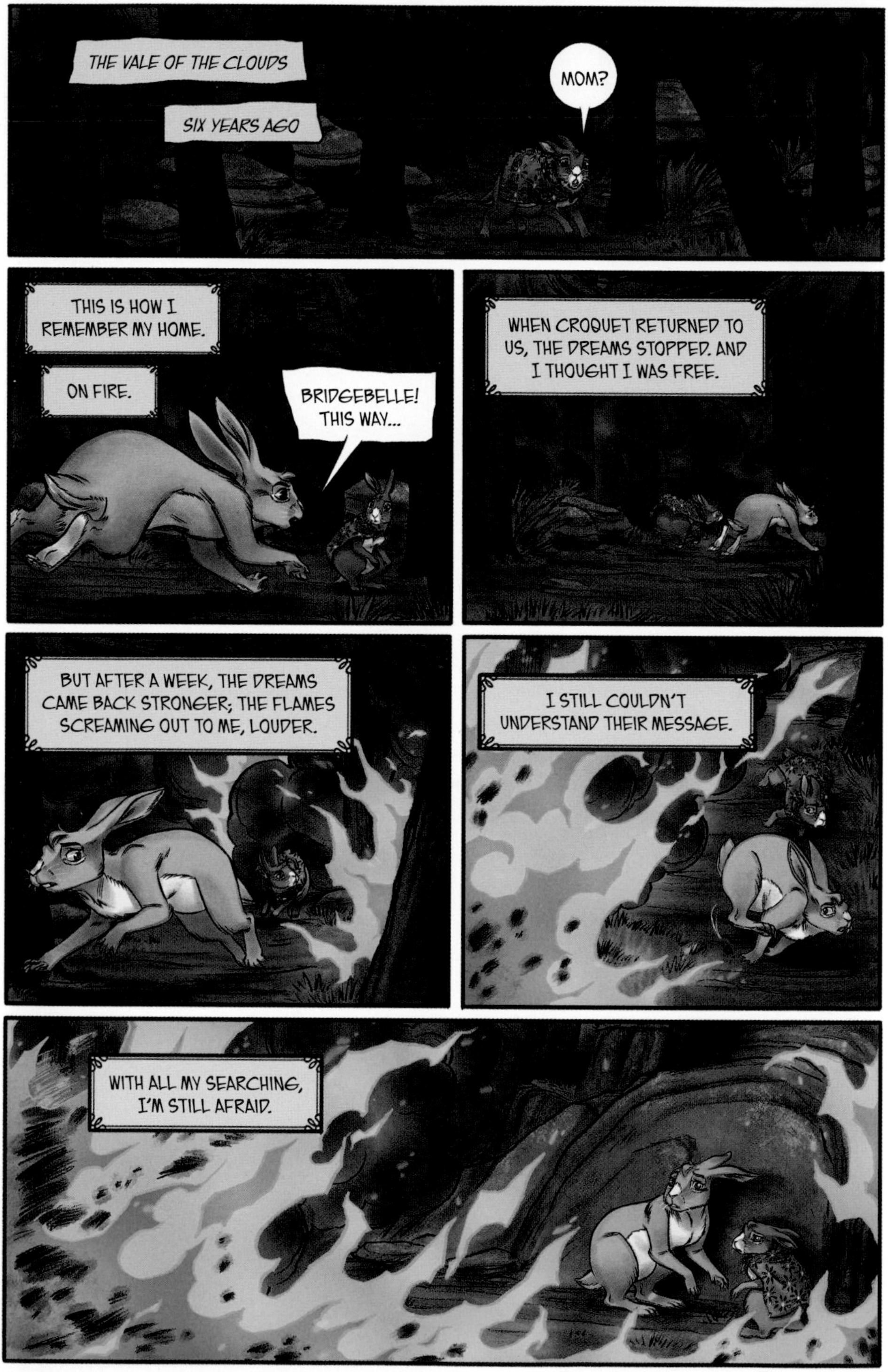
THE VALE OF THE CLOUDS
SIX YEARS AGO
MOM?
THIS IS HOW I REMEMBER MY HOME.
ON FIRE.
BRIDGEBELLE! THIS WAY...
WHEN CROQUET RETURNED TO US, THE DREAMS STOPPED. AND I THOUGHT I WAS FREE.
BUT AFTER A WEEK, THE DREAMS CAME BACK STRONGER; THE FLAMES SCREAMING OUT TO ME, LOUDER.
I STILL COULDN'T UNDERSTAND THEIR MESSAGE.
WITH ALL MY SEARCHING, I'M STILL AFRAID.

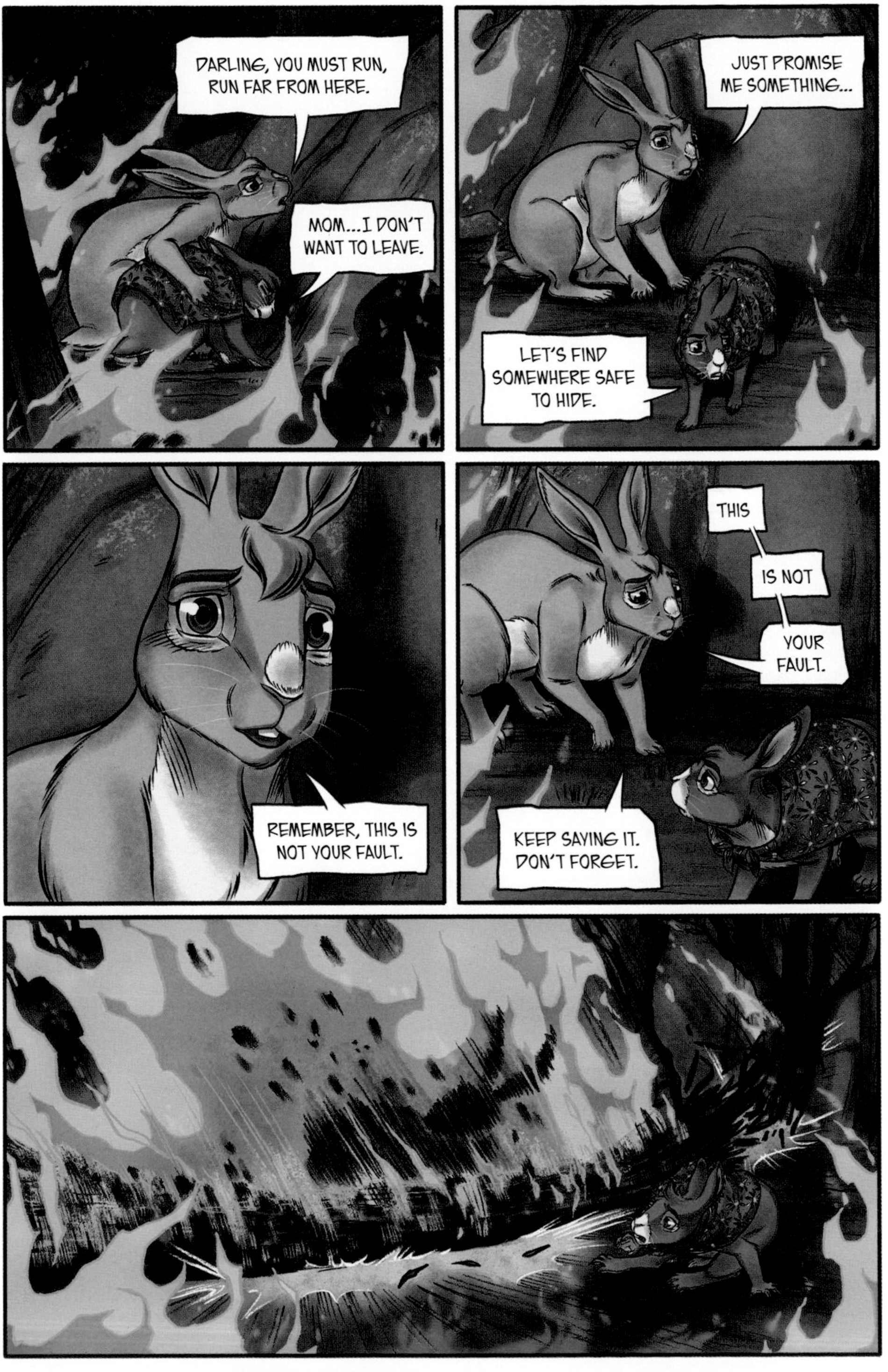
DARLING, YOU MUST RUN, RUN FAR FROM HERE.
MOM...I DON'T WANT TO LEAVE.
JUST PROMISE ME SOMETHING...
LET'S FIND SOMEWHERE SAFE TO HIDE.
REMEMBER, THIS IS NOT YOUR FAULT.
THIS
IS NOT
YOUR FAULT.
KEEP SAYING IT. DON'T FORGET.

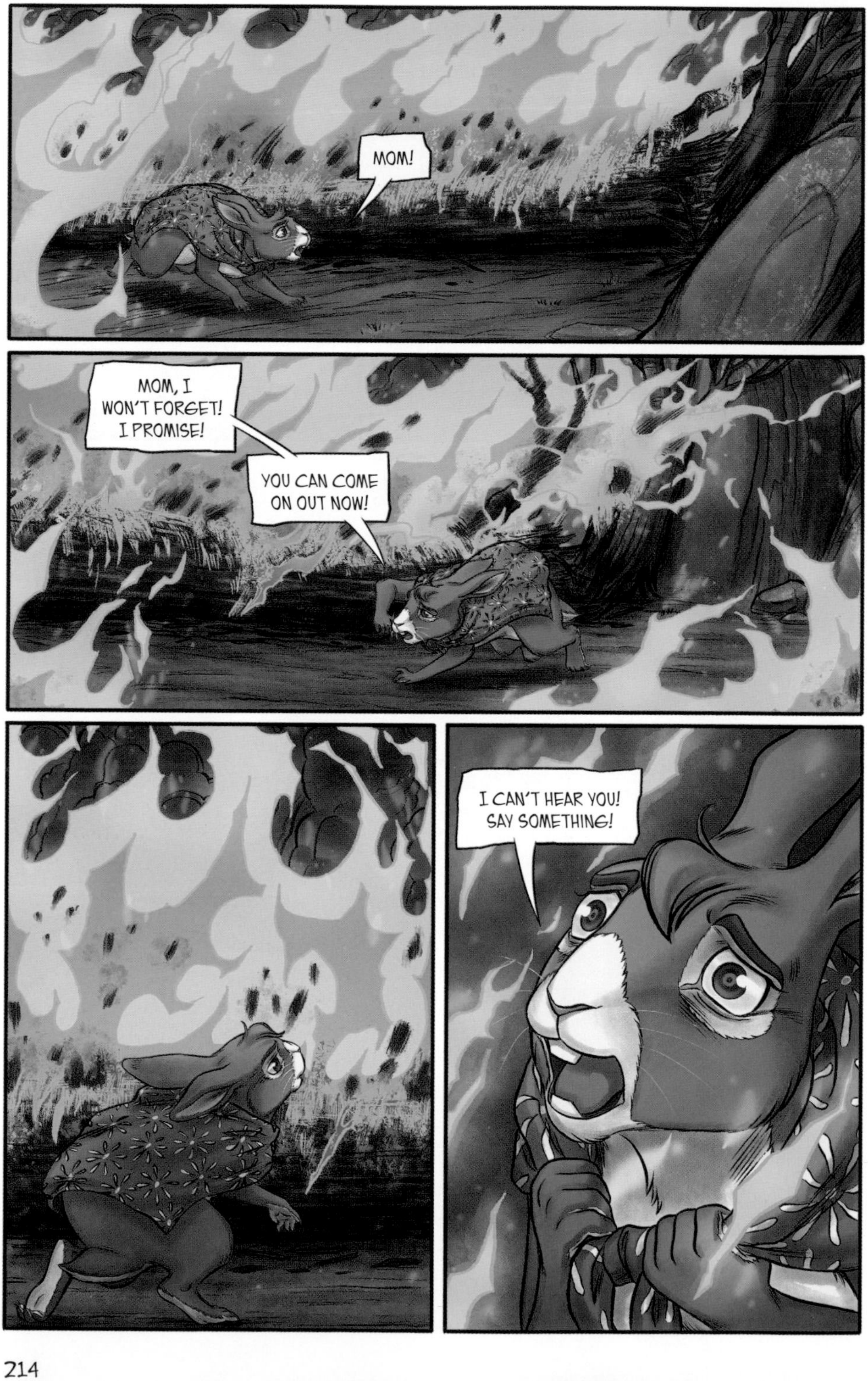
MOM!
MOM, I WON'T FORGET! I PROMISE!
YOU CAN COME ON OUT NOW!
I CAN'T HEAR YOU! SAY SOMETHING!

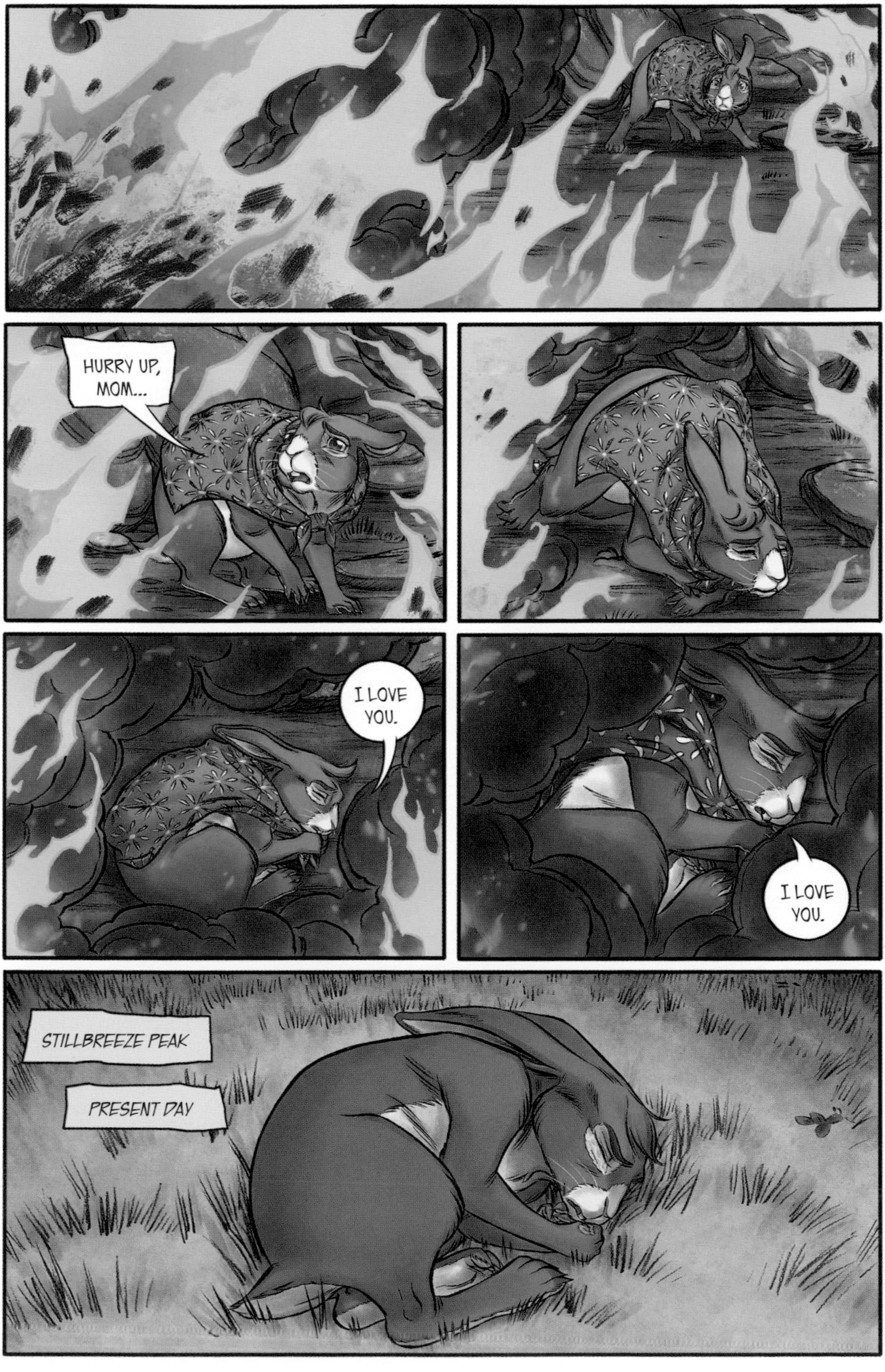
HURRY UP, MOM...
I LOVE YOU.
I LOVE YOU.
STILLBREEZE PEAK
PRESENT DAY

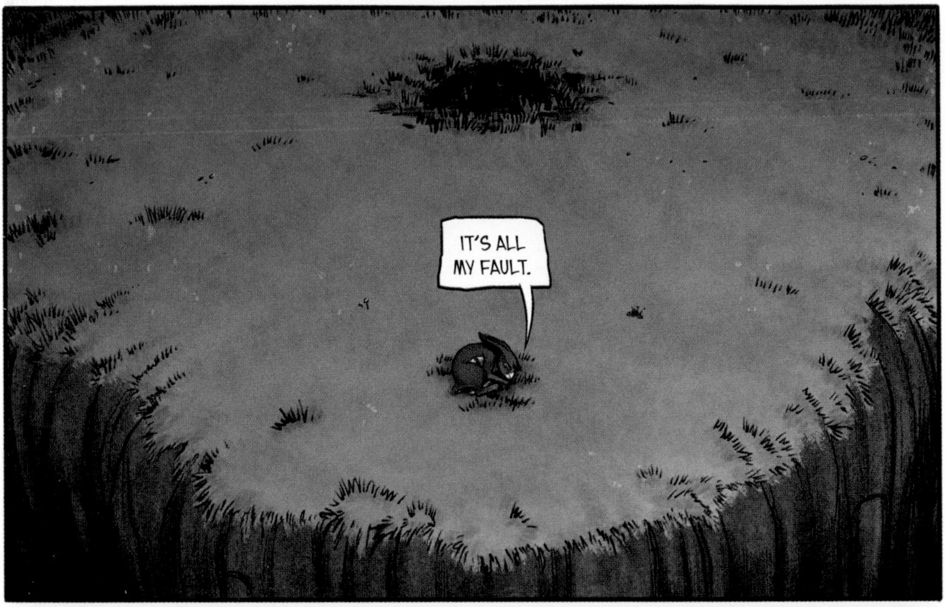
IT'S ALL MY FAULT.

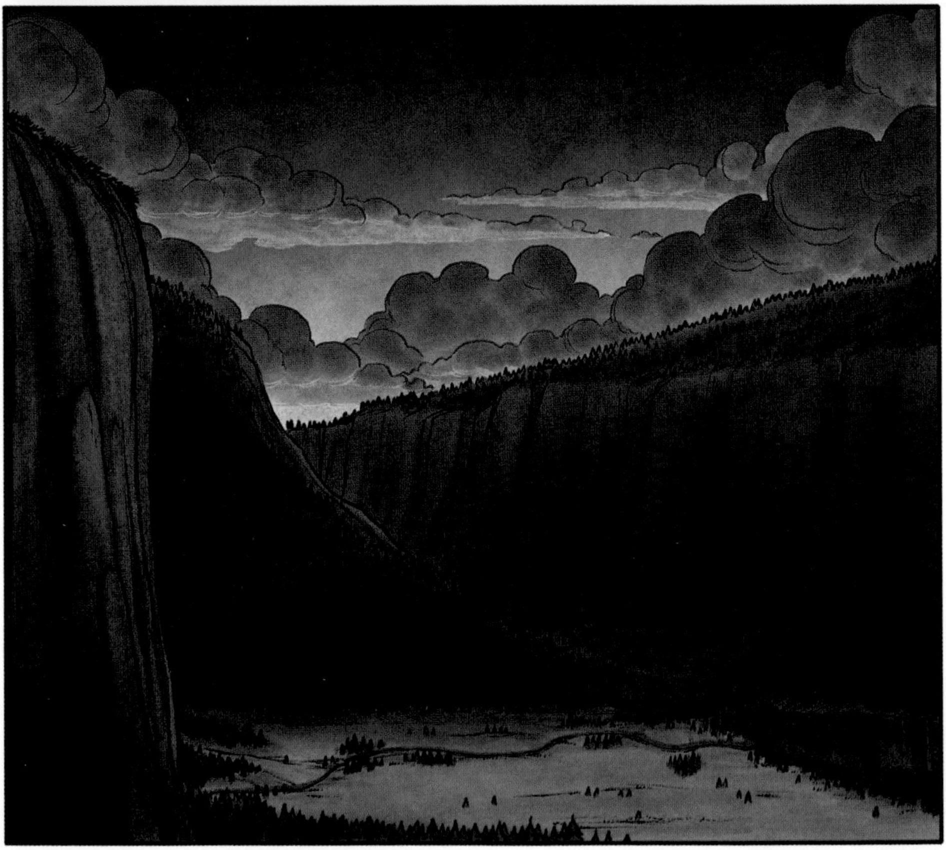

21.

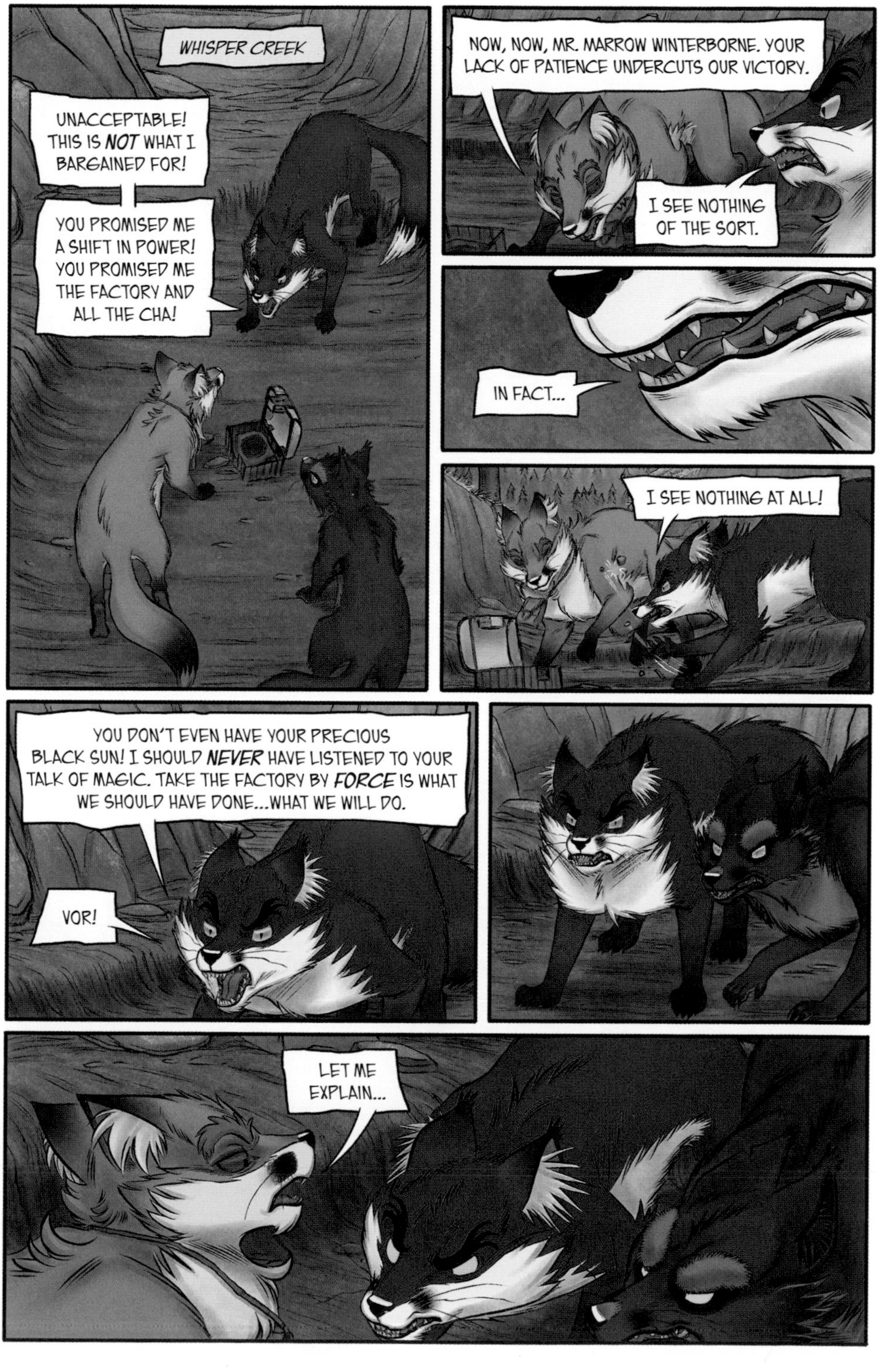
WHISPER CREEK
UNACCEPTABLE! THIS IS NOT WHAT I BARGAINED FOR!
YOU PROMISED ME A SHIFT IN POWER! YOU PROMISED ME THE FACTORY AND ALL THE CHA!
NOW, NOW, MR. MARROW WINTERBORNE. YOUR LACK OF PATIENCE UNDERCUTS OUR VICTORY.
I SEE NOTHING OF THE SORT.
IN FACT...
I SEE NOTHING AT ALL!
YOU DON'T EVEN HAVE YOUR PRECIOUS BLACK SUN! I SHOULD NEVER HAVE LISTENED TO YOUR TALK OF MAGIC. TAKE THE FACTORY BY FORCE IS WHAT WE SHOULD HAVE DONE...WHAT WE WILL DO.
VOR!
LET ME EXPLAIN...

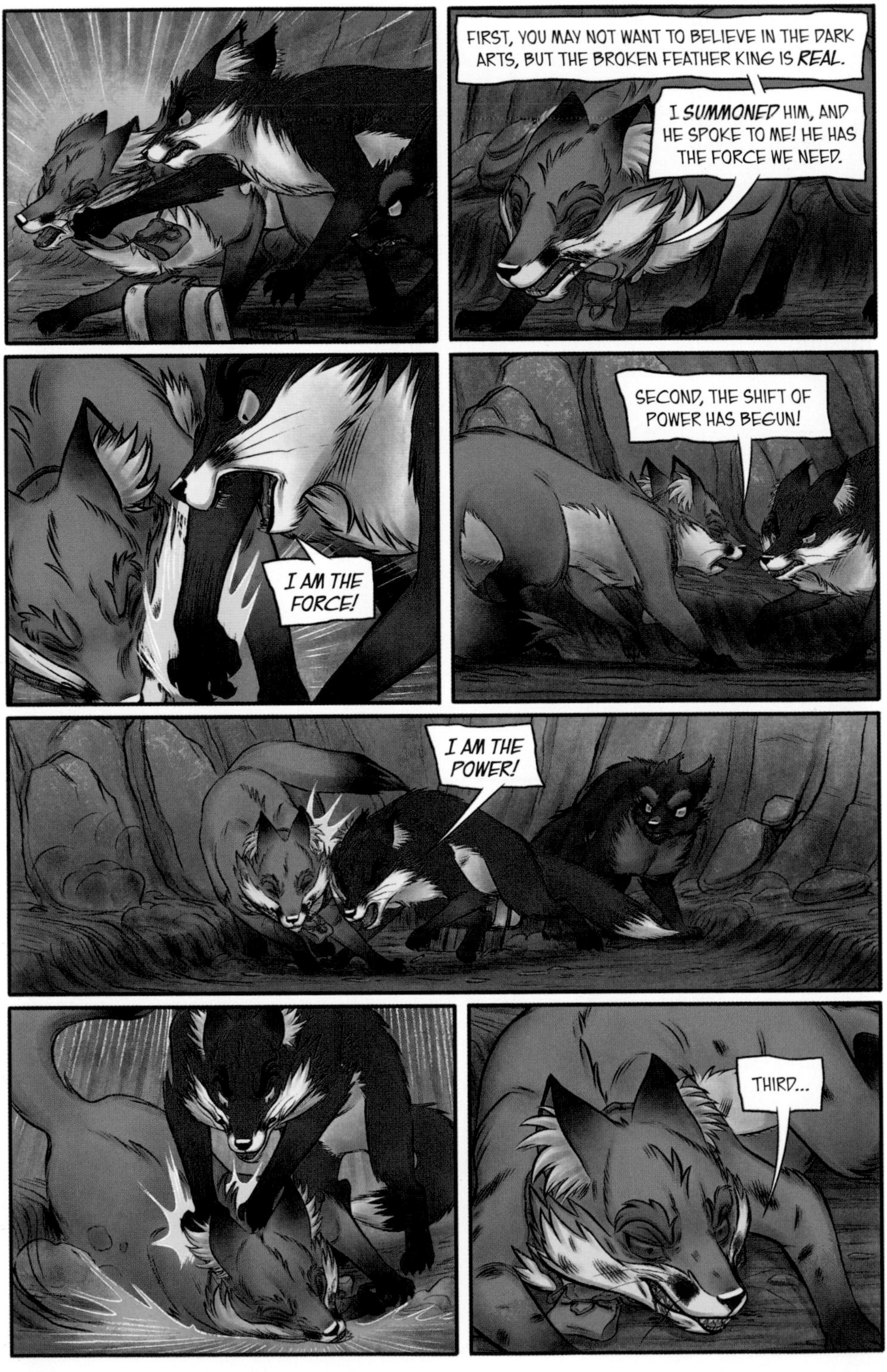
FIRST, YOU MAY NOT WANT TO BELIEVE IN THE DARK ARTS, BUT THE BROKEN FEATHER KING IS *REAL.*
I *SUMMONED* HIM, AND HE SPOKE TO ME! HE HAS THE FORCE WE NEED.
I AM THE FORCE!
SECOND, THE SHIFT OF POWER HAS BEGUN!
I AM THE POWER!
THIRD...

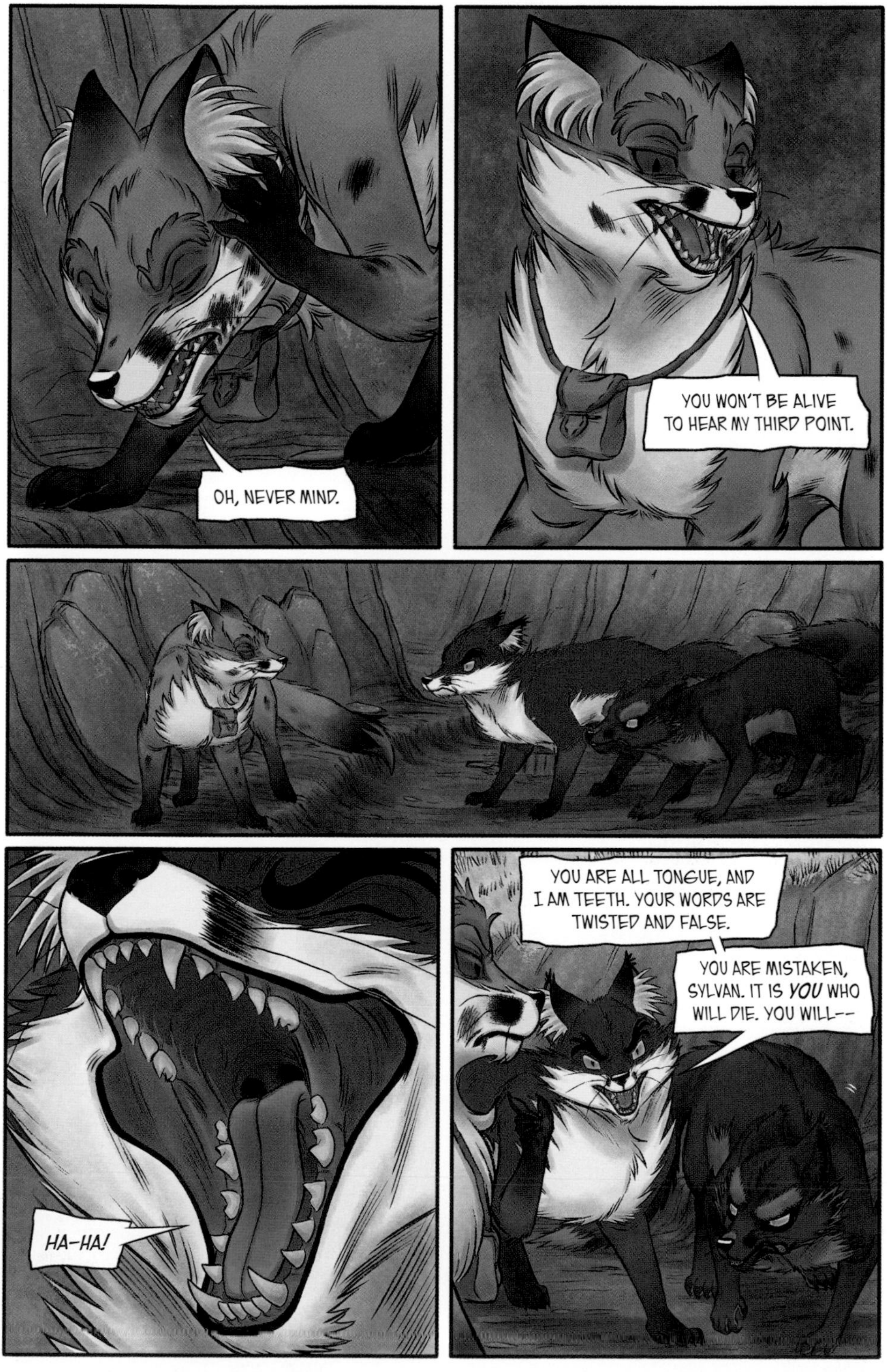
OH, NEVER MIND.
YOU WON'T BE ALIVE TO HEAR MY THIRD POINT.
HA-HA!
YOU ARE ALL TONGUE, AND I AM TEETH. YOUR WORDS ARE TWISTED AND FALSE.
YOU ARE MISTAKEN, SYLVAN. IT IS *YOU* WHO WILL DIE. YOU WILL--

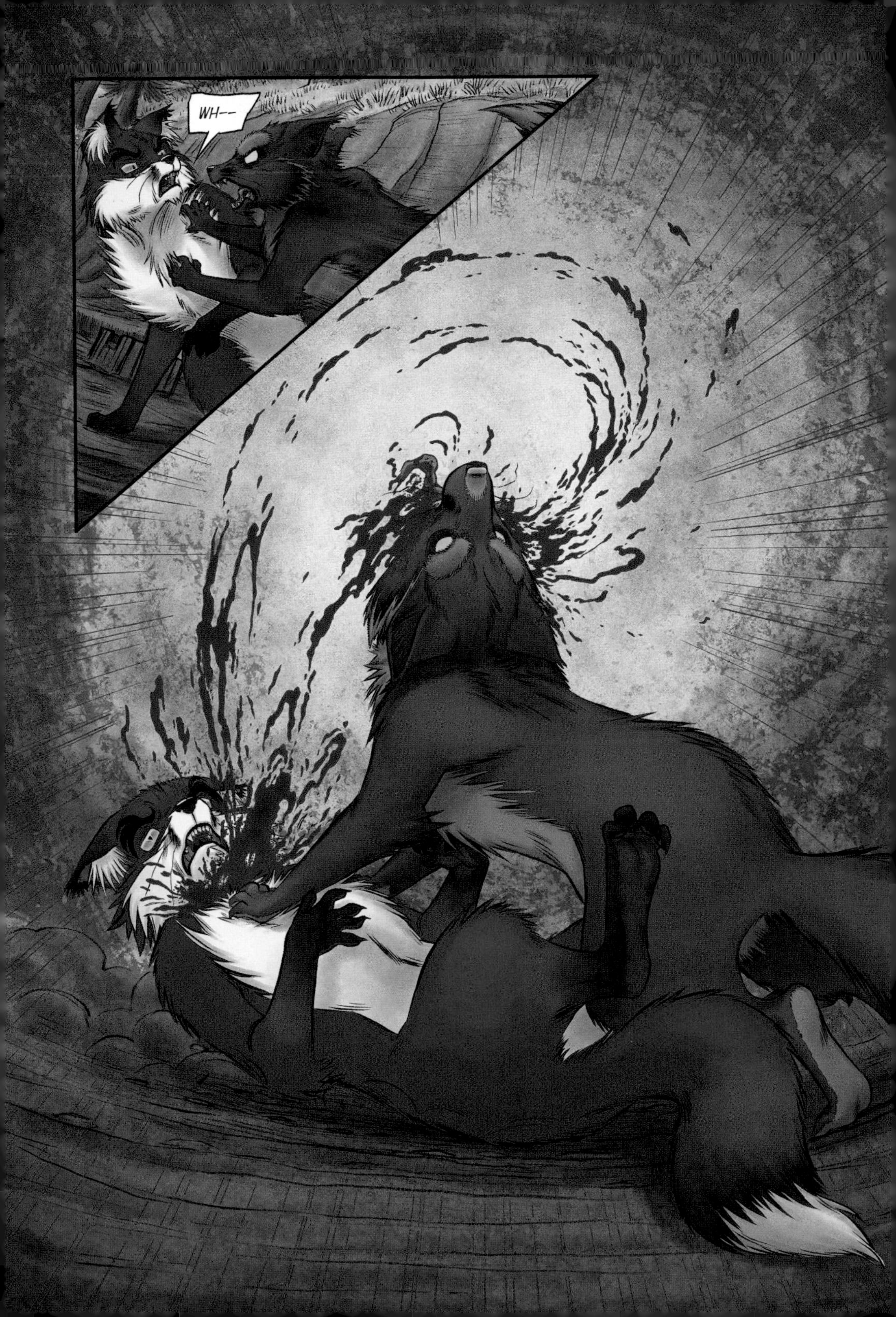
WH--

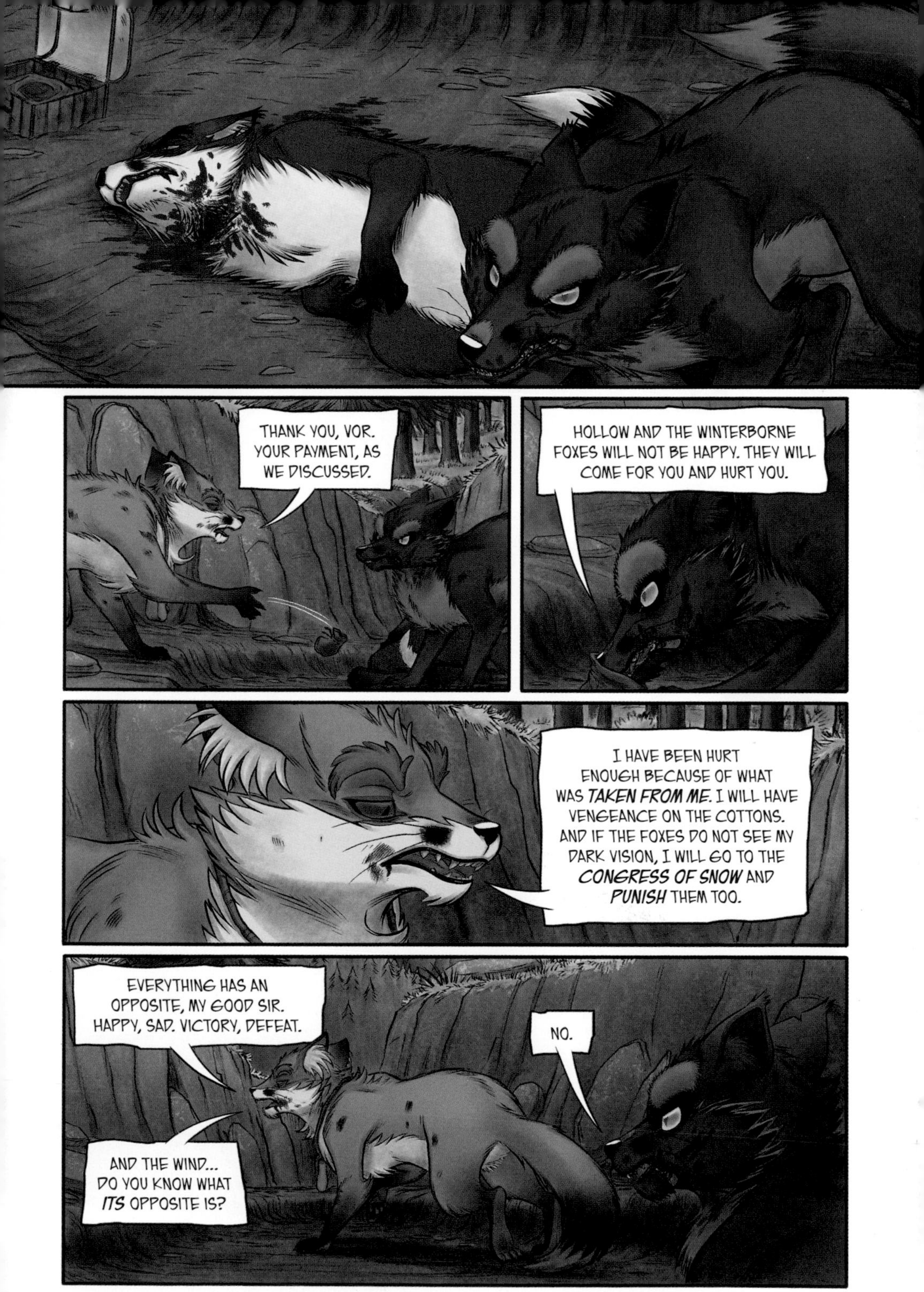
THANK YOU, VOR. YOUR PAYMENT, AS WE DISCUSSED.
HOLLOW AND THE WINTERBORNE FOXES WILL NOT BE HAPPY. THEY WILL COME FOR YOU AND HURT YOU.
I HAVE BEEN HURT ENOUGH BECAUSE OF WHAT WAS ***TAKEN FROM ME***. I WILL HAVE VENGEANCE ON THE COTTONS. AND IF THE FOXES DO NOT SEE MY DARK VISION, I WILL GO TO THE ***CONGRESS OF SNOW*** AND ***PUNISH*** THEM TOO.
EVERYTHING HAS AN OPPOSITE, MY GOOD SIR. HAPPY, SAD. VICTORY, DEFEAT.
NO.
AND THE WIND... DO YOU KNOW WHAT *ITS* OPPOSITE IS?

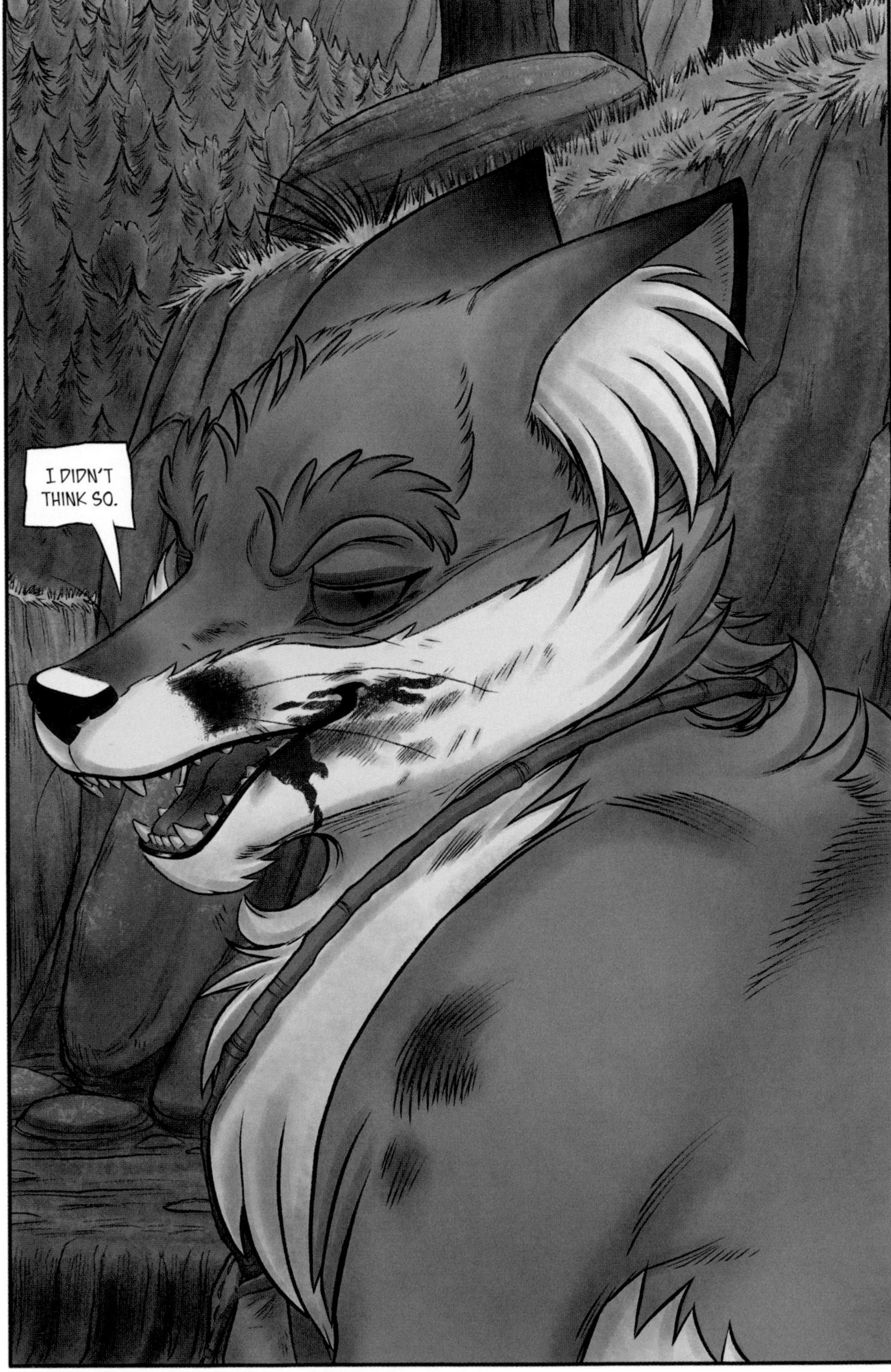
I DIDN'T THINK SO.

22.

THE GARDEN

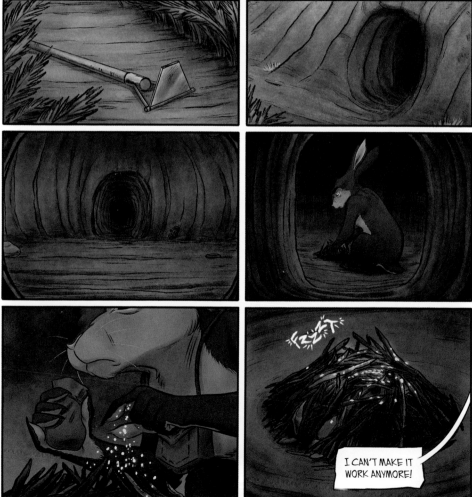

I CAN'T MAKE IT WORK ANYMORE!

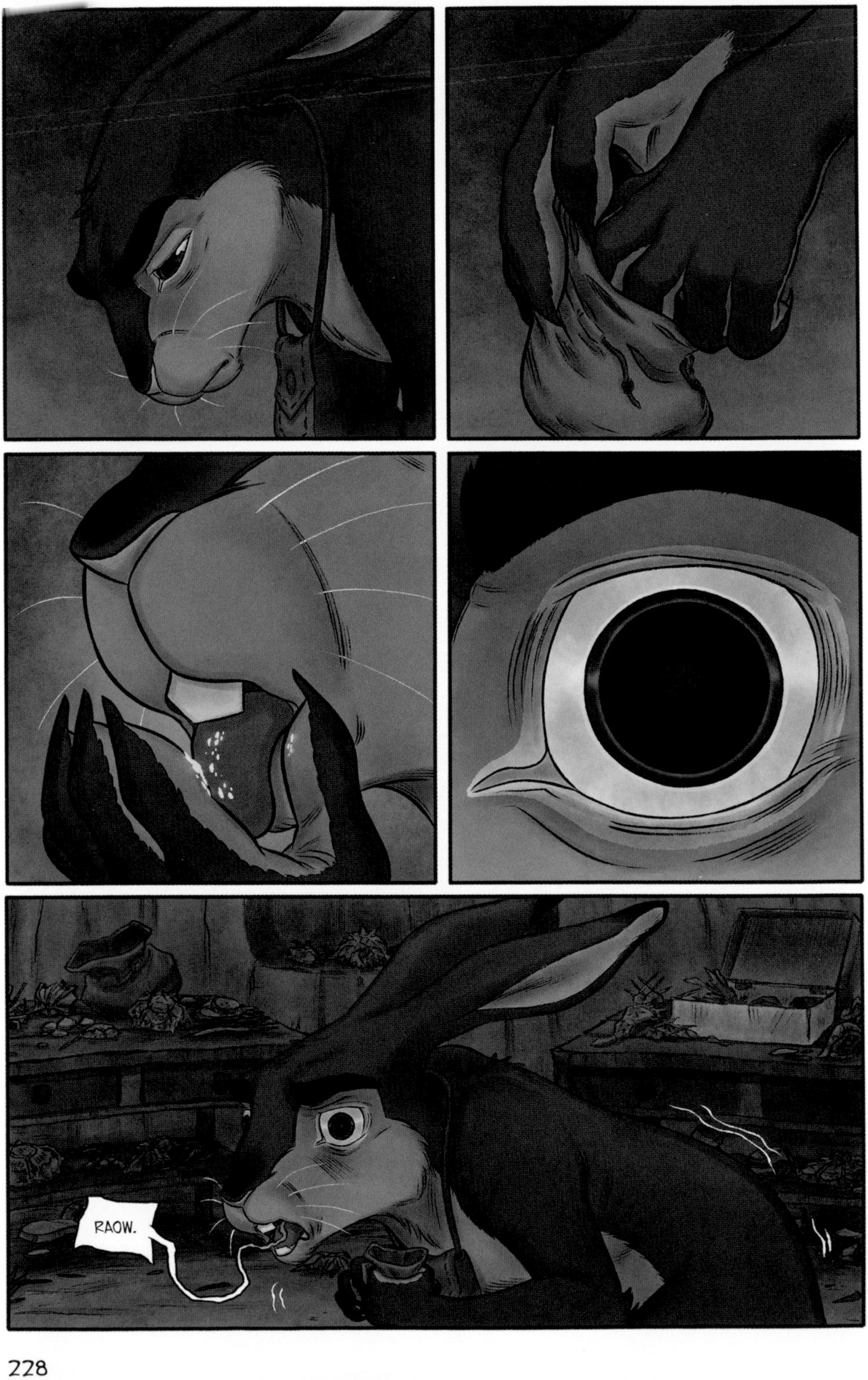
RAOW.

23.

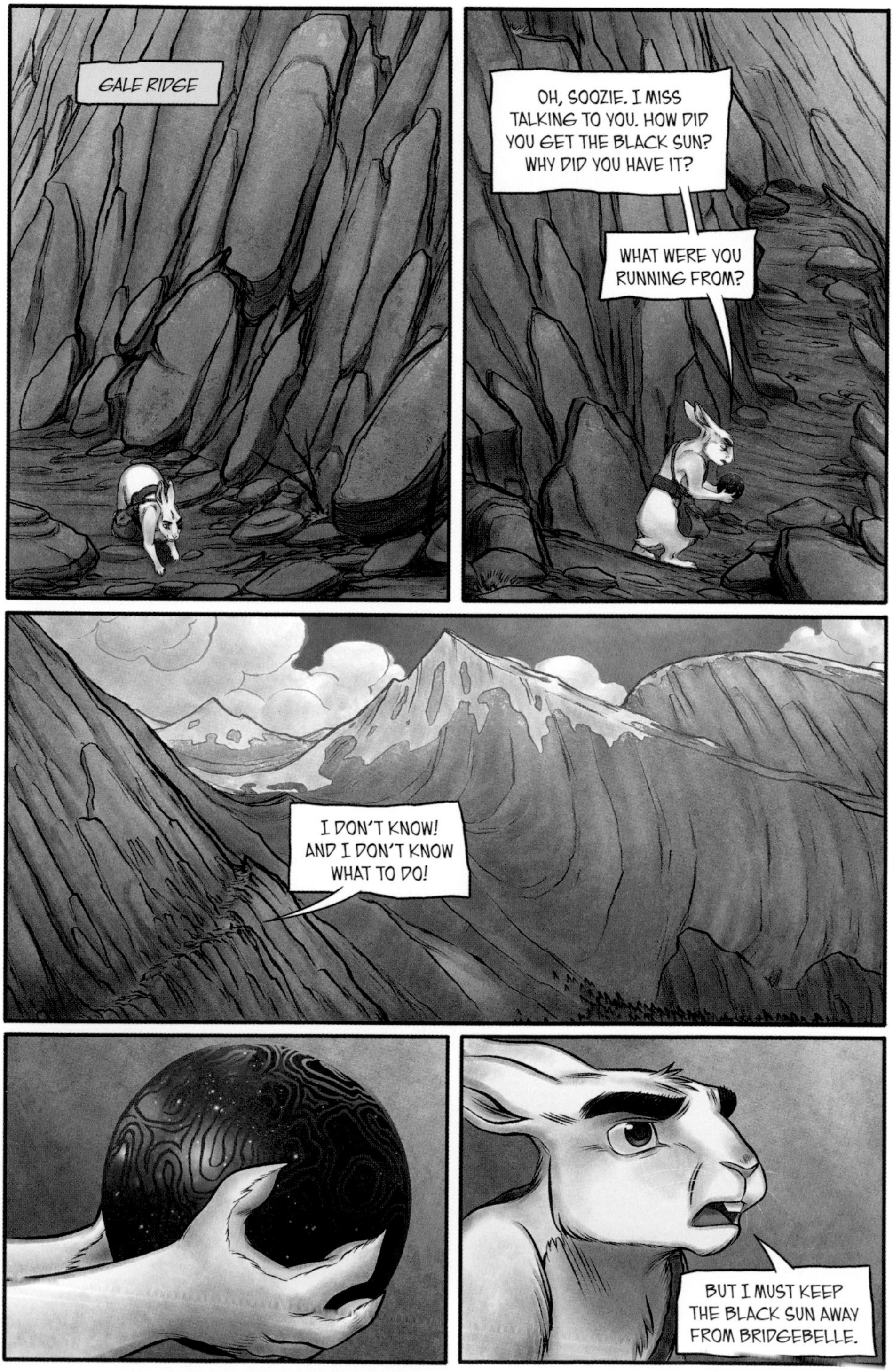
GALE RIDGE
OH, SOOZIE. I MISS TALKING TO YOU. HOW DID YOU GET THE BLACK SUN? WHY DID YOU HAVE IT?
WHAT WERE YOU RUNNING FROM?
I DON'T KNOW! AND I DON'T KNOW WHAT TO DO!
BUT I MUST KEEP THE BLACK SUN AWAY FROM BRIDGEBELLE.

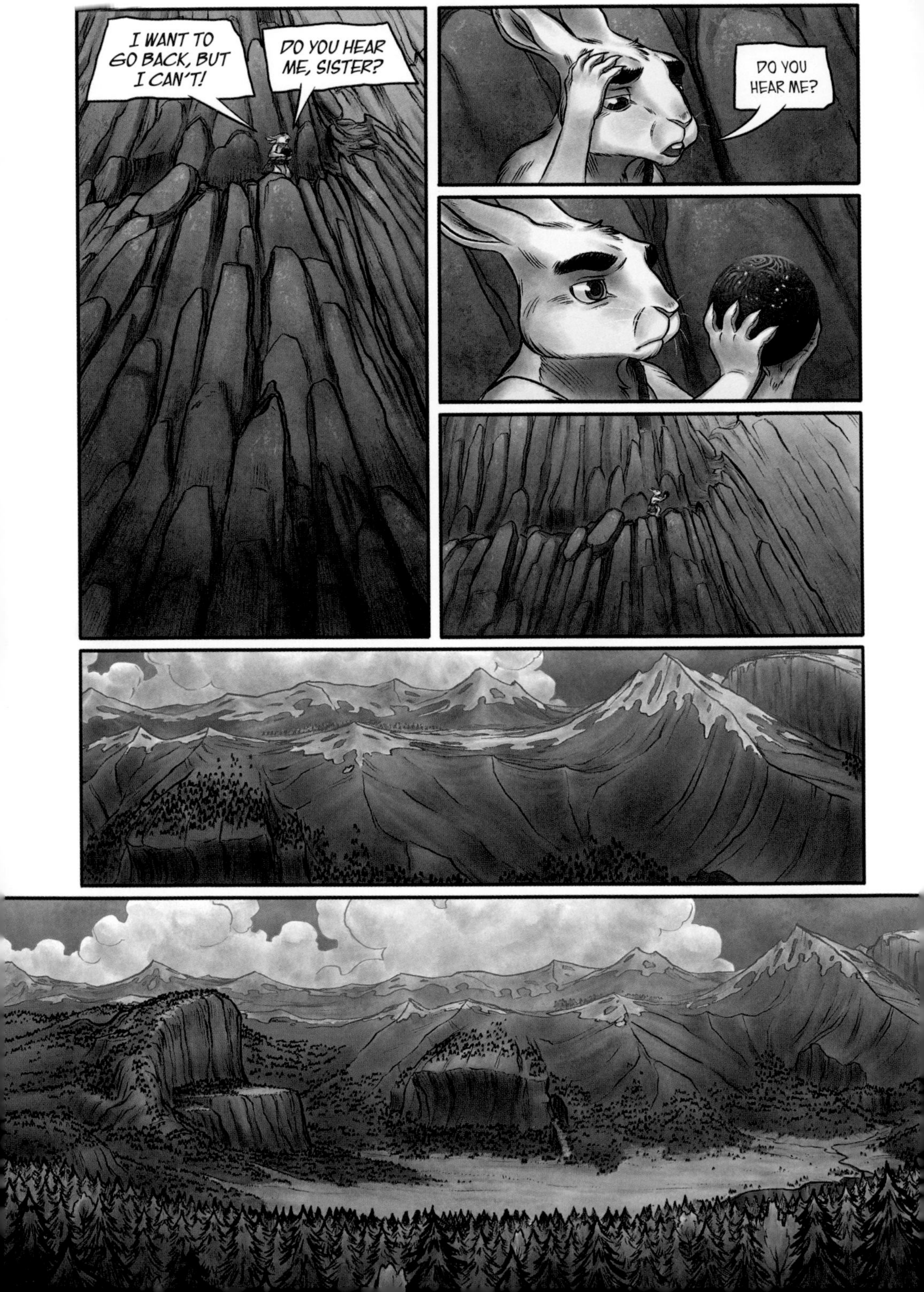
I WANT TO GO BACK, BUT I CAN'T!
DO YOU HEAR ME, SISTER?
DO YOU HEAR ME?

24.

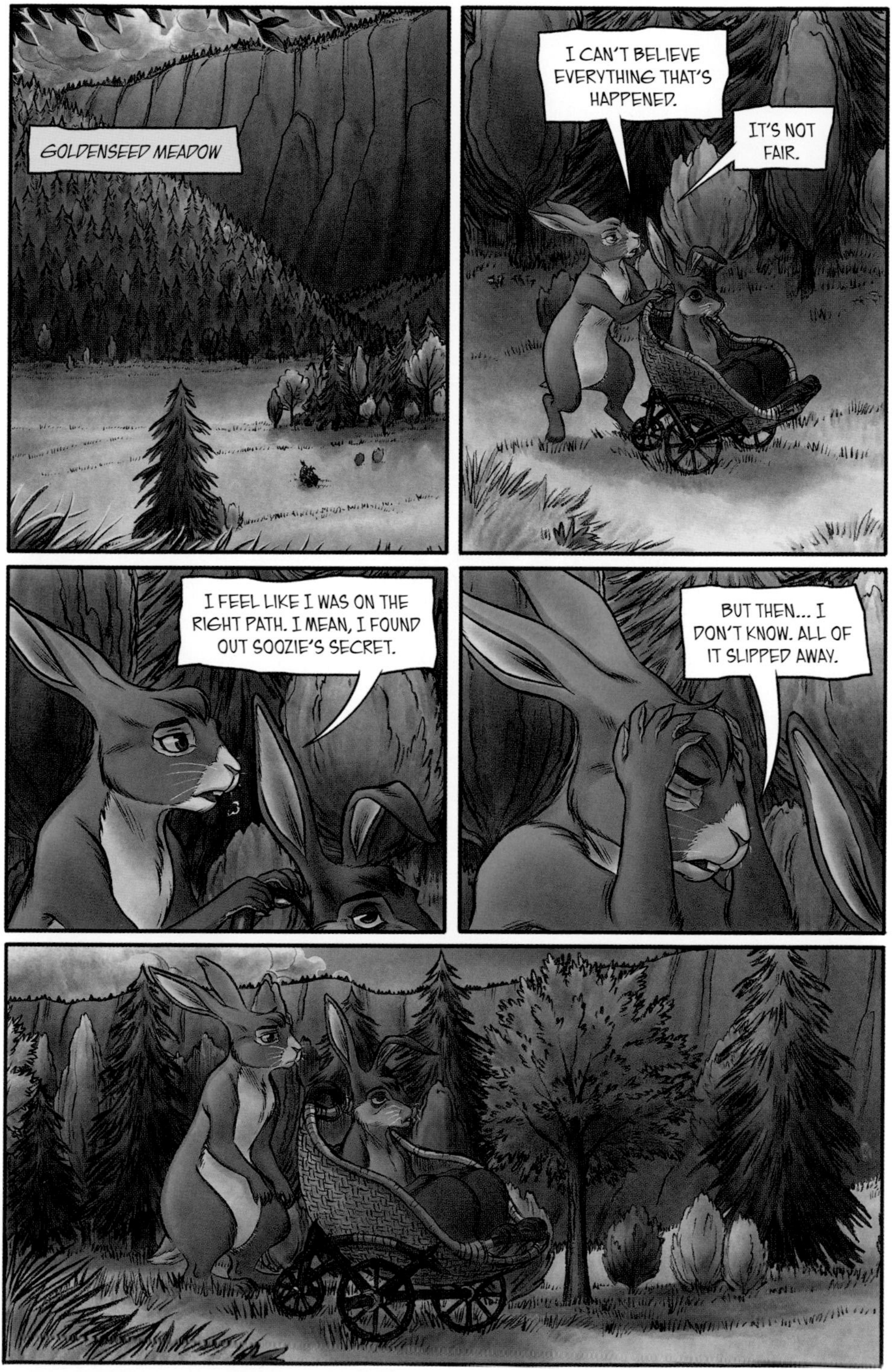
GOLDENSEED MEADOW
I CAN'T BELIEVE EVERYTHING THAT'S HAPPENED.
IT'S NOT FAIR.
I FEEL LIKE I WAS ON THE RIGHT PATH. I MEAN, I FOUND OUT SOOZIE'S SECRET.
BUT THEN... I DON'T KNOW. ALL OF IT SLIPPED AWAY.

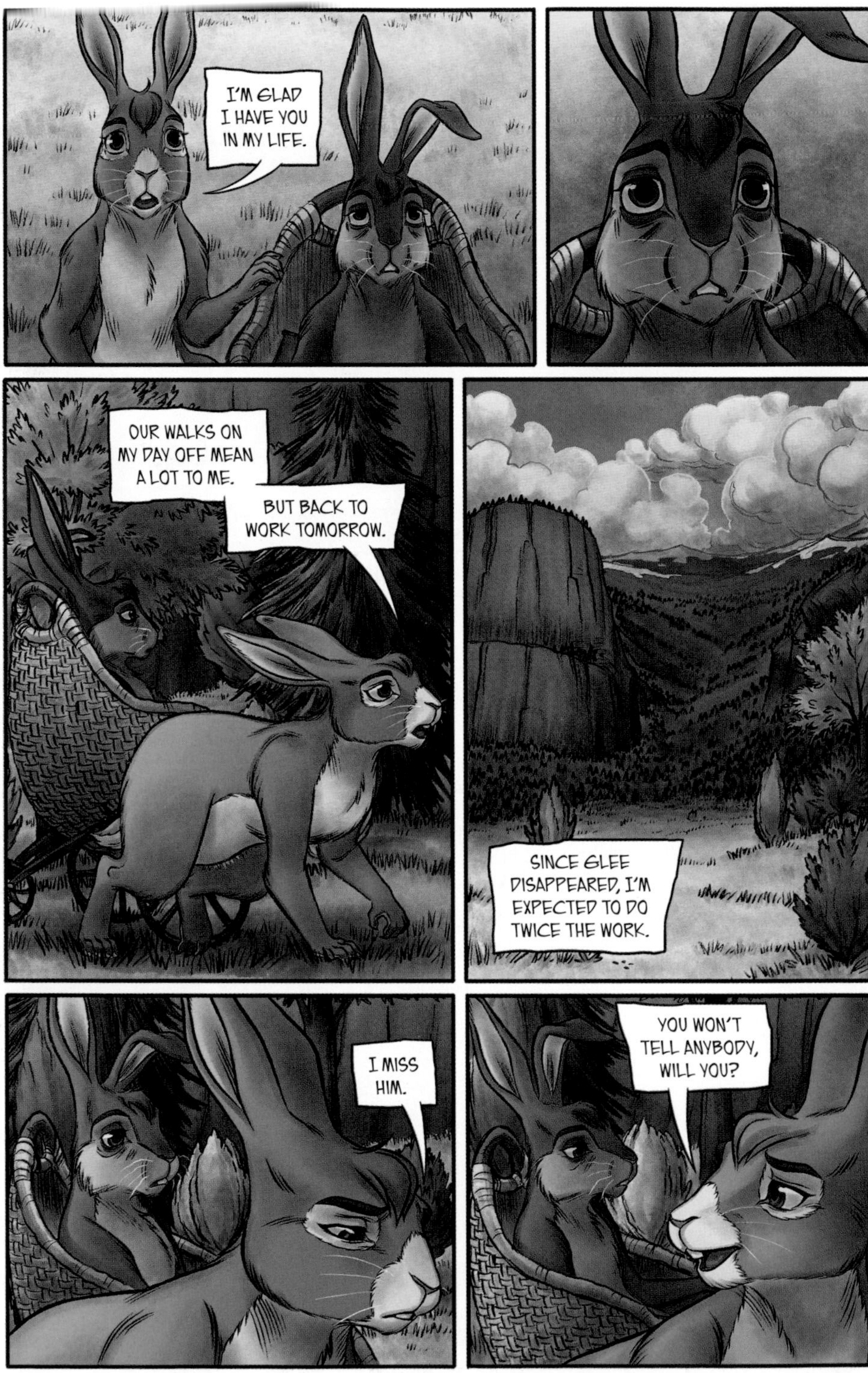
I'M GLAD I HAVE YOU IN MY LIFE.
OUR WALKS ON MY DAY OFF MEAN A LOT TO ME.
BUT BACK TO WORK TOMORROW.
SINCE GLEE DISAPPEARED, I'M EXPECTED TO DO TWICE THE WORK.
I MISS HIM.
YOU WON'T TELL ANYBODY, WILL YOU?

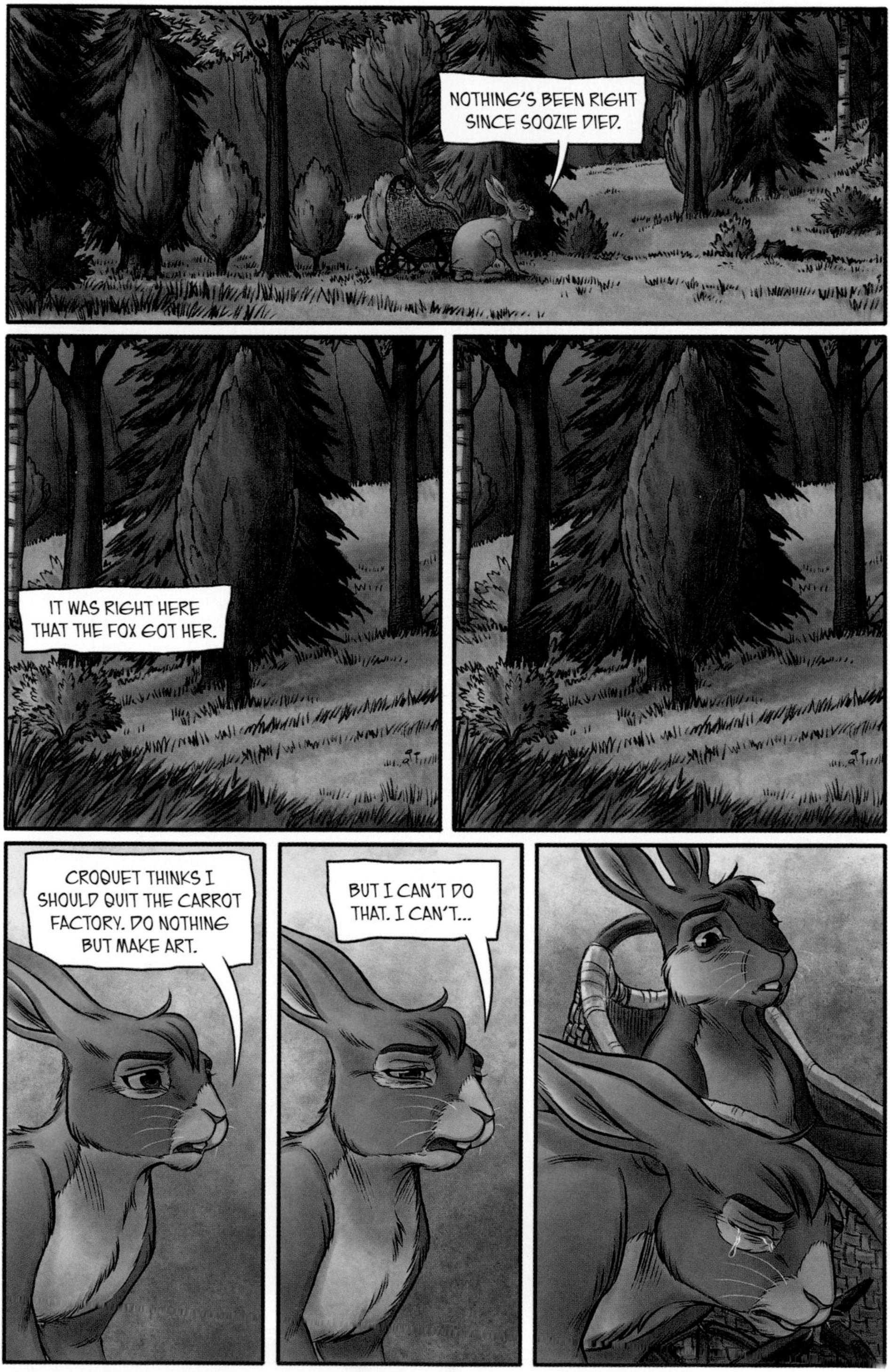
NOTHING'S BEEN RIGHT SINCE SOOZIE DIED.
IT WAS RIGHT HERE THAT THE FOX GOT HER.
CROQUET THINKS I SHOULD QUIT THE CARROT FACTORY. DO NOTHING BUT MAKE ART.
BUT I CAN'T DO THAT. I CAN'T...

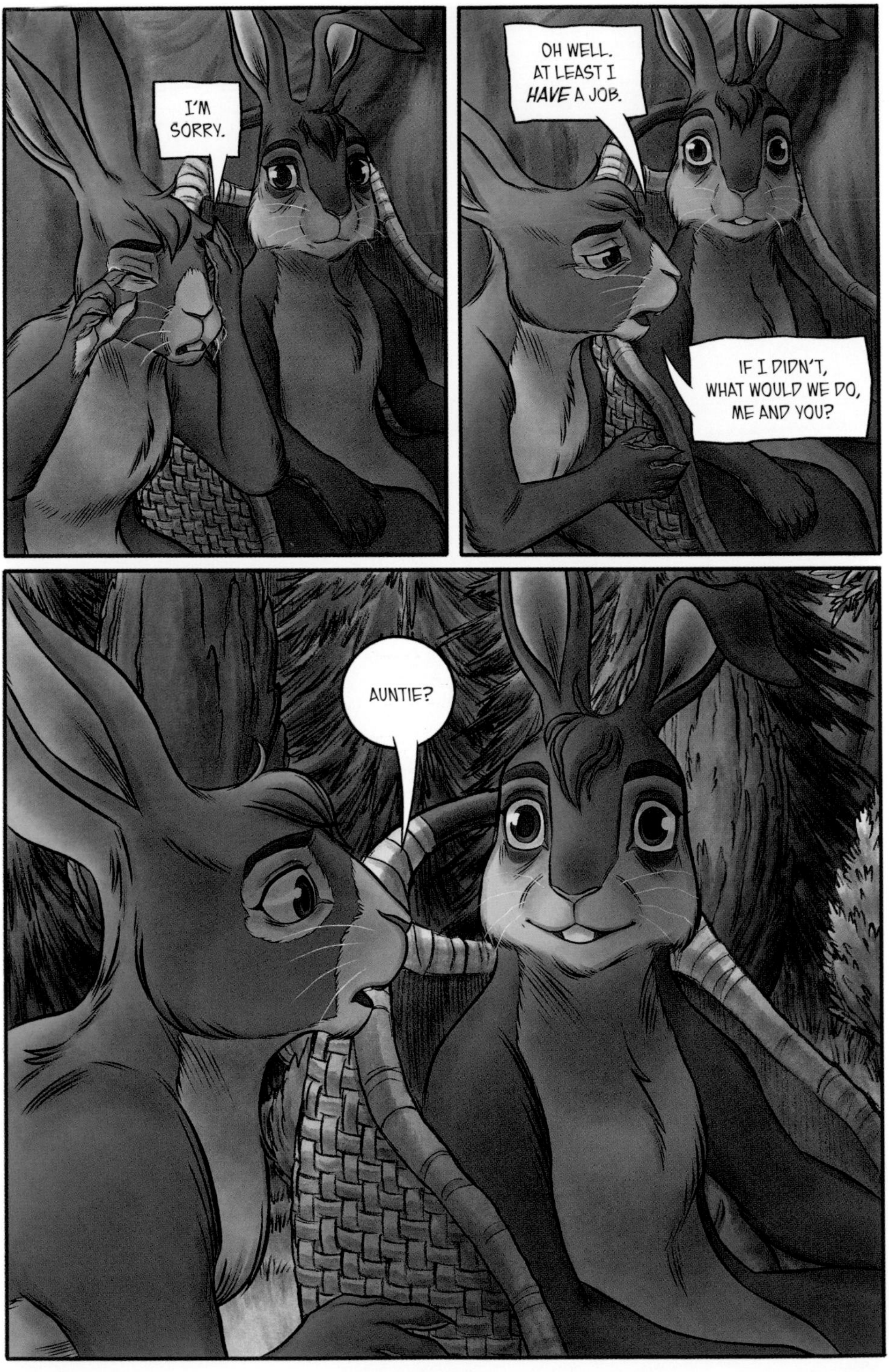

I'M SORRY.
OH WELL. AT LEAST I *HAVE* A JOB.
IF I DIDN'T, WHAT WOULD WE DO, ME AND YOU?
AUNTIE?

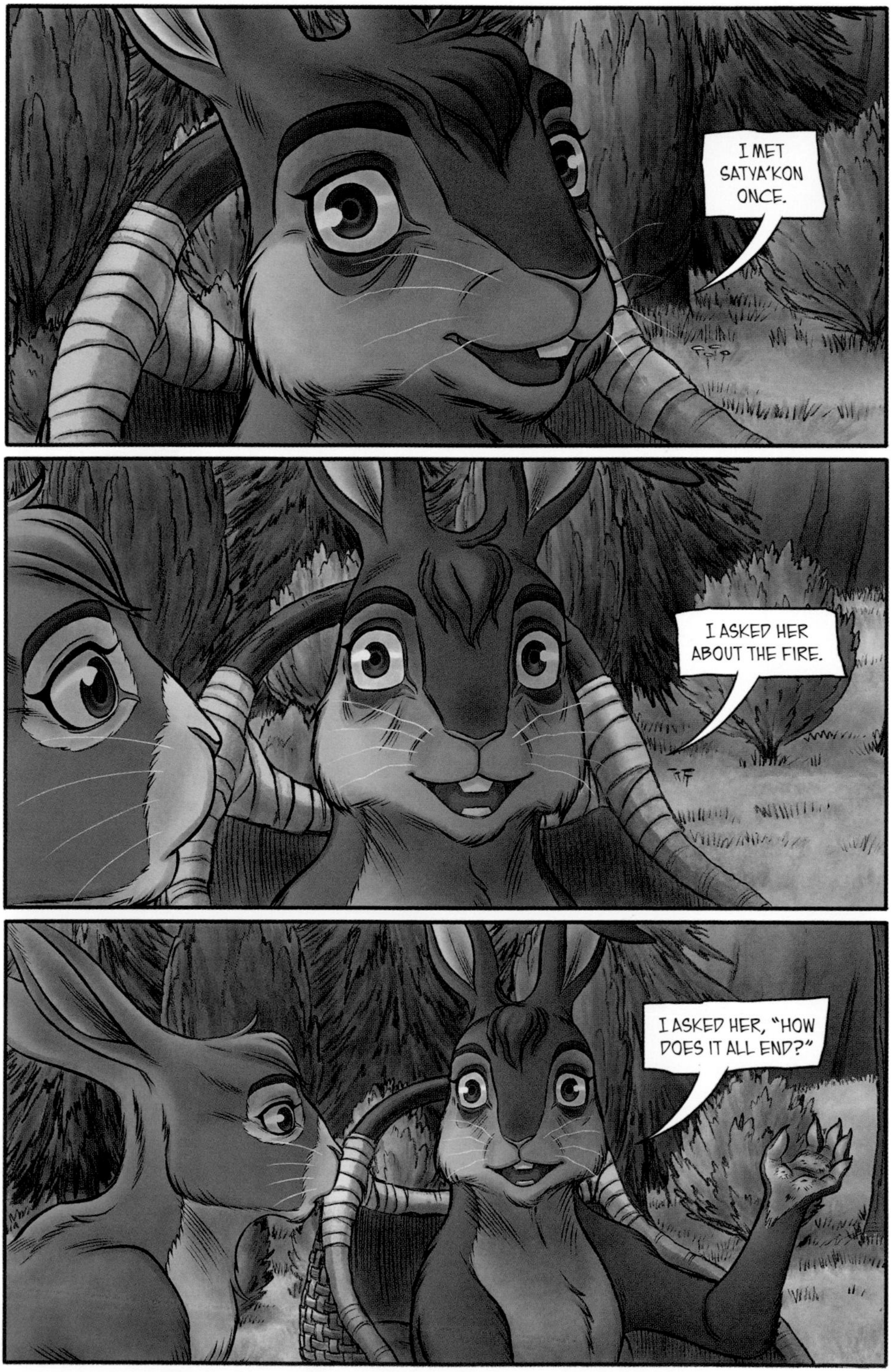
I MET SATYA'KON ONCE.
I ASKED HER ABOUT THE FIRE.
I ASKED HER, "HOW DOES IT ALL END?"

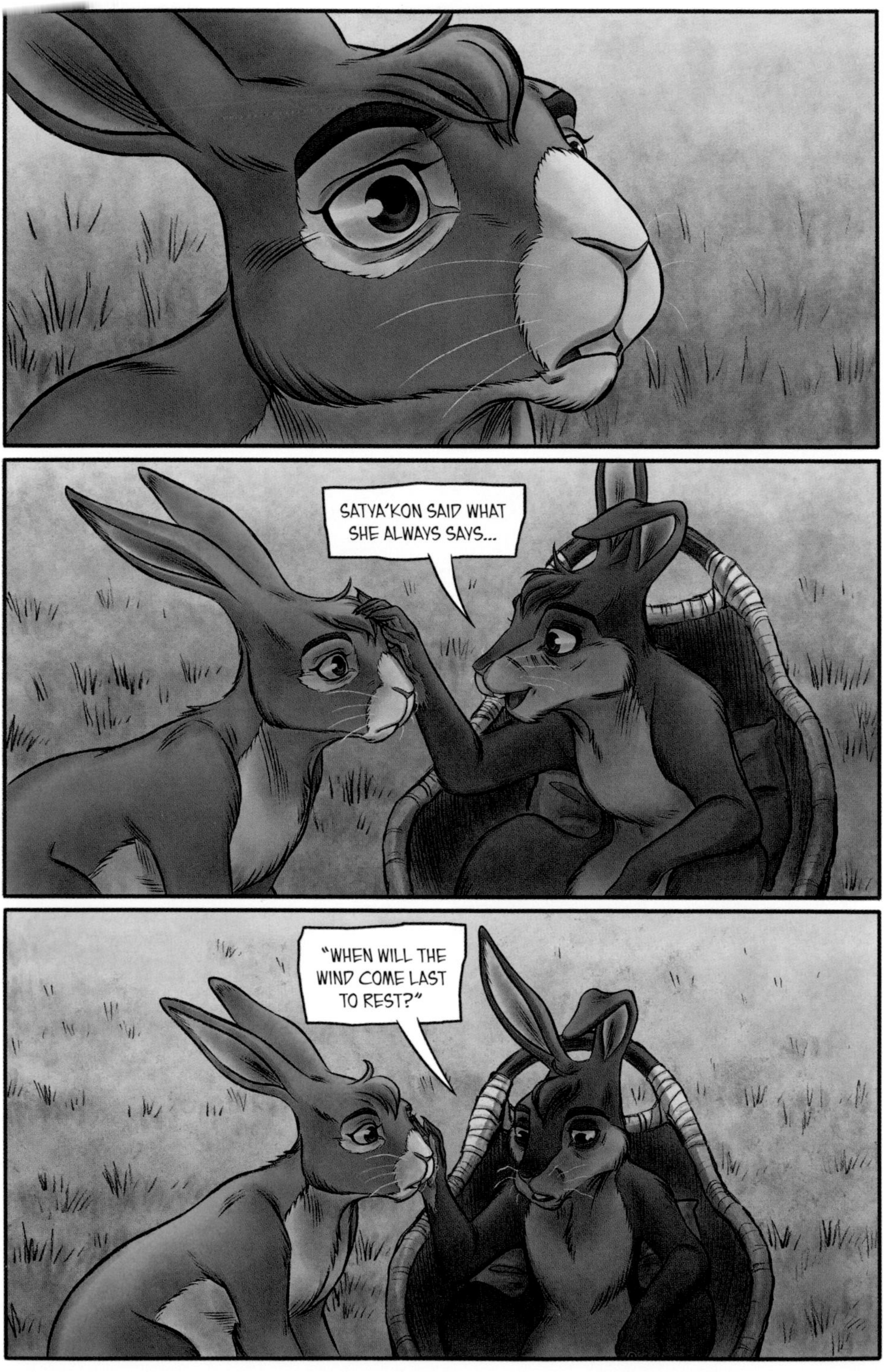
SATYA'KON SAID WHAT SHE ALWAYS SAYS...
"WHEN WILL THE WIND COME LAST TO REST?"

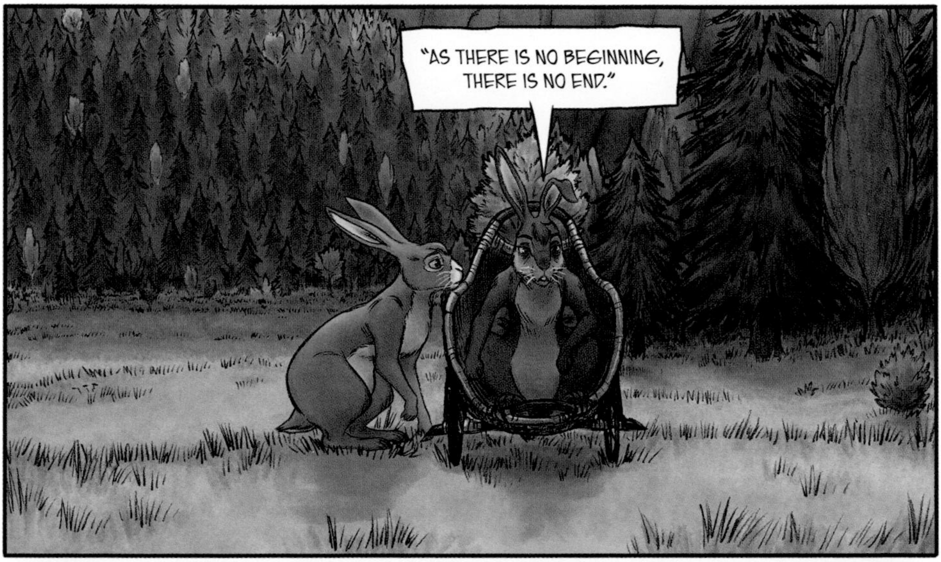
"AS THERE IS NO BEGINNING,
THERE IS NO END."

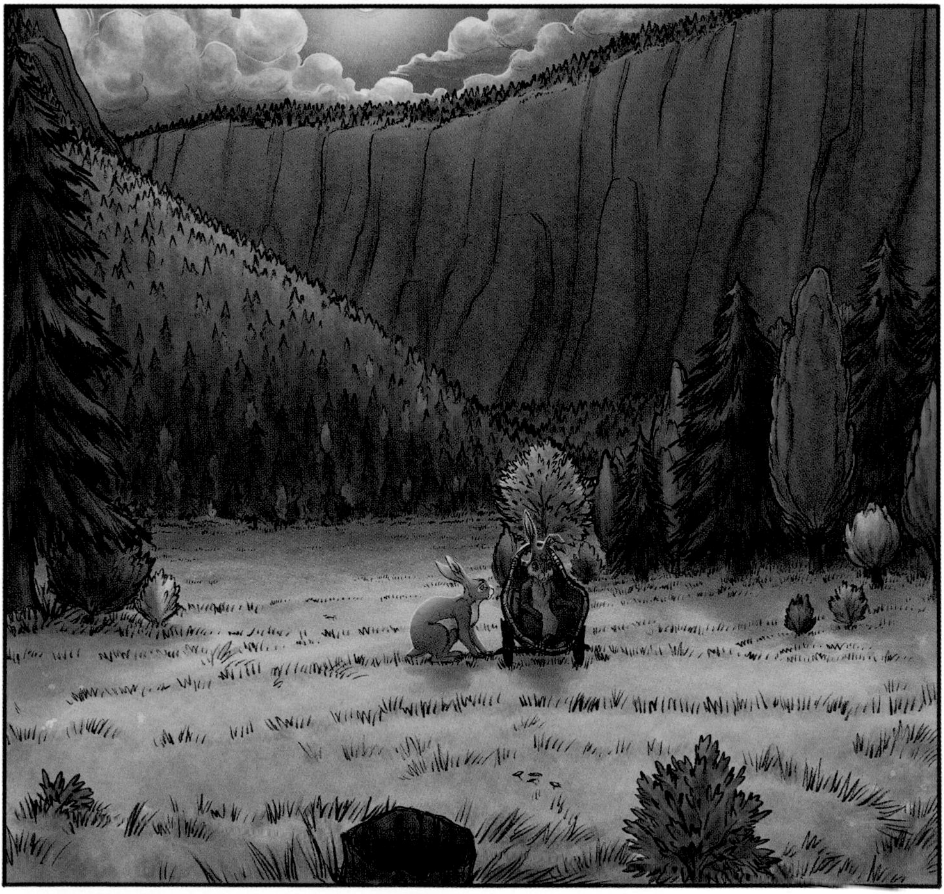

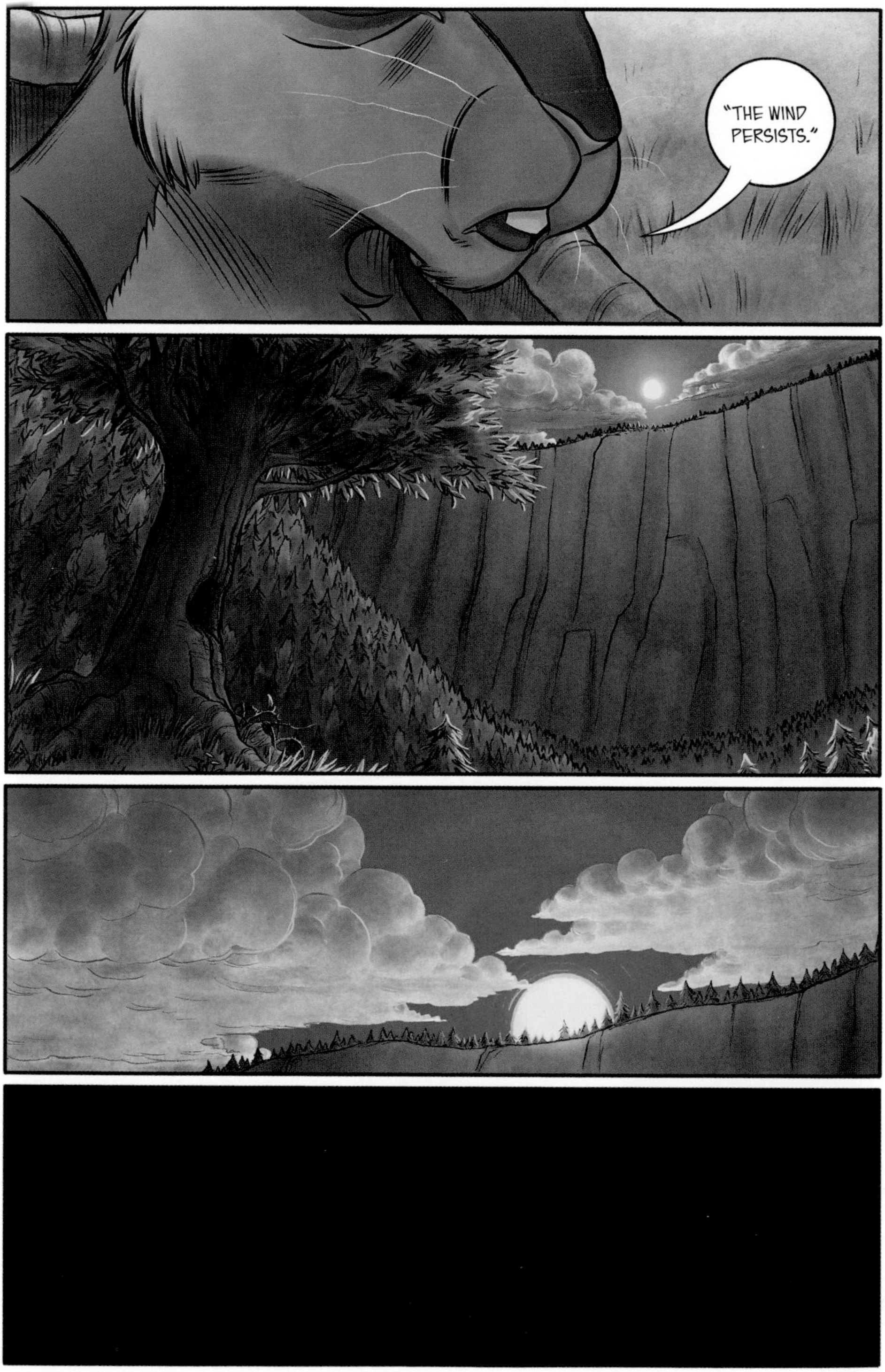
"THE WIND PERSISTS."

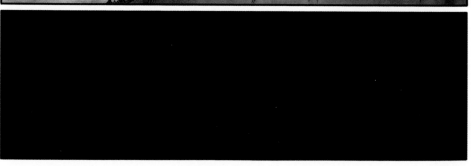

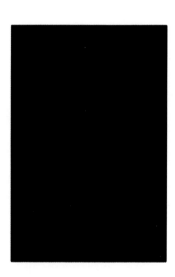

THE TWO VALES OF LAVENDER
prepared by the rabbit Woven

IN THE NORTHERN HEMISPHERE OF OUR WORLD LAVENDER, THERE LIE TWO VALES: *THE VALE OF INDUSTRY* AND *THE VALE OF THE CLOUDS.*

SEPARATED BY A LARGE MOUNTAIN RANGE CALLED *GALE RIDGE,* THESE TWO LANDS ARE HOME TO VARIOUS HARDWORKING RABBITS.

AS PART OF MY TRAINING, I HAVE BEEN ASSIGNED THE TASK OF PREPARING BACKGROUND INFORMATION ABOUT THIS UNIQUE PART OF LAVENDER, ITS CULTURE, ITS HISTORY, AND ITS CURIOUS INHABITANTS.

AS IS COMMONLY KNOWN, THE VALE OF CLOUDS SUFFERED A *DISASTROUS FIRE* THAT CONSUMED MOST EVERYTHING THERE. WHILE VARIOUS RUMORS HAVE SURFACED SURROUNDING THE CAUSE OF THIS DESTRUCTION, THE VALE OF CLOUDS REMAINS A LARGELY *UNKNOWN AREA.*

WITH THAT IN MIND--AND CONSIDERING THE TALE OF BRIDGEBELLE (AS IT'S ROUTINELY TOLD) TAKES PLACE IN THE VALE OF INDUSTRY--MOST OF MY RESEARCH WILL CENTER ON THIS ONE VALE.

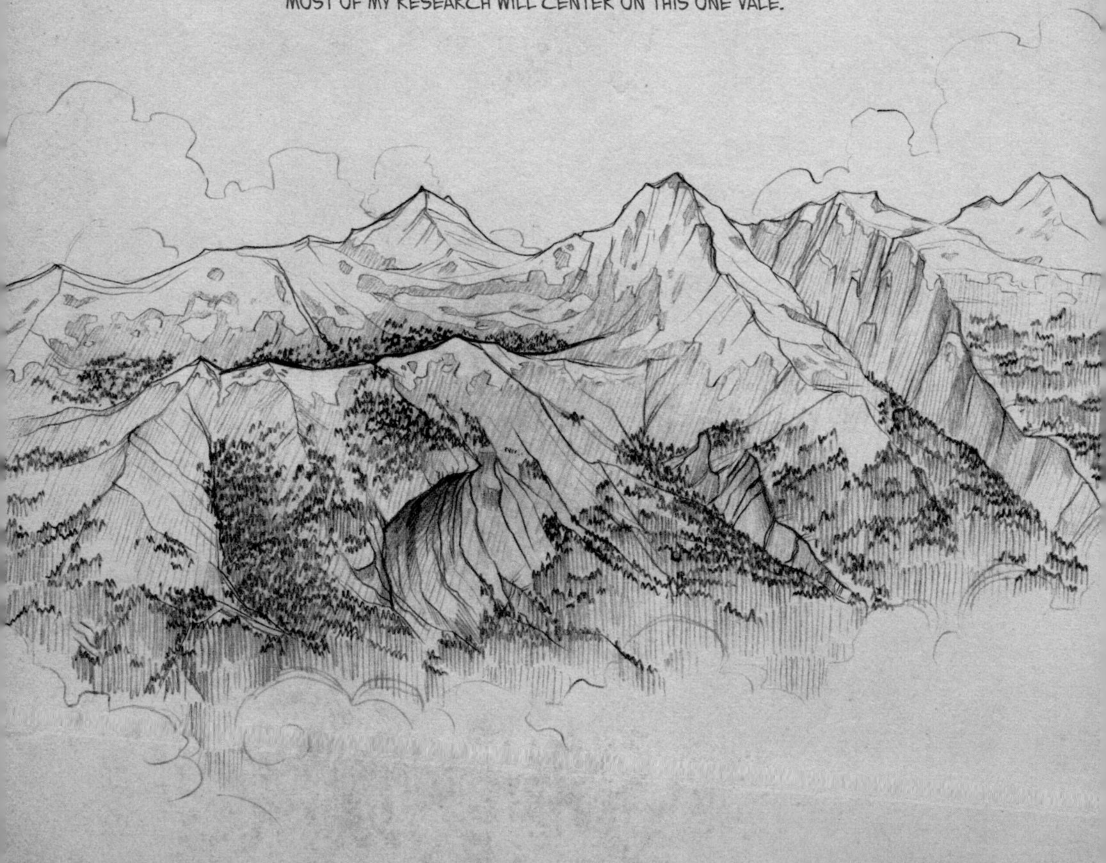

THE LAND

THE VALE OF INDUSTRY IS A *SIMPLE VALLEY* RESTING BETWEEN THE MOUNTAIN RANGE OF *GALE RIDGE* TO THE SOUTH AND THE *HIGHLAND PLATEAU* TO THE NORTH. THERE EXIST MANY NOTABLE LOCATIONS IN THIS VALE, SEVERAL OF WHICH ARE IMPORTANT TO THE STUDENT INTERESTED IN BRIDGEBELLE AND HER STORY.

GOLDENSEED MEADOW
THE MAIN GRASSY MEADOW IN THE VALE.

THE CARROT FACTORY
FORMALLY KNOWN AS *WAMPU INDUSTRIES*, THIS FACTORY--AND ITS *REFINING OF CARROTS INTO CHA*-- REPRESENTS THE MAIN INDUSTRY FOR THE COTTONS.

(PLEASE SEE THE FOLLOWING SECTION ON INDUSTRY IN LAVENDER, WHERE THE ACTIVITIES AT THE CARROT FACTORY WILL BE FURTHER DETAILED.)

TZARA CANYON
THE DENSE WILDERNESS BETWEEN *GREENAWAY FALLS* AND THE *BLUE HEART*.

CHIMBLEY SPIRE
AS THE HIGHEST ELEVATION ENTRANCE TO THE WARREN, THIS SPOT IS FREQUENTLY USED AS A PLACE FOR A CONTEMPLATIVE RUN.

CORNFLOWER
A FIELD OF CORNSTALKS IN THE WEST, GENERALLY CONSIDERED THE HOME OF THE FOXES. IT GETS ITS NAME FROM THE BLUE WILDFLOWERS THAT GROW BETWEEN THE CORNSTALKS.

STILLBREEZE PEAK
A TALL MOUNTAIN PEAK AT THE EDGE OF *GALE RIDGE* THAT FEATURES A WIDE-OPEN PLATEAU. OFTEN RECOGNIZED AS A PLACE WHERE COTTONS WILL BURY THEIR DEAD, STILLBREEZE REMAINS AN AREA OF STRONG SIGNIFICANCE TO MANY RABBIT SCHOLARS.

THE LAND CONT.

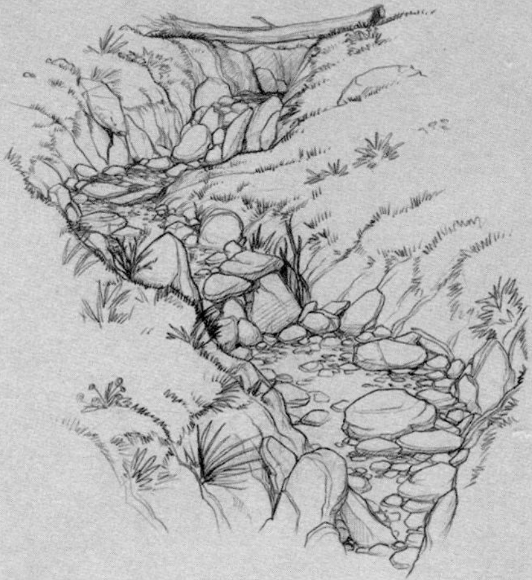

WHISPER CREEK

A DRY RIVERBED FILLED WITH RIVER ROCKS. WHILE THE MAIN SOURCE OF WATER IN THE VALE OF INDUSTRY COMES FROM *GREENAWAY FALLS*, THE SOURCE OF WHISPER CREEK SWELLS GREATLY WHEN IT RAINS, CAUSING A RUSHING, POWERFUL (IF SMALL) STREAM.

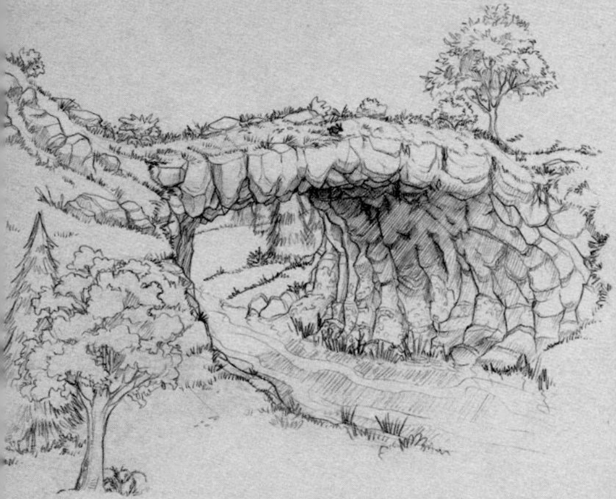

WAVERING WOOD

THE MAIN FOREST AREA NEAR *GOLDENSEED MEADOW*, WHERE BRIDGEBELLE LIVES.

ROARK'S SPAN

A NATURALLY FORMED LAND BRIDGE, NAMED AFTER A PROMINENT TOOTH-AGE RABBIT WHO BUILT MANY SIMILAR CROSSING STRUCTURES, MOST OF WHICH HAVE NOT STOOD THE TEST OF TIME LIKE THIS NATURAL FORMATION.

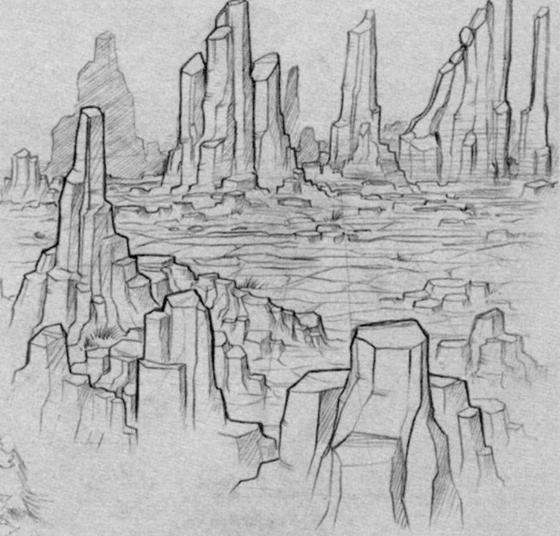

THE BASALT GATES

AN ISOLATED AREA OF COLUMNAR ROCK FORMATIONS, SURROUNDED BY THE HIGH CLIFFS NEAR *GREENAWAY FALLS*, WHICH CAPS THE WESTERN END OF THE VALE. SOME RESEARCHERS (MYSELF INCLUDED) BELIEVE THE EDGES OF THE WARREN ARE RICH WITH HAUNTED SPIRITS. (SEE THE *GLIMMER STICKS* ENTRY.)

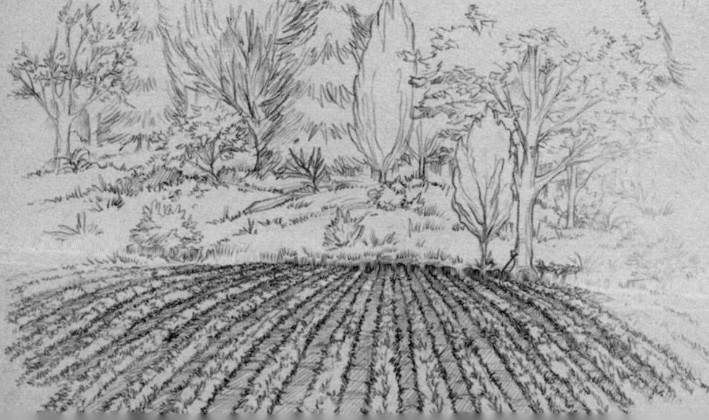

THE GARDEN

THE FIELD WHERE THE RABBITS GROW CARROTS, PRESIDED OVER BY JHON CROQUET, WHO TENDS THE FARM.

THE LAND CONT.

TENDERFOOT CONSERVATORY

A TRADE SCHOOL FOR RABBITS TO LEARN HOW TO REFINE CHA AT THE CARROT FACTORY. THOUGH NOT TECHNICALLY ALIGNED WITH A SPECIFIC PHILOSOPHY, THIS SCHOOL DOES PERHAPS OVERLY STRESS THE VALUE OF HARD WORK AS A MEANS OF SURVIVAL, THUS CREATING A DEVALUED SENSE OF ART. SOME CRITICS OF THE CONSERVATORY BELIEVE THIS IS OUTDATED THINKING FROM THE COLD AGE THAT HAS STOPPED PROGRESS IN OUR CURRENT NEW DARK AGE. FURTHER DISCUSSION OF THIS ISSUE IS NOT THE PRIMARY GOAL OF THIS REPORT.

THE GLIMMER STICKS

A DARK, HAUNTED GROVE, ALMOST MAZE-LIKE IN ITS MANY WINDING TRAILS. LOCATED ON THE EASTERN EDGE OF THE VALE OF INDUSTRY ON THE WAY TO WARREN'S END.

FOUNTAINGLASS

THE SEAT OF POWER IN THE VALE OF INDUSTRY, AND THE HOME OF THE RELIGIOUS SECT KNOWN AS THE *WINDIST CURATUS*. A STRANGE "FORGOTTEN" STRUCTURE FROM THE ERA 500 YEARS AGO. SINCE THERE ARE NO REAL RECORDS OF THE ADVANCED RABBIT SOCIETY BEGUN IN THE WIND AGE ON THROUGH THE TOOTH AGE, WE CAN ONLY GUESS THAT THIS RARE STRUCTURE MAY REPRESENT A GLIMPSE OF PAST RABBIT GREATNESS.

THE VAULT OF TIME

FOLLOWING THE RIVER EAST, BEYOND *WARREN'S END*, THERE IS RUMORED TO LIE A SERIES OF NATURALLY FORMING STONE ARCHES. NO RABBIT HAS VENTURED THAT FAR AWAY FROM HOME TO REPORT BACK ON THIS STRANGE LOCATION.

GREENAWAY FALLS

BECAUSE OF THE CHURNING WATERS AT THE BOTTOM OF THE FALLS AND ITS PROXIMITY TO BOTH *CORNFLOWER* AND THE *BASALT GATES*, THIS WATERFALL IS BEST VIEWED FROM A GREAT DISTANCE.

HISTORY

THE HISTORY OF LAVENDER CAN BE MARKED BY
FIVE DISTINCT EPOCHS.

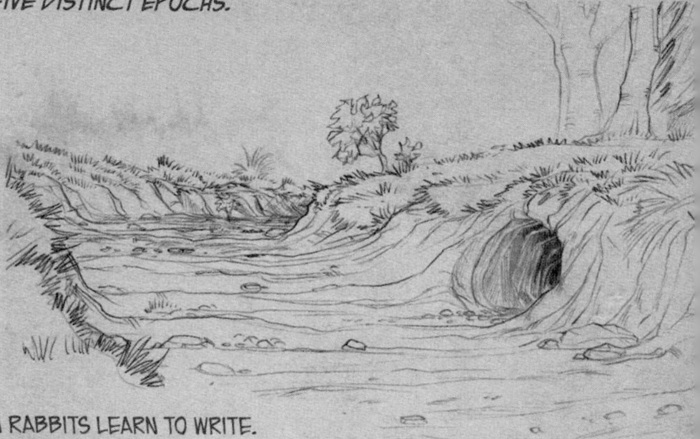

1. THE DARK AGE

THE EARLIEST DAYS OF LAVENDER, PRIOR TO RECORDED HISTORY, ARE CONSIDERED THE DARK AGE. DURING THIS TIME, RABBITS SLOWLY DEVELOP THE ABILITY OF SPEECH. *CIVILIZATION* BEGINS TO FORM.

2. THE WIND AGE

A PERIOD OF *ENLIGHTENMENT* BEGINS WHEN RABBITS LEARN TO WRITE. IT IS HERE IN THE WIND AGE WHERE OUR ANCESTORS FIRST WRITE DOWN *THE HOLY BOOK OF WINDISM--THE VERT LIBER.* SOCIETY BEGINS TO ADVANCE AS RIGHT AND WRONG ARE CODIFIED.

3. THE TOOTH AGE

A COMPLICATED ERA OF *INDUSTRIALIZATION* IS USHERED IN WHEN THE RABBIT *REKRA* DEVELOPS A PROCESS TO REFINE CARROTS, THEREBY DISCOVERING CHA. WITH THIS INDUSTRY COMES THE FORMATION OF THE *PENNY CURRENCY* AND A GROWING MATERIALISM. COTTONS BECOME OBSESSED WITH "THINGS" AND TAKE TO WEARING CLOTHES AND OTHER ADORNMENTS. (WHILE I HAVE MY OWN THEORIES, THERE IS NO WIDELY ACCEPTED REASON RABBITS HAVE NEVER REGAINED THE DESIRE FOR CLOTHING IN THE PRESENT TIME.)

CHA COMES TO POWER AN *ENERGY GRID* THAT SPREADS THROUGH THE VARIOUS VALES.

RABBIT PRIDE, AVARICE, AND GREED LEAD TO *GREAT CONFLICT AND WARS.* THREE MAJOR CONFLICTS--*THE GREAT GNASH I, II, AND III*--TAKE THEIR TOLL IN MASSIVE SHORT-TERM CASUALTIES. HOWEVER, LIKE IN MOST TIMES OF WARFARE, INDUSTRY THRIVES AND THE *RICH RABBITS* GET RICHER AND MORE POWERFUL.

THE END OF THIS AGE COMES WITH AN EVENT THAT IS DEBATED BY MANY OF MY CONTEMPORARY RABBIT HISTORIANS.

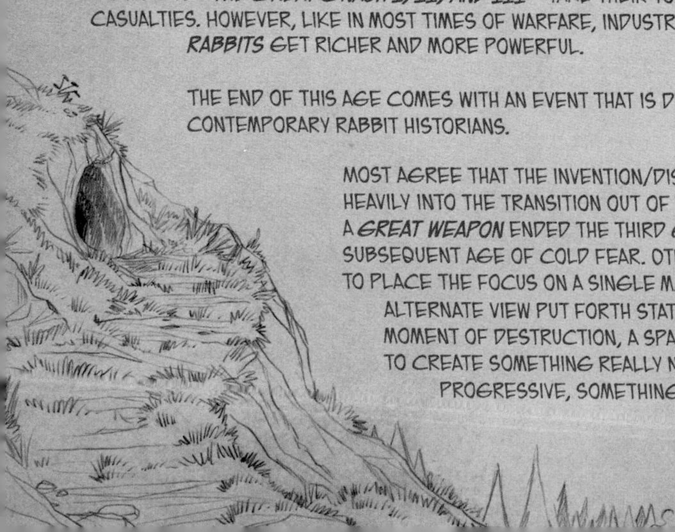

MOST AGREE THAT THE INVENTION/DISCOVERY OF *THOKCHAS* FACTORS HEAVILY INTO THE TRANSITION OUT OF THIS AGE. BUT SOME BELIEVE THAT A *GREAT WEAPON* ENDED THE THIRD GREAT GNASH, CREATING A SUBSEQUENT AGE OF COLD FEAR. OTHER RABBITS ARE LESS INCLINED TO PLACE THE FOCUS ON A SINGLE MASSIVE WEAPON--INSTEAD, THE ALTERNATE VIEW PUT FORTH STATES THAT DURING THE GREATEST MOMENT OF DESTRUCTION, A SPACE WAS CLEARED FOR A RABBIT TO CREATE SOMETHING REALLY NEW, SOMETHING AESTHETICALLY PROGRESSIVE, SOMETHING *ARTISTIC.*

HISTORY CONT.

4. THE COLD AGE

EITHER WAY, THIS DUAL DETONATION OF FORCES--BOTH A DESTRUCTIVE
EXPLOSION AND A *CREATIVE EXPLOSION*--FORMED THE BASIS OF THE MODERN
AGE. TECHNOLOGY RISES, INFORMATION SPREADS, AND RABBIT CIVILIZATION
PROGRESSES TO GREAT HEIGHTS.

HOWEVER, WHAT BEGINS WITH AN EXPLOSION, ENDS WITH AN IMPLOSION. A MASSIVE
BREAKDOWN IN SOCIETY--CALLED *SUNFALL*--CAUSES RABBITS TO LOSE ALL THEIR
GREAT ADVANCES, AS THEY SLIDE DOWN TO A SIMPLER STATE OF EXISTENCE.

NO RABBIT CAN FORGET SUNFALL, EVEN THOUGH IT HAPPENED 500 YEARS AGO.

5. THE NEW DARK AGE

YES, WE ARE 500 YEARS INTO A POST-SUNFALL ERA. SOME HISTORIANS ARE AGAINST
GIVING A NAME TO THIS CURRENT AGE, BUT IT'S HARD TO IGNORE THAT MOST RABBITS
CALL IT THE NEW DARK AGE.

IT'S NOT THE POINT OF THIS REPORT TO DETAIL EXACTLY HOW MANY *CENTURIES
OF APOCALYPSE* EXISTED BEFORE LAVENDER HEALED ITSELF ENOUGH THAT WE
RABBITS COULD BEGIN TO REFORM OUR SOCIETY. WHAT I WOULD LIKE MY READERS TO
TAKE AWAY FROM THIS HISTORICAL OVERVIEW IS *THE UNIQUE COMBINATION* OF OLD,
BROKEN "FUTURISTIC" TECHNOLOGY WITH AN ALMOST MYTHIC SENSE OF RENEWED
NATURALISM. THE FRICTION BETWEEN THESE TWO ASPECTS OF MODERN COTTONS IS
A KEY DRIVER IN THE TALE OF BRIDGEBELLE.

CHARACTERS

ONE MAIN GOAL OF THIS REPORT IS TO PROVIDE CLARITY AND CONTEXT FOR THOSE READERS LOOKING TO DELVE FURTHER INTO THE TALE OF BRIDGEBELLE. FOR THAT REASON, I PRESENT A QUICK GUIDE TO THE MANY CHARACTERS INTRODUCED IN THE TALE. NO DEEP CHARACTER ANALYSIS IS INTENDED. FOR THAT, I HOPE MY READERS REFER BACK TO THE TALE ITSELF.

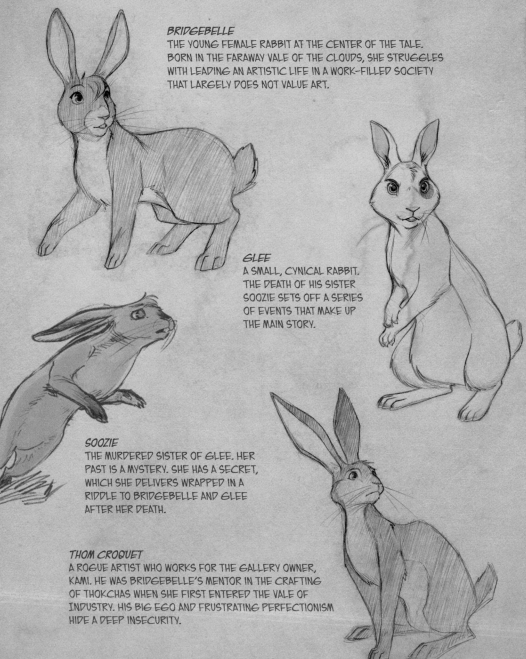

BRIDGEBELLE
THE YOUNG FEMALE RABBIT AT THE CENTER OF THE TALE. BORN IN THE FARAWAY VALE OF THE CLOUDS, SHE STRUGGLES WITH LEADING AN ARTISTIC LIFE IN A WORK-FILLED SOCIETY THAT LARGELY DOES NOT VALUE ART.

GLEE
A SMALL, CYNICAL RABBIT. THE DEATH OF HIS SISTER SOOZIE SETS OFF A SERIES OF EVENTS THAT MAKE UP THE MAIN STORY.

SOOZIE
THE MURDERED SISTER OF GLEE. HER PAST IS A MYSTERY. SHE HAS A SECRET, WHICH SHE DELIVERS WRAPPED IN A RIDDLE TO BRIDGEBELLE AND GLEE AFTER HER DEATH.

THOM CROQUET
A ROGUE ARTIST WHO WORKS FOR THE GALLERY OWNER, KAMI. HE WAS BRIDGEBELLE'S MENTOR IN THE CRAFTING OF THOKCHAS WHEN SHE FIRST ENTERED THE VALE OF INDUSTRY. HIS BIG EGO AND FRUSTRATING PERFECTIONISM HIDE A DEEP INSECURITY.

CHARACTERS CONT.

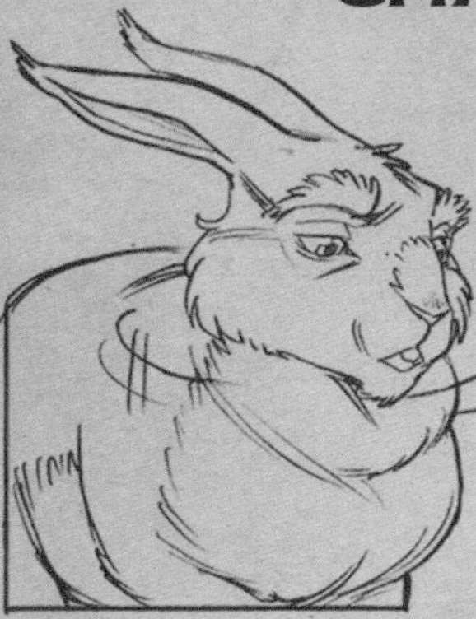

WAMPU
OWNER OF THE CARROT FACTORY. HE IS ONLY CONCERNED ABOUT THE PRODUCTION OF CHA. ALTHOUGH HE MAY ALSO BE A LITTLE CONCERNED ABOUT THE BEAUTIFUL KAMI.

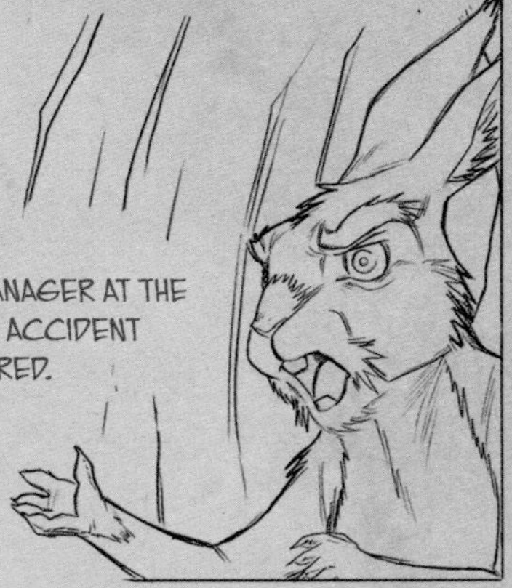

LAVIT
LEAD OPERATIONS MANAGER AT THE CARROT FACTORY. AN ACCIDENT LEFT HIS FACE SCARRED.

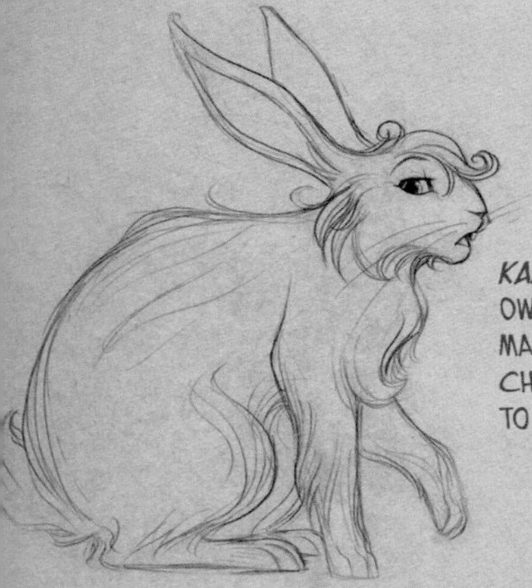

KAMI
OWNER OF A THOKCHA GALLERY. NATURALLY THIS MAKES HER AN OUTSIDER, BUT HER BEAUTY AND CHARISMA HELP CONVINCE OTHER RABBITS NOT TO IGNORE HER COMPLETELY.

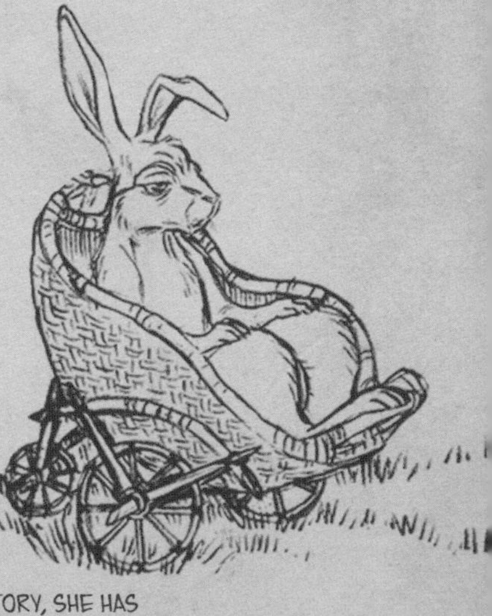

AUNTIE
THE ADOPTED GUARDIAN OF BRIDGEBELLE, AND A FORMER TEACHER AT TENDERFOOT CONSERVATORY. SHE HAS FALLEN GRAVELY ILL, SO THAT NOW INSTEAD OF TAKING CARE OF BRIDGEBELLE, BRIDGEBELLE IS TAKING CARE OF HER.

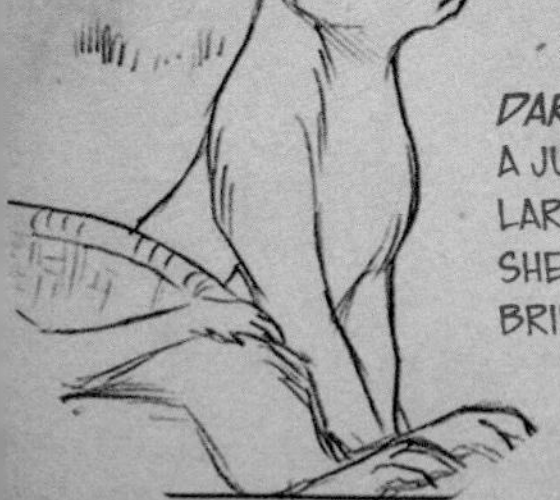

DARLENE
A JUNIOR TEACHER AT TENDERFOOT CONSERVATORY, SHE HAS LARGELY TAKEN OVER AUNTIE'S DAY-TO-DAY DUTIES. AS SUCH, SHE OCCASIONALLY HELPS LOOK AFTER AUNTIE WHEN BRIDGEBELLE IS BUSY AT THE FACTORY.

CHARACTERS CONT.

JHON CROQUET
THOM CROQUET'S FATHER,
AN OLD FARMER OF CARROTS.

LONIJI
THE MALE LEADER OF THE *WINDIST CURATUS*. HE
LEADS THIS GROUP MORE LIKE A SECRET SOCIETY
THAN A RELIGIOUS BROTHER/SISTERHOOD.

TORIJI
A DEVOUT MEMBER OF THE *WINDIST CURATUS*,
SHE IS PERHAPS THE MOST PURE BELIEVER IN
THE WIND. MORE CONCERNED WITH FAITH THAN
WITH FOLLOWING ORDERS.

SAMIJI
THE NEW APPRENTICE TO THE *WINDIST CURATUS*, BEING
MENTORED BY TORIJI. AN AURA OF GREAT ANGER AND VIOLENCE
SURROUNDS HIM, WHICH HINTS AT HIS SECRET PAST.

LEXA
A YOUNG, CAREFREE RABBIT WHO
FITS INTO THE MAIN TALE LATER.

DIGGERS
SMALL VOLE-LIKE CREATURES WHO INHABIT
THE TUNNELS OF THE WARREN. THEY ARE
EXTREMELY SUPPORTIVE OF RABBITS, AND
WHILE THEY ARE SOMETIMES ANNOYING AND
PLAYFUL, THEY RARELY CAUSE ANY HARM.

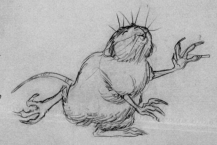

CHARACTERS CONT.

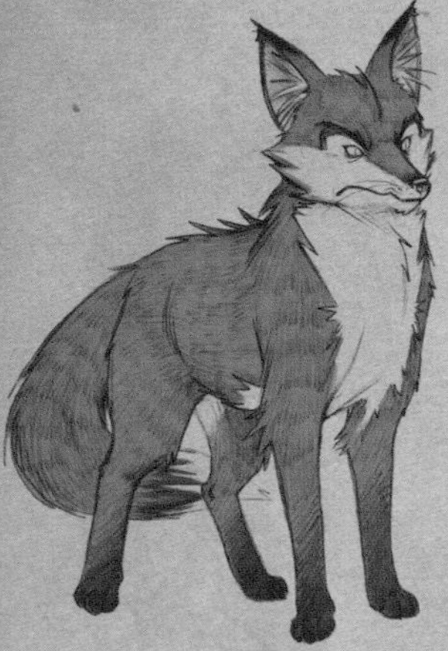

MARROW
A RUTHLESS RED FOX WHO IS INTENT ON GETTING CHA FROM THE COTTONS, BECAUSE HE FEELS THIS MAGICAL SUBSTANCE IS THE KEY TO HIS DOMINATION OVER THE WHOLE VALE. A KILLER.

SYLVAN
A CLASSIC SLY TRICKSTER, THIS SILVER FOX HAS A MASTER PLAN TO PERFORM AN OCCULT CEREMONY THAT WILL RESULT IN A KIND OF REVENGE FOR AN UNKNOWN GRIEVANCE IN HIS PAST.

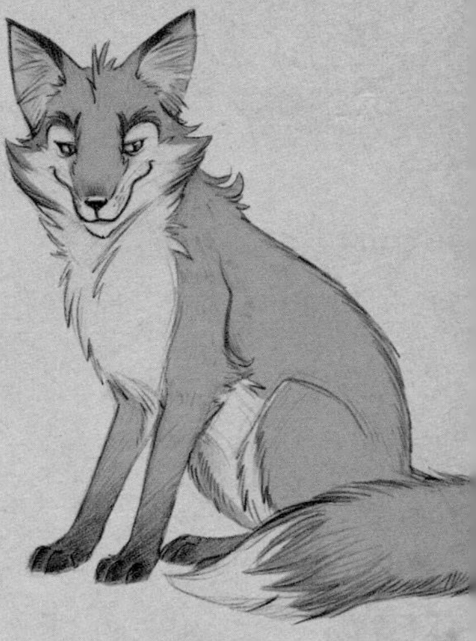

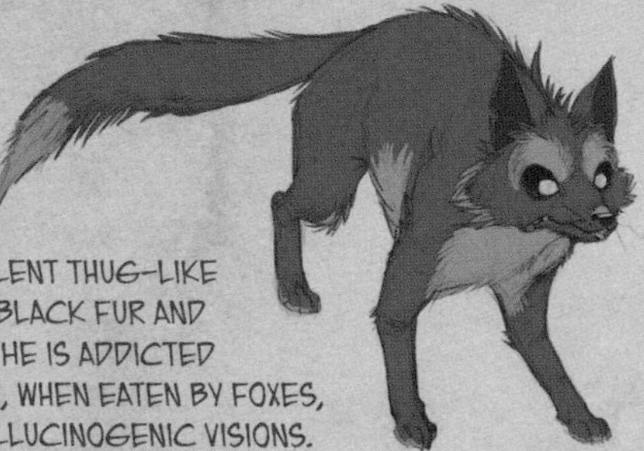

VOR
THE HYPERVIOLENT THUG-LIKE FOX WITH JET-BLACK FUR AND YELLOW EYES. HE IS ADDICTED TO CHA, WHICH, WHEN EATEN BY FOXES, PRODUCES HALLUCINOGENIC VISIONS.

THE BROKEN FEATHER KING
THE EVIL DEITY WHO LORDS OVER THE GREAT VOID OF EMPYREAN--A FLAMING WORLD ABOVE THE CLOUDS, WHERE RABBITS ARE SENT TO BE PUNISHED AFTER DEATH. THERE IS NO KNOWN IMAGE OF THIS BEAST.

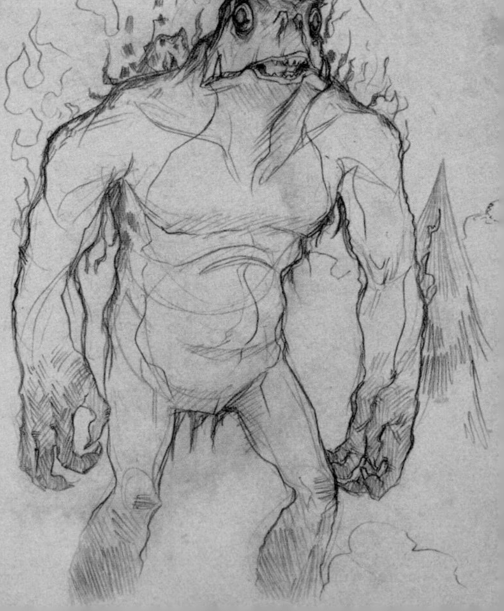

GRALALA
A STRANGE MYTHIC CREATURE THAT WALKS ON TWO LEGS AND IS CONSTANTLY ON FIRE. IF THAT SOUNDS SILLY, IT'S BECAUSE IT IS (PLEASE FORGIVE MY UNPROFESSIONAL COMMENTARY HERE). GRALALA IS A FOLK TALE TOLD BY MOTHER RABBITS TO SCARE THEIR KITS INTO BEHAVING. I FIND IT STRANGE THAT SOME SCHOLARS NOT ONLY BELIEVE IN GRALALA, BUT ALSO HOLD AN OPINION THAT HE IS SOMEHOW A BENEVOLENT SPIRIT OF THE FOREST. I INVITE READERS TO FORM THEIR OWN JUDGMENTS.

INDUSTRY

SOMETIME DURING THE TOOTH AGE, AN INDUSTRIOUS RABBIT NAMED REKRA HAD A WILD IDEA: IF RABBITS EAT CARROTS FOR ENERGY, THEN THERE SHOULD BE A WAY TO EXTRACT THE ENERGY OUT OF CARROTS IN A MORE PURE FORM. AFTER MANY FAILED EXPERIMENTS, HE DISCOVERED A METHOD OF REFINING CARROTS INTO A LIGHT ORANGE POWDER CALLED CHA.

MOSTLY USED AS AN ENERGY SUBSTANCE, CHA HAS MANY OTHER STRANGE (SOME SAY "MAGICAL") PROPERTIES. WHEN INGESTED, CHA CAN CAUSE DREAMLIKE VISIONS. HOWEVER, ONLY FOXES ARE KNOWN TO USE CHA LIKE THIS. (COTTONS PREFER THE WARM BUZZ OF HONEYSUCKLE TEA.) CHA IS ALSO USED IN THE CREATION OF THOKCHAS.

DURING THE REFINING PROCESS, ANOTHER SUBSTANCE IS PRODUCED: A DARK ORANGE PASTE CALLED PEH. MOST RABBITS ORIGINALLY TOOK THIS SUBSTANCE TO BE A WASTE BY-PRODUCT, BUT A CLEVER COTTON DECIDED TO COMPRESS IT AND POUND IT FLAT INTO SMALL DISCS CALLED PENNIES.

ORIGINALLY THE PROCESS TO GET CHA FROM CARROTS WAS A PAINSTAKING TASK DONE BY HAND. BUT AS DEMAND GREW, SO DID ENORMOUS UNDERGROUND FACTORIES. THESE CARROT FACTORIES HAVE FOUR MAIN SECTIONS:

INDUSTRY CONT.

1. THE RASPING ROOM

RAW CARROTS ARE FED INTO A LARGE HOPPER, WHERE THEY ARE CRUSHED BY GIANT WOODEN GRINDER WHEELS. THIS *CARMATCHA SLUSH* IS ROLLED OUT ON BROAD LEAF CONVEYOR BELTS, WHERE IT IS RAKED AND SEPARATED FOR UNIFORMITY. SMALL STONES, BITS OF ROOT, AND ANY CLUMPS OF DIRT ARE REMOVED BY HAND, EVEN TO THIS DAY.

CONVEYOR BELT
FOR SORTING - CAN BE LENGTHENED + WIDENED

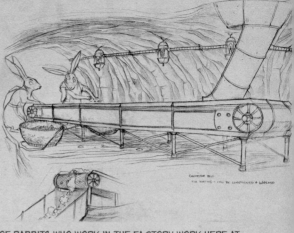

2. THE MAIN EXCHANGE

THE CARMATCHA IS THEN FUNNELED INTO THE MAIN PART OF THE FACTORY: A ***MAZE OF GLASS*** TUBES AND ORBS WHERE THE CARROT MASH UNDERGOES A LARGE SERIES OF HEATING, COOLING, AND EXTRACTING UNTIL IT IS FINALLY SEPARATED INTO ***CHA*** AND ***PEH***. THE MAJORITY OF RABBITS WHO WORK IN THE FACTORY WORK HERE AT LARGE CONTROL PANELS WITH SWITCHES, KNOBS, DIALS, AND LEVERS. THESE PANELS, CALLED *THE BOARD*, FACILITATE THE SMOOTH FLOW OF CARROTS THROUGH THE REFINING PROCESS.

3. THE MINT

THE PEH IS POURED DOWN A CHUTE FURTHER UNDERGROUND INTO A SECURE SECTION OF THE FACTORY, WHERE ***PENNIES*** ARE POUNDED OUT.

4. THE CANOPY

THE REFINED CHA IS SENT UP ON CUPPED BELTS TO THE TREETOP *CANOPY DIVISION*, WHERE THE CHA IS SPREAD OUT TO DRY ON LARGE, FLAT CAMOUFLAGED SAILS. IT IS EVENTUALLY COLLECTED AND PACKAGED IN SMALL POUCHES. AN UNEDUCATED RABBIT MAY THINK THIS IS THE ***EASIEST*** PART OF THE PROCESS, BUT WE ALL KNOW THAT CANOPY DIVISION WORK IS THE ***MOST DESPISED JOB*** GIVEN TO ONLY THE LOWEST CLASS OF COTTONS, SINCE RABBITS HAVE SUCH A ***GREAT FEAR OF HEIGHTS.***

CARROTS
RASPING WHEELS
EMPLOYEE AREA W/CUBBY SPACES FOR PERSONAL ITEMS
UNWANTED DIRT + ROOTS, ETC. SIFTED OUT OF CARMATCHA SLUSH COLLECTED IN BASKETS + CARRIED OUTSIDE
CONVEYOR BELT FOR RAKING/SIFTING CARMATCHA
THE CLEAR TUBES

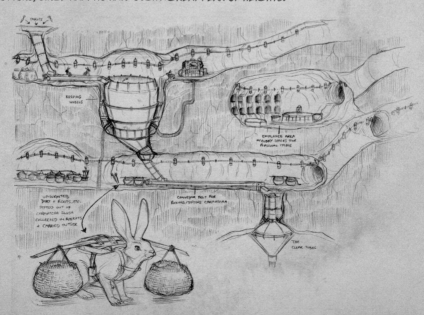

RELIGION

THE MAJOR RELIGION OF LAVENDER IS *WINDISM*. IT IS *TRITHEISTIC* IN NATURE.
THE DEITIES ARE AS FOLLOWS:

SATYA'KON: THE GODDESS OF TRUTH

APEP'KON: THE GOD OF CHAOS

CREPU'KON: THE GENDERLESS GOD OF INDECISION AND TWILIGHT

IT SHOULD BE NOTED THAT WHILE A COMMON RABBIT MAY BELIEVE THAT SATYA'KON HAS
A PRIVILEGED OR MORE PROMINENT ROLE IN THIS TRIAD OF KONS, WINDISM HOLDS THAT
ALL THREE DEITIES ARE EQUAL. THIS MAKES EVEN MORE SENSE WHEN YOU TAKE INTO
ACCOUNT HOW IMPORTANT "BALANCE" IS TO THE WINDISTS.

THE GROUP OF DEVOUT FOLLOWERS ARE CALLED THE *WINDIST CURATUS*. THIS
PRIEST/POLITICIAN CLAN OF BUREAUCRATS LAYS DOWN THE DECREES OF RIGHT AND
WRONG. ONCE A RABBIT IS BROUGHT INTO THIS CLAN, HE OR SHE ADOPTS A COMMON
NAME FORM, SUCH AS TORIJI, LONIJI, AND SAMIJI.

THERE IS AN EVEN STRANGER TRADITION AMONG MEMBERS OF THE *WINDIST CURATUS*.
EACH HOLY RABBIT MUST HAVE HIS OR HER EARS BOUND TOGETHER. THIS, OF COURSE,
GREATLY LIMITS THEIR EARS' EFFECTIVENESS, BUT IT'S PART OF THE STRICT WINDIST
BELIEF THAT INSTEAD OF PROTECTING YOURSELF, YOU PUT YOUR TRUST IN SATYA'KON,
AND SATYA'KON WILL TAKE CARE OF HER FOLLOWERS.

COTTONS ARE STRONG BELIEVERS IN LIFE AFTER OUR FUR BODIES FALL FOR THE
FINAL TIME. EVERY RABBIT, YOUNG AND OLD, DREAMS OF *YONDERFIELD*--AFTERLIFE'S
PARADISE, A PEACEFUL, PERFECT UNDERGROUND FIELD. BUT THERE IS ALSO A LAND
OF PUNISHMENT--*EMPYREAN*, BELIEVED TO BE FIERY CLOUDS IN THE SKY.

THE NAME OF THE WINDIST HOLY BOOK IS *THE VERT LIBER*,
ALSO KNOWN AS THE GREEN VERSES, OF WHICH THERE ARE 92.

[FROM THE BEGINNING OF THE VERT LIBER, VERSES 1-4]:

AND SATYA'KON SAID, "WHOEVER HARVESTS FROM THE LAND,
AND GIVES LIFE TO IMAGINATION, SHALL KNOW MY NAME AND THUS SHALL
NOT HEAR THE RINGING OF DEATH."

EVEN BEFORE THE BEGINNING THERE WAS CHAOS AND THERE WAS TRUTH.
TRUTH DID NOT ARISE FROM CHAOS; CHAOS DID NOT SPILL FORTH FROM TRUTH.
THEY DID NOT CREATE EACH OTHER, NOR WERE THEY CREATED AT ALL.
THEY EXIST IN THE ALWAYS ALREADY.

WE MAY CALL THE "ALWAYS ALREADY" BY ITS NAME,
AND THAT NAME IS THE WIND.

FORMLESS TRUTH, WHICH WE MAY CALL SATYA'KON, REACHED INTO
FORMLESS CHAOS, WHICH WE MAY CALL APEP'KON, AND SCATTERED BITS
OF EACH TO THE WIND. WE MAY CALL THESE BITS RABBITS.

THOKCHAS

THIS REPORT WOULD NOT BE COMPLETE WITHOUT A QUICK DISCUSSION OF *ART*.

THE DISCOVERY OF CHA AND THE CREATION OF THE PENNY ECONOMY ALLOWED FOR TREMENDOUS GROWTH AND ADVANCEMENT OF THE RABBIT CIVILIZATION ON LAVENDER DURING THE TOOTH AGE. THIS PROGRESS LASTED FOR HUNDREDS OF YEARS. THEN CHA WAS RESPONSIBLE FOR ANOTHER GREAT *TECHNOLOGICAL LEAP FORWARD.*

AN INVENTIVE RABBIT NAMED TURLING BELIEVED THAT CHA'S ENERGY WAS MAGICAL AND THAT IT HAD A DEEP POWER OF TRANSFORMATION THAT COULD BE HARNESSED INTO AN AESTHETIC ENGINE OF SORTS. TURLING WAS THE FIRST ARTIST TO USE CHA TO FASHION OBJECTS--JEWELRY, TOYS, CURIOS--OUT OF SIMPLE MATERIALS, LIKE STICKS AND STONES, MUD AND GRASS.

THESE DAZZLING OBJECTS, CALLED *THOKCHAS*, ARE BELIEVED TO HAVE EVEN MORE MAGICAL PROPERTIES, WHICH, WHEN ACTIVATED, APPEAR AS WONDROUS, EXPLOSIVE VISIONS. BECAUSE THOKCHAS HAVE THIS EXPLOSIVE ELEMENT TO THEM, THERE ARE THOSE RABBITS WHO BELIEVE THAT A LARGE QUANTITY OF CHA CAN BE TURNED INTO A *MEGATHOKCHA*, CAPABLE OF BECOMING A WEAPON OF MASS DESTRUCTION.

THE PURITY OF CHA, AND THE THOKCHAS MADE FROM CHA, ARE MEASURED IN A SCALE WITH UNITS CALLED *ROOTS*. THE PUREST CHA TOPS OUT AT 92 ROOTS.

MOST COTTONS BELIEVE THAT THERE IS NO WAY TO GET EVEN CLOSE TO THAT LEVEL OF CHA. HOWEVER, THERE EXISTS A MYSTERIOUS OBJECT--*THE BLACK SUN*--A POWERFUL MEGATHOKCHA THAT SOME RABBIT SCHOLARS CONTEND IS A PERFECT 92.

PERHAPS IT IS IRRESPONSIBLE OF ME TO INCLUDE SUCH A TALL TALE AS THE BLACK SUN IN MY WRITING. I AM AWARE THAT THIS INTRODUCES QUESTIONS THAT I AM, AT PRESENT, UNABLE TO ADDRESS.

THE ROLE OF THE INDIVIDUAL IN SOCIETY, THE IMPORTANCE OF BEAUTY, AND THE VALUE OF ART ARE TOPICS THAT ARE NOT WITHIN THE SCOPE OF THIS REPORT.

THOSE READERS LOOKING TO ENGAGE IN A DISCUSSION OF THESE MATTERS ARE ADVISED TO REVISIT THE TALE OF BRIDGEBELLE PROPER, WHERE SUCH ANSWERS *MAY BE* MORE FORTHCOMING.

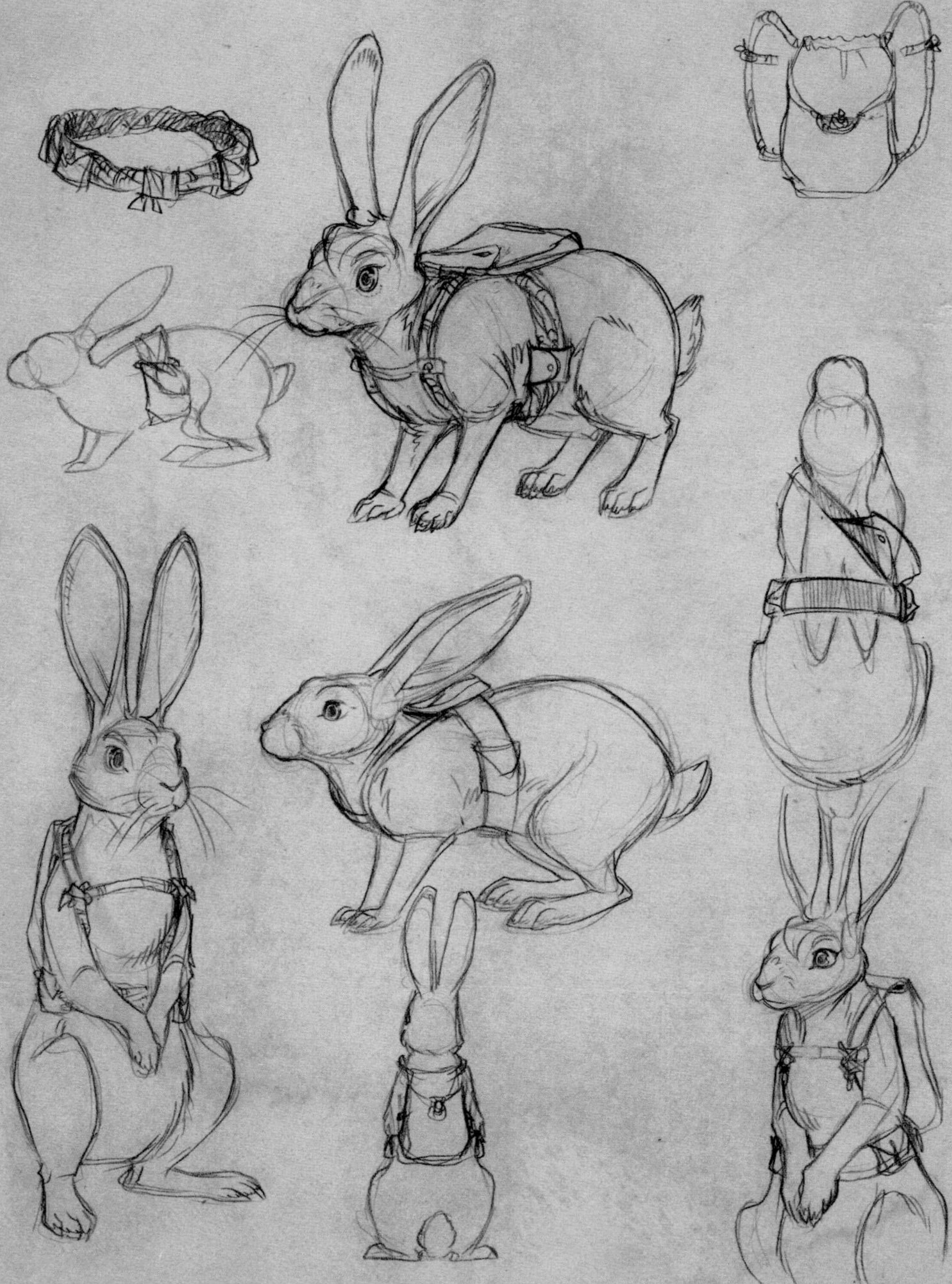

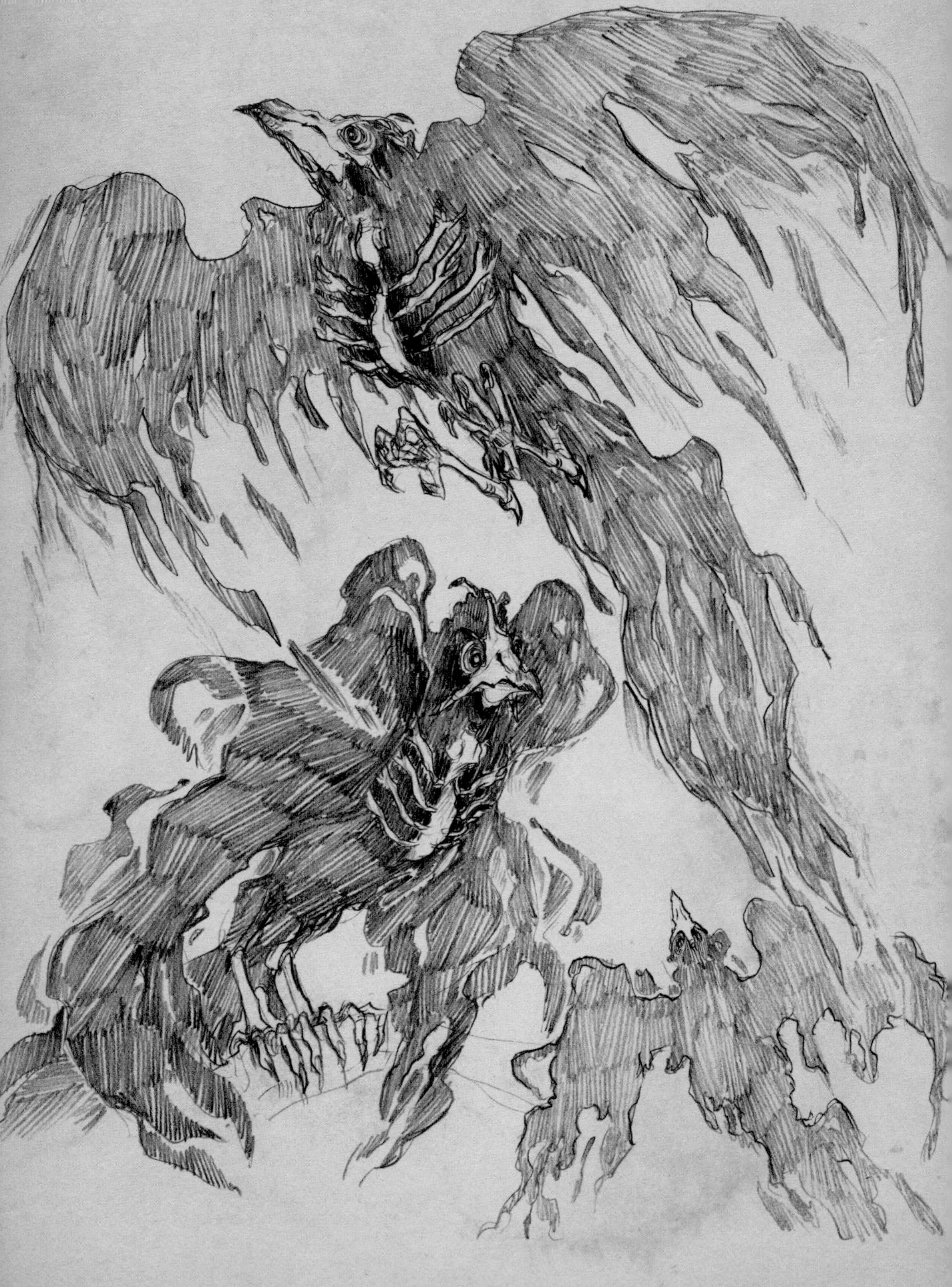

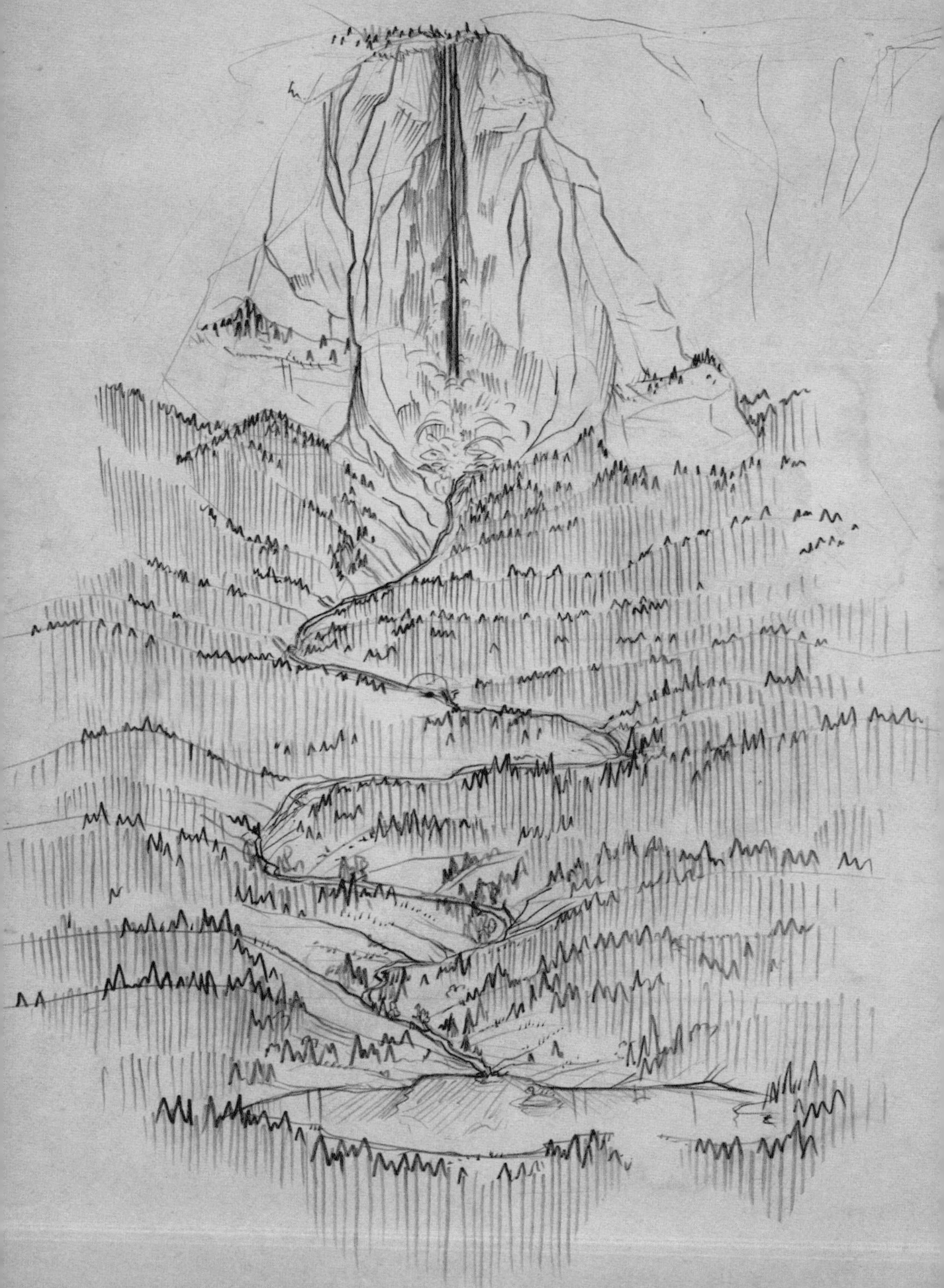

THE ADVENTURE
CONTINUES IN

COTTONS
THE WHITE CARROT

Acknowledgments

All my creative love to Heidi Arnhold. Your amazing collaboration has made my dream come true. Many thanks to Paul Pope, whose twenty-plus years of friendship have inspired and challenged me. You were the first true supporter of Cottons. You will always be my brother. Thanks to David Tibet. Your influence shines brightly in these pages. I would like to acknowledge Dr. Frank Zbozny, who told me the story of the man who wished to learn patience. Thanks to Mark Haskell Smith, Mark Yturralde, John Crawford, Tom Fassbender, Paul Morrisey, Jeong Joo Park, James Blackshaw, and Charles Brownstein. Thanks to Adam Waldman, Brad Hochberg, Brett Winn, Molly Kloss, Jeff Birch, and the rest of my work family at The Refinery, with special thanks to Nancy Julson for the hand-lettering on the maps. Thanks to the incredible Mark Siegel. Your belief in this project means the world to me. Thanks to Gina Gagliano, Calista Brill, Robyn Chapman, Andrew Arnold, and everyone else at First Second. Thanks to my wonderful agent, Mary Evans at the Mary Evans Agency. Thanks to John Lavitt, whose thorough and savage readings of my early drafts helped keep me from straying too far afield. Thanks to my mom, my dad, and my brother. And finally, many thanks to Gabrielle Pascoe, Paloma Pascoe, and Blaise Pascoe for their unending love and support. I love you all.

—Jim Pascoe

My heartfelt thanks to Mark Siegel, Gina Gagliano, Calista Brill, Robyn Chapman, Andrew Arnold, and everyone at First Second. To Mary Evans. To Jeong Joo Park and Yes Flats. To Jim Pascoe, for crafting the kind of story I've always dreamed of illustrating. To my family and friends for their encouragement and support. To my husband, Brandon Kraemer, for lending his shrewd editorial eye when I couldn't see the forest for the trees. To Josephine: Anyone who says that dog is man's best friend has never been loved by a rabbit. In memory of Bartleby, Five, Pixel, and Steel. To the wonderful people who work tirelessly at the Georgia House Rabbit Society. To God, for His inspiration and strength. I am forever grateful.

—Heidi Arnhold

Jim Pascoe is a writer, designer, and an award-winning creative director. For the past twenty years, he has been generating, collaborating on, and executing creative ideas. His comics credits include Buffy the Vampire Slayer, Hellboy Animated, and the original series Undertown—which was first published by TOKYOPOP, put out as a special edition by Scholastic, and distributed by Universal Press Syndicate to over fifty newspapers worldwide. He is the co-author of the crime fiction novel *By the Balls* (written with Tom Fassbender and illustrated by Paul Pope), which launched the cult publishing house UglyTown and was rereleased in 2013 in a deluxe fifteenth anniversary edition. Part of the original founding team of the entertainment advertising agency The Refinery, Jim Pascoe has worked on campaigns for every major Hollywood studio. He and his team have won multiple Clio Awards. He was also the creative director/producer on Disney/ABC Cable Network Group's interactive television program *JETIX Cards Live*, which won a 2004 Emmy Award (Outstanding Achievement in Advanced Media Technology). He lives in Los Angeles, where he drinks coffee, sleeps very little, and believes in magic.

Heidi Arnhold is an illustrator and sequential artist who trained at the Savannah College of Art and Design. Her previous comic work can be found in *Star Trek: Uchu*, *Legends of the Dark Crystal: The Garthim Wars*, *Legends of the Dark Crystal: Trial by Fire*, and *Fraggle Rock: Tails and Tales*. She began working on Cottons with her writer, Jim Pascoe, after a fateful reunion at San Diego Comic-Con in 2010. Since then, her whole life has been foxes and bunnies, which is far from a complaint as it finally gives her a professional excuse to draw those animals all day, every day. While visual storytelling is her passion, she also loves singing in her local choir, visiting and volunteering at the Georgia House Rabbit Society, and getting lost on long hikes as often as she can. Heidi currently lives in Atlanta, Georgia, with her husband and her adorable bunny muse, Josephine.

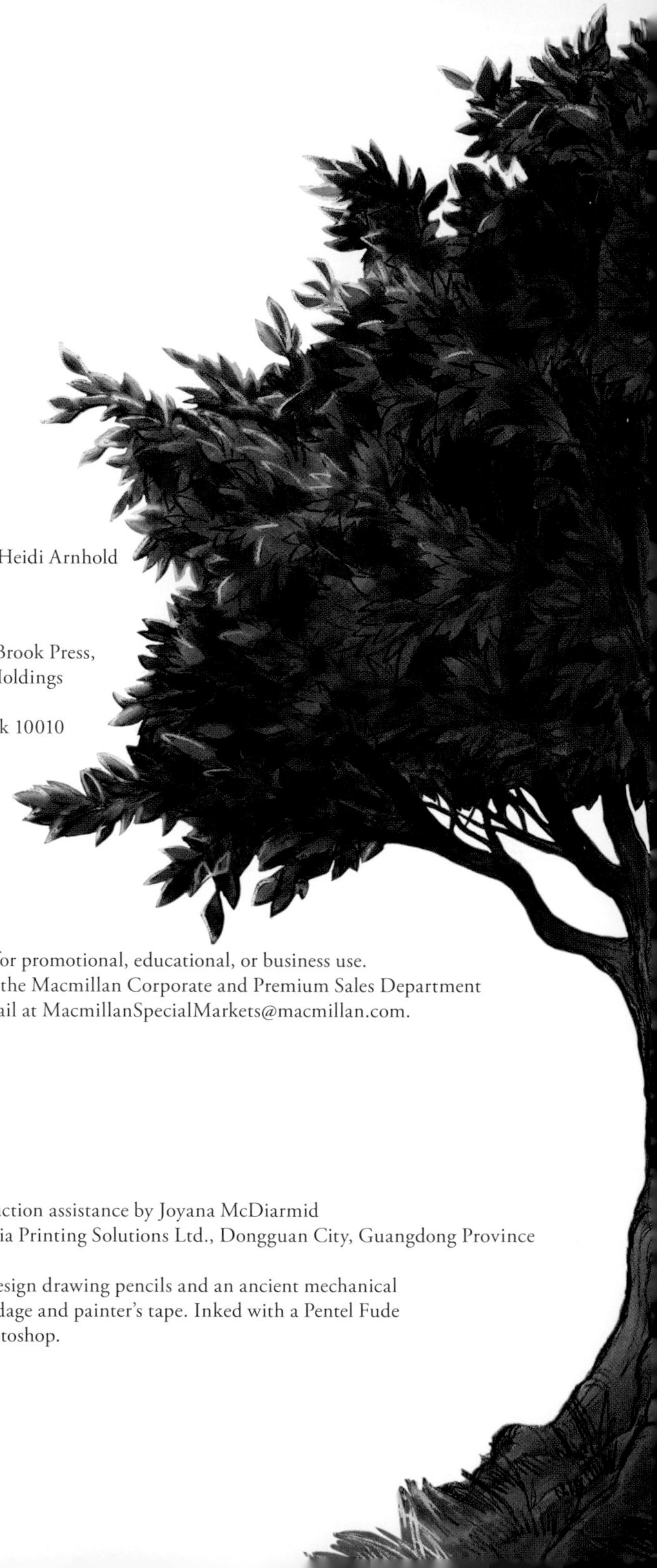

Copyright © 2018 by Jim Pascoe and Heidi Arnhold

Published by First Second
First Second is an imprint of Roaring Brook Press,
a division of Holtzbrinck Publishing Holdings
Limited Partnership
175 Fifth Avenue, New York, New York 10010
All rights reserved

Library of Congress Control Number:
2017946147

ISBN 978-1-250-15744-7

Our books may be purchased in bulk for promotional, educational, or business use.
Please contact your local bookseller or the Macmillan Corporate and Premium Sales Department
at (800) 221-7945 ext. 5442 or by e-mail at MacmillanSpecialMarkets@macmillan.com.

First edition, 2018
Book design by Jim Pascoe with production assistance by Joyana McDiarmid
Printed in China by RR Donnelley Asia Printing Solutions Ltd., Dongguan City, Guangdong Province

Penciled traditionally with Sanford Design drawing pencils and an ancient mechanical
pencil that is wrapped in an ACE bandage and painter's tape. Inked with a Pentel Fude
brush pen and colored digitally in Photoshop.

10 9 8 7 6 5 4 3 2 1

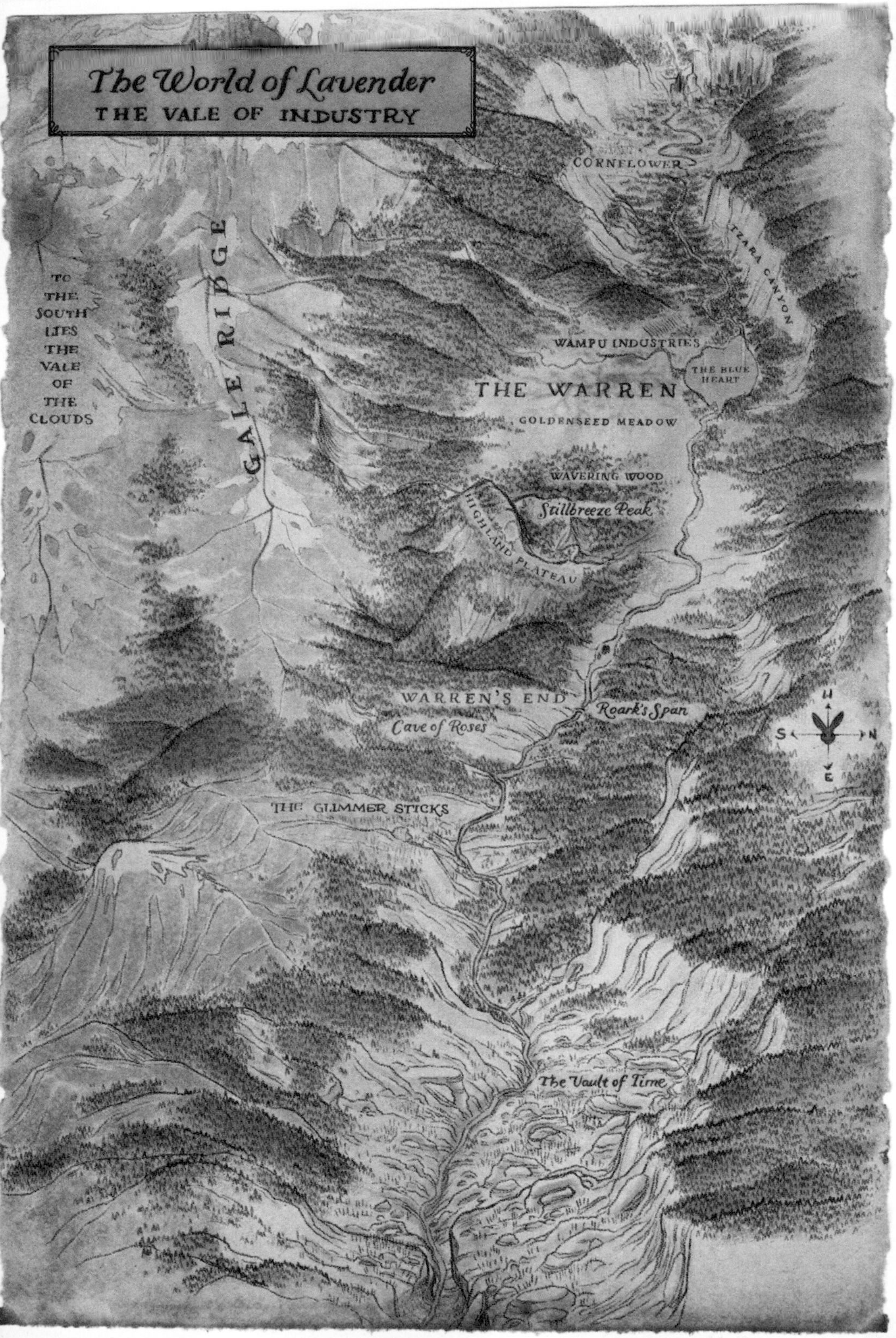

The World of Lavender
THE VALE OF INDUSTRY
CORNFLOWER
TZARA CANYON
GALE RIDGE
TO THE SOUTH LIES THE VALE OF THE CLOUDS
WAMPU INDUSTRIES
THE BLUE HEART
THE WARREN
GOLDENSEED MEADOW
WAVERING WOOD
Stillbreeze Peak
HIGHLAND PLATEAU
WARREN'S END
Roark's Span
Cave of Roses
THE GLIMMER STICKS
The Vault of Time
S
N
E